FALLEN EMBERS

BOOK ONE OF THE EMBERS SERIES

Lauri J Owen

PEARLSONG PRESS
NASHVILLE, TN

Pearlsong Press
P.O. Box 58065
Nashville, TN 37205
1-866-4-A-PEARL
www.pearlsong.com
www.pearlsongpress.com

ISBN-10: 1597190241
ISBN-13: 9781597190244

Book & Cover Design by Zelda Pudding. Zodiac/Sun image by Starblue.

Library of Congress Cataloging-in-Publication Data

Owen, Lauri J.
Fallen embers / by Lauri J Owen.
    p. cm.
ISBN-13: 978-1-59719-024-4 (trade pbk. : alk. paper)
ISBN-10: 1-59719-024-1
1. Women lawyers—Fiction. 2. Overweight women—Fiction. 3. Family
violence—Fiction. 4. Alaska Natives—Fiction. 5. Shapeshifting—
Fiction. 6. Alaska—Fiction. I. Title.
PS3615.W43F35 2010
813'.6—dc22
                                    2010014556

This book is dedicated in equal measure to
all the women and men out there who are big in all the right ways,
and to all the cats and dogs who do not get adopted.

CHAPTER 1

"**O**UCH!" KIERA FLINCHED FROM THE NEEDLE and, before she could quash it, shot her torturer a glare. His face carefully blank, he lifted the tattoo gun from her shoulder.

Kiera watched the tip draw away from her arm. Her eyes followed the single, ruby drop as it slid from the needle to plunk on the floor. She lifted her eyes to find Grant, her sandy-haired boss, hiding a smile.

"I should never have let you talk me into this, Grant," Kiera ground through clenched teeth.

"Oh, sure. Blame it on me." A grin lit his face. "You could have said no, you know."

Kiera found herself smiling back. "But if I had, I'd've never have gotten to fly to the big city of Bethel in Jim's Gulfstream."

Grant nodded. "That's true. And you certainly would never have another opportunity to submit to the ministrations of the renowned Harry Dogg." Grant inclined his head to the tattooist, who glanced expressionlessly at Grant as he wiped his gun. "And just think how impressed Jim will be the next time you wear that black dress."

Despite his teasing, Kiera knew he wanted her to be thankful, and she really should be. Okay, was. Dropping her eyes, she took a deep breath and lay back in the chair. It fit a bit too snugly around her ample curves, so she wriggled to try and keep the handrest from carving into her thigh.

Dogg, on whom almost no undecorated skin was visible, waited until Kiera looked up at him, his eyebrows raised in a silent question. She stared into his green and blue face for a moment before nodding. Her eyes slammed closed as the needles stabbed her arm, gently maiming her. Its unsubtle buzzing sounded too much like a damned dentist's drill and was just about as fun.

Grant leaned around the tattooist to watch.

"How close is he?" Kiera ground out.

"I'd guess another fifteen minutes."

Kiera made a face. Unless she further contorted herself, the position of the chair forced her to stare at the portrait mounted to the wall across from her chair. She could hide behind her eyelids, she supposed, but then there was nothing to distract her from the pain. Closing her eyes was almost worth it, though; the painted scene was downright eerie. Moonlit trees stabbed the nighttime sky. Half-changed werewolves slunk between the barren shafts, the whites of their teeth slashing their faces into ghostly masks.

Typical James Asana. Kiera wasn't surprised that Jim had chosen as his favorite tattoo artist some notorious Alaska Bush resident with a creepy werewolf fetish. Maybe all multi-billionaires had a penchant for the weird, since they never had to want for anything normal. Which might explain his near obsession with her, she mused, though despite his charm she couldn't find it in herself to return his admiration. There was something odd, odd and cold, about him that she just couldn't get past.

But despite his eccentricity Grant loved him, and Kiera didn't wonder why. She could only imagine how much capital his business poured into their little three-person law firm.

Two nights ago at one of the inevitable kiss-up-to-the-client dinners, she had made the mistake of admitting to Jim, while he openly admired her sleeveless black dress, that she had always wanted a tattoo. Here on her shoulder. Before she could say boo he had flipped out his phone and called Harry Dogg. She'd smiled, not really believing that he had really called anyone, but the following morning, not ten minutes after she'd arrived at work, a man had delivered a photobook containing Dogg's (unsurpassable, of course) works for her perusal, with flight arrangements tucked inside an accompanying folder. What could she say, indeed.

Kiera's teeth gritted as the needles cleaved rills into her arm, but she breathed out and tried to loosen the knot that used to be her stomach. She needed to keep Grant happy, and that meant keeping Jim happy. She had a little boy to take care of now.

ON THE FLIGHT BACK TO ANCHORAGE Kiera stared out her window. It was four days until Christmas, but the tundra snow looked gray and worn, like it had been lying too long but was too weary to get up. Her eyes shifted restlessly to her own reflection in the glass. Big brown eyes stared back from a softly rounded face, eyes that saw too much but never seemed to see enough. A full mouth, painted red, accentuated the auburn highlights in her long, brown hair. A package that as a whole might never be as beautiful as her sister, or as her mother had been, but should have been pretty.

She fidgeted, trying to ease the pinch of the seatbelt.

Without looking away, she said, "Grant, we should be back at the office by three. Do you mind if I leave a couple hours early today? Alex has a play tonight and I need to make sure he's at the school by five."

"Don't sound so enthused, Kiera," he chuckled. "Of course it's fine. You finished the Katmai motion?"

Still facing the window, she nodded. "This morning."

Grant turned in his seat to face her. "I hope I'm not prying, but are things getting any easier between you two?"

Kiera sighed, then shifted in her seat so she could look at her boss. "I don't blame Alex, Grant. He's six years old. His mother died less than six months ago, and we both know that I'm a pretty poor substitute for my sister."

Grant nodded but wisely kept silent.

"ALEX?" KIERA CALLED through the door. She pitched her voice to carry over the cacophony at Alex's babysitter's precisely because she was unwilling to brave the terrain to fetch him out of it. In moments he ran from some back area, grinning widely. Her breath caught. He looked so much like Julia. He had her wide brown eyes, her easy smile. A knot welled up in her chest.

Kiera tamped it down and smiled back. His genuine joy triggered a twinge of guilt at the annoyance she'd been feeling at having to get off work early, and for having to put off finishing her witness questions for her upcoming deposition, and all for what she had termed, but only in her mind, *the stupid Christmas play.* It was his first real interest since his mother's death and she knew she had to do all that she could to help him get on with his life. She owed that to him, and to her sister.

But it was hard sometimes. She often found herself pouring every spare thought into the frenzy of her cases, trying to get on with her life, to blot out the grief, to keep from being consumed by it.

Kiera helped Alex into his jacket and boots and led him out to the car. He babbled the whole way, recited one of his lines twice, reminded her that he'd be singing a song all by himself, asked her if his costume was in the car.

"Alex! Calm down a second! We have to stop at home and get your robes before we go to the school." He looked chagrined, so she added, "Don't worry, sweetheart. We won't be late."

As they turned off the road and into the driveway that snuggled up to her condo complex, Kiera glanced at the clock. 3:58. She pulled into the parking lot, then pushed the brakes. She glanced at Alex, who practiced whistling, and pushed open her door with her elbow because her arm stung when she moved her shoulder. Alex bounded out his, heading for the condo's common door at a lope.

Kiera shook her head as she climbed out of her seat. She pushed the door shut with her hip and started to turn.

Something slammed into Kiera at the same moment she registered some sound—was that a growl? The hurtling mass smashed her into the side of her car, knocking her feet out from under her.

Icy snow suddenly filled her nostril, caked her eye. Was she on the ground? Had she hit her head? Pain seared up her side, then into her neck. She wanted to panic, knew she should be panicked. Was she panicked? She heard screaming. Was that her? Was it Alex?

A softness brushed her face and white, spiky fur crowded the space in front of her eyes. Some bristles were black, she noted, black set in a patchwork of tan and white. She couldn't feel the snow, but cold seeped up from the ground into her back. She wanted to close her eyes but they stuck stubbornly open.

Something moved off to the side and she struggled to turn her head. It was Alex. He was running. She watched him throw himself on top of her. Her or the dog. She drifted for a moment and then the fur was gone.

Her breath caught and her heart suddenly pounded. She shifted her face out of the snowpack and tried to focus her eyes. Alex was pinned to the ground underneath a huge, snarling—dog?

It was a dream. It was real. Either way, she knew that Alex was going to die if she didn't do something. The tiny part of her that had been watching the scene unfold was screaming at her, screaming that she had to get up, had to save Alex, had to keep him from dying. *This is Julia's son! Julia, your dead sister's son! You swore you would take care of him! Damn you, Kiera! Get up, get up, get UP!*

Kiera's finger flicked. Her neck began to burn, then everything did. Sound came crashing back. As if she were a streambed in a flood, she was suddenly filled, overfilled, with more terror and rage than she could contain. And pain.

Oh, God, it hurt. Even the snow burned.

Kiera screamed her anger. She put her hands down into the snow, pushed up and scrambled to her feet. Hot blood rained down her coat. The world swayed as she turned.

The big dog had Alex by the arm. It bit and shook its head, pushed Alex down with one paw, then bit again, trying to get a better grip on Alex's coat as it dragged him across the snow and toward the woods crowded behind the condo.

Two steps separated them. Kiera howled a *kiai* as she took them, then kicked out at the third. Using the ball of her foot, she drove her boot into the dog's ribs as hard as she could. The dog let go of Alex, and its jaws just missed her ankle as she snapped her foot back. The momentum carried her back and she used it to power her second strike, this time a side-kick into the dog's hip. She chose force over technique, and though the blow landed, the dog did not leave Alex.

Kiera pulled air deep into her lungs and stepped back. Her heart hammered. The dog growled and crouched lower over Alex, who lay still and soundless on the ground. Kiera gritted her teeth. Set her feet.

A spear of sunlight divided the ground between them.

Kiera spat breath, lunged forward and drove her body's weight into her chambered leg. Screamed wordlessly with rage as she stomped down. The blow was hard enough to break bones, or teeth, and it slammed the dog's head away, down and into the snow.

The dog grunted and let go of Alex as it slid to its side. It lay for one heartbeat. Three. Shaking its head, it smoothly turned one yellow eye, then two, to her. Teeth flashed yellow as it lifted its lips. She gasped and stepped back involuntarily at that alien gaze, rage leaking away as quickly as it had filled her.

This was no dog. *What the hell is that thing?* her mind screamed.

Alex pawed the snow and scrambled away from the dog. The dog ignored him as it slowly raised itself to its feet and tilted its head to the side. Its eyes, eyes dark with death, never left Kiera's.

As soon as it regained its feet, it sprang, tackling her again. They went to the ground together. As she fell, it snapped at her face. She raised her left arm to keep it away and it bit deep into her forearm, shoving the back of her hand into her chin like a punch. The dog shook its head, trying to tear the meat from the bone. Her coat kept the dog from tearing pieces from her arm, but oh, God, it hurt.

She punched the dog in the face with her right fist as hard as she was able at that angle, which jarred her left arm so hard she almost fainted. She grabbed its shoulder, hugged it to her and kneed it in whatever part was nearest. Once, twice, thrice. No effect. Her ears roared as terror roiled through her.

She wrapped her fingers around the dog's lower jaw and tried to pry it off her, her blood clotting between its teeth. She managed to pull the jaw back a little, and it growled and tried to shake her off, then bit down and down again, driving a tooth through her forefinger as it tried to get a better grip. Tears streamed down her face but she refused to let go. Fire exploded in her arm.

This dog was going to kill her.

Breath whined as she started to hyperventilate.

Alex jumped on the dog from behind and battered its shoulders and the back of its head with his small fists. The dog released the pressure on her arm a little as it swiveled its eyes toward Alex.

Full panic had set in now. She couldn't fill her lungs, but managed to scream, "Alex, get out of here! Run! RUN!"

The dog snarled as it bit down again, deep into her shoulder, and red flames erupted around the three of them. Suddenly, before she could wonder why she wasn't burning, the world wavered sickeningly then faded away.

A HAMMER POUNDED inside Kiera's head. Her throat hurt and her mouth was dry, and she felt overheated and muzzy. She tried to turn but her arm cramped, and then her stomach churned and threatened to empty. A groan managed to find its way out, but she lay still and held her eyes closed. She breathed deeply, slowly, willing her body to settle.

Was she hungover? What had happened? Why couldn't she remember?

She heard the rustle of clothes and opened her eyes, then turned her aching head toward the sound. It was Alex, lying a few feet away on his back in the snow.

She tried to puzzle it out. Why was Alex sleeping in the snow, flat on his back with his arm across his face? As if he felt her gaze, he opened his eyes and turned them toward her. He yawned.

Spots of blood stained the front of his blue coat.

Memories snapped back. She gasped and pushed herself up as fast as she could, looking everywhere for the dog, hands up, horse stance, breathing heavy, heart hammering, ready for its attack, but it was nowhere in sight. She turned in a fast circle to her right, then the opposite direction in a second, slow circle, looking carefully at everything.

But everything was silent and cold and covered with snow. And no tracks. At least no new ones. A sketch of new snow had recently fallen, and it half-filled some animal tracks that meandered across the clearing, leading here and there, though none came near where she and Alex had lain. And none, she told herself with a swallow, were big enough to have been made by that big dog.

She blew a tremulous breath. Where was that damned dog?

And how bad was her neck? Keeping one eye on the ground around her, Kiera put a trembling hand to her throat, expecting gore. Although she found thick, scabbing mounds, the cuts had closed. Each puncture was sore, but she wasn't bleeding. She gingerly explored the skin all the way around her neck, finding only pinched tissue and a great deal of tenderness, but her skin felt as though it had been healing for several days, or even a week, and not a few minutes or hours.

She shook her head over and over. This just didn't make sense. None of it did. What the hell had happened?

She stepped over to Alex and dropped down in the snow. She lifted him and peeled back his coat. She pushed up his shirt sleeves and looked at his arms. Teeth marks dotted his left forearm, but they were minor, and closed, and looked days old. Up came his shirt, but his chest and back were clear. "Are your legs hurt?" she asked him, pushing his arms back into his coat.

Alex, whose eyes had gone wide, shook his head.

She had to get in the house and call the cops. Get them out of the cold and away from the dog.

Where the hell was the dog?

Kiera stood and lifted Alex to his feet. She took his hand, took a step, and then stopped.

Oh my God. Home was nowhere in sight. Gone was her three-story beige, nondescript condo building. Gone was the parking lot and the road and the noise and the town. She stood in the middle of—of a village or something. She and Alex had been lying next to a snowdrift, and they were maybe fifty feet equidistant from two series of ten or twelve round, squat buildings of some sort. Huts? Most were smallish, maybe twenty feet from side to side and fifteen feet tall, cast of wood and built with a triangular arch, and all were covered with snow. They looked like ones she had seen in a theme park her parents had taken her to when she was as a girl.

Darkness seeped from the windows of every hut, and all the doors were closed, but she needed a phone, and she prayed these houses were more than just props. Surely one of these places had a phone. A radio. Something.

Phone! *Oh,* she remembered, *my cell!* She patted her pockets with a shaking hand while she half-dragged Alex across the snow and to the closest hut. Before they got to the door she found her phone, so she pulled it out from a top pocket and flipped it open. She started to dial 9, then noticed there was no signal.

She willed herself calm as she snapped the phone shut, slid it back in the pocket, and smoothed down the Velcro.

"Come on, Alex," Kiera murmured as she reached and knocked on the door. "We have to go inside." She knocked again, then tried the door. It was open. She peered inside without going in.

This was no prop. It was a home of sorts, she guessed, or a place to camp, with a small, wooden table and chairs, and a metal stove set toward the back. Several gray and black blankets were tangled in a mess on the floor on the other side of the hut. There was no running water that she could see, no toilet, no phone, no radio. The house reeked of wood smoke, but not today's, and she backed out and closed the door. It certainly wouldn't keep anyone out who came to call, human or animal, and anything with eyes would see exactly where they were by simply following their tracks. Ugh. She grabbed a branch lying on the ground and tried to wipe the tracks away.

Fact: She had to find someplace for them to hide. But would hiding in one of these huts be safe? Now that they were closer, she could see that they were essentially lean-tos, maybe a fishing or hunting camp like the Bush natives used, roughly pulled together as a weather shelter but not meant for long term living. And any determined person—or dog—could push right through one of the walls.

But she wasn't ready to give up on the phone yet. She reclaimed Alex's hand and pulled him to the next hut, and the next, but all of the houses featured the same accouterments and setup as the first one. The sixth or seventh had a pile of what looked like hemp-brown clothes tossed in a pile toward the back of the house. She looked around the huts, watching for movement, stood completely still and waited ten seconds for sound, and then pulled Alex inside. She didn't know what animals were out here, and both she and Alex needed clean, blood-free shirts.

Am I dreaming? she wondered as she closed the door behind them. If so, this was one hell of a dream.

Sweat was pouring off her again, so she pulled off her coat and threw it aside. She stood next to the window and lifted her left fist to her shoulder so she could see the underside of her forearm. Yeah; she'd been bitten all right, but the tears had closed there, too, and had pinked with healing. Although her arm hurt like crazy, it certainly didn't ache like it should right after a fight with a big, crazy dog. Her shoulder itched where a bandage still haphazardly covered her tattoo, so she reached up her shirt sleeve and tore the bandage off. It was bloody, too, where the dog had bitten though it. Was it only this morning she'd suffered under the gun in Bethel? She put a hand to her forehead, then wiped her face and closed her eyes just long enough to take a breath.

She walked to Alex and squatted down. He opened his arms to her as she lifted him up and sat him on her knee. His eyes shone with fear, so she wrapped him in a quick, tight hug, then pushed him back so she could look at him. She helped him out of his coat, lifted and looked closely at each of his arms, but although his left forearm definitely bore the dog's teeth marks, the punctures were as healed as her own. She searched gently across his body, parting his hair, lifting his shirt, and pushing his pants-legs up, but his only wounds were those on his arm, which must have been what had bled on his coat. When she was finished, he pulled himself back against her chest and cried softly for a while against her shirt, and she let him.

While she rubbed Alex's back, Kiera rested her head on top of his and wondered again where they were and how the hell they'd gotten there. They were sitting inside a hunting camp in the middle of a village set God knows where. The walls of the little hut were made of thin, wooden strips tacked with mud, or something similar, and she again noted that they were more concealment than cover and would definitely not keep anything out. The stove in this one was huge and looked like a newer version of one she might find in an antique store. A metal pot sat cold and lonely atop the mammoth hearth. The table was raw wood and roughly made. Two low stools sat beside it. It looked more like a threshing table, perfect for cutting up fish or big game, than one you'd sit at for dinner.

Why weren't there any phones? Or radios? There didn't seem to be anybody around to ask. No one in any of the huts, and no footprints either. Well, no human ones, so no one had been here since the last snow fell, whenever that had been. And although she wanted this to be a dream, she knew it wasn't. For one thing, she never smelled the sharp stench of unwashed bodies or stale smoke in dreams, and those were what lingered in each hut they opened. And dreams just never made the same logical sense as life, or followed the same rules. And yet here they were. Had they flown? Been abducted by aliens? Fallen into a time machine? Were they dead?

And where the hell were the people? They had to have been here just a few days earlier. She could still smell them, for God's sake.

And was it Christmas here, too? There was snow, just like home, but there were no holiday decorations on anything.

What a crazy day. A crazy and terrible day.

When Alex stopped sobbing the house fell deadly quiet. Straining just a bit, she realized that she could hear something in the background, some irregular, pulsing, big noise in the distance, but she couldn't quite make it out. She sat Alex down on the floor, motioned him to stay quiet, and ghosted to a window. It was too smoke-blackened to see details through, so she tiptoed to the door.

Kiera held her breath, cracked the door open just a hair and peeked outside. She couldn't see anything, so she opened the door a little wider. It sounded like some big event, like a football game or something, was going on over a far hill. A huge bunch of people—hundreds, perhaps thousands—were yelling, maybe cheering. Dark was falling, but she didn't see any lights, though the direction of the noise was easy to discern. A huge pounding sounded, she jumped, and the crowd roared. Then again.

People. And people meant safety.

Stepping back inside, Kiera snicked the door shut and strode to the pile of clothes. She found a brown linen shirt that looked like it would fit Alex. After parsing through the pile, it became obvious that nothing here would come close to fitting her abundance, which meant that she was stuck wearing her bloody shirt. Well, at least it was red silk. And the blood was dry, which was a blessing. Even the blood on her coat, which she made a mental note to keep zipped, shouldn't smell too strongly in the sharp cold. She motioned for Alex to come over, and then to take off his shirt. She slipped the linen shirt on him. While it was a little big, it would cover his chest and arms and, more importantly, it wasn't covered with blood. His bloodied shirt she slipped into her coat pocket and zipped it closed before helping him back on with his coat. When he was finished dressing, Kiera stood up.

"Keer, where are we?" Alex whispered. She looked down to big, tear-filled eyes. "I want to go home."

"Oh, Alex," Kiera murmured, pulling him close. "I do, too." He sniffed. "I think we got lost somehow, and I've got to find a way to get us back."

Alex nodded into her chest. Kiera held him like that for a few moments, then pushed him back and stared hard at him for a second. "I need you to help me, Alex," she said. "Can you do that?" He looked scared and confused, but he nodded.

"Alex, while we're here I am going to be your Mama." Pain pinched his features but he didn't look away. "I know that's your Mama's name, Alex, but I don't want anyone else we meet to wonder whether you belong with me. Does that make sense?"

Alex nodded.

"I know this is very scary. I'm a little bit scared, too. So we need to work together so we can get home as soon as we can. Okay?"

"Okay," Alex said, and hugged her tight. He sniffled, but tried to smother it, and she found herself smiling into his hair.

Once outside, Kiera paused and looked both ways. Where was home from here? And where was that dog? She didn't think that it would lie in wait if it was close. The thought loosened the knot in her chest just a little.

She knew they needed to go toward the sounds and the people, but she couldn't shake a feeling of unease at the thought.

"Do you think that dog is still out there?" Alex whispered.

"Shhhhh. It might be," Kiera whispered, then wondered what else might be as well. "We'll have to be really careful."

Alex nodded and lifted his chin, looking out at the landscape. Despite her fear, Kiera felt a simmering of pride push some of the sick feeling away. He was very brave, just like his mother.

Too bad the man her sister had married had been a murdering bastard.

WITHIN FIFTEEN MINUTES Kiera and Alex cleared the village and headed into the forest that surrounded it. As soon as they hit the heavy trees Kiera scoured the snow until she found a stout stick. It was wrist thick, but about four feet too long, so she rested one end in a crotch where a low-hanging branch met a trunk and propped the other end on the ground at a forty-degree angle. She took a step back, lifted her right leg, then stomped down on the branch, breaking the bottom several feet off and leaving a fairly sharp point. It was better than nothing, which, aside from her pocket knife, was all that she had.

A fallen bough made a decent broom, and as she headed them toward the hill, and the sounds, she dragged the bough behind her, hoping to dampen their trail. To her relief, aside from a set of moose tracks they crossed and a pair of ravens who glared from a tree, she saw nothing.

The fear that had plagued her was softening, and the realization scared her anew. But why would a dog brazen—or sickened—enough to attack them in the daytime and right in her front yard hold off now? Wouldn't it attack if it were here?

Would anything else?

As they crested the hill through a gap in the trees, Kiera was startled to find a city below, nestled in the cleavage separating two sets of hills.

A city. A city and a phone. Kiera dropped the broom, grabbed Alex's hand and took the first steps down the hill. The snow deepened on this side, and it forced them to move more slowly.

As they descended, Kiera took in as much as of the city as the trees' growth and the diminishing sunlight permitted. Halfway down she stumbled over a snow-covered stump and nearly fell into a drift. Instead of going around it, Kiera climbed up and gaped through a breach in the branches.

A high unbroken stone wall squeezed the city into the shape of a teardrop. At least a dozen thin, gothic buildings raised ribbed vaults to worship the sky, while lower structures lay supine like sycophants at their feet. The city sprawl softened toward the middle, then stopped, leaving an open, octagonal area like a lidless eye. Streets north of the park arched before settling back into horizontal, marking raised brows to the eye and giving the city the look of a poxed worshipper enchanted by the sky.

A waning gibbous moon, which had risen as they walked, now shone the only light. None lit the city.

Where were all the people? And why the wall?

She jumped down and motioned Alex to follow her. The trees thinned as they walked, and the thick crust topping the snow crunched as they breached it. Kiera grimaced with every step.

Behind the city lay the other hills, at least as tall as the one they stood on, but unlike hers, those were bare of trees. Atop the tallest hill lay a big building, or series of buildings, inside its own wall, but all structures within lay unlit as well, and it was hard to make out the details in the growing darkness. The complex was not as big as the city, but it was bigger than many small towns she'd seen. It reminded her of the castles overlooking European towns she had visited.

Was this Europe?

Kiera jumped as a loud *whump* wound through the valley, then gasped as her eyes sought the source of the noise. From this angle she saw that north of the two cities lay an army.

A really big army. Five thousand people, and maybe more, some grouped in several squares that held hundreds, while hundreds or thousands of others snaked into the valley from the north in several thin lines. Torches lit the ranks at regular intervals, casting a circle of illumination from each source, rendering the plain above the valley into a round chessboard with too many squares.

Why an army? From where? Would they see Kiera as a threat? What should she do? Run? To where? She and Alex had to find someplace safe. Even if the city was truly empty, stone walls were more secure than those made from sticks. What was back behind them, anyway? She had no idea how far they were from the next inhabited place, and she was certainly not going to go traipsing around with Alex across the wilderness in the dark with just a stick and a pocketknife.

And she wanted a phone. Surely there would be a phone in the city.

Speaking of which, she thought, and pulled out her phone. She flipped it open and stared at the display. No signal. Of course.

Kiera pressed down her fear as they descended the last hundred yards of the hill. She kept them hidden at the edge of the trees for a long while as she looked around and listened. The area for a couple hundred yards around the city had been cleared. Anyone from miles around who was looking their way could see them when they made their way in. But they had to do it. She wondered if they should run the distance, then decided against it.

Taking a deep breath, Kiera gripped her staff firmly and pulled Alex out into the open. She put her head up and began marching toward an arched, seemingly deserted gate that had been cut into the wall almost directly ahead. The army remained on the opposite side, and she prayed no one would see them.

No one challenged them. Nothing attacked them. They made it through the gate, which was open, and all the way inside the city, which still seemed empty. No one was there. The street was unplowed and free of tracks. Some of the buildings sported what had to be rounded lanterns up at the second- and third-floor levels, but none of the lights were lit. True night had fallen, and it was hard to see much besides the gaping eyes of darkened windows and the shadows lurking in the lees of the buildings. There were no signs, nothing to tell her the names of the businesses or streets. She pulled Alex to one side and walked along the edge of the buildings so they could hide quickly if anyone passed. They began making their way toward the center of town.

A few blocks in, a loud whistle made her jump. Kiera yanked Alex behind an arch abutting a building they'd been skirting. They hunkered there for a minute, breathing hard. She didn't hear the noise again, so she peeked around the edge of the stone. At first she didn't see anything at all, but after a handful of seconds, and by the light of the moon, she saw an oddly dressed, slim man slip out from behind a large hunk of rock about fifty feet up the street, look furtively about, then motion to unseen others across the road.

The man was dressed in what looked like medieval clothes, including a cloak and what had to be a sword. As he moved the moonlight gilded the man's blond hair, but she couldn't see his face.

Kiera drew her brows down and tilted her head to get a better look.

Two young children, neither older than Alex, came running from the other side of the road. They moved in a quick shuffle, heads down, to the cloaked man, who wrapped his arms around them both and hurried them back the way he'd come. The light wasn't bright, but she had seen their faces, and they'd looked terrified.

What the hell was going on?

The cloaked man reappeared, gestured, waited, and then motioned again, impatiently this time, and three more young children came running from across the street. He grabbed them and pulled them behind the rock, hurrying them to wherever he was sending them.

Alex leaned out to try and see what Kiera was looking at, and she pushed him back. He made a sound of irritation and she turned to him and held up a hand for silence. He took two breaths before nodding.

She turned back to the street. The man was back, and again gesturing for more children. Two boys came running out, older this time. Perhaps ten.

One suddenly fell, and as he did the other screeched and made a wide turn as if he had suddenly lost his sense of direction. The cloaked man grabbed him and forced him to keep running. The fallen boy was trying to pull himself to the far side of the street, where the cloaked man and his confused comrade had gone. He struggled and then jerked, and Kiera went cold.

An arrow had blossomed in the boy's back.

Kiera pushed Alex further back into the dark, then scanned the area. Where was the damned bowman? The cloaked man came running back out, this time bearing something large, flat and round. Was that a shield? He dropped down next to the fallen boy and grabbed his shirt, wrapped it around his fist and began walking backward, keeping the shield up, up and facing the opposite direction from Kiera and Alex. He dragged the boy back toward the stone.

A very young woman, maybe a teenage girl, ran out from the far side of the road. The cloaked boy yelled something to her, his tone warning her to go back, but she ignored him and kept coming. The girl grabbed the fallen boy's hand. She, too, pulled him toward the large rock. The cloaked boy tried to cover the three of them with his shield, but arrows were flying now. One hit the girl in the thigh and she fell, holding her leg as she cried out.

"No." Kiera whispered. "Oh, no." Alex gasped from where he knelt down at her feet, peeking around the arch. She tried to push him back, but he jerked away from her hand. "Stay back!" she hissed.

As she turned back, Kiera caught movement on a roof across the street and down a hundred yards. The moon had captured the bowman as he leaned around a square stone to aim, or maybe just to get a better look. He was wearing a dark cape that danced around his thighs. He looked tall.

She watched him take aim and loose. Her eyes followed the arrow to where it pierced the girl, through her back this time. The girl screamed and convulsed when the arrow struck, then lay still.

Kiera looked back to the bowman and found more. At least two others had stepped forward to stand with him, bows drawn.

All Kiera could hear was the roar in her ears. She looked around, desperate to find something—anything—that could stop those men from shooting these people—the children!—down like deer.

A scream of anguish jerked her attention back to the street. The cloaked man ran back out into the street, into the danger, and grabbed the girl. He held up his shield with one hand, grabbed her shirt, and began to pull her across the road. All three bowmen had stopped trying to hide, instead standing boldly atop the edge of their building. One laughed and slapped another on the back. His cape fell back. He wore a uniform. They were soldiers. The third took a drink from a canteen. All three watched the man for a minute, then, as if choreographed, drew arrows, put them to bow and loosed.

One arrow screeched as it bounced off the man's shield, but the two that followed hit the disk with a thunk. Two from the next volley hit, and one cracked the man's shield in two. The next swiftly following arrow found its way through the gap and hit him in the side. He fell, losing his grip on the girl. All three bowmen stood at the edge of the building, bows down, watching the cloaked man writhe. The one with the canteen shook his head, then drew and nocked an arrow.

White hot rage filled Kiera. *How can they do this?* her mind screamed, and she found herself running from behind the archway. "Stop this!" she shrieked at the bowmen, who turned to look at her. "You bastards! How dare you shoot children! What the hell is wrong with you?" She picked up rocks and threw one, then two at the soldiers. They fell far short, and she gritted her teeth and threw the rest to the ground.

She ran to the fallen girl, started to lean down, panting, to check her, but Kiera froze when what she had done suddenly struck her.

Oh my God.

She looked up at the bowmen.

The three stood looking at her. Wordlessly.

Kiera still shook with rage, but now fear squeezed her chest as well. The one on the right end, the bowman who'd shot the final arrow into the man, turned and stared at the others. They looked back at him and his teeth flashed white in the moonlight. The first one reached over his shoulder, drew an arrow, put it to bow and aimed. At her. And held it.

Kiera's heart stopped, then pounded.

He waited.

Why?

She stared at his blank face, wondering why he didn't shoot her. She looked at the arrow. Stared at his face.

Oh my God.

It wasn't pointed at her. The soldier aimed at some point behind her.

And to the left. Water poured into her gut as she turned and saw Alex, who had crept out from the arch. And now he was too far away from the rock to hide and too far from her to shield from the arrow's path.

No! God, no!

She turned back to the bowman just as he smiled at her. And loosed.

"No!" Kiera screamed, and kept screaming.

And the world broke.

Without thinking, she lifted her hands as if they could hold off the arrow, and red fire erupted around her. "No!" she screamed again, wondering in the last thinking part of her mind if this was an illusion, if she was going crazy, if Alex was dead yet.

Rage, red rage, burned inside her, quelling the last of her rational thought. Time slowed. The buildings in front of her wavered, seemed to billow. She looked up, looked around at a surreal, undulating, dreamy world. A red world.

For a moment she seemed to remember seeing flames, feeling this way before, but the thought slipped away. She turned her eyes from the path of the arrow, which was traveling impossibly slowly toward her—no, toward Alex—and stared through the red fire into the ice cold eyes of the man who had loosed it. Time mocked them all. Made her think she could stop it. Made him think he could take it back.

Terror and rage seared anew. Kiera screamed again, words perhaps, but she didn't know what they were. She reached toward him, syrupy slow, wanted him to feel her hate and her hurt. She wanted him to suffer. To die. For all of them to die.

Red fire streamed from each of her hands, breaking through the undulating red wall in front of her and winding round each other, blazing strings forming an arm. It lashed out, lightning fast and deadly slow, slashing, crawling, toward the bowmen atop the building.

Wrapped in her rage, locked in stuttered time, Kiera watched the expressions on the men's faces, somehow crystal clear, slip from arrogance to clot with fear. To terror. Through the red veil she saw the men drop their bows and turn as if to run, but they, too, were trapped in time. The fire hit them before they could take even the first step away, and it wrapped itself around them like a blanket, like the embrace of an old friend. Their hair lit first, then their clothes, and then their faces and hands started to blacken. They fell to the ground, thrashing, screaming. She saw their mouths moving, singing obscene prayers, but she heard no sound other than the roaring in her own ears.

Oh, God! Alex! I have to get to Alex!

She tried to turn away, to let go, but it was too hard. She pulled herself back, but the world was thick and viscous, and she had no will to fight it.

I have to get to Alex. The thought was strong, but the need was stronger, and it held on to her.

She closed her eyes and turned her face, inch by inch, as if to wake from a dream. Suddenly the world—sounds, moonlight—came crashing back, and she stumbled.

And the red fire was gone.

The world went cockeyed and Kiera fell to the ground. She threw up, then threw up again. When the heaving stopped, she pushed back up and scanned the ground for her nephew. Alex stood behind her, exactly where she'd last seen him, staring at her with eyes the moonlight rendered both big and white.

Oh thank you, God. Thank you, thank you, thank you. "Are you hurt?" she called, stumbling over. She dropped to her knees and pulled him hard into her chest. Her heart pounded. She hoped she could get back up.

He shook his head against her shoulder.

"Did he miss?"

Alex shuddered and pushed himself farther into her chest.

Kiera lifted him away and looked him in the eye. "Alex, are you all right?" she whispered. He looked at the tears streaming down her face, then back into her eyes, and nodded.

She nodded back, hugged him tight, then pushed away and forced herself to her feet. She was still burning with heat, so she tore off her coat and let it drop to the ground, then turned and made her way to the fallen figures as quickly as she could.

CHAPTER 2

THE CLOAKED MAN WAS AWAKE, TO HER SURPRISE, but lying quietly. He looked up at her with stark fear in his eyes.

But this was no man. The cloaked figure who had risked his life to ferry children across the street was a boy of no more than sixteen. He was indeed blond, with striking, icy blue eyes and skin as pale as her own. His nose was strong and symmetrical, set well in his square, strong-jawed face. He was on his way to very tall, though now he was probably an inch short of six feet, and at maybe 175 pounds he still had some filling out to do. Kiera did not doubt that he would be a heartbreakingly beautiful man when he grew up.

"Hey, hero." Kiera lifted her hands in the "I give up" position and smiled down at him, wanting him to understand that she was no threat. "Can you understand what I'm saying?"

The boy swallowed, then nodded slowly, once. She smiled again, relieved, then leaned down. "Can I take a look and see what I can do to help?" He held her eyes, but nodded again.

She lifted his cloak very carefully. He was bleeding from the arrow lodged offensively in his side, but it seemed to be a sluggish flow. He would probably be fine if they could get him to a doctor. But they had to get that bleeding stopped. Now.

She turned to Alex, who stood where she left him. His eyes were still big. "Alex, will you please bring me your old shirt from out of my coat pocket?" It wasn't clean, but what else could she use?

Alex nodded and turned away.

Kiera turned back to the boy lying at her knees, and reached out a hand to stroke his forehead. The boy flinched, so she drew back her hand.

"What's your name?" she asked softly.

He lay looking at her for a moment before answering. "Marco," he finally whispered.

"Well, hi, Marco. My name is Kiera." She smiled at him. "It looks like you're going to be fine, so try not to worry, okay?" He stared up at her, tried to sit up, and flinched with pain. Kiera lifted a hand to keep him down. "Stay still, Marco. Now as soon as my boy comes back I'm going to try and stop that bleeding, but I don't want you to be afraid, okay? I'm going to try really hard not to hurt you."

He fought to keep the pain and fear from his face, so she looked away to give him time to get his feelings under control. He lifted his hand to his hair, revealing a small blue tattoo inside his left wrist, a triangle bisected by a horizontal line that pointed to his hand. "What does that mean?" she asked to change the subject.

When she met his eyes, he looked only puzzled. "A vata. My mark." Like she should understand.

She ignored him, instead glancing over at the girl, who hadn't moved.

"Is she dead?" the boy at her knees whispered.

"I don't know," she whispered back.

Marco begged her with his eyes. "Please, my lady. Please go see."

She nodded, then pushed to her feet. God. She did not want to do this.

Kiera walked to the girl and bent down to check the pulse at her neck. The girl was still warm, but she didn't feel a heartbeat. She hadn't expected to. She screeched and almost jerked away when the girl moved her head, and blinked open her eyes.

Oh my God! She's alive!

"Hey, you." Kiera whispered, then used a shaking hand to stroke the girl's face. The girl moaned, but didn't seem truly conscious. She had been shot twice—back and leg. One arrow had pulled the thin fabric of her bodice into the flesh of her back, and that wound did not bleed, but the first arrow had torn the thicker fabric of the girl's skirt when it pierced her thigh, and a finger's width of blood slid past the shaft to stain her skirt and color the snow beneath.

"Allie!" Marco called. "Are you all right?"

Alex came running up to Kiera, breathless and panting, and handed her the shirt. Her fingers found polyester and she knew at once that it wouldn't work. Keeping her back to the boy, Kiera stood, pulled off her coat, then unbuttoned her ruined silk shirt and tossed it down. She pulled her coat back on and zipped it up. She picked up the shirt and tried to tear a strip off, but she was too tired to start a rip. Reaching into her pocket, she pulled out her pocketknife, flipped it open and started a cut, then tore the strip off, not trusting her shaky hand that far with a knife.

Once the strip was free Kiera wrapped it twice around the girl's leg and pressed it hard around the arrow, willing the bleeding to stop. When her arms started to tremble she lifted her hands to cut a long strip off Alex's shirt. She wrapped it, too, around the leg, above the wound, then tied it tight.

She stood and turned back to Marco, who still needed his own tourniquet, but his eyes stopped her.

"Who are you?" he whispered fiercely. "Why are you helping us?"

"I told you, Marco. My name is Kiera. And this is Alex," she said, pointing to her nephew, who stood beside her. She lifted her hands, palms up. "I think most anybody would be horrified by what happened. And now you're hurt. What did you expect me to do? Run away?"

He looked at her for a long, measuring moment. Kiera waited until something relaxed in his face—maybe he found what he was looking for—before walking back. He continued to stare at her as she packed a shred of silk around the arrow in his side.

She chose to ignore it.

When she finished with the bandage, she tucked what was left of her battered shirt in her pocket and zipped it closed. Marco grunted, turned himself over, and started to stand. Kiera pressed on his chest, keeping him down.

Marco gritted his teeth. "Help me over to her."

"No. Lie here for a bit. I don't want that bleeding to start up again."

He lifted pleading eyes. "Please. I can help her."

"No, you can't."

He grimaced. "Well, not a lot, but I can help some. Please."

Kiera sighed, but helped Marco drag himself over to the fallen girl. He put his hand over the wound in her leg and closed his eyes. She couldn't be sure, but it looked like a faint blue light flowed from his hand.

No. She had to be mistaken. She swallowed and turned to watch the road but couldn't stop the shiver that slid down her back. Either her adrenalin was finally spent or maybe she'd been out in the cold too long. It seemed colder here than it had been back home.

Would she ever be able to go home? Maybe the more important question, the first question, should be finding out how they had gotten here. If she could figure that out, maybe she could reverse it. The dog at her throat was the last thing she remembered. Kiera closed her eyes. Had it done something besides bite her? If she had died, why was Alex here, too?

No; wait. The last thing she remembered was the fire. Did the fire have something to do with it? But that just didn't make sense. The fire had come again, here, but it didn't transport her back!

"What happened to your neck?"

Kiera turned back to Marco. "What?"

"You have bite marks on your throat."

The question sent a spark down her spine. "A dog attacked me and Alex."

Marco nodded as if this made perfect sense. "When?"

Kiera put her finger and thumb on the bridge of her nose. "I think it was just a little while ago."

His laugh was a strange sound that carried across the snow. "You think? Who healed you?"

What an odd way to put it. Feeling a little overwhelmed, Kiera dropped down next to the girl's feet and looked around for Alex. He was thirty feet away, building a snowman in the middle of the street. "No one." She rubbed her face with both hands. "What is this place called, Marco?"

His voice held a measure of surprise. "What do you mean?"

"What is the name of this city? This country?"

Marco turned with an unreadable look on his face. "What strange questions, Kiera. Where are you from? Did you lose your memory? Is your head injured?"

A thin sigh escaped her. "Where am I from? In relation to here? I don't know, though I certainly wish I did. I don't think I hurt my head, though it's as good an explanation as any, I suppose." Kiera pushed her hands down into the snow and squeezed the slush into icy balls. She knew her smile was ironic. "And I don't think I lost my memory, but then how would I know?"

Marco smiled back with equal measures of warmth and amusement. "This city used to be called Nakeetna. Is that familiar?"

She pulled her hands from the snow and shook them off. "No. What state are we in?"

His brows furrowed. "I don't know that word."

She sighed. "Okay. In what country, then?

"Do you mean deconn?"

The snow felt cold beneath her legs. Jeans. No long johns. "No. Have you heard of the United States, or Canada, or Britain? I mean, you speak English, so it has to be in an English-speaking country, right?"

He opened an arm and held it aloft. "The greater area is called Alaska."

Kiera rocked back, then leaned toward him, heart hammering. Maybe they hadn't gone far at all. "Alaska. We're in Alaska. The forty-ninth state?"

Marco's voice was a shade short of patient. "I don't know that word."

"Alaska, the great landmass north of Canada? Blue flag, big dipper?"

He gave her questions due consideration. "No. I don't think the area to the south has been named. No one lives there." To her surprise, he blushed a little. "Well, I mean, Alaks probably live there, but there are no Skani settlements south of Alaska."

Of course none of this made any sense. Maybe she *had* hit her head. "Anchorage. Which way is Anchorage from here?"

Now he looked suspicious. "Did you come from Anchorage? Is that where you were attacked?"

What was wrong with Anchorage? She shrugged. "It's a familiar name."

His smile said he didn't believe her. "Anchorage is an Alak deconn about a moon's ride south and west of here."

Skon-ee? Al-lack? Day-con? A moon? Kiera closed her eyes for a moment, willing some of this to be less mad. "Marco, do you have a phone I can use?"

He shook his head to show he didn't understand.

"A phone, landline or cell. Or do you know where I can find one?"

He shook his head. "I'm sorry. I don't know what you mean."

"It's a device used to contact people far away. You talk to them and they hear your voice. Maybe you call it something else here. You hold a receiver to your ear," she mimed the motions, "and push buttons with numbers on the other part, and the line rings and someone talks to you at the other end."

Marco looked at her for a moment, then smiled with obvious amusement. "There is nothing like that here."

Kiera felt flummoxed. How could this be Alaska? If there was an Anchorage here, would it be the same? How could there be so many coincidences with names? But there were no phones. And he had a sword! Those soldiers shot arrows!

Kiera shook her head. Maybe they'd gone back in time. But how could this be back in time? The Russians came to Alaska just a few hundred years ago, and they sure didn't speak English. Further, this kid was no Native. Was this an alternate universe? Some sci-fi dream?

She just didn't know.

When Kiera opened her eyes, Marco was watching her. "Who are you, I wonder."

It wasn't a question, but she answered anyway. "My name is Kiera. I told you."

"You speak Skani, Kiera. You're Skani but you have no mark." He pointed to his left wrist.

Kiera's brows drew together. "I'm sorry, Marco. I don't know what you mean."

"You're a fire mage with no mark?"

"I still don't know what you're talking about."

He half-smiled. "Tell the truth. Where are you from?"

Kiera looked past him to a building in which a big open window faced the street. Had it once been a store of some kind? A meeting place? Empty now, its door hung crookedly open like a gaping maw, gulping in the darkness but taking none away.

"A city very far from here," she whispered.

"How did you get here, Kiera?"

She looked at him. "What a good question, Marco. I wish I knew the answer."

"What happened?"

She shouldn't tell him. She knew she shouldn't, because he would think she was crazy, and maybe she was, but she was also alone in a strange place, she was afraid, and she had no answers to any of her questions. And she wanted a friend. Even one familiar face.

Alex slipped up and plopped down beside her. He hated it anytime she was less than serene, and things worked well between them because she was rarely anything else. Well, on the surface, at least. So she pushed her feelings aside and smiled down at him, showing him that everything was all right, or as all right as it could be under the circumstances. Alex smiled tentatively back but his eyes stayed assessing.

She took a deep breath and squeezed his hand. "This is going to sound completely crazy, Marco, okay, but Alex and I came home earlier tonight. We got out of the car and this giant—dog just attacked us." Kiera tried to suppress a shudder. "I have no idea why." Her hand went to her neck. "It meant to kill me. I'm sure of that. Anyway, I don't know what happened, but I must have passed out, both of us did I think, and this is going to sound even more crazy, but when we woke up we were lying in the snow in the middle of some deserted village just over the hill from here."

"Probably Kelktok," Marco murmured.

Kiera shrugged. "Anyway, the dog was gone when we woke. I don't know where it is, but I pray to God it doesn't find us." Kiera looked back at the store. "We heard noises, people, and made our way through the forest toward them. We found the city, came in, and found you. The rest you know."

"So what are you going to do?"

"I'm trying to figure out how to get home, Marco." She let her teeth show as she lifted her numb legs and pushed to her feet. "But right now I need to find a doctor for you and the girl. And by the way, what about the other boy they shot?"

"Others took him."

"Will he be all right?"

He sighed. "Yes. It wasn't as bad as it looked."

"Okay. How do I find a doctor for you two then?"

"A doctor? If you mean a healer, you don't need to search."

Kiera stared down at him. He had to be cold. "Why not?"

"In case you didn't notice," he smiled drily, "there is an army outside the city. A patrol will come through here by morning. They'll find us, I'll ask for a healer and they'll bring us to one."

"Is this city completely deserted?"

"Yes. Mostly. But there is no one here who will help us. Who can."

Kiera blew out a breath. "After what happened you're going to trust the army?"

"Kiera, I have to." He pressed his lips together. "I think those three were just having some fun." He slid an elbow underneath his chest and pushed halfway up. "A patrol will come this way fairly soon. They'll check all the streets." He sounded incredibly weary. "And soldiers always have healers."

"Is that really a good plan?" she demanded. Alex squeezed her hand and she forced herself to relax.

Marco closed his eyes. "There are no healers left in this city."

"Will they kill us?"

He turned to her, face grim. "Kiera, Allie will die without a healer."

Kiera put her free hand over her eyes and wiped her face. "Well, I'm just not willing to let any of us die if I can help it. Tell me how to even the odds."

Marco shook his head. "You even the odds, Kiera. If they try to hurt us, you call fire long enough to hold them off and we'll make our way out of the city."

Kiera stared at the boy. "Marco, I didn't make that fire." Her eyes flickered to the blackened wall where the bowmen had died, and she shuddered. That fire had almost gotten her, too, hadn't it? "I have a little martial arts training, but I am most definitely not a warrior and I don't have any weapons, real or magical. That means that I can't protect you that way if the bad guys come back. That also means that I am going to have to move Alex, Allie and you to someplace safe so I can hide you."

"Aren't you Skani, Kiera? A Skani sunwyr mage?" Marco suddenly demanded.

Kiera struggled to keep the exasperation from her voice. "I told you, Marco, I'm not from here, so I don't know your words. I don't even know what you're asking. I'm sorry."

"I don't know how it is that you speak fluent Skani and don't know who we are, Kiera, but maybe you did come from some faraway place." He held her eyes. "But you can call fire. Summon it. Kiera, I saw you."

Kiera snorted, then turned and walked away, Alex trailing behind her like a pup.

This whole day was utterly crazy.

Or was it she who was crazy? If not from her, where in the hell did that fire come from? It felt like it knew her, or that she knew it. Like it knew what she wanted.

Kiera let a bitter laugh escape. This was a plot from a bad movie.

"So what's a sun-weer?" she asked as she scanned the buildings for a safe place to pull him and the girl into.

He looked up at her. "There are four sorts of sunwyr. You can be a fire-fire, like you. You can be an air-air, earth-earth or water-water. Sunwyr are the most powerful mages, mages who can summon their element. Call and manifest their element into the known. There aren't very many."

She didn't laugh, but it was a close thing.

He glared at her.

"So are you a sunwyr, Marco?"

"Yes." He turned away, leaving her to gape at his back.

KIERA FOUND A SECLUDED NICHE on the far side of one of the buildings that would hold all four of them, and that no casual looker would find. She hoped. A long-abandoned shop whose doors had been easy to pop open would protect their front, and the high wall lining the far edge of the alley would guard their backs. She laid out some musty blankets she had scavenged from a nearby store, then went back for the kids. She helped Marco in first, stumbling with him through the empty rooms and out the back door. He could limp, after a fashion, with support, and once there she wrapped him up cocoon-style and made him as comfortable as possible. Alex helped her move Allie, but that part was hard, terrible and slow going.

After everybody was safely ensconced in their little hidey-hole, Kiera went out to wait in the building in front of the children. No one seemed near, so she went back to tell the kids where she was going to hold up.

She stopped just short of the back door to listen. Marco was talking.

"Well, Alex, those kids lost their mothers and fathers, and I was trying to help them get out of the city."

"Why?"

"So they could find the rest of their families to go live with."

Alex's voice was small. "Where did their parents go?"

Marco sighed, then spoke so softly that Kiera had to strain to hear him. "Many fled. Some were killed."

"Who killed their parents?"

"The soldiers. These or some others."

"Why?"

"Because the soldiers serve tyrants."

"What's a tyrant?"

"A man who wants everything and shows no mercy to those slow to give it to him."

Kiera listened because she'd wanted to ask those questions, too, but this was too much for a six-year-old. She walked in and cleared her throat. Shooting a glare at Marco, she spoke quietly. "Let's not talk about this anymore, all right?"

"Can I ask one more question, please?" Alex begged.

Kiera waffled. "Let's hear the question first."

"What would the soldiers do to the children if they caught them?"

Before Kiera could object, Marco told him, "Probably take them for slaves."

"All right, Alex, come out here with me. Now." Kiera shot another glare at Marco, but he had closed his eyes.

ABOUT THIRTY MINUTES LATER Kiera heard noises that only people, a lot of people, can make. She couldn't see anyone yet but the sounds were growing louder, and she didn't doubt that they were coming this way. She dragged Alex to the back and sat him with Marco. "Stay quiet!" she told them both, noting that Marco's mouth looked pinched, probably from pain. She glanced over at Allie, who even in the reflected moonlight looked both too pale and motionless. She wondered again, briefly, about the other boy who'd been shot.

"Kiera," Marco said, "promise me one thing."

She turned to look at him. "Depends."

"I beg you."

"It still depends."

Marco frowned. "No matter what happens, please don't tell anyone my or Allie's names or what we were doing. Call us other names, or tell them we wouldn't tell you. Tell them you found us already hurt."

"Why?"

"Just please, Kiera. Please."

Exasperation snaked through her. "Why did you tell me your names,

Marco, if I'm not supposed to tell anyone else?"

He smiled a little ruefully. "I admit it was a stupid decision. I'll blame it on being hurt," he dropped his eyes, "and that it seemed disrespectful to lie to the person who had just saved us."

For some reason that hurt, a little, but whether it was for him or because of him she wasn't sure. She nodded before making her way back to the front of the building. Since no other option presented itself, she hid herself behind the door. With it partly open, she could stand behind it and see out—with one eye—through the crack where the hinges connected to the wall. She fervently hoped that no one could see in.

How would she tell a doctor if she saw one? And what the hell was she going to do anyway? Call out? She shook her head. Maybe after these soldiers left, their tiny, ragtag group could continue to hide out until the girl was better and then they could try to make their way to a city. One with people in it.

Within minutes she made out the first soldiers. None looked terrifying, but she wasn't about to fling herself into anybody's arms. Soldiers had shot Marco. How could she tell who would do such a thing and who wouldn't?

Dozens of soldiers now marched down the road, perfect in their formation. No one looked her way.

She slid further back into the shadows anyway.

When she peeked out, she had to stop herself from jumping back. Some of the soldiers had peeled off the main lines and were walking far too closely to her doorway. One dark-haired, heavy-shouldered man jumped up on the stone walkway just outside her entry and she froze, held her breath, and fervently wished that it was darker where she stood.

He glanced inside, then turned to go. She breathed a sigh of relief.

Suddenly he turned back, grabbed the door and, before she could blink, pushed it back, trapping her against the wall. He peered through the crack at her and flashed an ugly smile.

She gaped at him in shock. He looked her up and down, slowly, leeringly. His grin widened, then disappeared. His boots shushed as they passed through the doorway. She tried to push the door open, but it wouldn't budge.

He was holding it shut.

As he reached the crack between her and the wall, she kicked the door as hard as she could, catching him in the face with its edge. He let go of the door to grab his face and she slid by, then ran through the open room that fronted her hiding spot.

Stupid, stupid, she chanted to herself, nearly in a panic. *It had to be the footprints. I forgot to hide the goddamned footprints.*

She had nowhere to go but out into the throngs of soldiers in the front or back to where the children were hidden. The soldier was now sputtering, and angry, and he called out to others, a move that helped her make her choice. She ran out the back door and looked for a place to run.

But they have to see me, she thought wildly, *or they'll search.*

Her spotter came through the back door, grinning at her with no amusement at all. She started to run away down the back edge of the building, but another solider appeared in the alley down the way she'd planned to run. The fifteen foot wall she'd previously considered a source of protection ran behind the alley and as far as she could see, keeping Kiera from the buildings one street back. With the alley now blocked she had nowhere else to go except back toward the children, and that she would never do.

She made a little noise of frustration and put her hands up.

Oh, please. Let the children be all right.

The soldier from the doorway smiled broadly. He let the point of his sword—when had he drawn a sword?—drop down toward the ground. He walked leisurely toward her, looking her up and down, slowly, baring his teeth, and Kiera felt herself stiffen with fear.

The soldier was almost to her when she heard Alex scream. And scream again.

"No!" she yelled. "No!" She tried to push past the soldier to get to the children. He grabbed her arms and crushed her to his chest, where his arms encircled her like a lover's. He barked out a laugh, but his eyes held ice.

Kiera kneed him in the groin. As he started to double over she punched him just below the eye with a closed fist. He let go and slid to the ground, hands wrapped in his crotch, moaning, and she ran past him.

About a dozen soldiers surrounded the children. Some held long spearlike things and others had swords, and all looked decidedly unfriendly. Alex lay curled up on the ground, clinging to Marco.

Kiera crashed past one of the soldiers and grabbed Alex. "Leave them alone!" she panted, holding a whimpering Alex close to her chest. "We haven't done anything wrong. Please don't hurt us. We need a healer. Please."

She closed her eyes for the briefest of moments and prayed they'd be merciful.

When she looked up, a hard-looking, blond man in his thirties watched her. "I want to know who murdered my men."

Kiera looked away, heart sinking.

"Who killed the men?" The soldier stepped closer and knelt, but Kiera refused to look up. "Three of my men were murdered here less than a mark ago. I know you saw it."

Kiera glanced at Marco, who stared at the ground. Allie lay partially uncovered behind him.

She turned, still holding Alex, to the soldier who'd spoken. "I don't know what you're talking about, sir. I don't even know what you mean."

He stared at Kiera. She wondered if he could hear her heart hammering. "Look, soldier, these children are hurt. Will you please send for a doctor? A healer, I mean? Please?" She gestured behind her. "This girl will die if she isn't given medical help and the boy has got to get an arrow out before infection sets in."

The soldier turned to Marco. "Who shot you?" he asked.

Marco kept his mulish expression intact and his eyes on the floor.

The soldier stood and walked over to where Marco sat. "I asked you, boy, who shot you?"

Marco closed his eyes.

The soldier kicked Marco in the side. The side he'd been shot in.

Marco screamed and writhed back, pulling one leg up. Alex screamed and tried to climb up Kiera's chest.

"Stop it!" Kiera shouted, pushing Alex into a corner as she jumped up. "Don't hurt him!"

The soldier spun around and backhanded Kiera so hard that she lost her footing and slammed to the ground. Her head landed next to Alex's feet. She lay in the snow for a moment, looked up into Alex's terrified eyes, then pushed up on one elbow. In the same calm, cold voice, he again asked, "Who wielded the fire? Man? Woman? Who?"

"No one knows anything, you asshole!" she screamed, pushing up, and tried to tamp down the terror. Before she could rise the soldier kicked her in the face with the toe of his boot, bloodying her nose and mouth, and knocked her head back and into Alex, who slammed into the wall behind him with a solid *thunk* and started to cry.

The world caught fire, but this time she felt the origins of the Armageddon. It came from her middle, from her chest, from her fingers. From her rage and her fear and her pain. Time seemed to stand still while red silk, tangible strands of her rage, slipped from her body to form a solid wall fifty feet high around her and the children.

Fury consumed her, comforted her, caressed her. The fire was her heart, and it was burning. She wanted to strike out, ease her fear, but time had slowed to an almost sleepy pace and she couldn't seem to remember anything but the rage. The world was encased in red. As red as her fury. She felt the blood on her face and her anger redoubled, rekindled, the fire growing brighter and hotter.

She turned her head and soldiers were burning. Two, then five, then twelve. She saw them screaming, retching, panicking, but couldn't hear their voices. They burned.

More came, and more, from someplace, from everywhere, and tried to get to her, to Alex, to Marco and Allie, but when they came close they burned, too, and a part of her rejoiced.

Time passed—minutes? hours?—and she grew weary, but soldiers surrounded them, some distance away, and she was furious, and afraid to let go, to let it come back into her.

Could she do that? How could she make it stop?

Even as she wondered she knew those men waited to kill her and the children and her rage boiled again. The wall of fire expanded, reaching its fingers toward the soldiers, who broke rank and ran, so slowly, some too slowly.

The world tilted. Her strength suddenly waned, and she sank to her knees.

She would hold the fire as long as she could. How soon until she fell? Until the fire was gone?

As she watched the billowing vista, a man strode towards her, through the ranks of running men, his form undulating on the far side of her flame's red curtain. He was a very big man. Was he a soldier? She should stop him. Shouldn't she? Kiera felt confused, ambivalent, and she shook her head, trying to clear it.

He didn't frighten her, and she didn't understand why. She sat back on her heels and rubbed her aching eyes. She felt so tired. But she couldn't let go. If she let the fire go out, these men would kill her and take the children. Enslave them.

The man paused at the edge of the fire, and stared into the flames for a few heartbeats, intently, perhaps looking for its source. Then he bowed his head as if shielding his face from the wind and walked unscathed through the wall of flames.

Kiera forced herself back up, legs shaking, as the big man breached the fire. She swayed once, fisted her hands at her sides, and held firm. Her fire did not burn him. And yet. And yet she wasn't afraid. She wondered why, or wanted to wonder why, but the thought squirmed and wriggled away. Did it really matter? She was running out of strength and soon it wouldn't matter, anyway.

She rested one hand on her knife.

The man walked half of the dozen feet separating them inside the borders of the ruby dome, then dropped to one knee. They were close to eye level now. He bowed with his head, then called, "Greetings, my lady." His voice was low and gritty, and it sounded as though it came from far away.

Kiera stared at him but said nothing. Even kneeling, he was tall. And very, very big. He wore some sort of uniform. His shoulder-length, dark hair blew in a breeze she could not feel. The light of the fire behind him shadowed his features.

She held her breath and waited.

"Lady, I am here to ask you to cease this fire."

His words surprised her, but it drifted up in a slow, sticky way, infusing the anger but not diminishing it. She bared her teeth. "Why? If I do, these soldiers will kill me and take these children." To her ears, her voice sounded bigger, stronger, stranger. For some reason it made her feel even angrier. The dome reflected her, squeezing tighter, tendrils reaching inward, toward the man.

Either he didn't notice, or didn't care. "No, lady; no one will harm these children or you. I propose an accord. Stop the fire. Agree to hold the fire from us, and you have my oath that you will come to no harm from this army." He nodded and the air rippled around him, in the way of dreams, making her dizzy. "Those who offended you are dead."

She drew her wits together as best she could and spoke sharply. "Soldier, who the hell are you to make this promise? Do you think I'm stupid? As soon as I stop the fire you'll kill me and take these children! Wounded children. And do you know who hurt them? Can you guess?"

Her breath felt short. The world canted, or maybe she just lost her balance, but Kiera lost her footing, stumbled back, and sat down hard on the ground. Her strength was nearly gone. The man waited until she looked up at him, then lifted his right hand and let his fingers rest on the edge of the emblem embroidered on the left chest of his uniform. "Lady, I am the captain of this army. There is no higher authority within three turns' ride. You have my oath that should you agree, we will not harm you or the children."

Kiera considered this for a moment. What the hell. It wasn't like she really had much choice. She nodded, then fell back in the snow.

CHAPTER 3

WHEN KIERA WOKE, THE SUN SHONE on her face, her head ached, her throat hurt, and she felt like she might burst into flames. *Déjà vu all over again*, she thought, then opened her eyes.

She'd been sleeping in the bed of—was this a covered wagon? It was certainly moving. Alex lay snuggled up to her, his face peaceful in sleep. A heavy blanket covered both of them. She sat up, shrugged off the blanket, then moved Alex gently away and covered him back up.

Kiera scooted over to one side and pulled back the canvas flap. She looked around. And gasped.

Definitely a wagon. A wagon surrounded by an army. Ahead, a column of men, ten wide, stretched as far as she could see. All carried a long weapon of some kind. Behind her a squad of about forty men followed her wagon, and behind them trundled several other wagons.

The wind blew in her face. Bitterly cold air. She closed her eyes for a moment and let it leach some of the heat from her cheeks.

The train wound its way through some sort of valley. Heavy-bottomed, rugged mountains jutted spikes high into the sky on either side of their party, leaving only a narrow space between their feet. Hoar-frosted pine trees lined the snowy road, thick as a fur coat, and others who'd lost their leaves clung together, as if for warmth, in the few spaces the pines left bare. An unseen raven called. The cold began to sting, so she zipped her coat all the way up.

Kiera leaned back into the swaying wagon and let the flap drop. Just feet away, Marco and Allie still slept in separate bundles, their breaths even puffs of white smoke. Someone had tended Allie. She looked better. Clean and better.

A sound intruded. A discordant *clop-clopp*ing. Coming closer. She scooted back to the window and pulled open the flap. Behind the wagon a large black horse trotted forward, outside the lines, carrying a soldier.

It was the soldier from the fire. She was sure of it. She swallowed and tried to smooth out her face.

He caught her looking and nodded, holding her eyes, his face expressionless.

She blew out a breath. This soldier—didn't he say he was the Captain?—was for certain a beautiful man. *In fact,* she thought, *he may be the most beautiful man I have ever seen.* He was as big as she remembered, maybe bigger, about half again larger than any man she had ever seen. She guessed he would stand several inches over six feet tall and weighed a very easy three hundred pounds. *I'll bet he's strong,* she thought, judging by the way his body molded the many bands of metallic armor that V'd down his chest, ending just under a thick belt that encased his sternum. The same bands wrapped around his forearms. Was that for protection?

Even in this bitter cold, though, he'd left his shoulders and upper arms bared, and his waist nearly so, wrapped only by two straps of thick leather. His thick, nearly black hair just brushed the top of his shoulders. He had dark olive skin and two or three days' growth of beard. As he got closer she could see that he had a very strong jaw. He was somewhere between thirty and forty. And wow, he had nice eyes. Dark eyes rimmed with thick lashes.

Whoa there. She leaned back inside and dusted her hands on her pants. *I'm lost in this crazy place. I need to go home. And it isn't like I'm hoping to embark on a fiery affair in the interim.*

Or like he would even consider it, a voice inside her chided.

The soldier nodded when he came abreast of the wagon. "Good morn, my lady." His voice was as gritty as she remembered it.

"And to you. Are we your prisoners, sir?"

He shifted slightly in his saddle. Frowned. "No. You are not."

Kiera flushed. "I apologize, sir, if I seem abrupt. It was a shock to awaken in a wagon surrounded by an army."

He wrapped a rein around his hand. "I am sorry if we frightened you, my lady, but we must return on time."

"I see. Well, I owe you my thanks for allowing your healer to look at the children, so thank you, sir."

He nodded.

"By the way, my name is Kiera."

"I am pleased to know you, Lady Kiera. I am Captain Laszlo."

She tried to keep her eyes from his chest. Wasn't he cold? "Are you headed to a city?"

"Back to Fairbanks, my lady," he answered, eyes scanning ahead of their train. Their wagon was creaking so fiercely that she nearly missed Marco's groan. She kept her eyes on the man riding flush with the wagon.

But Fairbanks? She almost laughed. Was there a Barrow, too? Bethel? Well, at least Fairbanks was a city. "May we accompany you?"

The soldier turned back to her. "Yes, my lady. Do you have business in Fairbanks? Do you travel to meet your husband?"

Kiera wondered what business someone might have in Fairbanks. "Well, uh, I guess my answer is 'no' to both questions. I don't have a husband, and my son and I can't get where we want to go right now, so a city seems like our best bet." She closed her eyes for a moment. That had to sound as crazy to him as it did to her. She let out a breath. "So we will travel with you for now, if that's all right. Why are you returning to Fairbanks, if I may ask?"

He was staring at her. "We return to Lord Vayu." His gaze flicked to neck, then back to her face. "I would hear your story."

Her hand went involuntarily to her throat. "A dog attacked Alex and me, but we're fine now." She smiled and hoped it didn't look nervous. "So who is Lord Vayu?"

"The governor of Fairbanks."

"And why are we going there?"

"He is my lord." He nodded toward the column. "I return his army."

That made sense, so she nodded. What she wanted to ask might not, but she had to. Where else could they go? She had to find someplace safe for them until she could figure out how to get back home. It wasn't like they could ask to be dropped off someplace, and all she had was her phone and the clothes on her back. No wallet. No money. "Oh, okay. Uh, would the accord you offered possibly include lodging once we get there? For a time, I mean."

He seemed unsurprised. "I am certain that my lord would be pleased to offer his hospitality to you."

Oh, thank God. Kiera crossed her arms, rubbing the sore left one with her right to keep him from noticing her shaking hands.

"Are these children," he nodded to indicate the people in the wagon, "your family, or did you meet them in the city?"

"The small boy is mine. The other two I met in the city. They were hurt and we hid together."

"Did they tell you their names? Or what had happened?"

Her heart thudded in her chest. "No, Captain. They were hurt and we weren't together very long before those soldiers found us."

The Captain stared at her for a long moment and she knew he knew she was lying. "What can I have brought for you? Food? Water?"

She smiled a little. "I would love water and food. Enough for all of us, please, and thank you."

Laszlo nodded, then turned and rode off. Kiera watched him ride away until she couldn't see him any longer. She sat back down in the wagon. After tucking the blanket around Alex and herself, Kiera looked at Marco, who was still pretending to be asleep. "Marco, who to you is Lord Vayu?" she murmured.

"My father," he whispered.

She sighed and closed her eyes.

THE FOOD WAS HORRIBLE. It consisted of some foul-tasting dried fish and nearly rotten berries. Alex cried and begged Kiera not to make him eat it, and she shushed him and finally told him he didn't have to after she discovered that she couldn't force it down either. Marco, still wrapped in his blankets, eyes mostly closed, watched them gagging and grinned. Kiera shot him a black look, but put the tin bowls down and pushed them as far away from Alex and her as she could. Marco pointed at the food and then himself and Kiera nodded, reaching with her foot to kick the bowls the rest of the way to him. He scooped them inside his blankets and ate everything.

Alex was restless and bored, so Kiera tore a frozen branch off a tree they passed and broke it into pieces he could play with.

A soldier dropped off a second set of water jugs. After he left Kiera took one to Marco and knelt down. "So why doesn't he know you?" Kiera whispered.

"He's only been the captain for a cycle and I've only seen him from a distance. I didn't involve myself with the army."

That made sense. "So what names do I call you two?"

"Call me Roke and her Jana," he whispered softly.

Kiera nodded. She lay back and closed her eyes, debating how far to trust this young man. Would helping him hide his identity get her into trouble? He seemed like a decent kid, and she couldn't just turn him in when she didn't know what he was running from. To survive here, though, she needed information. She decided to stick a toe in the water.

Without opening her eyes, and in a tone she hoped conveyed idle boredom, she asked, "So Roke, how long has it been since Lord Vayu's son ran away? And why did he run? I can't seem to recall."

She opened her eyes to find him staring at her in horror. He flicked his eyes toward the driver and shook his head, and she smiled in what she hoped was an encouraging way.

In the same tone, but in a far lower voice, she said, "Remember that I'm new here, Roke, and it would be good to get to know a little more about what's going on before I end up offending someone who might throw me in the dungeon."

A flurry of emotions passed over Marco's face, but he finally swallowed and nodded, though his eyes stayed hard. "Well, Kiera—" his voice was quiet, but not quite a whisper. "As I heard tell, Lord Vayu's youngest son disappeared about a moon ago. They'd had a falling out. I don't know why—" he glared at her—"but Marco, that's Vayu's son, he left. I'm sure that Lord Vayu looked for him, but things keep him pretty busy, so his son is still missing."

Kiera wanted to ask about Allie, but Marco's face told her not only that he wouldn't answer, but also that if she pushed him, she might lose the fragile friendship they'd built. She needed a friend, and she liked him, so she switched topics.

"Why does Lord Vayu send his army out? Is he at war?"

Marco relaxed and closed his eyes. "Yes." He opened his eyes long enough to shoot her a significant look before laying back, arms behind his head.

"Oh my God! Are we at risk?"

"We're in the middle of the army, Kiera. How much safer can we be?"

Kiera made a face. "How much more can we look like targets?"

"No. It's all right. Lord Vayu's army can hold off just about anybody and they're not going to throw us out for bait."

"Oh, good," Kiera said weakly. "So who is Lord Vayu at war with?"

He considered. "We're not technically at war with anybody."

"I am completely confused here, Marco."

He grinned. "War is a Skani tradition, Kiera."

"What do you mean?"

He shifted his legs, trying to get comfortable. "About a hundred cycles ago our people came to this land from across the mountains." He gestured vaguely eastward. "They—we—are the Skani. We came because we were facing extermination. Our people had been at war with people we called the Shatru for so long it doesn't even matter anymore now.

"We came because we were dying out. They hunted us down, killing everyone they found. Women, children, animals, everything. They wanted our land and we had to leave. We fled in secret, and traveled far away. We came to this land." He rubbed one hand on the blanket. "The Alaks were living here at the time, and they didn't welcome us. It may be that there were some massacres on both sides. Who knows now. I do know that war broke out and it lasted for maybe a span of cycles. No one really won, but the Skani drove the Alaks west. West and south.

"Everybody got pretty tired of fighting. No one was winning. So the Skani and the Alaks finally agreed to a treaty. They agreed to split the land and stop fighting. There were four factions and they claimed what are now the four deconns. They renamed the great land, Alaska, and gave each other the promise of safe passage through each other's deconn. Deconns are off limits and no one is allowed to fight there. It's still tense, though, even after all this time, and there's still a lot of fighting in the interior. No governor can really hold more than his deconn and he can't promise safety to anyone outside it."

Marco laughed, but there was no humor in it. "But the war never really ended, Kiera. It just goes on and on. They all want more land, more slaves, more everything. So the fighting goes on and on and no one ever wins." He paused to take a breath. "But lots of people lose." He looked out at the trees. "The people who live outside the deconn, that's about a two turn ride outside each city, they have no protection. And most people have no magic, so when a governor needs slaves, he sends a team out to scout and scour a village." His face grew hard. "They mostly take children."

Kiera didn't understand all of what he said, but what she did made horror roil through her. In a quiet voice, she asked, "So why don't they move inside the, uh, deconn?"

He turned abruptly around, his features harsh. "Why should they? They choose to live free, to grow and hunt what they will, and to marry as they wish. Some in the nadeconn, outside the deconns, have lived on the same land for generations. Why should they have to leave?"

Well, that explained a lot, and she certainly agreed, so she nodded.

"So there are four deconns?"

"Yes. Fairbanks and Barrow are Skani-reigned and Anchorage and Bethel are Alak. The Skani have magic. Alaks are shifters, and they're strong and fast and meaner than the four hells."

Kiera's head was reeling. "'Shifters'? Shapeshifters, like werewolves?"

Or big dogs?

"I don't know what you mean by 'were,' but, my f—I mean someone told me that shifters are half animal and half human. They can shift into their animal form, whatever they are, and some are wolves. I know they live in tribes. By animal, I mean, like wolf with wolf, even though the Alak all speak the same language. It's not Skani. They have their own language. I heard they have wars with each other, but I don't know if that's just something people say. In truth, Kiera, I really don't know that much about them. Sorry."

"Jesus Christ." She whispered. Was the big dog that attacked them a shifter? If so, how had it gotten to her Anchorage? And why, for God's sake, had it attacked them?

"What?" Marco asked.

"Nothing. So Skani, your people, have magic?"

"Yes."

Alex, apparently bored, threw a piece of a stick, which hit her in the arm and slid to the wagon floor. She smiled, picked it up and tossed it back. He grinned at her and continued building whatever he was building.

Kiera wondered what being a Skani meant. Here it seemed to mean that you weren't a shifter. But was it cultural, too? Racial? If only Skani had magic, she must be a Skani, too. Or genetically similar. Maybe something here triggered it? "So how does magic work?"

"Well, there are four elements. Fire," he nodded to her, "water, earth and air. Everybody is born to their sunsign. It has to do with the place the planets and stars are on the date they're born. Every mother tries to birth a fire or an air since they are the most powerful mages. During brooding moons things get pretty crazy." He wriggled his eyebrows.

'Sunsign'? Planets and stars? Was this just some astrology thing? How could that be? She most definitely had some affinity with fire here, but was that because of the date she was born? She wished she could get on the internet. She knew she was a Leo, but was that a fire sign? She'd never gotten into astrology. Who did that in the 21st century? Did anyone?

Whoa. Wait a minute. "Brooding moons?" Moons? Months?

He grinned at her. "Well, a woman carries her child for nine moons, right?"

"Uh, yeah."

"Well, fire belongs to those born in the fourth, eighth and twelfth moons. Air to those of the second, the sixth, and the tenth. It's every other moon cycle. So women breed to give birth under a favorable moon. First, third, fifth and so on. During those moons even oaths of fidelity are waived for unproved women."

"What?"

He shrugged. "It gets crazy during those times."

She shook her head. "Wow. But let me ask you about something else. I heard you say something about fire-fire, air-air, and so on. You said it twice. Fire-fire. For, uh, sunwyr. What does that mean?"

"Each person has two signs, their sunhouse and moonhouse. Their sign is determined by the date and time of their birth. Like I said, there are four sunhouses. There are twelve moons, and four cycles of elements, earth, air, water, then fire, so each element dominates for three separate moons before the cycle closes. Those are the sunsigns. Do you understand?"

Kiera nodded. This was definitely astrology.

Alex brought his sticks to Marco, offering them. He smiled and took one, and Alex sat down next to him.

"What should we make, Alex? Will you help me build a house?"

Alex nodded. "Sure." Marco motioned Alex down and they began propping sticks together.

Marco continued to talk as he built. "Within three turns after birth every child born in our deconn is tattooed or branded," Marco continued, eyes on his construction, "with their sunsign inside their left wrist. I know that sounds gruesome," he said, correctly interpreting the look on her face, "but it's done because a person's sign is very important, maybe the most important thing in their life. That mark guides their life choices. Not only can they work with their element, they have certain talents that they're born with."

Kiera lifted her eyebrows.

"Kiera, nothing is more important than the influences a person was born under. It shapes who they are more than any other force. Life stretches some talents and suppresses others, but who you are at birth is your destiny."

Kiera pressed her lips together. "Ever heard of a self-fulfilling prophecy?" she asked.

"No."

"It's when someone does something, sometimes going to very great lengths to get it done, because they believe ahead of time that's the way things will turn out."

"That isn't what this is, Kiera."

She frowned, but changed the subject. "So what about the moonhouses then?"

Instead of answering, Marco turned back to Alex and the house and struck up a conversation with him.

"Since the boy's decided to sulk, I'll tell ya," boomed a voice from the front of the wagon. Startled, she looked up and into Grant's face.

She gasped.

No. Wait. This wasn't Grant.

But this man, the driver who had pulled the canvas back so he could see her, looked enough like Grant to fool a casual looker. This man, like Grant, was fiftyish, and tall and thin like a runner. Like Grant he had a proud face, slightly rounded, but where Grant's nose was too prominent this man's was hooked, and Grant's eyes were grey, not a startling blue.

And Kiera couldn't imagine seeing Grant sitting in the front of a wagon wearing a black army uniform branded with two large vertical red stripes.

God, she'd been stupid. He'd been quiet so long she'd nearly forgotten he was there. And could hear.

"Want me to tell ye?"

Well, this particular cup was officially spilled. "Uh, sure. Yes."

He spoke with an odd accent, one she had never heard before. "The moonhouses, moonsigns, ye see, are named by birthmark. Ye know there'r four elements. The first mark of the turn, the one from nighttide till first mark past, is filled with fire, so children born durin' that time are firemoons. Earth fills the second mark, air the third, and water the fourth. Then they cycle again. Six times. Fifth mark is fire, sixth is earth, and on ye go."

"I'm sorry but I'm a little confused. 'Mark' is a measurement of time?"

The driver nodded.

"Have you heard the term 'hour'?"

"Nah."

Kiera blew out a breath. "How many marks have we been traveling?"

"'Round seven."

Kiera pulled back her sleeve and looked at her watch. It was 2:10 P.M. Had she been up for seven hours? She didn't think so.

Maybe reading her frustration, Marco spoke from behind her. "It's just into the fourth air hour, Kiera."

It took Kiera ten seconds to do the math, but then she smiled. Marks were hours. Marks were hours and moons were months. Thank God. Vocabulary she could learn, but trying to decipher new concepts of time would make trying to get by in this place a hell of a lot harder.

"Thank you, Marco. Can I ask you guys another question?" She paused, but spoke again before either could answer. "I know my questions might seem silly, but I've never studied this stuff, so I really appreciate your patience with me. I'm new here, and there's so much to learn."

The driver nodded once. "Where are ye from then, if'n I might ask ye?"

A logical question, and one Kiera wished she knew how to answer in a way that didn't sound insane. She sighed. "We're from a city far from here, and I'll save you the next question. I'm still not sure how we got here, soldier, but I can say that I want to go home. I'm just not sure how to do that yet."

The soldier's eyes were kind. "What would ye know, lady?"

Kiera smiled gratefully at his tact. "What impact does this moonsign, birthmark, have on children? I mean, what does it have to do with life? And the, uh, element they have this affinity for?"

"Moonsign," Marco said from behind her, "is the balancing half of your magic. Water, earth, fire or air. If they're the same, you have the strongest power in that element. If they're compatible, like air and fire, you will have some skill in both."

"And if they aren't?" Kiera asked.

"Then both halves of your magic may cancel the other and if they do you will never be a mage."

"Nobody has to ask ye which sun or moonhouse you belong to, do they?" the driver snorted. "Now, fires canna call fire, right, like you can, 'nless they're fire sun and moon, but most control their element somewhat, dependin' on the man, but then ye're gettin' to know that, I s'pose." He winked at her.

Kiera didn't know what to say. "I, uh, thank you for the information, soldier, though I don't think you told me your name."

The driver bowed in his seat. "I thank you for the invitation to know ye, Lady. I am Mosha. It is my pleasure."

She paused a moment, then answered, "And I am Kiera. I am pleased to make your acquaintance as well, Mosha. And now I'm cold so I think I'll lie down for a bit. Thank you again."

"'Twas my pleasure, lady."

"It's Kiera. Just Kiera."

"Kiera, then." He smiled and turned back to the horses.

Kiera moved back to her blankets and climbed into them. "Alex, are you cold?" she asked, but he shook his head, still caught up in building his house with Marco. It couldn't be ten degrees out here.

"Roke, would you bring me that water so I can have a drink before it freezes?" she asked, and when he brought it over, she touched his arm to catch his eye, and pointed down. *Sit. Please,* she added with her eyes.

He sat.

"I need to know some things, Roke. Will you help me?" she whispered.

"Depends," he answered with a smile.

Kiera took a drink from the water jug, then laid back and pulled the blankets up to her neck, trying to ward off a chill.

She motioned him down and he lay back, head in hand and elbow on the ground, looking at her.

She dropped her voice as low as she dared. "So what do I say when people ask me where I'm from? Everyone now knows that I can call fire. Is that going to get me in trouble? Who should I say I am?" Kiera gathered her courage and asked the question that most scared her. "Marco, are they going to enslave me and Alex? Please tell me the truth."

Marco frowned as he stared at her for a minute, thinking. "I don't know what you can say that will keep you safe, Kiera, but you're a powerful woman, and everyone knows it, or will, and that may be more important than anything else."

"Powerful? Because I can call fire? But, Marco, I don't even know how I did that! I don't know if I can do it again, or how to stop it if it happens again, for chrissake."

"That you can is all anyone will care about. Trust me."

"And what does that mean?"

"It means," he hissed, "that full fire mages are very rare. It means that, at worst, the governors will vie for you. You asked the captain if Lord Vayu would be willing to provide you with a bed like you were a beggar and I nearly laughed. Vayu, any of them, would do anything to get you into his retinue." Marco scooted closer. "Kiera, I have never met, no, I've never even heard of a full fire mage. I don't think anyone would dare try to enslave you, but you would be a powerful addition to any deconn, and especially to an army. They may do about anything to keep you. Why do you think the captain was so generous?"

She was stunned. "I don't know. How could I know?" Tears rose in her eyes. "I just want to go home, Marco. I don't want to be part of anything here, especially a war. And I will never join anybody's army!"

He patted her hand. "Well, keep that part to yourself, okay? The best way to keep safe is to keep quiet and stay mysterious."

"So what should I say? When someone asks, I mean, or they introduce themselves to me. Who should I be?"

"Say that you're a nadeconn. No ties. It will help explain your ignorance."

"All right." She sniffled. It was mostly from the cold.

"And why was I there? In that village?"

"I can't answer that one. Make something up, but make it believable. You could say you were brought here by magic." He winked, then rose and went back to Alex, who was trying to listen while pretending he wasn't.

Kiera closed her eyes and tried to rest. Her thoughts were tumultuous, keeping her from sleep, but she wanted to be alone with them so she kept her eyes closed.

A while later a warm body snuggled up to hers. She opened the covers and Alex wriggled in. "Keer, I wanna go home. When can we go home? I don't like this wagon."

"Me, too, Alex." She pulled a hand out and smoothed his hair, and he snuggled against her. He was cold. "Why don't you get under the blanket?" she sighed. "I haven't figured out how to get us home yet. Hold on, okay, and we'll keep trying."

She paused a moment. "I'm sorry we missed your play."

"Yeah." His voice was unhappy.

"What did you miss, Alex?" Marco asked, sliding over so he could hear better.

"Aw, I was gonna be a wise man in the Christmas play at my school last night. I was gonna get to sing a song all by myself, too, in front of ever body."

Kiera flashed Marco a grateful look, and he smiled.

"No way! A wise man?"

Alex smiled shyly. "Yeah."

"Well, how about your mom and I pretend we're at your play and you can tell us what you'd say there, and then you can sing us the song."

"And for me, too," called Mosha.

Kiera grinned. "Well, Alex, let's hear it."

IT GOT DARK EARLY, in mid-afternoon. Before long Kiera and Alex were both cold and hungry. Kiera knew how Alex felt because he told her. Repeatedly. They stayed snuggled together under the blanket and tried rather unsuccessfully to stay warm.

The army stopped and put up a sort of camp in the early evening hours. The men, so quiet before, became animated, chatting and laughing amongst themselves as they constructed their little town for the night. Tents went up everywhere, quicker than Kiera would have thought, and apparently in some kind of pattern.

As soon as the wagon had stopped Mosha dismounted and promptly disappeared.

Kiera waited until the men seemed to settle down, but Mosha didn't come back.

"Keer, I'm hungry," Alex whined.

"All right, Alex," she said, stifling impatience with Mosha, and with everything, and got out of the blankets. "I'll go see if I can find something to eat."

Marco uncovered. "I'll come with you," he told her.

Kiera shook her head. "You don't need to," she said. "Stay here with Alex and uh—uh—" She gestured at Allie.

"Jana," Marco mumbled as he pulled the blanket over Allie and tucked it around her face. He pulled on his coat and hopped over the lip of the wagon, landing with a thud.

Kiera sighed. "Alex, stay here with Jana. I'll be back as soon as I can. Do not get out of this wagon, do you hear me?"

Alex nodded, pulling the blankets up.

Kiera climbed out of the wagon and looked around. It looked as though a city had sprung up around them. There were tents the size of her living room laid out in such even rows that Kiera wondered, amused, if someone had marked lines in the snow. Apparently fires were rationed, too; there was one for about every five tents.

None of the ones she could see had pots or any other cooking implements.

Up ahead, maybe ten rows, she could see some larger tents, easily twice as big as the ones erected around their wagon. Kiera put her hands in her pockets and headed that way. Marco could come or not as he pleased.

Marco joined her as she walked, and men came out of the tents, or stopped chopping wood, or ceased poking the fires. None challenged them or asked what they wanted, but they all stared.

Kiera wondered briefly, belatedly, if this was a good idea, then shook her head. Alex shouldn't have to go hungry because these men forgot them.

After a good fifteen minutes of walking, about the same time her legs had started to burn from the cold, Kiera found herself facing one of the biggest tents she had seen. She skirted it, then stopped. Around her about ten other very large tents circled a central area like the prongs of a gem. Fires roared inside rocks set in front of each of the tents. A-shaped stands held bubbling pots. Each held something, hopefully edible, though she couldn't smell anything from where she stood. She predicted it would be something short of delicious, but at least it would feed Alex.

She took a couple of steps toward the nearest fire, lifted a hand to signal the cook, but a movement to her right caught her eye and she stopped and turned to look.

The area in the middle of these tents was flat and bare of trees, but it wasn't empty. In fact, it was filled with a couple hundred men. She felt slightly shocked that she hadn't noticed before, but it slipped into curiosity as she noted that they seemed to be watching something, silently, and that none had turned to her or Marco.

Unable to stop herself, Kiera took a step toward the men. Marco grabbed her arm. She flashed him an irritated look and pulled free.

Kiera walked across the snow to the edge of the men, who had formed a four-man-deep wall, then peered through a gap to see what was going on.

And stopped.

The soldiers all stood outside a single line of torches. Inside the line were two men.

One of the men, the one closest to her, had his back to her. He was naked. His knees were bent in a sort of crouch, his hands were up and open, and he was making small moves back and forth like a cat getting ready to spring. Kiera followed what must be his line of sight to another man, who stood across the ring and as straight as a tree.

It was the captain.

He wasn't wearing a shirt. She looked down. Or pants. Just some sort of brown cloth wrapped round his, uh, loins.

And wow.

The man in front of her sprang so suddenly that she jumped back. He flung himself at the Captain, who stayed frozen until the man was almost to him. While the man was still in mid-air, Laszlo took one step aside as he lifted an arm with sinuous grace and stunning speed; he was almost too quick to be seen. It looked like he spent no effort, but his blow not only stopped the man's trajectory, it knocked him completely out of the ring, and the attacker went flying into the crowd across from Kiera. As if choreographed, the watchers parted like water. The man landed in the snow, on his back, and wheezed.

Laszlo rolled his shoulders, then raised a hand to wipe his forehead. He turned and the torchlight reflected off the sweat on his chest.

His very large, muscular chest.

"Wow," she breathed. "Wow." She felt a smile pulling her face. She tried to stifle it, but it would not be banished. She covered her mouth with a hand, feeling like an idiot, and pressed her lips together.

She took a deep breath through her nose, trying to ease the funny feeling in her stomach.

Laszlo was rolling his neck. He suddenly stopped and stiffened. He started to turn his head—toward her!—and Kiera panicked. She did not want this man to see her acting like a—an idiot.

She took a step back and then one to the side to hide behind the group of soldiers. Marco took her hand and she looked at him. He was laughing silently. "Shut up!" she whispered, embarrassed, then hid her own laugh behind her hand.

A sound startled her. Kiera jumped, then whirled around, hands up.

Laszlo was standing behind her. In front of her, now. Well, Laszlo's chest, anyway.

How in the hell had he done that?

She flicked her eyes to the right. Marco was staring up, mouth open, looking as much the idiot as she must.

She felt a cold rush of something clench her sternum.

She looked up. Laszlo's face was hard and so angry that she flinched. He stared down at her. "Did you come to watch the animals fight?" His voice was as glacial as his face.

Kiera furrowed her brows, flummoxed. "What?" she said. Of all the things she expected he might say, or be mad at, this made no sense at all.

He took a breath and opened his mouth to say something else, but then stopped. He closed his mouth and looked at her for a long moment.

The ghost of a smile flitted across his face.

Kiera felt herself flush.

He knew.

How the hell did he know?

She closed her eyes, completely mortified. She wanted to be anywhere, anywhere but right here. Where was that magic now?

Without looking at Laszlo again, she turned, took Marco's hand and led him away. They would ask someone on the way back how to get Alex something to eat.

CHAPTER 4

MUCH TO KIERA'S RELIEF, SHE DID NOT see Laszlo all the next day, her third day there, and it passed uneventfully. Within an hour after full dark fell she heard someone outside talking about lights ahead. She sat up, uncovered, and crawled over to the edge. She opened the flap and peered into the darkness.

"I'll bet that's a mayor's place. If we're lucky, we'll stay there tonight," Marco commented from behind her.

"No need to wonder. We'll stay at the manse tonight." All three jumped. The captain had ridden up.

Kiera turned and faced him, the man who had apparently been riding behind the wagon. He was watching her. His gaze flickered to her clothes, then back to her face. His intense scrutiny made her feel a little uneasy. He urged his horse forward until he was even with the flap. He peered inside until he found Marco.

"So you finally woke. How are you faring?" he asked the boy.

Marco bowed his head and stared at the wagon bed. "Much better, Captain, and I thank you for letting your healer tend my sister and me."

Marco was acting strangely, fawning like a peasant boy to a king.

The captain nodded, though Marco couldn't see. "What is your name and what business took you to the city?"

Marco looked up, then back down. "Well, sir, I am Roke and this is my sister, Jana. I traveled to escort my sister back to Fairbanks, sir, as she was visiting a relative, and I'm not sure who shot us. I can tell you that we sure didn't know the governor's army would be out or I'd've waited to fetch her back."

"No doubt." The Captain's gaze was flat, and Marco went a little pale, but Laszlo left the matter, instead turning his gaze back to Kiera.

"Was the food not to your liking, my lady?" he asked. "You ate none of it."

Kiera paused, emotions warring in her chest. God, he was beautiful. How did he know she hadn't eaten? Was he watching her? He probably wasn't exactly a nice guy, but was this man a monster who let his soldiers shoot down children? If so, why wasn't he angry at her for protecting them? Or maybe he was.

She sighed. This was probably not the best time to prod into this morass, she supposed. "Alex and I are used to different food is all, Captain."

He was staring at her again. Or still. "There will be a wider variety at the manse. We'll be there within a mark." He nodded to her, then turned his horse away.

When he was gone, Kiera sank back and put a hand to her heart.

"Oh, he likes you, too," Marco smirked.

"Don't tease me, Roke. I never said I liked him."

Marco hid a grin and nodded his head. "Sure. Whatever you say."

WITHIN THIRTY MINUTES the house came into view, or rather the lights of the—what had he called it? The manse? As the miles passed the building revealed itself to be a flat-topped not-quite pyramid, three hundred feet to a side and perhaps four stories tall, which builders had cast of some dark stone. Lights shone from the two dozen arched windows she could see on two sides, beckoning and promising warmth. She shivered in anticipation.

Shouts went out among some of the soldiers as they started setting up camp. Her wagon didn't stop, though, but continued to trundle through the half-made camps, more fully erected the farther they went. Wherever they went, soldiers stopped and stared. Some flashed what might have been hostile looks before turning back to their tasks, but most just looked blandly interested. It was a little frightening, but she refused to hide inside the wagon bed. Instead she sat up straight, met their gazes and kept her face clear.

They soon rolled past the last of the soldiers and into the courtyard surrounding the manse. Mosha hopped down after they stopped, then came around. Smiling, he offered her a hand down. She smiled back and took it, stepping carefully over the wagon's edge and dropping down to the crushed snow carpeting the ground. She took a moment to gain her footing. Except for the two quick rest breaks her hosts had so graciously provided throughout the day, she hadn't been on her feet since she woke. She turned and helped Alex out, who clung to her like static to a blouse. She turned back to the wagon. The driver offered a hand to help Marco down, but he declined with a slight smile to Mosha. "I can't leave my sister."

"I'll bring you something to eat later," Kiera told him, zipping her coat, then leaning over to zip Alex's. "Wrap up in our blankets."

"Thank you, lady mother, but there is no need." He grinned. "I ate your food, remember? Go in, eat well and sleep. We would have been sleeping outside anyway, Kiera. We will be fine." He smiled warmly at her, but it was tinged with just a hint of sadness, and she wondered how long it had been since anyone had really cared about this kid.

Kiera hesitated, but finally patted the wagon twice, turned and followed Mosha, Alex's hand in hers.

She entered the house and found herself impressed with the décor. Hardwood framed the doorway, old but wide, and carved with figures of flying fantasy creatures, many with bows. Inside the entry lay a wide open room, two stories tall and forty feet wide. The floors were marble. Small, rounded tables held some kind of lanterns, but they didn't look electric and they didn't flicker like fire. There was a plush, muted white and gold runner on the floor, inlaid with what looked like a bunch of triangles that reminded her of the mark on Marco's arm. The rug bisected the room, leading entrants through double doors into the recesses of the house.

Kiera could hear people laughing inside, and she twinged with uneasiness. She opened her mouth and turned to Mosha, but he smiled at her and let himself out. She let out her breath and led Alex to one of the couches, one of four, all gold and silky, and sat down. She had slept in her clothes—her bloody, torn, filthy clothes—and she hadn't brushed her hair since who knew when. She knew she looked terrible and she didn't really want to go into a strange house looking this way. What was she supposed to say? "Hi. I'm here to eat. By the way, please ignore the way I look. And oh, would you mind if I borrowed your bath?" Hardy har har. Maybe she should wait for someone she knew to come through the door to go in with.

Oh. Yeah.

Kiera started to laugh, and Alex looked at her strangely. She patted his hand and stopped herself before it became hysterical. She knew exactly one person, and he had stayed in the wagon. Well, she kind of knew Mosha, too, but he was already gone.

This was ridiculous.

Maybe she should just go back outside. She stood, pulling Alex up, and pulled him toward the door. It opened before she got there. Laszlo stepped in and stomped the snow off his boots. He started to remove his jacket, caught sight of Kiera, and stopped in mid-motion.

He looked at her for a moment, then finished taking off his coat, hung it on a rack, and walked to her. He stopped a few feet away and inclined his head.

"My lady, why have you not gone in? Are you no longer hungry? And your son as well?"

Kiera grimaced. She had ridden in the goddamned wagon all day. She was too tired, and grumpy, to play polite games. "Well, Captain, after I came inside I realized that, one, I don't know the anyone here, and two, neither Alex nor I are exactly dressed to meet nice company. I am wearing filthy clothes, I probably stink and my hair hasn't been combed in two days. I can't imagine what I look like. And so I am taking Alex back to the wagon. If you would be so kind, will you ask someone to bring us something to eat and drink? Water is fine, but fish is not. But I won't complain no matter what if it's even remotely warm."

Laszlo stared at her for a long minute, face unreadable, then nodded once. "I have been thoughtless. Please let me have someone take you to where you can have a bath and a change of clothes. You can eat after you bathe."

Kiera exhaled through her nose. "Captain, I thank you for the thought, but I don't have any spare clothes, nor do I seem to have my wallet with me. I can't pay for anything. So while I again thank you, I must decline, although I do ask that you have someone bring my son something to eat."

Maybe it was the sense of helplessness, maybe it was because she'd been strangling her fear for days, or maybe it was just because she was tired and cold and wanted to go home, but then, and to Kiera's great shame, she began to cry.

Deeply embarrassed, wishing she could make it stop, she turned away and pulled Alex toward the door.

Alex wailed and dug in his feet, for what purpose Kiera could not fathom. She stopped and patted his shoulder, trying to calm him, and struggled to get herself under control as well. "I am so sorry," she broke out, apparently apologizing to both of them, "I didn't mean to cry," and, retaking Alex's hand, moved toward the door.

From behind her Laszlo grabbed her shoulder, hard but not hurting her, but certainly holding her in place. He shouted a word she didn't understand. Annoyed, she wiped her eyes and tried to pull away. Before she could break free a woman came running, then another, and he barked something else to them. They—young, blond, and indistinguishable in apricot-colored livery—took both of Kiera's arms, patted her and murmured soothing sounds. She opened her mouth to refuse, then closed it because she knew she didn't want to. One took Alex's hand, and the women led the two of them around a corner and into a hallway she hadn't been able to see before.

A few doors down they all stopped. One woman let go of her arm, opened a door, and motioned Alex and Kiera inside. Kiera stepped into a luxurious bedroom plush with russet carpet, antique furniture, and a high sleigh bed. The room was sparkling clean, which made Kiera feel even filthier. Someone had set fresh flowers in a bowl on one table, and their spicy, sweet odor tickled her nose.

After the door snicked tight one of the women pulled off Kiera's coat and the other began unbuttoning her shirt. Kiera pushed her hands away, shaking her head with a rueful smile. She had nothing to change into. The woman let go and stood back. The door opened and some round pine thing rolled in, followed by two more women.

Alex stared with huge eyes. Kiera thought hers probably were, too.

Even more people—men this time—strode in one by one bearing buckets of hot and cold water, which they dumped into the wooden vat. A fifth, or sixth, woman wrestled in a smaller tub and others filled it as well. An older woman followed the small tub in, walked a circle round Kiera, left, then returned soon after carrying a gold gown and a heavy purple overrobe. She left them on the big bed. The clothes-bearing woman motioned for the others to leave, then caught Kiera's eye and with gestures made plain that she should use the tub and put on the clothes.

"That high-handed bastard," she murmured, helping Alex out of his clothes and into the bath, then slipped out of her clothes, determined not to let the hot bath go to waste even if it was technically capitulating. After the last thirty-six hours, she needed the bath like a junkie needed a fix.

She washed her hair twice, then her body, with soap that smelled like exotic flowers. Then she laid back and closed her eyes. When the water chilled, she reluctantly got out. She found Alex asleep, his knees curled up and his head resting atop them. She scooped him out, laid him on the bed, dried his hair some, and covered him up. Still naked, she used the bath to wash his clothes, then hung them along the sides of the tubs. She washed hers, too, and spot-cleaned her coat, and hung them all on the backs of chairs.

She stood up, dried her hands, and looked at the dress. It was sure pretty. She pulled it on, and to her surprise, it fit. Rather well. She strode to stand in front of a mirror atop the one dresser to see how it looked. She smiled at herself in the glass, but it slipped away as her glance slid down.

The dress. The dress was glorious. It was also more than a bit on the risqué side. It hugged her lavish hips, which made her cringe, and even with the purple overcoat, which she shrugged on, the neckline bared a lot more cleavage than she ordinarily felt comfortable showing. She toweled her hair nearly dry with the little cloths they'd left for her, then found a wide-toothed wooden comb atop one of the dressers. She pulled it through her hair and wrestled the snarls out. Someone had also laid out a rather old-fashioned looking toothbrush, but she would have used a bottle brush right then.

After scrubbing her teeth she smiled again at her reflection in the mirror. She looked better, but looks were ashes compared to how amazing she felt. She swore to herself that she would never, ever take being clean for granted again.

One of the women who'd led her in from the hall came in—and curtseyed. Kiera frowned, shook her head and motioned her up. The woman rose, then walked to the dresser, pushed back the chair, and motioned for Kiera to sit. Curious, Kiera complied.

The woman walked over to a second cabinet on the right and pulled some small items out of the top drawer, then came back over and motioned for Kiera to push her chair farther back.

The woman knelt in front of Kiera and began putting makeup on her. Kiera let her. She was too tired to argue and it felt too much like pampering to really want to anyway, so instead she closed her eyes.

After a while the woman tapped her shoulder. A sleepy Kiera opened her eyes and looked at the woman, who smiled and motioned to the mirror. Kiera turned and stared for the third time at her reflection. All in all it was a bit more than she normally used, but it wasn't bad. And it made her feel better. Silly, maybe, but cleaned and made up, she felt like she could face anyone now.

The woman motioned toward the door, and Kiera smiled and pointed to the bed, where Alex lay. "I need to stay here," she said quietly.

"I'll stay with the boy, my lady," the woman answered, equally soft. "The mayor awaits you downstairs. They've held dinner for you."

"What? "Kiera wailed, getting up. "Why would they wait for me? They shouldn't have done that!"

The woman's head dropped down as she nodded.

"I'm sorry," Kiera said, touching her arm. "I don't mean to sound harsh. It's been a trying week." She stepped back and wiped the wrinkles out of her dress. "So I really have to go, huh?" The woman nodded again, still staring at the floor. "Well, it's going to ruin the effect of this dress with my snow boots," she grumbled, "but there you have it."

The woman pointed at something under the desk. "Oh no, my lady. Your slippers are there."

Kiera pulled out a pair of slinky yellow shoes and held them up. They looked like hospital slippers except that they tied at the top. "Oh-kay." She slipped one over one foot, then the other, and tied them. The bottoms were so slick she could slide across a smooth floor with them. She supposed that would ruin the effect of the nice dress, but the thought made her smile.

"Well, I guess I'm ready," she said, spreading her arms, "unless there is something else I need to put on?"

The woman pressed her lips together and shook her head. She pointed toward the door she'd come in. Kiera took a deep breath and walked out the door.

A MAN, A SOLDIER, AWAITED HER in the hallway outside the room. A tall, dark haired, and handsome man. He smiled down at her in obvious pleasure and offered his arm, which she took. He escorted her swiftly through a hallway, around a corner, through double doors, then into a central dining area. Only the carpet kept her feet from slipping as she tried to keep up. Heart beating fast, Kiera stopped at the doorway for a second to look around.

The room, massive, rectangular, and completely open, had been lined with black stone walls. It was at least four stories high and a hundred feet long. Huge, sparkling chandeliers hung down every twenty feet or so. An open gallery ran around the two sides of the room opposite her, but two stories up, and she didn't see any stairs.

Across the room from her and to the left stood a narrow stage, set above the crowd perhaps ten feet. Upon it a band played a soft, perhaps romantic song. To the right of the band a another stage had been erected, a bit higher and maybe thirty feet from one side to the other, with black tables set upon it. Maybe fifty long picnic-like tables lay half-full below the two stages. Some people in very nice clothes milled around in front of the tables, drinking drinks in fluted glasses and talking in groups. Some of the women were much larger than the current convention back home, she noted, yet seemed confident, and she relaxed just a smidge.

Kiera licked her lips, then straightened her back, which, to her chagrin, made the purple overcoat pop open, revealing her cleavage and much more of the form-fitting dress. She wished she could think of some dignified way to hold the coat closed. *Ignore it,* she advised herself, and nodded to her escort to continue. He led her ahead and toward the stairs to the higher tables.

She suddenly noticed that nearly everyone had stopped talking to watch her as she approached. Some seemed to be talking about her and others pointed her out to others. It took every ounce of self control not to look down or away. Instead she smiled at them, and although she couldn't help tightening her grip on her escort's arm, she hoped she showed no other signs of strain as she paraded to her seat.

The soldier led her up the stairs and to an empty chair between Captain Laszlo—*of course,* she thought, and hid a grimace—and another well-dressed man. She flashed a genuine smile at her escort as he held her chair for her, and his return smile was both warm and inviting. A blush crept up her cheeks, and she ducked her head.

After she was seated she looked to Laszlo, who stared at her but did not smile. Nodding to him, she turned to the gentleman on her left, intending to smile a welcome, but he was too busy staring at her cleavage to look at her face.

Disgusted, she smiled anyway for the benefit of those who were watching and who had awaited her for dinner, and turned back toward the table, praying someone would soon bring out the food so that people would have something else to look at.

Thank God they did. Within moments servers brought out dish after dish and laid them on the tables. Kiera tried to watch the others without turning her head to see how they did things, and when others started dishing for themselves, she did the same. Some of it smelled good—well, kind of good—and she was hungry. Much of it was soupy or in sauces, and she fervently hoped she didn't make a mess on the dress.

Laszlo leaned in and murmured, "You look lovely, my lady. And I hope the bath was a help to your spirits."

Kiera tilted her head to the side, wondering whether to say what she thought. Mind made up, she turned to him and said, "Yes. It was. And although I'd like to complain about your strong arming me, I won't. Instead I'll just say, 'thank you.' For everything."

The Captain leaned back, brows raised, and for a moment Kiera wondered if she had offended him, but then he nodded. "My apologies. My intent was to help."

"I know it was. And I do thank you."

They ate in silence for a while. The food wasn't very good – perhaps it was the spices, or that everything tasted like fish – but it wasn't rotten either, and it was hot. She drank a glass of wine, and then another. It was a good, sweet red, not too strong, for which she was thankful.

A few bites later Kiera turned to the Captain and said, "I also want to say 'thank you' for inviting me to dinner."

His gaze slid over her shoulder, then back to her face. "It was my pleasure, my lady." A flat voice.

What was that about? "Kiera. Please." She smiled.

"Kiera, then." He did not. In fact, he looked like a man putting a great deal of effort into smothering annoyance.

"So, uh, Captain, what happens after dinner?"

"Dancing," he replied, looking out at the room.

"Not your favorite?" she guessed.

"No." He took another bite, eyes on his food.

"Mine either. Am I allowed to go to bed after I eat?"

He turned and faced her. "If you're asking my permission, my lady, you don't need it." He grabbed his mug and downed the drink.

Kiera gave up and turned to take in the room, but the man on her left's smile, obviously directed at her, caught her attention and she turned to him. He was in his forties, strong shouldered, with short dark hair and keen blue eyes. Some might call him handsome, but something in his eyes belied it, and she had not forgotten his perusal of her, uh, attire. She noted, perhaps belatedly, that he wore an ensemble that featured the same gold and purple as her dress.

"Lady, I would be most pleased to make your acquaintance. My name is Nickinum, and I am Mayor of Talium, the city here." He flashed another smile. His teeth were very white. "Your very great beauty flatters my house, and I welcome you to it."

He held her eyes a little too long, a little too intently, and so Kiera laughed, a little uneasily. "It's my pleasure to meet you as well, Mayor Nickinum. I am Kiera."

"Nick, please. Call me Nick. Well. Where are you from, when did you arrive, and how long will you be here with us?"

Everyone within hearing was trying, some not very subtly, to listen in to their conversation. Despite her best efforts she stiffened a bit, and Nickinum caught it. He took her hand and lifted it to his lips, and lingered over her wrist a handful of heartbeats, as if taking in her scent. "Perhaps you would walk with me? I will show you my home. You have finished eating, I see."

Kiera wasn't sure how to politely decline without being completely ungracious to the man who had apparently fed her, allowed her to bathe, provided her with clothes, and allowed one of his employees to sit with her son while she had dinner. Even if he was a little creepy, he'd been very generous. She nodded and stood with him.

He motioned to the band as they stood, and the band, as if syncopated with the mayor, began playing a slow-paced, violin- and buttery-rich song.

He dismounted the stairs first and offered his arm, which she took, and he led her to a doorway on the far left of the room. Once outside the hall he stopped and patted her hand. "I apologize if my behavior seemed abrupt, Kiera. You seemed, may I say, surprisingly uneasy with everyone hanging on your every word." He winked at her. "It must be challenging for a woman as beautiful as you to take dinner in a strange house." He started walking, pulling her along. "Of course, some women get used to it, I imagine, but it's that much harder to be both arrogant and charming, isn't it?"

Kiera stumbled and Nick grabbed her arm to steady her.

"Uh, thank you, Nick. You're very kind."

"Nonsense. It's plain truth." He paused, pointed to a mural of a woman on the wall. They turned to look at the painting. The woman was seated outside on a royal blue bench, a bundle of peach flowers dropped carelessly at her feet. She was golden haired, plump, and heartbreakingly lovely, and she wore a version of the gold and purple ensemble Kiera had on. In this likeness she laughed gaily and pointed at something behind the painter's shoulder. "My mother, gods rest her."

"She is beautiful."

He smiled, a baring of teeth. "So, you're a visitor to Fairbanks. Where are you from, my lady, how long will you be with us, and if you're married, you must tell me your husband's name so I can have him murdered." Nick laughed, and after a moment Kiera did, too, but even to her it sounded a bit forced.

"Um, yes. My son and I are visiting Fairbanks. We've come east and I don't know yet how long we'll stay. It's, uh, so lovely here."

"From close to Anchorage then, or Bethel?"

Nosy bastard. Kiera wished she had another glass of wine. "No. My son and I are from the nadeconn. We're just travelers passing through. I don't know where we'll end up."

"Well, for all of our sakes I sincerely hope you decide to stay in our deconn. And I'd love to guest you here, Kiera. Please consider it." He smiled, and she smiled in return, but tried to keep it as neutral as possible.

"If I may be so bold, Kiera, may I say that you have some very interesting scars on your neck." He leaned closer. "Would you think me too forward if I asked you how you acquired them?"

Kiera stopped their procession and looked at him, a snake of annoyance winding through her. "Believe it or not, a very large dog attacked me."

"A large dog? My goodness!" He put a hand to his heart. "How frightening that must have been! And who came to your rescue?" He looked thoughtful for a moment. "The large captain, I'll bet." Nick tried to look sly. "And just in the nick of time, by the look of things." He patted her hand, shaking his head with admiration, apparently imagining Laszlo's courageous feats. He tried to pull her toward the path again but Kiera held her place, pulling him to a stop. He looked at her, surprised and perhaps a tad annoyed.

That makes two of us.

"Well, I am not sure exactly how it ended, Nick. The details are a little foggy in my mind. No one else helped, though. That's for sure."

A look of surprise washed over Nick's face, but he covered it quickly with a smile, then took her arm and led her onward. "You defeated a wild dog on your own?" He shook his head. "An impressive feat, my lady." He chuckled and rubbed her hand. "I'm afraid we're not accustomed here in the east to such ferocity in our women." He squeezed her hand. "You are such a delight."

Kiera raised a brow, but chose to keep her thoughts to herself.

NICK ESCORTED HER around the hall, showing her his collection of paintings, and then back to the main room.

"Would you honor me with a dance, Kiera?" he asked.

"I would love to, Nick, but I need to go check on my son first." She smiled brightly and prayed he'd forget by the time she returned.

Pleased, perhaps at her smile, Nick patted her hand. "Certainly, Kiera. Certainly. I'll see you soon, then, my dear." He pulled her hand up and kissed it, smoldered up at her over it, then turned to make his way across the floor.

Kiera stared at him for a moment, laughing a little, then looked around and tried to gain her bearings. Unfortunately the room had a door set into the wall about every twenty feet. Gauging the direction of the tables when she came in, she narrowed it down to three or four and headed that way.

She got lost.

She pushed through a door too quickly and ended up outside. She turned and tried to grab the door, but it was heavier that she'd thought and slid past her fingers and shut behind her. Of course it had no handle on the outside. She swore softly. It was damned cold out here without her coat, but she walked out from the manse, rubbing her arms, to get far enough away from the wall to find another way back in. Twenty feet out she slipped in the snow in her silky slippers and nearly fell. Once she regained her balance she gritted her teeth and walked carefully, putting one foot down firmly before lifting the other.

The sky loomed thick and black above, and the waning moon shone down from a nest of sparkling stars. The air felt sharp and cold, but it tasted clean. She lifted her face and closed her eyes, breathing deeply.

The sound of a slap, hand to skin, sung out, crisp and strong. Her eyes flew open and she tilted her head to hear better. She heard other noises, softer sounds, but couldn't make them out. Whatever was happening was near, but it was hard to tell from what direction. She considered then dismissed the sounds of the army camp. Too far away.

She heard a man snarl. Then another slap, and someone cried.

Crossing her arms across her chest against the cold, Kiera made her way across the snow, away from the house, looking left and right.

There. The sounds came from a squat, darkened building behind the manse.

She tried to hurry toward it, but the moment she stopped paying attention to her feet she slipped and fell. Gritting her teeth, Kiera pulled herself back up and kept going.

When she got close she saw that it was a stable, long and narrow and built of rough wood. She'd come to the back, so she walked round the corner and found the door, which was propped open. She stepped inside, grabbed the nearest wall, and shook some of the snow from her frozen slippers. It stank of manure in here, almost beyond bearing.

She was in an office of sorts, but it sat darkened and empty, and a few steps past another door opened out into the main section. Beyond the door a long, poorly lit hallway lined with stalls led further inside. She walked through the door and into the hall. With each step her feet burned as they warmed. The sounds of a struggle sounded much clearer now.

A stifled scream sent her heart thudding.

Thoroughly pissed off, she started a jog down the hallway, peeking into each stall she passed, but found only empty spaces and a few dozing horses. With each step Kiera found herself surprisingly thankful for the slippers. They kept her footfalls nearly silent.

Near the end of the hall, she found them.

A man had a woman pinned on her back on the ground. He had pushed her skirt up past her waist, baring her legs. The woman, a young woman, eyes squeezed shut, turned her face back and forth like someone trying to wake from a bad dream. As she twisted the dim light reflected off tear rivulets that further etched gaunt, pink cheeks.

The man shifted, and the woman tore an arm free and hit him with it. He didn't seem to feel it, or it wasn't hard enough to matter. With one hand he held her other arm. His weight held her body down, his legs pinned hers, and he was using his free hand to work off his pants.

The woman slapped him hard in the face, and the sound stung Kiera's ears. The man stopped moving, grunted, then punched her in the mouth.

Effortlessly, seemingly, but the woman's head flew back to bounce against the ground. A ruby-red stream gushed from between her teeth, spilled down her chin and dripped into the hay.

Kiera went cold, then adrenalin made her hot.

Julia's mouth. The last time she'd seen Julia, her mouth had been bloody. She clenched her hands.

At that moment the woman saw her and froze. Kiera slowed her breath and forced her hands to unfist. She shook her head and held a finger to her lips, then turned around. A shovel hung on the wall a few stalls down, a large metal shovel with a long, white wooden handle. She walked over and lifted it carefully down from its rack.

She walked back to the grotesque floor show, cocked her head for a moment, set her feet, then raised the shovel above her right shoulder. She paused to take a breath, then swung from the hip and stepped in with it. She brought the shovel down as hard as she could upside the man's head, but he moved at the last moment, rendering it a glancing blow.

Kiera grinned. That was okay. She'd done it to get his attention, not kill him.

Yet.

She stepped back. The man bellowed and pushed off, and the woman pulled her skirt down and skittered backward into the corner like a wounded spider. Wiped the blood from her mouth. Before the man could gain his feet Kiera hit him again, hard, baseball style, this time in the upper back, and he fell face first to the ground. He was drunk; the rancid stench of stale beer wafted from his clothes and his filthy breath. She switched her grip so that she held the shovel like a golf club, blade down, and she sang out as she clouted him once more in the head. He shuddered and lay still.

Kiera let the shovel head drop to the ground and motioned with her free hand for the woman to come out, but she shook her head, eyes wide. Kiera took a breath and motioned again, exaggerating her movements, making big Os in the air with her hand. "Get out of there. Come on! Before he wakes up. Get up! Get up!"

The woman sat up, twisted over and crawled out on her hands and knees, staying as close to the stall wall as she could. She crabbed her way to Kiera, where she collapsed on the floor and hugged Kiera's legs. Kiera patted her back briefly, then gently pushed her away. She knelt down so that their faces were even, and felt her stomach clench. Jesus. This girl was maybe seventeen, and sickly thin. "Go in the house and get cleaned up. Go, go! Before this piece of shit wakes up." The girl let out her breath as she let go a sound of relief, then stood up on shaky legs, using Kiera as ballast.

Kiera turned to watch the girl go, and a big hand grabbed her left leg and pulled it out from under her. She pushed the girl away before she fell, but grabbed hold of the shovel.

She landed on her hip and cracked her head on the side of the stall, shooting stars across her vision. Before she could draw a breath the man punched her in the middle of her back. Some part of her noted that even drunk he was apparently quite strong, since it hurt like *hell*.

"You asshole!" she screamed as she turned over onto her very sore back. She still held the shovel, but her legs were far stronger than her arms. She mule-kicked him in the head with her right foot and followed the kick all the way down, trying to break his neck.

To her chagrin it apparently didn't work. Instead of conveniently dying he grabbed her dress and dragged her toward him. She struggled to get free but he punched her again, this time in the kidney, a solid blow, and she writhed and almost threw up. She swallowed several times rapidly, then flipped to her side and kicked him in the face with the ball of her right foot. And all of her might. He slid backward, losing his hold on her dress, his nose broken. She hoped he'd lost some teeth since several would be imprinted into her heel for the foreseeable future. He slithered back another foot, sat up and grabbed his nose, which was spurting blood all over his shirt.

She flipped over and pushed up to a sitting position. Her back was singing with pain and she didn't know if she could get to her feet, but she shot him a withering glare.

"You whore!" he snarled, but because of his nose it sounded like "ew nor!" and so she laughed at him.

"Yeah, I'm a whore and you're a rapist," she spat. "Touch me or that girl again and I swear to God I'll break every one of your goddamned teeth out and ram them down your shit-stinking throat!"

He snarled and lunged for her. She lay back and sideways and cocked a kick, but instead of coming toward her, he went up. She twisted around, jarring her back, to see what was happening.

Someone's hand was holding him off the ground by the back of his shirt.

Stunned, she looked up, and up, and into Laszlo's furious face.

He dropped her gaze and stared down at the man dangling beneath him—whom he held completely off the floor with one hand, she noted in some cold part of her brain—and as Laszlo's gaze met his prisoner's, his face transformed into the most frightening expression Kiera had ever seen.

The man she'd been fighting with, who had to be six feet tall and well over two hundred pounds, went ashen, cringed, planted his feet on the floor and tried to scoot away. He brought his hands up over his head, palms out. "No, Captain. No. Please."

Laszlo stared at him for a few seconds as the man babbled and whined. Suddenly, without warning, Laszlo punched him in the side of the head, his huge fist flying inhumanly fast. Bones crunched, the man fell limp, and Laszlo's eyes glittered.

He turned back to Kiera, the man's limp body still hanging from his hand. He pointed at the floor with the other. "Stay right there," he growled. Abruptly he turned and dragged the man like a ragdoll down the hall and out of the stable.

When he had gone Kiera pushed herself back to the wall of the stable. She reached up above her head and grabbed a board. Pain made her gasp when she tried to pull herself up and she froze, panting, and then let herself back down. Waiting a minute wouldn't hurt a thing.

Laszlo returned within five. Alone.

He walked right into the stall, squatted down and lifted her face with an impersonal hand, turning it from side to side.

"So you left the festivities to go rescue a slave." His tone was odd, and Kiera wondered whether he was making fun of her.

"A slave? That girl is a slave?"

He dropped his hand and leaned back on his haunches. Raised his head and stared at her.

She stared back defiantly.

He looked at her for a long minute. "Are you hurt?" he finally asked.

"I'm fine."

"He hit you," he said, as if pointing out a foible.

"I've been hit harder than that before. It's not that bad."

He laid a hand on her shoulder. "Let me see it."

"No. I am fine." She pushed his hand off and started to stand, but staggered, and he caught her arm and helped her up. "I need to get back inside. I have to go check on Alex."

"May I escort you back to the hall?"

"Yes. Thank you," she gritted through clenched teeth, trying to stand straight, then twisted a little, testing the pain in her back. It was bearable, though it would hurt like the devil tomorrow.

"Your back is bruised."

Kiera snorted. "Thanks for the diagnosis, Captain. I wouldn't have guessed."

When she could stand by herself she followed him down the hall and out the door. Once outside Kiera forgot to set her feet and slipped in the snow. She caught herself before she fell, but pain doubled her over. She took two quick breaths, trying to stifle a scream.

Laszlo reached down as if to carry her, but she put one hand on his chest and pushed him back. "If you try to pick me up, I'll break your goddamned nose." She took a deep breath and stood. "Besides giving you a hernia. Will you please just let me lean on your arm?"

He held out an arm, which she took, and he led her indoors.

She made a slow path to see Alex, who was still sleeping. The maid, or whatever she was, bowed her head as Kiera entered, but stayed silent. "Has he woken?" she asked, but the maid shook her head.

Kiera pulled out the chair in front of the desk for a minute and sat down. She crossed her arms atop it and dropped her head down, willing the ache to lessen. She twisted and held it, stretching her back, and after a few minutes the pain began to recede, which meant a muscle was pulled or bruised and her kidney was fine.

She sat up and looked down at her dress, which was miraculously un-marred by her little adventure. She stood and brushed a few stray pieces of straw off with shaking hands, stretched again, then picked up a brush with a trembling hand and ran it through her hair. She pulled her hair back into a ponytail, then wrapped it round and round into a roll. There were a col-lection of straight, brown sticks in a cup on the dresser. Kiera pulled two out and used them to anchor her hair.

There. Fresh as a daisy.

Well, except that she suddenly had an urge that she had to deal with now. She turned to the maid and smiled a tad awkwardly. "Uh, is there a bathroom I can use?" she asked. The maid smiled, looking faintly puzzled.

"Uh, a chamber pot then, or someplace where I can urinate?" she asked. The maid still didn't answer. "Pass water, piss, pee?" She made a motion to show something coming out from the crux of her legs, and the maid stood and nodded. She went to the far side of the room, stood in front of a screened off area, and pointed. Kiera made her way behind the screen, then groaned when she saw the little ceramic pot with a towel lying next to it.

Oh. My. God.

She did her business with less mess than she expected, then pulled her-self back together, straightened her back, and walked to the door. As she opened it she turned to the maid and said, "If he wakes, please send some-one to get me."

The woman nodded. Kiera let herself out the door and made her way back to the hall.

CHAPTER 5

KIERA FELT THE HEAVY DRUMBEATS BEFORE she reached the door. She crossed the threshold without pausing, nodded politely at the people who glanced her way, and looked around for a place where she could sit.

It seemed darker than before she'd left, but she could still see across the floor. A great many people, two hundred at least, were standing and talking in groups or walking to some destination. Many held goblets filled with dark or golden liquid. Some were laughing or trying to talk over the band. All looked glamorous. Men—many handsome—wore well-cut dark jackets over slim-fitting pants, which she sincerely appreciated. The women all wore dresses of various styles and colors, but most were close-fitting and jacketed like her own.

An uncarpeted dance floor lay below the band. Dancers slid across the floor, faces intent on the music and each other, couples, men and women and women and women.

She spotted three or four empty seats together at a table between the dance floor and the band's podium and, walking wide to avoid the groups, made her way there. Kiera took off her jacket and hung it on the back of one of the chairs, then sat down carefully, gritting her teeth to keep the pain from her face.

Before she settled a man in gold and purple livery rushed up and offered her a glass of wine. Surprised, she smiled and lifted a glass from the tray, then held up her hand for him to wait. She drank it all down, took another, and waved the server away.

She finished her second glass and set it down on the table. As the warmth seeped through her she closed her eyes and blew breath through her mouth.

Feeling better, Kiera opened her eyes and watched the dancers. Some were definitely following some sort of pattern, but many were moving in an eclectic way she didn't recognize.

A strange thing occurred to her as she watched the crowd. She was, she freely admitted, a fat girl. A plus size. Big and beautiful. And so on. She was usually the largest woman in the room, even bigger than the men sometimes, and men's gazes usually skittered away from hers in social situations. But here, many of the women—at least the ones in nice dresses—were close to her size. Some were smaller, some were larger, but all of the men seemed very interested in meeting their eyes and in watching and touching their bodies, especially the soft flesh their dresses revealed.

This was going to take some getting used to.

Her eyes found Nick, who seemed to be making his way over to her. A center of attention, he stopped here to say "hello" and there to kiss a hand. She tried not to grimace as he approached her table.

To her surprise, he sat down. He eyed her hair, her gown, her cleavage, then his gaze lifted back up to her face. "How is your son?" he asked.

She wondered if she was supposed to feel more flattered and less like slapping his face.

She answered without smiling. "He is well. Thank you."

Nick motioned to a waiter, who brought him a glass of wine that he flourished with a little bow. Nick took it, then turned back to Kiera and lifted his glass, eyes appraising. "Will you dance with me?" he asked, his face as serious as her own.

She sighed. "Uh, I'd like to wait for something slower if you don't mind. My back is a little sore tonight."

"Something slower? Oh, of course, my dear." He leaned back and laughed, delighted, and gave her a slow wink.

Alarmed, Kiera shook her head a little and raised a hand. "No, Nick, really. I've hurt my back."

"No. No. I understand." He rose, still smiling, and offered his hand. "Come with me and I am certain we can arrange something more appropriate to your mood."

With a sigh, she rose and took his arm. Nick walked her to the edge of the dance floor. He raised her hand, kissed it, then let it go. "Wait right here, my dear."

He skirted the dance floor until he stood directly in front of the band, and raised a hand. The music died. He said something and the man in front nodded once, sharply, then turned to the others and spoke a few words. The leader raised his hand and another man on his left raised what looked to be a violin, drew the bow, and began playing slow, haunting, Celtic-sounding music. After a measure the others joined, and a woman began singing in a language Kiera didn't understand.

Nick returned and bowed to her. When she smiled he stepped in, placed a firm hand around her waist, pulled her close, and led her onto the dance floor.

Pressed inside the throng of people, the song seemed to pour into her, notes like fingers piercing and twining inside her chest, filling her but leaving her wanting. The threads pulled her, smoothed the lingering unease. A bead of sweat trickled down her back, and she opened her mouth and breathed deeply. Eyes closed, her heart seemed to slow until it, too, echoed the rhythm. All the while Nick moved with her, led her, their bodies crushed together.

The music smoothed and softened. The room seemed darkened, somehow, and Kiera let her thoughts drift. She felt Nick's hand on her hip, his chest against hers. Notes danced in the air above them, then swirled down like a pregnant wind to wrap around her, around them, each sound a touch. An invitation. Kiera moved, Nick moved, a dance of lovers, and the music led them.

The tempo increased and she felt Nick laughing as he swung her in time with the song. Nothing mattered but the music, its pleasures and pains, and she knew them all. The touch of her lover, the burn for his hands, the ache for his kiss, the pain of his loss. She closed her eyes and felt tears coursing down her heated face.

Her body swayed. The fabric of her dress caressed her too-tight skin as she moved, sending shivers of pleasure down her spine. She arched her back, ran her hands over her chest, down her sides, sparks following her fingers. She groaned, and Nick pulled her closer, hands on her, pressing his body against hers, wanting her, burning for her. She leaned into him, needing his touch, the music filling her, leading her on.

Nick's breath brushed her neck, and she arched against him. He pulled her face closer and touched his tongue to her ear. She gasped and opened her eyes.

The crowd, a clash of colors and shapes, moved with her as she turned. Everyone was dancing, swaying, touching, eyes closed, or glazed open, unseeing, mouths open, teeth gritted, hands pulling and grasping and stroking. She felt what they felt, the need, the ache, the strain to sate it. Erotic, sensual, it enveloped her, made her want nothing but to touch and be touched. The music played inside her head, the notes inflaming her need.

As she turned, her eyes caught Laszlo's. He stood outside the throng, outside the dance floor, and he stared at her with ebony eyes set in a granite face. Nick pulled her a half turn away, breaking her view, leaning into her, rubbing her back, breathing on her bared shoulder, and her head fell back.

They turned once more and her eyes again found Laszlo's, still staring, black holes boring into her soul. Her heart throbbed in her groin, wet and heavy. She arched and gasped as all the need inside her coalesced into something hard and hot, a need more dear than a breath. Before Nick could turn her away, she lifted an arm toward Lazlo in supplication. In invitation. "Please," she mouthed to him. "Please."

Laszlo's gaze never wavered, his mouth stayed hard, but Kiera felt his need erupt, so hot it hurt, but God, God, she wanted that heat. She wanted his arms crushing her, his mouth on hers, his bare chest pressing her down as he took her.

Nick turned her again and Laszlo's face slipped away. Nick's teeth found her ear, his fingers her breast, and she moaned and leaned into him. The song slowed and changed, and she stumbled, feet forgotten. She felt drunk, drunk with lust and aching and need. Images of writhing, naked, of rubbing her flesh against bare flesh filled her. Nick grabbed her bottom and pulled her in, and closer, until his erection pressed flesh to bone, and she surged into him, eyes closed, mouth open.

Strong fingers dug into her shoulder and jerked her back and away from Nick. She lost her balance, but before she could stumble someone wrapped an arm around her chest and leaned into her from behind. Her head fell back, drunkenly, and she started. Laszlo! For a moment they stood motionless in the middle of the sea of writhing bodies.

A need as sharp as her own shone in his eyes. She reached up, pulled his head down, and pressed open lips to his, biting him hard when their mouths met. He jerked, then grabbed her hair and deepened the kiss. With rough hands he turned her around, and she let her body sink into his. He kissed her harder when her fingers dug deep into his back, and she moaned into his mouth.

His body felt hard and strong, and the urgency in his hands sent wet need pulsing through her. He kissed her jaw, her neck, and she raked her nails down his arm, needing him to hold her harder, pull her closer.

Abruptly, without warning, Laszlo pulled away, breath harsh and fast, and rested a hand on her chest. Kiera made a sound of displeasure and tried to move his hand. He held her there, gently, far enough away that they couldn't touch.

His voice was hoarse. "No, Kiera. Wait. Please."

"You are so beautiful," she whispered, staring into his eyes. "Please, Laszlo. Please don't stop. I need you."

From behind her a hand reached around her waist and jerked her backward. Her back screamed in agony, tearing a gasp from her as she stumbled.

The music had stopped. For a moment silence thundered, then, like a wave, sound crashed as people began talking. Kiera managed to keep her feet and turned to face the grabber. She wasn't surprised when Nick's angry gaze met hers, but his features smoothed as he took in her face. "Come with me, Kiera. Leave the captain and dance with me." His touched her hand and she felt herself melting. His voice was sultry, sweet, and her lips parted as she felt the pull begin again.

Laszlo's hand fell on her shoulder, stopping her. From behind her he snarled, "Mayor Nickinum. Did you bespell this woman without her consent?" He wrapped his arm around Kiera's shoulders and pulled her gently back into him.

And into his erection.

Startled, Kiera stiffened, but didn't move away. Everyone had stopped talking and gathered around to watch. Kiera felt her face heat and looked down.

The fog had begun to lift, but her body still ached with need. She breathed through her mouth, trying to slow her pounding heart. As her mind cleared, she stared at Nick, wondering if he had made her feel this. A trickle of anger wound through her.

For his part, Nick looked sullen.

Laszlo's voice made her jump. "You will answer me, Mayor."

Nick went a little pale. "No, Captain," he answered, looking at Kiera when he spoke. "I did not. I asked her to dance, but it was upon her request I played the Danse."

This just didn't make sense. The bastard was blaming her? What had she done?

"Wait a minute," Kiera said. "When did I ask—"

Nick cut her off with his hand and squared on Laszlo. He snarled, "You let her speak? She is a woman, and nadeconn. Twice her word carries no weight in my hall."

Kiera's mouth fell open. She wasn't allowed to defend herself because she was a woman? She glared at him, but he kept his gaze pinned to Laszlo's.

Kiera slapped him as hard as she could. Laszlo grabbed her shoulder before she could strike again.

"I will consider Lady Kiera's opinion."

Nick rocked back, outrage large on his face.

Kiera pushed the anger out of her voice. "You asked me to dance, Nick. I said no and went to check on my son. When I returned, you asked me again, and I told you that I prefer a slow song because my back is hurting." She paused, considering. "Is that consent?"

Above her shoulder, Laszlo's voice rolled low and hard. "No." He paused to draw a breath. "Mayor Nickinum, as you admitted, Lady Kiera is not yet a member of this deconn. Unless you explained the Danse to her, or unless you believe your Danse renowned throughout the nadeconn, it is not possible that Lady Kiera knew what you offered."

Nick struggled to look contrite, but only managed to look affronted. "I believe we have misunderstood each other, Lady Kiera." He bowed low. "I beg you to accept my most humble apologies." He did not rise.

Everyone's eyes watched her, and Kiera suddenly realized that they were waiting for her to grant her pardon, or not. For a heartbeat she wondered what would happen if she refused. Half of her wanted to. "Yes, Nick. I accept your apology."

He stood and faced her, lips pressed into a straight line. "You may name your recompense, Lady Kiera."

She pretended to consider for a moment, then pasted on her most meaningless smile. "None is necessary."

"Very well," With a raised brow, he turned and stalked off.

"Was that the wrong thing to say?" Kiera asked Laszlo, who still hadn't released her.

He was silent for a moment. "No. Not wrong."

Kiera nodded, and Laszlo let go of her. She stepped out and made herself turn around.

She looked up at him, up from his arm which still bled from her nails. She closed her eyes for a moment, trying to keep embarrassment from flowering into full mortification, then took a breath and opened them. He was staring at her, waiting, his face impassive.

"Captain, I am hoping that later you will deign to explain to me what happened here. I think once I have all my own feelings back I am going to be really, really pissed off." She clasped her hands together. Her eyes flickered to the floor, but she forced herself to look back up at him. "In the meantime, I believe I again owe you my thanks for your help. I also owe you an apology, Laszlo. I am deeply sorry and very embarrassed to have acted like a complete wanton in front of everyone, and most especially for dragging you in to whatever spell Nick was casting on me." She took a lusty breath. "And for scratching your arm."

Laszlo looked at her for a long, long time, and it was impossible to tell what he was thinking. "How is your back?" he finally asked.

"It hurts like hell."

"Can I help you back to your room?"

She smiled. "I think I can manage. What I am worried about is riding in the wagon tomorrow."

"I'll find you something."

"Thank you."

She left the hall alone.

THE DOG HAD KIERA PINNED to the ground, its teeth ripping flesh from her neck. She howled in rage, punched, arms flailing, trying to get it off, desperate to win free. She struggled, kicking, punching, biting, but its teeth sank deeper. Fire erupted. It was everywhere. She turned her head, and everyone she knew stood inside a ring of flame, and all burned. The men from the wall were there. All the soldiers she'd seen through the fire. She struggled to her feet and ran to the fiery veil, reached through, tried to grab their hands, but their bodies were writhing, twisting, blackening, shriveling. Mouths open, their agony filled her ears even after they burned. She took another step toward them and stumbled. At her feet was Julia, reaching out through the fire. Julia lying in the dirt in her red party dress, blood on her face. Kiera lunged, tried to grab her, but when she touched Julia's hand, it turned to ash.

Kiera screamed.

Someone grabbed her shoulder. She jerked away and flung herself out of bed, back to the wall.

"Kiera. All is well." A man's whisper cut through the fog, and strong arms pulled her to a hot, hard, and decidedly naked chest. She stiffened, but didn't pull away. A hand stroked her hair. "It was a dream."

Kiera lifted a hand to her face and covered her eyes. The arms felt safe, and she relaxed into them, pulling in breath after ragged breath.

Strong hands helped her find the bed, sat her down. The hands left her, then a lamp was lit. She looked over. Laszlo, wearing just a pair of soft-looking brown pants, looked back.

Embarrassed, she put her head in her hands. Breathed out.

Alex woke then, looked around. Seeing her, he jumped off the bed and launched himself into her lap. "Keer, Keer! Don't cry!" he wailed. Kiera pulled him in and hugged him close as she struggled to rein in her raging emotions.

She let out a heavy breath. "Hey. I'm okay, Alex. It's okay. I'm not crying. Honest. I just had a bad dream." Alex hiccupped, let his legs relax, and lay resting against her.

After a few minutes Laszlo patted Alex's back, then drew him away. He helped Alex back into bed and tucked him in. In moments he was asleep again.

Kiera leaned over, staring at the floor, forearms on her thighs. "How did you happen to be here?" she asked without lifting her head.

His voice was quiet. "I'm in the room across the hall. I heard you."

"By request or happenstance?"

"What do you mean?"

With one hand, Kiera waved it away. "Never mind. I'm fine now. You can go back to sleep. Thank you for waking me."

He didn't move. "What were you dreaming about?"

She stared down at her hands. "I don't remember," she lied.

They sat there in the peace for a minute, then two.

Kiera sat up. Shook out her hair. It was just a nightmare. "So. Laszlo. Exactly why don't you hate me?" She grimaced. "Or maybe you do."

He didn't answer right away. "For killing the men?"

She frowned. "Yes."

He stood up and walked to the dresser. Put his hands on the back of the chair. Kept his back to her.

"Should I hate you for it?"

"I don't know," she whispered.

His voice was mild. "Why did you do it?"

"I didn't mean to. I—didn't want—they were—were hurting the children—" She grasped for words. "I—I don't even know how it happened." She put her head in her hands, drawing ragged breaths through her mouth. "I just want to go home."

"What happened to your neck?"

"I told you. A—a big dog attacked me. Me and Alex." She took a deep breath, willing the memory, the dream, away.

"When?"

"Two days ago." She laughed a little. It was a bitter sound.

"In Nakeetna?"

"No. In front of my house. Someplace else."

He turned to her, hand still resting on the back of the chair. She couldn't read his face. "Was that the first time you called fire?"

She rubbed her forehead. "Are you interrogating me?" She was beginning to feel a little annoyed. A little like he was taking advantage of her vulnerability. "Well, Captain, I object."

"Answer the question."

"Screw you." She said it without rancor. "Screw you and screw Nick and screw all of you manipulating bastards. I didn't ask to be here. I didn't ask for any of this."

He sighed. "Kiera—"

"Allow me to repeat myself. Screw you. Now get the hell out of my room before I lose my temper and break your goddamned nose." She stood, pulled the blankets back, and slid in next to Alex. "And turn off the light on your way out."

She turned away from the light and let sleep gulp her down.

CHAPTER 6

ALEX WOKE HER BEFORE THE SUN BREACHED the sky. He was singing, softly. A Christmas song.

It made her profoundly sad.

She was cold, so she pulled the blankets up.

Alex stopped singing. "You awake, Keer?" he asked, his voice hopeful.

"Yup. Wanna get up?"

"Yeah!" Alex scrambled out of bed, then pulled the covers off Kiera.

Her back twanged as she sat up. She bent over and let herself wish for a moment that she had a bottle of pain relievers.

Alex watched her with worried eyes.

"I'm okay," she assured him. "I hurt my back a little bit last night."

He twisted his mouth. "Where are my clothes?"

Kiera opened her mouth to tell him, but they no longer hung where she'd left them. Maybe the maid had moved them last night. She looked until she saw them folded neatly and laying on a chair. After she pointed them out he went over and pulled them on. "Where're yours?"

She looked around but didn't see them. "I don't know, kiddo. Let me look."

Her clothes lay folded on the dresser. They, including her coat, had been washed again and pressed. Someone had found the remnants of her shirt and had tried to sew it, but the shirt had shrunk with the wash and now there wasn't enough left to cover her. With a shrug she pulled on her coat and stuffed the rag into her pocket.

She looked at Alex. His clothes had been cleaned again, too.

They dressed, they took turns using the chamber pot, then made their way back toward the hall. Instead of going in, she went out the front door and walked toward the camp. She'd eat—make Alex eat—rotten fish before she sat at the same table with that bastard Nick again.

It was a long, cold walk, better than a mile, but Alex didn't complain.

Thank God. She was glad to see that the tents were still up. As she got closer she saw that there were several large fires going. Soldiers milled around, looking purposeful.

A young soldier stepped out from his hiding place in the trees when they were still a hundred yards out from the nearest tent.

"Good morning," she said.

He looked at her, then down at Alex. "Going back to the wagon?" he asked. He shivered, and she felt a twinge of pity for him.

"Yes, sir. We sure are. Would you point the way?"

He gave her directions and she thanked him. She pulled Alex, who stared at the soldier with a look of awe, and headed to the wagon. Mosha was nowhere in sight. *Probably off having breakfast,* she thought as her tummy growled. She could imagine how hungry poor Alex must be.

She peeked in the wagon bed and found Marco asleep, but, to her surprise, Allie lay awake. She looked maybe fifteen, which was younger than Kiera had thought she was. She had long blonde hair, big blue eyes, and a generous mouth. She was quite thin and still had a child's face, but she was very, very pretty, and the set of her mouth made Kiera think she knew it. She also looked haggard, though, and every bit like she had just beaten death.

Not wanting to frighten her, Kiera stood back from the wagon. "Good morning, Jana." She smiled. "I rode with you and Roke yesterday. It's good to see you awake. How are you feeling?" She walked to the wagon then, and lifted Alex inside.

Allie nodded. When she spoke her voice was low and sweet. "Roke told me. I am some better thisturn. It's my pleasure to meet you, lady."

"And this is Alex." Alex blushed, and Kiera rolled her eyes as she pulled herself into the wagon. "No food yet, huh?" she asked.

Hoofbeats drew her eyes back outside the wagon. Laszlo rode by at a trot. He turned his head to look at her, and her heart turned over in her chest. She watched the back of him until he was out of sight, then shook her head and laughed at herself.

Allie looked puzzled.

Kiera smiled, trying to find the bright side. "Oh, I'm just making fun of myself. Pay no mind to me."

She sat down on the blankets she and Alex had been using and leaned back against the rail.

Marco opened his eyes and yawned. "Good to see you back, Kiera. How was your night?"

She looked at Alex, who was looking at her. "It was an adventure. But

77

we did get a bath and clean clothes out of it."

"I'll be right back and then I want to hear all about it," he grinned, pushing out of the blankets. He gave Allie's hand a squeeze before sliding over the lip and loping off.

Kiera wrapped blankets around Alex, then herself, grimacing when her back cramped, and snuggled in. Allie lay covered up and looked at Alex. A thought occurred to her. "Do you want me to help you up so you can use the bathroom, uh, I mean, go, uh, get rid of the water, uh—do you know what I mean?"

Allie blushed and Alex giggled. "Yes. Thank you."

Ignoring them both, Kiera scooted over and peeled back Allie's covers. Kiera got down first, then helped Allie, who seemed a bit shaky, climb down, then looked around for a sheltered spot. Kiera helped her to the treeline, then behind a tree.

Her back was a solid ache by the time they returned, and Marco was already in the wagon, so she let him help Allie back in. He had brought food. It was fish again, this time in strips, and it smelled terrible, but Kiera made herself eat. Alex whined, but he was hungry, too, and he ate the stinking strips without as much fuss as she'd feared.

When they finished she told Marco what had happened, softening the hard spots so that Alex wouldn't catch on.

Marco whooped when she told him about the slap, but then looked serious.

"Nick's not a nice man, Kiera. Be careful."

She waved her hand, dismissing it. "Marco, how did Nick do that?"

Marco gave her a meaningful look. "Nick is a water mage."

Kiera shrugged and lifted a hand to show she didn't understand the implications of his portentous warning.

"A water mage can use his magic to make people feel things. I would say that he has created some kind of lust spell and bound it in a song, but it was likely keyed to his touch. Did he touch you?"

"If by keyed you mean that's what triggered it, I think it was something else. While Nick held me, I was, uh, very interested in Nick. But when I saw Laszlo, it made me focus on him, and then it jumped from me to him. I could feel it in Nick, and in all the people around me, and then in Laszlo. It affected everybody around Nick. Maybe everybody who heard the music."

Marco laughed.

"What?"

"Oh, I don't doubt that everybody on the dance floor, or at least those close to you two, caught some of the reverberations of Nick's spell. Lust is very powerful. But it doesn't work like you said. Those kinds of spells require a trigger, like the touch of a hand."

He smiled mischievously. "The feelings you had for the captain, well those had to be your own, and what he felt for you, and his decision to come to you, were his."

Heat flamed Kiera's face. "I think you're wrong. He's a jerk."

His grin was mischievous. "Wanting me to be wrong won't make it true."

"Okay. Enough of that. So, do you think we will we make it to Fairbanks today?"

Before he could answer Mosha came marching back. Instead of going to the front he climbed into the wagon bed and stepped across Alex to get to Allie. Kiera started to rise, but he held a hand up.

"I just wanna take a look a'her and make sure she's healin' up."

"You're the healer, too?"

Mosha smiled widely. "Yup. Hard ta believe I can drive *and* heal."

Before he left he reached inside his coat and pulled out a small gray pillow, which he handed to Kiera.

"What's that for?" she asked, not taking it. Was this a peace offering? An apology? Just keeping his word?

Shrugging, Mosha waved it in front of her until she reached out and grabbed it from his hand. She laid it in her lap and wiped her fingers across the velvet, flattening the fabric. It looked suspiciously like one of the pillows from the room she'd slept in, and a laugh escaped her before she could catch it.

"Canna look at yer back?" he asked.

She shook her head without looking up.

They left a little while later. Tents had been taken down much more quickly than she'd have thought, and the men had fallen in to ranks, some in columns and some in lines on horses.

Even with all those people, it was eerily quiet. The mountains loomed large, snow-covered giants, and fresh powder clung to the trees. Everything looked clean and new. A new day, a new chance.

They traveled until after dark, stopping only twice to rest and eat. The first time they stopped, Kiera helped Alex make a snowman. The second time Mosha helped, too, and Marco and two other soldiers each made their own.

While they rode Kiera used the pillow and tried to doze, but the road was rough and the bumps made zings of pain scuttle across her back.

When the sky was fully black, Marco crawled over to Kiera. He sat next to her in a companionable silence for a while. Just as she started to doze he nudged her and she opened her eyes. He motioned to the slice of sky they could see through a gap in the wagon cover. A green patch of what she would call the northern lights glimmered magnificently.

She sat up and they watched the lights for a while. Marco patted her hand, then leaned close and whispered, "We're going to leave tonight. I don't need you to do anything except not make a fuss when we do."

She pulled her head back and glared at him.

He shook his head stubbornly, so she leaned close and whispered back, fiercely, "That girl is not half healed. If you take her out in this cold, she'll die. You'll both die."

He looked at her with a strange look on his face. Strong emotions flickered in his eyes, but it was too dark to make them out. "You don't understand. And I won't explain it to you because you're safer not knowing. We have to go, Kiera. I don't have a choice. If I don't get to tell you later, thank you for all you did for us. I'll never forget it." He kissed her cheek.

"Then let us come with you!" she hissed, grabbing his arm to keep him close. "We can take care of each other."

He shook his head. "There is no way four of us can get away. I pray that two can."

"We're not prisoners! The captain said so!"

He laughed softly. "Just try to leave and see what happens. You're going to see Lord Vayu, Kiera, and that's all there is to it. The captain won't let you get away. Vayu would kill him."

"Then stay, you idiot!"

He grabbed her hand and looked into her face. "I can't. My father will kill me if he finds me, and I don't want to imagine what he'll do to Allie. Just don't ask, okay? I have to go. Please don't do anything to stop us."

She continued glaring at him as he scooted away and tucked himself back in to the blankets. She closed her eyes and tried to pull her temper in. It wasn't that she was mad, exactly, but the whole thing scared the hell out of her. She had no idea what she could do, and everything she could think of would just endanger them further.

They stopped less than an hour later, but this time there was no warm mansion with warmer beds to retreat to. She sat in the wagon as the soldiers began putting up tents, wondering where she should go to find something to eat.

"Mosha," she called, "if you'll tell me where to go, I'll go get food."

He jumped down off the box and stretched. "No, no, my lady. Let me," he called, then stalked off toward the tents.

Kiera climbed out of the wagon. It was colder than hell. If hell were cold, anyway. "Alex, get down, sweetheart. Let's go potty."

Alex jumped down, grinned up at her, proud of himself, and they made their way into the trees. They hid behind separate trees. He finished first, and when she stood to pull up her pants, he threw a snowball at her.

When her pants were zipped she grabbed a handful and threw it back. She was laughing when the next one hit her mouth. Alex ran up, so she grabbed him and twirled him around, and he shrieked with delight. When she stopped and put a hand on her aching back, he tackled her. He wasn't strong enough to take her down, but she faked a stumble and they went down together. She tickled him until he said "please," and then they made snow angels on the ground.

A noise niggled at the corner of her hearing. She stopped, sat up, and motioned for Alex to be quiet. She stood and made her way to the edge of the trees. Alex followed behind her.

Groups of soldiers ran in different directions, as organized as ants. Some stood at the junctions between rows and bellowed. She couldn't make out the words.

What the hell?

She saw Mosha running to her a long time before he got there.

She stepped out of the trees. "Lady," he called when he saw her, "come quickly. You need ta come back ta the wagon."

She took Alex's hand and they jogged back to the camp. When they got there Mosha helped them back into the wagon. "Wait here, lady, and keep the rest here, too."

"What's going on?" she demanded.

"Just stay here," he ordered, voice gruff, and left.

She covered Alex up. His eyes were huge. Marco and Allie lay together. The noises became louder.

"Is someone attacking us?" she asked Marco.

"I'd say yes," he answered, looking grim.

"Warlike." Kiera said, and blew out a breath. How much worse could this get? "Are you still going to go?" she asked.

He shushed her with a hand.

She heard hard hoofbeats, and suddenly Laszlo was there. He had on his armor and wore a really big sword across his back, but he'd left his head uncovered.

"Kiera, step out, please." She'd never heard his voice sound that hard before.

She climbed out of the wagon as he dismounted. He took her arm and led her out of hearing distance of the wagon.

He grabbed her shoulders in his hands and looked at her. He looked hard. Hard but brimming with energy. It was strange. "Kiera, no matter what happens, do not call fire."

"What's going on, Laszlo?" she countered.

"We're being attacked. I do not expect them to get this far, but if any do, you must rely on us to stop them. You must not call fire."

She opened her mouth, then closed it. Then opened it again. "Laszlo, I don't know how to stop it."

He leaned so close their faces were almost touching. She could smell his hair. It smelled fresh, like sun-warmed clover. This close, she could see that his irises were brown lined by black. "Get everyone down under the wagon. Take the blankets. Build up some berms under the wagon so no one can see you're under it. If things get bad, turn your back. Close your eyes. But stay down and out of the way. Give me your oath."

"Why are you asking me this, Laszlo?"

"You can't control it yet, Kiera. You'll kill my men. You must not. Give me your oath."

She rocked back, then nodded her head once. "You have it."

He let go of her, mounted and rode off at a gallop. She walked back to the wagon and started pulling out the blankets.

MARCO LEFT. He helped her build berms, then he took Allie and they crawled away in the snow. The wagon seemed empty as soon as they left, and Kiera's heart ached as she watched them slip away. She kept Alex quiet, and he helped her get the blankets situated. They walled up the rest of the area under the wagon, then crawled in their blankets and huddled together, trying to stay warm.

It was like a nightmare. It was too dark to see anything under the wagon. People were screaming. They were too far away for her to tell if they were screams of rage or of pain, but they were terrible all the same. Alex huddled up with her. He was silent. She made him lie down, and then she lay beside him. Her breath steamed. Her nose ached from the cold. She covered her face, and Alex's too.

A long time passed. Or maybe it just seemed that way. She tried to think of something pleasant, but her thoughts were like water, running here and there, and all she could do was hold on to the boat. She listened to her breath, and to Alex's.

Someone screamed, close to them. They both jumped. It was a sound of rage, she thought.

Clang, clang. Crash. People were fighting. With metal. She reached in her pocket and pulled out her pocket knife. She opened it.

She heard herself breathing fast and tried to slow it down. She closed her knife and put it back. There was no way her four-inch knife would help her keep Alex safe. Alex was shaking now, and she pulled him close and rocked him, petting his hair. She closed her eyes and willed herself to stop trembling.

They jumped again when something hit the wagon. Someone screamed, but this time it was pain. The sounds stopped, and she stayed very still. Maybe they would move away.

It was getting hot in here.

A shushing sound started, then stopped. Goosebumps raised on her arms. It started again.

Oh God. Someone was digging down the berm! She pulled Alex as far away from the noise as she could.

It was getting hotter. What the hell was going on?

A piece of the berm fell away and she could see a sliver of red light through it. It was a reflection of a fire.

She breathed slowly through her mouth and put her hand lightly over Alex's lips to keep him quiet. Her breath seemed so loud. She prayed the blankets would hide them.

Snapping jaws suddenly pushed through the hole, clacking each time teeth came together. The mouth pulled back and the dog yipped twice, then pushed its head in further, twisting as it came to make the hole bigger. Its claws came through next, into the hole it had made with its head. It was the dog, the dog that had attacked them, and it was digging in.

Alex screamed. Kiera turned her body and kicked out the berm farthest away. Once, twice, three times and there was a hole big enough to get out of. She grabbed Alex and pulled him out, then looked around wildly.

Where was the dog? Where the hell was the dog?

She looked down and saw a long staff, some kind of weapon, lying on the ground. She picked it up as fast as she could and looked around. The staff had a metal tip. A spear. Good, providing she could keep the bastards far enough away to use it.

The wagon was on fire. As she looked at it the dog jumped over the top, wailing a frightening cry, and tried to land on her.

Kiera pivoted from the hip and kicked it as hard as she could in the chest. She swung her body with it and the dog went flying. When it landed, she screamed a *kiai* and stabbed it in the guts, not slowing her arm, trying to pin it like a bug. It screamed, screamed like a man, and she put a foot on its leg and pulled the spear out, then shoved the spear through the dog's throat.

"Motherfucker!" she screamed, high on terror and adrenalin.

If it was a shifter, it did not turn back into a human when it died.

She turned to find Alex kneeling on the ground, throwing up. She looked around, but saw no one. She went to him, keeping the bloody spear, and squatted down beside him.

"You okay?" she asked.

He threw up again.

"Oh, baby. I'm so sorry," she said, rubbing his back. She was shaking so hard she almost dropped the spear. She didn't feel sick; she felt elated.

Sick would come later. She was sure.

The noises were close.

What the hell was she going to do? Hiding under the wagon was no longer an option.

The moon glistened on the snow, casting the world in a white pallor. She looked across the wagon and saw another dog, slinking up, just inside the line of the trees. Another was behind it. They were staring at her, stalking her like lions.

Oh God, oh God. Sweet Jesus Christ! How many of those things are there?

"Alex," she murmured. "Alex. Stay down. Sit down and stay there, okay? No matter what happens."

She couldn't look at him, couldn't make sure he understood. Couldn't make him feel better.

Couldn't make him safe.

She wished she knew how to call fire. She strained, tried to remember what she had felt like when the fire came. She felt nothing. No spark, nothing.

Goddamnit, she spat, and spun the spear. She'd tested to brown belt, and trained with staffs. Back in the real world. She laughed, but it was strangled.

Two, no four more dogs were in the trees.

They were bigger than great danes, she noted. Big and grey, with a patchwork of darker markings circling their torsos and faces.

Then there were five. Then too many to count. Twenty at least.

They were going to die.

"Alex," she said, not turning around, "I love you more than anything in the world. Your mama loved you even more than that. Don't you ever forget that."

He didn't answer. She risked a glance back, and he was sitting crumpled in the snow. Sitting looking forlorn. His eyes were huge. She could see the whites, even in the dark. "I love you," she said again, and turned back to the dogs.

One was coming. A second one followed a heartbeat later. She set her stance. Pulled back her shoulders. Took a breath. Held it. Released it. The spear shook in her hands. It was adrenalin, not fear. Not yet.

The first dog made wide to her left and the second one came straight at her. She turned slightly, in basic stance, and waited.

The first one fell even with her left side, four yards out, when the second one leapt. She hit the leaper in its right shoulder and followed through, knocking it down and to her right. She spun up, not wasting motion, to meet the dog she knew was leaping from the left. She rammed the spear point into its face and pushed down. It writhed on the ground, then pulled back and tore free.

A third dog was almost on her. She spun a quarter turn to her left, and *kiai*ed as she kicked it in the chest. It flew backward.

Dog number one jumped her from the right, but she dropped the spear, grabbed the dog, spun, and threw it to her left, using its own energy to teach it to fly.

Another dog hit her, then another, and another, and she went down. She was pinned on her right side, so she wrapped her left arm around her face and pulled her head down to keep them off her neck, and used her right hand to wriggle out her pocketknife. She passed it to her left hand, flicked it open and stabbed the dog biting her left arm over and over. It didn't seem to have any effect.

Blood was everywhere.

Alex was screaming.

Black sparks danced in her eyes. Where was the fire?

Suddenly she was jerked to the side, then up a foot to come crashing down. One of the dogs went flying. Then another.

She stabbed the third in the eye, and it shrieked. She pushed it away and jumped up. It did not move. Her vision was fuzzy, and she realized she had blood in her eyes. As quickly as she could, she wiped her face with the back of her arm, then tried to turn, stumbled and nearly fell back in the snow.

The dogs were streaming out of the forest, but they weren't headed for her. She turned and saw Laszlo, sword raising then falling, dancing the swordsman's dance, fighting dogs from all sides. There were ten at least. He was inhumanly fast, and it was beautiful.

Behind him, other soldiers were running up, swords out. A dozen. Maybe.

She knew it wasn't enough.

At least fifteen more dogs were loping toward them, out of the forest.

She looked and found Alex, still in the same place she'd last seen him.

The fire was nearly out in the wagon.

She picked up the spear and went to stand in front of Alex.

"Keer, Keer," he wailed, and started to get up, but she motioned for him to stay down, then turned to face the fight.

The dogs from the forest met the men coming up and the dogs attacked ruthlessly, quietly, and made ridiculously short work of it. In minutes all the men were dead, and none of the dogs. One stood over a dead soldier, looking around, taking in the scene like a human would, and Kiera shivered.

Its eyes met hers. It cocked its head a little, then turned and started making its way across the snow, lifting its feet delicately as it walked.

Kiera gripped the spear tightly. Terror had come. She tried to find the fire, pushed, held her breath, but nothing. Not a blessed thing happened except that the dog got closer and closer. And there was just her and Laszlo to protect Alex.

And Laszlo was a little busy. He was making headway—hell, half the dogs he'd been fighting were dead, but he'd never fight free in time to help her.

And it didn't look like anyone else was coming.

At about twenty yards out, the dog stopped and sat down.

Kiera took a deep breath, blew it out, then pulled in another.

The other dogs had followed this one and waited behind it. Some paced back and forth.

The lead dog yipped at one of the pacing dogs, and it went wide and to Kiera's right. Another went left without a signal. Yet another followed. Soon all of the dogs were moving, surrounding her.

She was hyperventilating. She opened her mouth and tried to slow it down.

The dog who'd been watching her sprang first, and she swung the spear, knocking it to the left, but one hit her from the right, and then another, and she knew it was over.

She hunkered down, curled in a fetal position, trying to protect her head and neck. One grabbed her leg and jerked it out, tearing flesh, and she screamed. Another had her arm and was pawing at her coat, trying to get inside her arms to her face.

Another bit her on the back of her neck and she screamed again, and writhed in agony. The dog at her arm wriggled its head far enough in that its wet nose hit her face. It tried to open its jaws but she pushed down as hard as she could.

One bit her side. She shrieked and kicked out.

The dog on her face suddenly catapulted off. It went flying and landed with a yelp. Another was pulled away, then another. She lay there panting, trying to pull the pain in.

Alex! she thought, and pushed herself up.

One of the dogs was almost to him. Alex sat in the snow, eyes huge with terror.

She reached down to claim the spear and nearly passed out. Blood rained off her. It dripped from her neck and her arm, and she could feel a warm wetness at her side and down her leg.

She picked up the spear and jogged, limping badly, the twenty steps to the dog stalking Alex. It turned when it heard her and leapt, all in one motion, but she was ready. She rammed the spear through its throat, then wrestled it to the ground like a fish on a line. She held the dog pinned until it stopped moving, then jerked the spear out.

Alex backed under the still-smoking wagon and hid under the blankets.

Good boy.

She turned to look for Laszlo, but he was gone.

She tried to scan the trees, but her vision was blurry. She shook her head, trying to clear it, but dizziness made her stumble.

A sharp snarl sounded. She snapped her head around to find the source.

There was movement coming from the area behind the wagon. She moved a few steps and stopped to gape. A dark brown bear was fighting the dogs back there.

Using the spear as a cane, she made her way around the wagon.

The bear was enormous. Unreal. It had to be over two thousand pounds.

And vicious. Every time it swiped a dog with a paw, the dog went flying, bloodied. Some got back up.

The bear caught one of the dogs in its enormous jaws. It worried it until bones snapped, then tossed it aside. It flew through the air, then plopped in the snow and lay still.

Six, ten of the dogs lay dead in the snow, but at least eight more were attacking it, sniping at it from every angle. Light from the fire glistened off its hide, probably marking the blood.

The snow had pinked all the way around the bear, and she knew it was only a matter of time.

Then the bear turned and looked at her, and for a moment time froze.

Those eyes.

The bear was Laszlo.

For that moment she saw his fury, felt his pain.

She couldn't breathe.

When Laszlo was dead, the dogs would kill her, then Alex.

He turned his head, and sounds came rushing back.

With it came the fire, but more slowly this time. She felt it start in her chest, then arc up, through her face, down her legs, into the snow, which fizzed and melted away.

She leaned her head back and closed her eyes. The pain was fading now, fading until it was just a gentle memory.

She opened her arms wide and the fire flowed out, softly, gently, caressing her skin, easing her aches.

She heard more dogs coming. She opened her eyes and saw them. Hundreds. Coming from behind Laszlo.

"No!" she screamed.

Laszlo swatted a dog away, looked at her, then stood up on his back legs to see what she was staring at.

He bellowed a challenge, dropped down to all fours and charged into them.

In moments they covered him like flies, covered him until she couldn't see him anymore. The pile wriggled and fell to the ground, grey bodies writhing all over it like maggots on meat.

"Nooooooo!" she screamed, and the fire leapt from her, but she was too far away. She ran toward Laszlo, sending the fire ahead of her, until its fingers found the first dog.

It screamed as it burned, twisting and writhing as it blackened. A second dog caught fire from the first, and she sent more fire.

The fire encircled Laszlo, and all the dogs were burning.

She started to laugh.

Tens, hundreds came.

She sent the fire out, sent it to kill them all. Hatred flowed from her fingers.

Fifty died, and she rejoiced.

She reached Laszlo and knelt down to him. He was human, and naked, and lying on his stomach. Rips and tears covered his body. And blood. So much blood.

Shaking with rage, she lifted her face and closed her eyes, willing the fire to consume them all.

Hundreds were dead, and the rest turned and ran, but stopped a thousand yards back from the wall of flame.

They were a wall. A plague.

She knew they were waiting for her to tire.

"More!" She screamed, and reached out, but they were too far.

She closed her eyes, lifted her hands, reached up, and found fire in a hole in the sky.

She tried to grab it, but it slipped away. She tried again, sank her fingers in deep, and it came crashing back, into her, filling her. She stumbled, then fell across Laszlo.

She pushed back up. Her nose leaked blood, but the power sang through her. Fire from the sky.

She laughed. She wrestled it, let it fill her, shaped it, and sent it out. It drove her to her knees again but she did not let go.

Lightning flew from her hands and fell from the sky, both finding the pack of dogs. Sharp cracks followed each strike.

They burned. The dogs, the trees, everything.

She stood, closed her eyes and sent more of the fire. She felt the flames around her and Laszlo sputter and die, felt the wall sink to the ground with the slow ease of a veil falling from a bed.

She held tight to the fire in the sky, sending it out ten times, and ten more. She sent it until all of the dogs were gone. Dead or gone.

When there was nothing but ash she tried to push it away, but it surged back into her, knocking her flat on her back. It was like trying to swallow a storm.

She tried to let go of it, let it drift back, but as soon as she loosened her grip, it crushed her. She pushed back, but she couldn't hold it for long.

It was going to devour her.

She could hear herself wheezing, fast and shallow. She started to shake. She struggled against it, but she couldn't open her eyes.

Laszlo's hand found hers, clasped it tight, and strength surged through her. "Send it into the mountain," he rasped.

She opened her eyes and focused on the peak. She pushed up to her knees, lifted her arms and strained, pushing the fire away, pushed it into the wall of rock.

Lightning struck the mountain top once, nearly blinding her, and rock flew and boomed. Then it hit again. As each stroke hit the pressure lessened. After an eternity, it was gone. The power, the elation, the fear. All had gone.

She fell onto her back, panting.

And then Laszlo was on top of her, kissing her. His tongue licked her lips, then met hers. She moaned into his mouth.

His hands found her coat, tore it open, his fingers like fire on her skin. She kissed him back, dug her fingers into his shoulder and pulled his body close.

Without warning her head throbbed, the world spun, and she knew was going to be sick.

She pushed him away.

She turned over and threw up once, twice, shuddered, then fell face first into the snow.

CHAPTER 7

KIERA WOKE TO THE DARK. Blankets covered all but her face, but still she shook with cold. She opened slitted eyes to a tilting, hazy world. She tried to speak, but her tongue wouldn't work because her mouth felt too dry. She tried to moisten her lips. Was she in a tent? What had happened? "Alex," she whispered.

"Shhh," a voice soothed, and a hand touched her face. "Alex is fine." It was Laszlo. "Sleep."

"Please. Water," she rasped.

A warm hand lifted her head and helped her drink. The water was cold, and it eased her burning throat.

She slept.

When she woke again, she could hear Alex talking. He sounded serious, but not upset. Like he was telling a story.

Her head throbbed like seven kinds of hell. She rubbed her face with one hand to fight the blurriness back and opened her eyes. The curve of a tent arched above her. Shafts of daylight speared in, but she lay on and under blankets pushed back against the wall where none could touch her.

She pushed the covers back and found herself wearing someone else's scratchy shirt. Alarmed, she looked down. She still had her pants on, thank God. She pushed up to her knees, then had to wait until the dizziness passed before she could climb to her feet. She made her way outside the tent and stood for a moment, hands on her knees, to catch her breath.

Alex screeched when he saw her and came running. She braced for his impact, but Laszlo popped out from behind the tent, reached out a hand and snapped him up before he could hit her. He lifted Alex until they were face to face.

"She is still sick, Alex. You have to go slowly."

"Okay, okay, okay," Alex said as he squirmed.

Laszlo let Alex down and he wrapped his arms around her leg. Smiling, she patted his back. "Are you okay, Alex?" she asked. She suddenly wanted to cry, and she wasn't sure why. And she needed to sit down.

Perhaps reading her face, Laszlo took her arm and led her to a stump in front of a roaring fire cupped inside a circle of stones. She sat, closed her eyes and soaked up the heat. Alex plopped down on a blanket next to her and wrapped one hand around her calf.

"You don't have any coffee, do you?" she asked.

"I have something good," he said, and handed her a cup. It was almost too hot to hold. It was also the best thing she had ever tasted. She drank it all.

"Broth?" she asked, setting the cup down.

"Yes. How are you feeling?"

"Like sh—I mean, not terribly well yet." She was still a little dizzy, but when she looked up at Laszlo his smile seemed very warm.

She looked away. "Are we all that's left?" she asked.

He reached over and took her cup, then stood up. "No. Do you want more?"

"No, thanks. In a bit, okay? I'd like to see if this stays down first."

He gestured toward a hill to the west. "The main body of the army is camped over the hill. I brought you here to escape the noise."

"How many are left?" She stared at the ground.

"We lost about a thousand."

She closed her eyes. "Mosha?" A shadow blocked the sun. She opened her eyes to find Laszlo standing in front of her. She looked up at him. With the sun shining behind him, he looked like a god.

"Mosha is fine. Worried about you." He paused. "And we have Marco." He put a hand on her shoulder. "But Aliyah. Aliyah is gone."

"Gone as in *missing,* or gone as in *gone?*"

"They took her."

She put her hands over her eyes. "Wait. Marco?"

He sighed. "Yes, Kiera. Marco."

"Is he your prisoner now?"

He didn't answer.

She was suddenly furious. "You know what, Laszlo? He is a boy. A decent, innocent boy who is terrified of his father. He doesn't deserve to be hurt."

"That changes nothing."

"So you're going to give him back to his father."

He walked over to a kettle hung over the fire and scooped out another cup of broth, which he handed to her.

She took it. When it was gone, she pushed off the stump. When she stumbled he reached for her, but she avoided his hand.

WHEN KIERA WOKE AGAIN, it was night. She still hurt, but her stomach felt a little steadier, and her body felt better than it probably should have. She took a deep breath, trying to lift the heavy weight that had settled in her chest. She turned over to her side. Something brushed her arm and fell onto the blanket next to her. She picked it up; it must have been lying on top of her.

She shifted back onto her back and held it under the scant light drifting in through the open door. It was small, hand-sized, and prickly, but it was hard to see what it was meant to be in the dark. It might be a star.

She had to go to the bathroom *now*. She pushed up and looked around. Alex was snoring softly in blankets near the back of the tent. His breathing was soft and deep, and it made her feel comforted in a small way.

It was very cold in the tent. She looked for her coat, found it lying on the floor just out of reach. Without getting out of the covers, she lunged and grabbed a sleeve and pulled it over. She put the star-thing into her pocket and pulled on her coat. The zipper made a sharp sound in the darkness.

Kiera stood up. There was a blanket covering most of the door, which she pushed back before limping outside. The fire still burned, sparks spiraling into the darkness, but she didn't see Laszlo. Maybe he was asleep.

She didn't care.

She stepped out and into the trees and searched out a suitable place. Snow fell, lightly, sluicing through the holes between branches. She saw very few footprints, but she still chose to make her way into a place with new snow.

It was almost oppressively silent, except for the crackling of the fire and the crunching of her steps. The trees stood tall, painted lines drawn on a black canvas.

She unzipped her pants and felt vaguely annoyed about the lack of facilities, but it came and faded away. She finished her business, then pulled up her pants, resettled her coat and stood staring out into the night. She ran a hand through her tangled hair, then began combing out the ends with her fingers.

She felt so tired. Tired and sick at heart. She wondered if Grant was worrying about her. What her friends thought. If the flowers she'd laid on Julia's grave were dead yet.

The dead. All the dead. All the people she had killed.

Julia. Lying on the floor. Eyes open.

She shuddered and closed her eyes, willing the images away.

Her face burned from the cold, so she turned and made her way back to the fire. The tree stump was still there, so she let herself gently down and pushed her feet out in front of her. Sparks from the fire jumped and skipped in the air. Still chilled, she leaned forward and put her hands out. A tendril of fire snaked over and wrapped around her hands.

Startled, she jerked back, and it evaporated like mist.

After a moment she stood, took a few steps forward, and reached a hand out again, willing it to come. Nothing happened.

Annoyed, she scooped up a handful of snow and threw it at the fire. It hit the flames in a spray, hissing as it melted. She wanted to go home. She wanted all of this to be a dream, but the ache in her leg proclaimed it was not. She wanted—

A hand grabbed her shoulder and spun her around. She stumbled, caught herself, and found herself staring into Laszlo's chest. Slowly she raised her eyes to his face. His jaw was clenched hard, his eyes filled with heat.

Eyes on hers, he put his hands on either side of her face and lowered his lips to hers. Slowly. Giving her time to pull away. To say "no."

She did neither.

He kissed her softly, a feather light touch of mouth to mouth. Heat roiled through her belly. She closed her eyes and kissed him back, equally soft. He groaned, and deepened the kiss.

A flurry of thoughts passed through her. How good he felt. How beautiful he was. How many women he must have.

I can't do this, she thought. *I just can't.*

She pulled her head back and pushed him away, gently. She didn't look at his face, but instead hobbled back and sat on the stump. "I'm sorry, Laszlo. That just isn't what I want."

"What do you want?" His rumble made her jump; she hadn't heard him come up behind her.

The fire writhed and popped, casting tendrils of light across the snow.

"I want to go home, Laszlo." She leaned forward and rested her elbows on her knees, then squeezed her thumbs under her fingers. "I want Alex to be safe." She made a vague motion with her hand. "I want this horror to end."

"Where is your home?"

She sighed. "I don't even know anymore."

"How did you come here?"

"I don't know that either." She leaned forward. "It's far away. I seem to be stuck here."

"Where is your husband? Your son's father."

She picked up a handful of snow, crushing it into a ball. She threw it into the fire. "I haven't had a husband for a long time, Laszlo."

"Lie with me, Kiera." His words were soft, authoritative.

Kiera picked up another handful of snow. "No."

"You desire me."

She let out a breath. She thought about denying it, but he would know. "Sure."

"Why, then?"

She dropped the snow on the ground and crushed it with her foot. "For many reasons."

He took a step and stood where she could see him. "Name them."

She glanced at him, then looked back at the fire. "No."

He snorted, then laughed.

His laugh embarrassed her, and the awkwardness she felt turned her words sharp. "Screw you, Laszlo."

He smiled. "You say that every time I anger you, Kiera."

She shot him a glare and looked back at the fire.

He stepped away and walked to the far side of the clearing. He pushed his hands out to warm them, then rubbed them together and held them up again.

The snow kept falling.

"So you're a bear, huh?" Kiera asked.

Laszlo's hands went still.

Kiera looked away. "Look, if you don't want to talk about it, that's fine." She hated that she sounded embarrassed. She shouldn't be embarrassed. Shifting wasn't like a disease. Right?

He turned his back on the fire. "Yes. I am a bear."

He had a beautiful back, she mused. A beautiful shape.

"So are there many shifters here? In Fairbanks?" It was getting colder, so she stood and took a step closer to the fire.

"Yes, there are shifters both in the army and in the deconn."

"Are they all bears? Well, bears or dogs?"

His voice was flat. "No, Lady Kiera. There are many kinds of shifters."

Kiera shook her head, annoyed, even though he couldn't see it. "Why do you keep calling me that, Captain?"

"My apologies if it offends you." He did not sound apologetic.

She decided to ignore that. "So when did you join up? The army, I mean. You must have been doing this for a while, being the captain and all."

He turned and faced her, but she couldn't tell what he was thinking.

"What do you mean?"

Kiera looked at him for a moment, brows down, not understanding what he didn't understand. Finally she shrugged. "I guess I wondered what would motivate someone to want to become a soldier." She smiled. "No offense. It's just not something I would ever consider doing."

Something passed over his face, but he was too far away for her to make it out. Then he laughed, a little wryly. "You say you don't know."

She lifted a hand in an *I don't know* gesture. "I don't know what?"

The wind whipped up white powder, dusting her head and shoulders. She looked up to the half moon peeking through a break in the clouds.

His voice drew her back. He was smiling, but it wasn't with pleasure. "I didn't 'join,' Kiera." He spread his arms. Spoke matter-of-factly. "None of us did. I was taken as a child, as was every man in this army."

"What?"

He took a step closer to the fire and turned his back to her. "All of the deconn armies are made up of slaves," he told the trees. His voice said it didn't matter, but Kiera didn't believe him.

She walked around the fire until she stood in front of him. "So your 'lord,' Vayu, what? Owns you? Like property?"

He looked at her face, her mouth, then nodded once.

"Are they all, uh, shifters?"

"No. Some are nuwyr, Skani with little or no magic. Like Mosha."

"Skani are the lords then? They have magic, like me?"

He nodded, watching her face.

"My God," Kiera whispered. She reached out and took his hand. He looked down at their hands, then up at her face. "I am sorry."

He pulled his hand away and pushed past her, stalking toward the trees. "Don't pity me, Kiera."

"Why the hell shouldn't I pity you?" she spat to his back. "That is absolute bullshit! Slavery is bullshit! No one should be forced to join a goddamned army!"

He laughed. Stopped. Turned around. Stalked back to her. She lifted her chin and prepared to shoot back at whatever he said. If wanted to argue, fine.

He surprised her. "Tell me why you won't lie with me."

Lingering anger made her reckless. "Well, Laszlo, we both know that someone like you wouldn't choose someone like me to fuck unless pickins were pretty damned slim. And, to tell you the truth, I would rather not be one of the doubtless many women who've graced your bed and will undoubtedly continue to do so. I don't do the casual, one-night-stand-type sex." She turned her back on him. "Sorry." She limped around the fire and let herself down on the stump.

Laszlo threw a log onto the fire, shooting sparks into the sky. The log caught, and the fire burned brightly, casting shapes onto the trees.

The crackling of the fire made the only sound for a long, long time. *What would it be like to be a slave?* she wondered, and snuck a glance at Laszlo, who again faced the fire. *It must be beyond awful knowing that someone owns you.* She looked at him again when he turned to stare off into the trees. *I wouldn't have guessed,* she mused. *He is not what I'd expect a slave to be like.* She felt her lips curl. *He's too arrogant. And bossy.*

The fire had warmed her and her eyes felt heavy. "I should go back to sleep," she commented, but didn't make any move to get up. *In a minute,* she thought.

Laszlo walked over and squatted down in the snow in front of her. She leaned back a little to take in his face. He was still taller than she was. He reached out with both hands and pulled her head close, like he was going to tell her a secret. She could feel his breath in her hair.

"Sleep with me," he murmured, and bit her ear.

She jerked back, startled, and he let her, but then he turned his head and nudged her nose with his. He leaned in and opened his mouth over hers, breathing her breath.

He kissed her then, hard, and pulled her to his chest and then down to the ground. They landed on his back, and his mouth never lifted from hers. He growled and thrust his tongue against her lips, then into her mouth. Before her heart could beat once, she arched, moaning softly. He nipped her lips, her jaw, her neck, her ear. He pulled an arm free, brought up his hand and cupped her face.

"No," she whispered, and pulled back. She laid one hand on his chest and felt the muscles roll under her touch. She opened her eyes and looked into his.

His eyes were golden brown. Inhuman. Beautiful.

She took a deep breath. Let it out. Took another. "Laszlo, God knows it isn't that I don't want you." Even though she still laid on his body, she looked into his eyes, willing him to understand. "But I meant what I said. I don't do casual sex. I do not meet men, even really sexy men," she smiled ruefully, not meeting his eyes, "and fall into their beds."

Laszlo slid her off, then propped himself up on one hand, elbow on the ground. "I am not asking you to provide me with sex for a night," he told her. Hot desire burned in his eyes, and he leaned forward, breath hot on her face, to kiss her again.

She put her fingers on his lips.

"You're relentless, Captain."

His voice was husky. "And you are beautiful."

She rolled her eyes. "What I am is here, and what you are is wanting. But what will happen when we get back to Fairbanks?" Kiera scooted back. "Once we get there you'll hand me over to that lord of yours and go back to, to, whoever you usually see, and, uh, tumbling maids and all that. I can't do that, Laszlo. I'm sorry."

He grinned. "You would be jealous."

She glared.

He ran a finger down her face. "Kiera, I'm an Alak, not a Skani."

"Whatever the hell that means!"

His face was serious. "It means that lying with you will not be casual."

She smiled. "Tell me about the shifters, Laszlo."

He drew his brows down in mock anger, reached out and grabbed her arm, giving it a shake. "Woman, you ask more questions than anyone I've ever known."

She laughed. "I can't help it! I just can't stop wondering, so I ask."

He pulled her close, nipped her lower lip. "No more asking," he murmured into her mouth, then kissed her.

She let him.

She wanted him. She wanted him so much she ached. He was so beautiful. So strong. So—everything. *What the hell,* she thought recklessly, wrapping her arms around him and deepening the kiss. *It's only my heart.*

He tried to pull her down into the snow, but she pushed him back, laughing. Before he could object, she said, "I will not have sex with you outside, Laszlo. And not in with Alex. Do you have a tent?"

A smile erupted, broad and wicked. He stood, grabbed her hand and pulled her smoothly, if a little too quickly, to her feet.

Pain shot through her back and down her leg when she stood—she'd been off it too long—and she leaned over, grimacing, and held up a hand for him to wait a minute.

Laszlo reached down and scooped her up into his arms.

"Goddamnit, Laszlo," she said, outraged, pushing back from his chest with both hands, "put me down. Right now. I'm not a swooning schoolgirl."

"No." He walked past the fire and into the trees, grip hard. Like his chest.

"Put me down right now or I swear to God I will punch you in the nose."

He grinned. "No you won't."

"I'm a big girl, Laszlo. You'll give yourself a goddamned hernia."

He looked down at her. "Stop."

She shut her eyes. "Shut up, you jerk."

He laughed, and it was a joyous sound.

LASZSLO'S TENT STOOD about twenty yards uphill from hers, nestled into the lee of a trio of pines. He pushed through the cloth across the door and laid Kiera gently on the mess of blankets lying on the floor.

It was dark inside. Too dark to see.

Kiera's heart was pounding out of her chest. Was she really going to do this?

Yes.

She heard the rasp of fabric pulled against skin and knew Laszlo was taking off his clothes. The door-cloth suddenly drew back, and she saw him tie it back, just a little to let in the light. The snow had stopped and she could see the moon through the trees.

He turned, and for a moment, silhouetted against the light, he looked like one of the old gods. The moon shone through the tendrils of his hair, giving the shape of his face a sculpted, ethereal look. His shoulders were huge, his chest only slightly less so. It V'd to a smaller, but still very large waist. His thighs were rounded with muscle.

He came and knelt smoothly beside her.

She felt his hands on her shoulder, lifting her up, helping her out of her—his—shirt. He pulled the bra from her shoulders, and she unsnapped it. He tossed it to one side. He pulled at her pants, but got caught trying to figure out the zipper, so she reached down and opened them. He pulled them off her in one long movement, lifting her legs off the ground. He reached up and slid her underwear down her legs, then tossed them off into the dark.

Laszlo moved to one side so that he wasn't blocking the light. It shone on her and her hands flinched, then fisted, wanting to cover her rolling belly, her generous thighs, her bulging breasts.

He reached across her and took her hand. "No," he whispered. "Let me see you." He let go and sat up.

Kiera swallowed and closed her eyes.

His lips touched her stomach, feather light, and she flinched. He laughed, low in his throat, and licked her skin. Licking and nipping, he made his way to her breasts. He took the edge of one into his mouth, and suckled her, licking and nipping. She arched and moaned, and reached for him. He pushed her hands back. After an eternity of torment he took the other nipple into his mouth, his fingertips skimming back and forth across her torso, sending shocks skidding across her skin until she gasped.

He left her there, shaking with need in the moonlight, and shifted so his head was at the juncture of her thighs. He leaned over and took her into his mouth, his tongue finding just the right spot. She arched her hips up, and he rode her with his mouth. His fingers found her wetness and pushed inside, and she arched again. He made love to her that way until the waves of climax washed over her, until she lay gasping and trembling.

His lips found hers. He bit her lower lip, and she opened her mouth to his. He tasted warm and brackish. His tongue touched hers, hot and slick, and she moaned and wrapped her arms around him. He pulled back, licked her face, bit her ear, her jaw, then found her lips again.

He moved over her, pushing her legs apart with one knee, then the other, holding his weight off of her. He pressed his hardness against her, but didn't breach her. He kissed her, pushed his hand through her hair, pinning some of it, and her head, to the pillow.

"Kiera," he whispered against her lips, and in one long, hurried stroke, pushed all the way inside her. He stopped and held himself there, seated as deep inside her as he could go. He was very large and it hurt, a little. He murmured words she didn't understand like a secret into her mouth, then kissed her again. He began to move, pushing deep, pulling slowly, letting the flavor fill her, the longing begin to burn. She arched against him, digging her nails into his back, pulling him in with every stroke.

He felt her need and moved to meet it, moving with her as she climbed again, pushing her on. He reached between them with his hand and stroked her, making her weep with need. Harder, faster, he plunged until she cried out, lifting her hips to take him deeply, begging with her body for more. Into her he thrust, again and again and again until she peaked, sparks dancing in her sight. He grabbed her hard, groaning, plunging deep, once, twice, and spilled into her with a shudder.

They lay gasping, his weight pressing her down into the blankets. He moved off of her, and pulled her into his arms. She nestled her head on his chest and wrapped one arm over his stomach. Her breath was still ragged.

The wind ruffled the cloth covering the door, and three drops of moonlight splashed across them. Kiera looked out through the crack. The moon had slid sideways while they had made love, now almost gone from sight except what splayed through the trees.

The world lay so quiet, and a sense of peace stole over her. Of safety. She knew it was crazy, but she savored it anyway, raised her face and bathed in it, letting the stillness fill her chest, slowing her heart and quieting her worries.

Laszlo's fingers painted absent swirls on her back. "Sing for me, *a'kala*," he murmured.

She lifted her head and started to object, but he put a finger on her lips. "Please."

After a moment she laid her head back on his shoulder and closed her eyes. He let his fingers slide through her hair and rest against the nape of her neck. He wrapped a strand of hair around his hand and continued to trace a pattern on her bare skin.

All right. A gift for a gift.

Poring through her memories, she tried to choose the right one. Surprise washed through her, pulling a smile to her lips as Kiera remembered a song that her mother used to sing when Kiera was small. Keeping her eyes tight, she softly sang the words it had taken twenty years to understand, but could never forget.

Beneath a Van Gogh sky,
We stand watching, you and me.
We wait for stars to sing the song,
To seal our destiny.

They light the sky on fire,
The sound of bloody light.
Our shadows stretch, immortal;
Devouring the night.

The stars, they burn the skies,
Burn my eyes, white December.
My heart, it floats like ashes,
Fallen embers, blowing embers.

We stand so strong and purposeful,
Our hands stretched toward the moon.
And who would blame me if, perchance,
I gave my heart so soon?

Fiery stars streak toward us,
Shooting, spinning through the skies.
Flame chars the past to soot,
We see through newborn eyes.

The stars, they burn the skies,
Burn my eyes, but I remember.

The stars, they float like ashes,
Fallen embers, blowing embers.

Against the blazing heavens,
We lie watching, you and me.
The sky too small to capture us;
Love is infinity.

The stars, they burn the skies,
Burn my eyes, white December.
The stars, they float like ashes,
Fallen embers, blowing embers.

Fallen embers, blowing embers
Love burns all life to ashes.
Resurrection. Rising embers.

When she finished, Laszlo pulled her chin up with his fingers and kissed her softly on the mouth. She fell asleep, her head on his chest.

CHAPTER 8

THE SKY HAD JUST BEGUN TO PINK when Laszlo woke Kiera. She groaned and pulled the covers over her head.

"Alex will be up soon," he said. "I didn't think you would want him to wake without you."

She pushed the blankets back and he handed her her clothes. He watched her as she pulled on her underwear.

It made her feel uneasy. "Do you have to stare?" she asked.

She heard the smile in his voice. "Yes."

She groaned and turned her back to put on her bra, then pulled her shirt on.

"Are you sore this morn?" he asked.

"Oh yeah. All over," she answered. "I'm healing pretty fast, but my back and my leg still hurt."

"That's not what I was asking."

She stilled but did not turn around. "Oh. You mean—"

"Yes. That is what I mean."

"I'm fine." She said, pulling on her pants. "Well, a little sore," she admitted. "But I'll be fine."

Kiera turned around. He squatted down in front of her and took one of her hands. She looked up at him. He looked very stern. "Kiera, by tonight we will be in Fairbanks. Things are very different there than they are outside the city."

She leaned back and looked up at him. She wasn't sure what that meant, or how she felt about it.

"Be cautious, Kiera. If you will listen to my advice, you will keep your secrets close, including last night."

"Why?" she asked, feeling a little hurt but trying to push it away as premature. "Why 'including last night'?"

He stood up and walked over to the door, then pulled the cloth back and looked out. He scanned the forest for a long second, then turned back and looked at her. "Because the fact that we are lovers won't make you any friends among the Skani." He leaned down and kissed her, then stood and offered her his hand. "Go wake Alex, and then we'll return to the main camp."

Kiera's heart thudded, for one reason or many she didn't know, but she took his hand and stood. She walked downhill to the Alex's tent while Laszlo took down his. Dawn had broken, but night's chill still lingered. She shivered in her insufficient coat.

Alex woke when she entered the tent. She sat down and he crawled into her lap and told her about his dream. Laszlo poked his head in a few minutes later. She dressed Alex, then Laszlo started taking down the tent while she took Alex behind the trees.

While Alex did his business Kiera pulled her fingers through her hair and tried to wrestle through the tangles, but she simply couldn't get all the small ones out.

When they got back, Alex's tent lay in a pile in the snow. As she watched, Laszlo rolled the canvas into a cigar shape, doubled it, then used rope to bind it to his tent. The bundle they made looked too heavy for a horse. Still kneeling, and perhaps feeling her gaze, Laszlo glanced up, grinned, then stood. He walked right up to her and kissed her lips, then lifted her face with his fingers. "Where's the comb I made you?"

"Yuck! Why'd you kiss Keer?" Alex wanted to know.

He turned to Alex, but she saw his eyes crinkle. "Because she's so pretty."

"What comb?" Kiera asked, ignoring that. "You didn't give me a comb."

"I left it on your chest yesturn while you were sleeping so you would find it when you woke."

What? "Oh!" she said, and patted her coat pockets. She pulled the little stick-thing out of one and held it up. "Uh, Laszlo, I don't know how this is supposed to work."

He took it from her hand, turned it back and forth to show it to her, and took a lock of her hair in his other hand. With overdramatic gestures, he pulled the device through her hair, taking tangles as it went.

She snatched it back, scowling. He laughed, then went back to the tents. He knelt down, picked the bundle up and slung it over his shoulder.

"Wow!" Alex sung out. "You're strong."

Laszlo turned and grinned at him. "Naw. It's not that heavy. Want to help?"

"Sure!"

Kiera watched Alex run down the hill. At the moment he reached Laszlo the sun crested the mountaintop, its yellow rays bleeding down the slope and washing them both in sunlight. Laszlo handed Alex some pegs in a bag and said something Kiera couldn't hear. Alex laughed.

Embers of dust ignited, then danced and swirled in the breeze.

Kiera's chest felt tight. *I could fall in love with this man.* She lifted her face to the sun, took a breath, and then opened her eyes to find Laszlo staring at her. She smiled, a little tremulously, and he smiled back.

Laszlo started for the army camp. Alex kept at his heels the whole way, chattering, and she followed behind, trying not to limp.

THEY CRESTED THE HILL TOGETHER and made their way toward the camp.

Someone saw them and shouted. Men came running from all over to crowd into the rough formation that was forming in front of the camp. She was heartbroken to see so many missing. Laszlo had said a thousand, but she hadn't really known what that meant until she saw how many were gone.

Before she could ask Laszlo what the hell they were doing, they broke into cheers. Wave after wave washed over her. Laszlo stopped about fifty yards out from the camp and dropped the bundled tents on the ground. He turned and flourished a courtly bow to her, and she felt her face flame as the soldiers screamed and pounded the ground with spears.

When the noise had died down, Laszlo picked up his bundle and motioned Kiera and Alex to follow him. They did, and the ranks spread to let them pass, but when she breached the ranks, the men swarmed around her, patted her back and her arm, squeezed her hands. She smiled at everyone and pushed her way through, holding on to Alex by the back of his jacket. He was jostled and pushed, but he laughed.

When Laszlo had passed the last of the men, he turned and roared, "Back to it! All of you! We leave in half a mark!" It was the loudest voice Kiera had ever heard.

Men scrambled to obey.

"Why did they do that? What was that for?" Kiera asked from behind him.

Laszlo stopped and turned back. His voice was deadly serious. "You saved their lives, Kiera." Her puzzlement must have shown, because after a moment he added, more quietly, "Your fire saved all of our lives."

Laszlo led her to a wagon, then lifted Alex inside, but motioned for her to wait. He pulled her aside and said, "Marco is inside. He was hurt very badly by the Shunakah."

She held up a hand. "The what?"

"The shifters that we fought."

She nodded grimly. The dogs' name.

He looked at her. "Mosha thinks that he will live, but he is hurt very badly, and he is grieving. He loved Aliyah, I think, and feels her loss is his fault."

She let out her breath. They stood looking at each other for a moment. Finally, she motioned him down so she could whisper in his ear. "Are you still going to give him to his father?"

He gritted his teeth and whispered back fiercely, "Woman, I will not discuss this." He motioned her to the wagon and stalked off.

She flashed a glare at his back.

Kiera climbed into the wagon. Marco lay inside, under blankets. His eyes were closed but he wasn't sleeping.

He looked like he had been beaten. The left half of his face was red and swollen where a swath of claws had raked down his face. Both of his eyes had been blackened. Kiera shuddered to think what he must look like where she couldn't see.

Mosha poked his head over the side. "Lady, yer lookin' well," he said. "I'm that glad ta see it." Kiera smiled at him. "I'd heard ye fought a pack of Shunakah with just a spear and took a couple bites o' yer own." He grinned. "Ye trying ta make us look bad, Lady?"

"No, no." Kiera waved a hand dismissively, embarrassed.

Mosha patted her shoulder. "Well, ye know we all thank ye for the fire. It killed them all, the whoresons, if you'll pardon me for saying so. Saved Marco, too, here."

The silence felt a little awkward.

"Have ye eaten?" Mosha asked.

"No, we sure haven't. And I'd love a jug of water for the trip if you can spare one. Oh, Mosha, where did these extra blankets come from? They're lovely, but they're not ours. I think ours burned up with that other wagon."

"Some of the lads donated 'em," he said with a wink, then turned and marched toward the front of the column.

Touched, Kiera turned back and helped get Alex bundled into the blankets. She looked at Marco, but he was still holding his eyes closed.

She sat on top of the blankets until Mosha got back. He climbed in and ate with them, then put an extra blanket under Marco's head before he climbed back out.

"Keep the boy covered and lemme know if he is in too much pain," Mosha said before climbing up on to the driving board.

Kiera nodded to his back, then scooted over to Marco.

"I know you're awake, Marco." She brushed the hair from his forehead.

"I can't imagine how you must be feeling about all of this. But it isn't your fault, you little dimwit. You didn't do anything but what you thought was right. The truth is that sometimes the world just isn't fair."

"Leave me alone," he rasped, not opening his eyes.

"I will leave you to soak in self-pity in just a minute. But I want you to think about this: You should be proud. You gave everything you had, Marco, for her, to free her. You can only give everything you have. There isn't anything else. Grieve and be sad, and plan how you'll do better next time, but don't give up. There are few strong enough to offer everything and have it taken, and even fewer courageous enough to stand up and offer it again."

Kiera sighed. "My *kwan jang nim*, the man who taught me how to fight, used to say something that you need to hear. He used to tell us, 'every time you stand up for someone else, you give them the chance to stand for another.' And he was right. Maybe the person they stand for will be you, Marco, or someone you love when you can't.'"

Marco turned his head away.

Kiera leaned down and kissed his forehead, then went back and tucked herself into the blankets.

THE AIR WARMED as the sun climbed the sky. A few clouds scuttled past to slink off the horizon. Alex was restless, so Kiera sang and played games with him. Some of the soldiers drifted by. They smiled and teased Alex, and when the train stopped for a break, forty men built fifty snowpeople in a clearing. Some, Kiera noted with amusement, had chests too well-endowed to be called snowmen. While Kiera was working on hers, Alex threw a snowball and hit her in the back of the head.

"Ouch!" she cried, rubbing the snow out of her hair with one hand. She turned to find a dozen faces staring at her, some looking faintly scared. *Do they think I'm going to beat him?* she wondered. She picked up some snow, rolled it in her hand, whooped a war cry, and threw it at Alex.

Alex ran. Trying not to limp, Kiera chased him around the snowpeople, lobbing snowballs. He screeched with glee. He stopped behind one of the figures, grabbed snow and tossed it.

"Lame!" she called, and hoisted another. He ducked behind a snowwoman and she missed.

She ran up behind him, grabbed him, and pulled them both the ground. He was breathless from laughing. "Snow angels!" she called, and they both flopped to their backs and waved their arms and legs in the snow.

She helped Alex up and they turned to admire their work. All the men bunched up behind them, too, faces solemn. She felt faintly embarrassed, but kept her eyes on the snow.

"What's that for?" one asked.

"Fun," she answered, and smiled broadly. "Want to try? I'll do another one with you."

The speaker, a young, blond man in his twenties, looked at her, then at the other soldiers. "Naw," he finally said, but she could tell he wanted to.

She grinned and put her hands on her hips. "Oh, come on now, you guys!"

Another soldier sat down in the snow, then laid back. He moved his arms tentatively.

"You have to move your legs, too," she said, leaning over to look. "You're making an angel. Your arms make the wings and your legs make the gown."

"My angel ain't no girl," he replied, and she laughed.

"Very well." She grabbed Alex's hand and tipped them back into the snow. "Snow angels!" she called. Thirty-nine bodies hit the ground, and for a moment all could be heard was the swish, swish, swish of arms and legs breaking the snow.

A roar of laughter made everyone sit up, then bodies were scrambling to stand.

"Don't ruin the angels!" Kiera cried. "Be careful!"

She turned and saw Laszlo, seated on his horse about fifty yards away and laughing so hard he was in danger of falling off it.

"Oh you're just jealous!" she called and made a face.

He climbed off his horse, pulled off his helmet and wiped his eyes. He hooked the helmet over the saddle horn.

The soldiers stood at attention. Silently.

He stood for a moment. Took off his sword and stuck it into the ground. Then he took off at a dead run. At her.

She gulped.

Laszlo was there in three seconds. Faster than any human could ever be. The rank of men parted to let him through. From ten feet out he leapt, catching Kiera in his arms and pulling her to his chest, one hand behind her head. They tumbled across the snow, turning over and over until they slid to a stop.

They landed on his back. She looked down at him, mouth agape. He put his hands on her cheeks, then pulled her face down and kissed her. Softly, just a press of lips to lips.

Apparently uncaring that forty-odd pairs of eyes watched the show.

His voice was very serious. "My angel is bigger than your angel."

She blinked. He suddenly grinned like a schoolboy, surprising a laugh out of her. She reached down, picked up a fistful of snow, and shoved it down his shirt.

He yelped and pushed her off him, then tossed a handful of snow at her face.

Kiera got up and ran back to the snowpeople, stopping every few feet to toss snowballs at him as he walked behind her. Alex came running, bearing his own arsenal.

Laszlo stood and let them pelt him four or five times, then held up his hands in surrender. He reached down and grabbed a handful of snow, which he tossed at one of the soldiers who still stood at attention. The soldier flinched when the snow hit his leg, and his eyes opened wide.

"Let's go!" Laszlo bellowed, and the soldiers fell out.

MARCO SLEPT, REALLY SLEPT, for the rest of the day. The troupe trundled into a narrow valley, and the army now marched on what looked like a frozen river. The mountains drew closer here, craggy and snow-covered, with hints of black granite peeking through here and there like shy children. The crunch of feet breaking snow made the only sounds, occasionally punctuated by the creak of the wagon and the sounds of Marco's breathing.

When the sun slunk behind the mountains, Kiera and Alex snuggled into their blankets and tried to rest. She knew they were close to Fairbanks, and she was too worried to sleep, so she sang. She kept her voice quiet so she wouldn't wake Marco, but when Alex knew the words, he sang with her.

When her voice fell silent, Mosha called, "Sing the one about the stars again," he called. "Ye put so much heart in that one it brought me a tear."

Kiera sat up, embarrassed. "Mosha, you are far too kind. My singing is average at best. I love to sing, though you're the first person who's ever asked me to do it some more."

"It's fair lovely," he said, his voice a little sad.

"Don't you all sing?" she asked. "You could teach me a song and we can sing it together."

His voice was gruff. "I don't know any songs, Lady. Only ones who sing here are mothers ta children or wives ta husbands."

"So are you proposing marriage then, Mosha, or asking to be adopted?" she teased.

He was silent so long that she began to worry that she'd offended him. *Oh God!* She suddenly realized, and it felt like a fist slammed into her heart. *He's a slave. He can't marry and some monster probably took him from his parents when he was just a kid.*

She took a deep breath. "Mosha, that was the most insensitive thing I have ever said. I cannot apologize humbly enough, and I beg your forgiveness. I was embarrassed about my poor singing and somewhere while I was thinking about myself I stopped thinking about anything else." Her voice dropped to a near whisper. "I am so sorry."

Mosha did not answer.

Kiera sat back and put her hand over her eyes.

"I do not remember my mother," Mosha said, after a while, and his voice was so low she had to strain to hear it. She sat up, and scooted across the box. Marco's eyes were open.

"I should say that I remember her, but na her face. I canna see it." He paused. "I remember her singing. Her voice was, I dunno, higher than yern. And her songs were more sad. But she sang ta me when I was small."

Kiera's eyes prickled. Marco reached out of the blanket and took her hand.

She looked down at his hand in hers. His arm was completely bandaged. His hand looked black and three of his fingers were broken.

Kiera stared at those fingers. A tear fell.

"Mosha, what can I sing for you?" She said, voice thicker than she might have wished.

"The one about the falling stars," he said.

Kiera closed her eyes and sang.

CHAPTER 9

AS IF A STAR HAD FALLEN AND CONTINUED TO BURN, the lights from the city blazed from miles away. A wall encased its hulking girth, and someone had cut the trees away for more than a mile outside its perimeter for as far around as Kiera could see. Overbright mushrooms of individual lights blossomed over some of the taller buildings. Most of the structures stood too short to poke more than a dozen feet above the battlement, but one, set at the far end of town, a stone-colored mass composed of three giant, attached domes, rose above them all and flared like the sun.

A palace, she thought.

The army crossed the clearing and breached the city through what must have been the main gate. Uniformed guards waved them through a post set just inside, but no one tried to stop them or asked any questions. As they passed through the gate the marching men veered left, following a path along the wall.

The mounted soldiers and her wagon continued forward.

They passed under a poled lantern that bathed them in yellow light. Marco groaned as it sluiced over him. Kiera gently patted his hand, which he'd left next to hers. Alex dragged himself close to her, dropped one hand on her leg, and stared out at the city. Many feet had trampled the snow until it lay flat and nearly black on the road. A few people scurried down the sides of the streets, but none cast more than cautious glances their way.

Mosha drove them up a round driveway that led to the domed castle. Light fell from dozens of windows, down patchwork stone walls to splash across the crushed snow. A frozen garden lay off to the right, bisected by a narrow walkway. Off to the left stretched a flat, unbroken yard. Someone had shoveled the snow from the drive and the area in front of the door, revealing small black rocks underneath that sparkled when they caught the light.

Mosha hopped off the front, his feet crunching in the rocks. He said a few words to the two soldiers who had already dismounted, then strode to the side of the wagon. Kiera climbed out, then stood by in case someone needed help with Marco. Alex slid over and crushed himself against her leg. Kiera's heart beat hard in her chest, too, but she smiled down at him with what she hoped was reassurance.

Four women and three men, all wearing blue and grey livery, rushed out of the house. Two of the men carried what looked like a stretcher. The third, a heavy-set brunet, climbed in and lifted Marco up. He stepped gingerly over the edge, then dropped down to the ground. Kiera flinched when Marco groaned, but the man didn't seem to notice. The others lifted the stretcher, and the brunette laid Marco atop it and tossed a blanket across him. As silently as they had come, they took him into the house. And away.

Kiera's eyes slid from the now-empty doorway when one of the women, the youngest, approached her, then curtsied deep. From this angle, Kiera could see that she had knotted her dark blonde hair behind her head.

Kiera stared at her. The woman kept her head bowed. Kiera shifted her weight to her other foot.

Mosha stepped close and whispered, "She wants ye ta follow."

"Thanks," she whispered back. She took a step, then turned back and said, "Take care, Mosha. I hope to see you again soon."

He grinned at her, a tad sourly, then climbed back into the wagon.

KIERA AND ALEX FOLLOWED the young woman through the door and into a very grand hall. Kiera tried not to gape like a country cousin, but it was hard. Even compared to Nick's home, this was truly a palace.

The melting snow on Kiera's boots dirtied a yellow marble floor inlaid with ornate blue tiles. Two pillars stood just inside the entryway, carved of the same marble, reaching up to at least three stories of open space to prop up the edges of a rounded, bowed out ceiling, which an enormous skylight sliced in half. Dark, nearly black wood covered walls adorned with cubbies and intricately carved moldings.

Halfway down the hall life-sized, marble statues of winged men perched on pedestals. Twin stairways led to the upper story winding around either side of the hall. The woman led Kiera and Alex up the right stairway. They turned left at the top, then walked around a corner, turned right, and walked down to the end of a long walkway. The woman opened a door on the left and entered, and after a moment Kiera and Alex did, too.

Kiera gaped. The room was larger than her entire condo. She took a step and sank into thick blue carpet. Someone had painted the walls a soft blue, except for a single panel of paintings directly opposite the door, lined vertically, flowing upward from the floor to the fifteen-foot ceiling. Each showed a different bird in flight. Three tall walnut dressers edged against the wall off to the left, and what looked like a closet lay behind them. *Like I'd ever need that much room for clothes,* she thought, shaking her head. Off to the right, in which the bulk of the apartment lay, Kiera found a sitting area in which two earth-toned, velvety couches crouched around a brightly burning fireplace. On the far right side, thirty feet past a dining table, an enormous canopy bed squatted atop a soft, yellow rug, and a smaller, trundle-styled bed had been tucked behind it and close to the wall. Kiera guessed she could walk twenty steps between them. A door marked the wall behind the small bed, and Kiera prayed it led to a bathroom. And not to a chamber pot.

The woman said something, but it was so close to a whisper that Kiera couldn't hear her. "Pardon me, ma'am?" she asked.

Startled, the woman looked up. "No, no, my lady." She said, then bowed her head. "I'm just Emmy. What can I bring you, my lady?"

"Can I take a bath?" Kiera asked. "Would that be all right?"

"Yes, my lady," Emmy said softly, "right this way," and pointed at the door behind Alex's bed before scampering toward it. Before Emmy opened it, Kiera called, "Wait." Emmy stopped. "Could we also have something to eat and drink?"

Emmy curtsied again. She turned and made her way back to the main door, then closed it softly behind her.

Kiera walked through the apartment and into the door Emmy pointed out. It was a huge bathroom—and a bathroom in every sense of the word. There was a big tub, of marble, and a smaller one, also marble, laid into the floor. With drains. Both had some mechanism by which running water was dispensed, and Kiera felt herself smiling. And behind those sat a beautiful, glorious toilet. It looked like it covered a hole in the floor, but she could have hugged it.

After Kiera and Alex bathed and ate, they lay on their beds. Alex started snoring almost instantly, but Kiera couldn't sleep. Thoughts tumbled and bounced in her head. She wondered what tomorrow would bring.

She wondered if Laszlo would come.

A creak pierced her thoughts, and she sat up in bed. Her door was opening, slowly. She got out of bed, thankful nothing in the mattress made noise, and jogged across the carpet on her toes. She stopped behind the door, wishing that she had something in her hand. It was too late; the door swung open and a man walked inside. He turned and shut the door, then dropped a bar she hadn't seen.

It was Laszlo. She let out her breath.

He turned and swept her up in a hug. *"A'kala,"* he whispered into her hair. His kisses came a moment later. He led her back to the bed, his mouth never leaving hers.

WHEN KIERA WOKE it was morning. She reached across the expanse of bed and found Laszlo gone. She felt a twinge of sadness, but then reminded herself that this was her first night in a strange place and it probably wouldn't do to flaunt their affair to the household. She wondered at Laszlo's warning. What would they say?

It was cold enough to see her breath. "God, I miss central heating," she groaned, and pulled the blankets up to her neck. Alex stirred, ruining her plans to laze. "Stay in bed," she told him, and forced herself to get up.

She pulled her coat off the back of a chair, then sank her feet into her boots and skipped to the beautiful bathroom. Alex was sitting up when she came out.

"It's cold," he complained, still sleepy.

"I know, sweetheart. Stay in bed until I get a fire going."

She walked over to the fireplace, tossed a couple of logs inside, then looked for something to light them with.

She growled. There was nothing. No lighter, no matches.

Before she could start a second search, someone knocked at her door. She peeked out to find a woman standing outside. She was not one of the women who brought things, of that much Kiera was certain. This fifty-year-old woman wore regal like a second skin. A long white dress hung gracefully down, cinched tight at the waist with gold ties. Pins pulled her blonde and gray hair into a sweeping style, leaving icy blue eyes and strong cheekbones to dominate her face.

A small frown formed between the woman's brows as she took in Kiera's blue coat draped over her shoulders, which barely covered the white nightshirt Kiera had found on the bed last night.

Kiera felt her cheeks heat. "Um, hello."

"May I come in?" Chill colored her voice.

"Please do," Kiera said, opening the door and standing aside. "But please let me apologize. The room is very cold. I was about to light a fire."

The woman looked slightly puzzled. "Have you not called your girl?"

"Nooooo," Kiera responded, drawing out the sound. "I don't know how to call anyone." She smiled.

The woman did not smile back.

"So, how may I help you?" Kiera asked, sneaking a quick glance behind the woman to see if anyone else stood behind her.

"What is your name?" the woman demanded.

"My name is Kiera," she snapped back. "What's yours?"

The woman stiffened. "I am Leith, Lady Vayu, and I came to welcome you to my house."

Kiera closed her eyes for a heartbeat, then opened them. "Please allow me to apologize, Lady Vayu. I am a visitor here and am unfamiliar with your customs." She inclined her head. "I thank you most sincerely for your hospitality."

Lady Vayu nodded once, looking slightly less ruffled.

"Would you like to sit down?" Kiera asked.

"No. I would not. We will be formally introduced during court, which you must attend in one mark. You have time to bathe and dress." She paused. "And I also wished to thank you for saving my son's life." She turned to go, but stopped and looked back. "I will send your girl to tend to your needs. She will tell you how to call her." She strode out into the hall.

Court? Kiera swallowed, then leaned out the doorway. "You're welcome, Lady Vayu. Marco is a very good boy and I am honored to know him."

Lady Vayu paused without turning around, then walked away, the back of her dress sweeping the floor behind her.

TEN MINUTES LATER Emmy entered without knocking. Barely slowing to curtsey, she hurried over to the fire. She held a candle in one hand, which she waved her fingers over, and the wood in the fireplace burst to life.

Kiera's mouth fell open. "How did you do that?"

Emmy froze.

"No, no. I'm not angry," Kiera told her as she walked over. "I have just never seen anything like that before."

Emmy whispered to the floor. "It's going 8:30, my lady. A fire mark."

Kiera wondered what that had to do with anything. "Um. Okay."

Without looking up, Emmy waved her free hand at the lamps perched atop the tables, each of which popped as they lit.

Alex slid from under his covers, mouth open, and stood next to his bed. He looked over at Kiera, who shrugged and made an *I don't know* face.

"May I bring my lady's breakfast?" Emmy asked. "And after, a fitting?"

Alex hurried over to the couch. "I'm hungry!" he announced.

Kiera flashed him a grin. "Um, breakfast is fine, but what fitting, and for whom?"

Emmy still hadn't looked up, but the face that showed looked confused. "I mean who is going to be fitted? Me?"

Emmy nodded her head.

"For what?"

"A dress for court," Emmy answered.

Ah. "Is there something for my son to wear?"

"I will have something sent," Emmy replied. "If you need me, my lady, pull the gold cord behind the door." She curtsied and skittered out.

Within an hour Kiera and Alex had bathed, eaten, and dressed up in lovely clothing, Kiera in yellow and gray silk, and Alex in a gray, rather medieval-looking outfit. A trio of servants—slaves, she assumed—had come to silently fix Kiera's hair and makeup. Now she sat on the couch carefully, not wanting to wrinkle the dress.

Perching on the edge of the cushion quickly lost its charm, so Kiera got up and made her way to a spot on the floor where she could stare at her reflection in the full-length mirror mounted to the wall next to the smallest dresser. She looked like someone out of a Victorian photo. The dress trapped her upper torso inside a nearly too-tight bodice. Strategically placed contraptions inside it mashed her breasts together, creating cleavage nearly up to her chin, but the neckline left her bare almost to her nipples. Below her chest the smooth gray fabric clung like fingers to her waist. Three rows of silver ruffles wound round each other as they circled her middle, then flowed down the center of her billowing skirt to flare a foot above the hemline.

The bare skin on her chest drew her eyes back, and Kiera had to fight to keep her hands from covering it. She slipped on her one protection, a pale yellow, lacy shawl, and let out her breath.

As if cued, the door opened, Kiera turned, and Emmy ducked in. She left it open, though, and Kiera peered over to see why.

A man in red livery stood outside.

"Hello," she called, and took a step forward. "Are we supposed to go with you?"

The man looked at her dress before meeting her eyes. With a quirk to his mouth, he nodded once.

Kiera sighed. "Alex!" He came running, and she took both his hand and another breath, trying to loosen the knot in her chest.

Once outside the apartment the man offered his arm. She pulled her shawl more snugly across her shoulders before laying her free hand atop it.

He led them down the hall and the same stairs they had ascended last night. They exited through a vaulted doorway into a remarkable room, and Kiera paused to take it in. They stood at the threshold of a concave-ceilinged triple-story hall that stretched at least three hundred feet deep. A delicate-looking rug done in middle-hue blues clutched the floor. Elegant eight-foot arches decorated either side, each marked with statues of winged people. Above the arches a second story wrapped around both sides of the room, with blackened double doors set every ten feet. Large round lamps jutted from irregular spots on the walls. The most impressive feature, however, and the one that drew the eye, was the enormous rose window that left over half the wall opposite the entry open to the sun.

An ornate ten-foot high platform rose below the window. Two chairs graced the podium—or rather one backless stool had been positioned next to what appeared to be an elaborately worked throne. Lady Vayu, now in a stunning blue gown, perched on the stool and stared down at her hands.

The man standing on her right must be Lord Vayu. He looked both tall and august with his ramrod back and shoulder-length white hair, but she couldn't make out his face from this far. His clothes, however, she could see—a long, kingly black jacket slashed in half by a shimmering gold belt and quartered by the blood red sash that flowed over his shoulder.

Kiera let her gaze drop to the floor. A yellow runner bisected the room, and perhaps a hundred people milled between the stage and the door, most standing in groups on either side. All seemed to be quiet, slightly tense, as if waiting. She wondered if they waited for her.

She nodded, and the man at Kiera's arm led her in, past the waiting people, down the aisle and up to the front of the stage. Alex still clung to her hand. The man bowed deeply to Vayu before he retreated.

Kiera stood up straight. Swallowed. Lord Vayu strode to the edge of the platform. She could see him now, and how much Marco favored him. *The idiot boy,* she thought. *As if no one would see it.* But there were differences. Where Marco was boyish and thin, Vayu looked hard and athletic, and wore fifty well. Marco had light blond hair, but the utter lack of color in Vayu's startled the eye. Marco's eyes warmed her heart, while Vayu's left her chilled.

A second ticked by, then another. Kiera curtsied, a little unevenly. When she rose she whispered to Alex to bow, and he did.

"We greet you," boomed Lord Vayu, and both she and Alex jumped. The room's designer had apparently engineered the acoustics to amplify volume. It worked.

"Greetings, Lord Vayu," she answered. "My name is Kiera, and this is my son, Alex. I am, uh, I mean, we are pleased to know you."

Vayu lifted a hand. "No, no. The pleasure is Ours." Vayu wiped that hand with the other, then pulled them behind him. "Kiera, we understand that We owe you our thanks for the life of Our son, and for intervening on behalf of Our army."

"You are welcome, Lord Vayu," she answered. Her hand was sweating, and Alex tried to pull away. She squeezed to tell him to hold on.

"You called fire."

It seemed to be a question. "Yes, Lord Vayu."

His leaned forward. "So you are a mage."

Kiera looked up at him. She paused to let out her breath. "I don't know if it's fair to call me a mage, Lord Vayu."

"Pray tell Us why not."

The sun shifted, and variegated light washed across the stage to spill on the floor.

Kiera opened her mouth. Shut it. She couldn't think of a suitable lie. Should she lie anyway? What would it gain her? "I, uh—uh, well, Lord Vayu, calling fire is something new."

His brows arched. "New?"

She looked up at the window. "The first time was less than a week ago."

Vayu nodded. He walked back to his chair and put one hand on the arm. "Who is your master, Kiera?"

Kiera shook her head a little. "I have no master, Lord Vayu."

Vayu turned and looked at his wife. She glanced up at him and nodded, once.

Kiera went cold. *Jesus Christ. Can she tell if I lie?*

"From where do you hail?"

Kiera weighed several possible answers before finally deciding on, "I am not from this area, Lord Vayu. We traveled a great distance before coming to Fairbanks." Well, that was certainly the truth.

A smirk skittered across his face as he straightened. "And where were you going?"

Did he just say "were"?

Kiera pulled her hand free of Alex's and clasped both together in front of her. "We plan to continue to travel, Lord Vayu."

Vayu walked back across the stage and stared down at her, eyes cold. "And where is your husband, Kiera?"

Kiera lifted her chin. "I have no husband, Lord Vayu."

"So it is just you and the boy?"

"Yes."

Vayu tapped his lips with a finger, as if considering her words. "We owe you recompense, Kiera, and in this deconn We are generous to Our allies. In light of your feats, and your status, We offer you a name and a house, and a place at Our table."

Kiera swallowed. "I am sorry, Lord Vayu, but I don't understand."

Vayu leaned forward, his face very serious. "Kiera, in recompense, We offer to ennoble you, and your son, to mark you a member of this deconn, and to permit you to live here, in this house," he spread his arms, "under Our governance. Do you have a response?"

Kiera pulled in a breath. "Lord Vayu, I am honored and humbled by your offer. I thank you for it. As I mentioned, though, I am a traveler, and hope to eventually find my way back home."

The silence thundered.

"You reject Our offer?" He sounded outraged.

Kiera was liking this less and less. "Lord Vayu, I would be pleased and honored to accept a place, uh, at your table, and lodging for my son and me for the time we are here, and perhaps the use of a magic teacher, if that is permitted. I will of course submit to your rules while I remain in this house." She took a breath. "Is that acceptable?"

"You do not wish to be ennobled?" he demanded.

A brisk sigh escaped before she could catch it. "I am not prepared to respond to that question, Lord Vayu. May I defer my answer?"

Anger flashed across Vayu's face. "We will permit you to consider Our offer and will return to this matter at next court-turn." He stalked back to his chair.

Kiera curtsied again, and Alex bowed a moment behind her. She led Alex to the now left edge of the hall, and started winding her way to the door.

"Bring in the boy!" Vayu bellowed, and Kiera's feet froze. She yanked Alex into an empty alcove and turned to face the stage. God! She had almost forgotten Marco.

From a doorway on her left two men carried in what must have been her friend, bundled in blankets on a stretcher. A white cloth wound around the top of his head and covered one eye. The men laid him on the floor directly in front of the stage, then stepped back and bowed at the waist.

Lord Vayu strode to the edge of the podium. Lips pursed, arms crossed, he peered down at Marco for a handful of seconds. While he deliberated, Lady Vayu arose and stood behind him, then slid her hand over his arm.

Vayu let his arms drop as he straightened, dislodging Leith's hand, and glowered at the men behind Marco. "He is injured how badly?"

One of them, the oldest, wearing a blue frocked coat, stepped forward and bowed again. "His leg, my lord, both arms, his shoulder, his wrist and eight fingers are broken. His tripes and inside his head are injured. Claws tore his face, arms, back, belly, chest, and both legs. He has infections in his arm, hand and leg. He is bruised extensively."

Vayu barked out a laugh. "Perhaps it would take less time to describe what parts of him are not injured." He leaned to stare down at Marco again. "Will he live?"

Kiera's jaw clenched. A hand touched her arm, and she turned to find Laszlo shadowed in the alcove behind her. He was dressed in finery, all blues and black leather. His eyes flickered to the stage and back, and he shook his head, a tiny motion. She glared and shook off his hand.

She turned back around, Alex's hand clasped in her own.

"I believe that he will, Lord Vayu."

Vayu nodded. "Well, that is a shame."

Kiera's jaw dropped. Lady Vayu seemed to have gone pale.

"Marco, can you hear me?" Vayu bellowed, startling a flinch from half the audience.

If he answered, it was too softly for Kiera to hear.

"Marco," Vayu called, looking down into Marco's face, "You betrayed me, you whoreson. You took my mistress and fled the deconn without my consent." He paused to draw a breath, then spat, "I judge you a fool. A fool and a traitor."

A murmur went through the crowd, and Kiera's gasp got lost in the noise.

"In my deconn, a traitor's sentence is slavery or death. Since you are in no condition to work a plow, it will be death."

Kiera flushed cold, then hot with anger. She turned to Alex and whispered, "Stay here. Do not move from this spot. Do not go with anyone. Do you hear me?"

Eyes huge, Alex nodded.

Laszlo reached a hand out to grab her, to stop her, but she ducked out of his reach.

She ran down the side of the hall to the stage, then across the open floor to Marco.

Breathless, she stood panting for a moment, one hand on her thigh.

Vayu straightened and pressed his mouth into a thin line. "Did you wish to address Us, Kiera?"

"Yes, Lord Vayu. I beg an audience."

Whispers erupted from the audience at her back.

He enunciated every word. Slowly. "At this very moment?"

Kiera pushed down her panic and dropped to one knee. She bowed her head and folded her hands. "Yes, Lord Vayu."

When he finally spoke, Vayu's voice was glacial. "This is not the wild nadeconn, Kiera, where women run as they please."

He paused to exhale. "No. In this deconn women do not dishonor their masters by interrupting them; however, We excuse you this once for your ignorance. You may speak."

Kiera remained kneeling but raised her eyes. "I would claim my recompense."

Vayu stiffened and narrowed his eyes.

"I ask that you spare this boy's life."

She struggled to hide her surprise when he laughed. "You would trade the favor We offer you for the life of this traitor-child?"

She held his eyes. "Yes, Lord Vayu."

Kiera watched him pace back to his chair. Lady Vayu still stood at the edge of the stage, staring expressionlessly at Kiera.

The room was silent. A trickle of sweat dribbled down Kiera's back.

Vayu turned and stalked back. "You spend your coin cheaply, Kiera." He stopped and shook his head, as if trying to understand. "However, since it is your coin to spend, you may do so as you wish."

His face grew grim. "Our favor, however, for saving Our gods-damned army and my traitorous son is not so great that it covers the cost of his life, so We counter your offer." He paused again, and peered over so that she could see his face clearly. "In exchange for his life, you will accept ennobling and a place in Our house."

He clasped his hands behind his back. He lifted his eyes to stare out at the audience. Spoke to them. "We took a grave loss when Aliyah was taken, Lady Kiera." He shook his head mournfully, then turned to look at her and held up a hand, as if to ward off her words, should she have any. "We admit that she was yet unproven."

Vayu must have read the confusion on her face. "She had not yet birthed a son," he said, waving such trifles away, "and was therefore of less value than one such as yourself. But as you know the price owed this turn is for far more than replacement of a stolen chit. It is also to spare the life of my treasonous son, and for the sum of those two we find Our favor insufficient."

He paused meaningfully and a stab of fear wound through her.

"Therefore, to recompense Our grievances you will also agree to either permit Us to find a suitable husband for you, or spend you as a war mage. Which We choose will depend on whether appropriate skills emerge during your training, which you will undergo with due diligence."

He paused again and stared at her, eyes hard. "We will not accept less."

Kiera's breath turned to dust. A part of her, locked tight inside, was screaming. She bowed her head and looked at Marco, who stared up at her.

"I agree," she whispered.

Vayu nodded, looking satisfied.

Kiera closed her eyes. She took a breath, then stood. Without looking at Vayu again, she turned and stode out of the hall. She dragged Alex back to their room and barred the door behind them.

CHAPTER 10

WAS SOMEONE PLAYING A DRUM? Kiera opened her eyes to darkness. The banging continued. Ah. The door. She pushed out of bed, head throbbing, and pattered over to open it. She slid back the bar. The knocker pushed open the door and slipped inside, spilling light from the hallway across the carpet.

Laszlo closed the door behind him and barred it.

He turned to her, and stood silent, stiff, not touching her. His face was impossible to read in the inky darkness.

A snake of unease slid through her. What is this? After a handful of seconds of quiet, she crossed her arms under her breasts. She could feel her heart beating. "What do you want?"

He stared at her for a moment, jaw hard, then leaned forward. "Do you know what you have done, Kiera?"

Kiera scooted around him. She pulled up the bar and dropped it to the floor. "Get out," she said, hand on the handle. "Get the hell out."

She put a hand over her eyes to try and ease the throbbing behind them.

Suddenly he was there, wrapping her in his arms, and after a moment's hesitation, she leaned into him. She caught her breath, then pushed back and wiped her face.

"What the hell was I supposed to do, Laszlo?" she demanded, then turned and walked to the window. She pushed open the curtain, splashing pale yellow light into the room. She leaned her hands against the window. The cold pressed into her fingers. "I had to do something. I didn't know what else to do."

She heard him sigh but didn't turn to look at him. Instead she looked at Alex, sleeping peacefully in his bed. One of the spears of the moonlight had painted a stripe across the mound of his feet.

Laszlo sounded as tired as she felt. "He will never let you go."

"Would he have anyway?" she shot back.

He walked to stand behind her and put a hand on her shoulder. "Not willingly," he admitted.

"Why did you give him back?" Kiera whispered to the window.

He sighed. Reached around her and wiped some of the ice from the glass. "Kiera, I did not believe that he would put his own son to death."

"Would you have let him go if you had known?"

He lifted his hand from the window, then reached across her chest and pulled her back into him. Nestled her head under his chin. "Yes."

Kiera closed her eyes. "Laszlo, he said he was going to marry me off or make me a war mage."

His voice was hard. "Neither will happen, *a'kala*. Nothing you do not want will happen."

"You can't promise me that," Kiera whispered. "What are you going to do? Spirit me away? You can't do that, and I can't abandon Marco." She sighed. "Laszlo, I don't want to talk about this anymore."

Laszlo tensed, then relaxed. "It will not happen," he said again. Before she could argue, he lifted her chin and covered her mouth with his.

THE NEXT MORNING Kiera woke to Emmy scurrying around the room, lighting lamps. She pushed out of bed and slipped her feet into her boots.

Emmy rushed over. "Here, my lady," she said. She laid some blue slippers on the floor, then stepped back.

They were beautifully wrought, and a rich shade, but had been fashioned out of some animal's fur. Kiera cocked an eyebrow. She reached down, picked one up with two fingers and held it up to her face. Was that bear? Wincing, she dropped it.

"Sorry, Emmy. I don't want these. You can take them back to wherever you got them."

Emmy's huge eyes met Kiera's. Kiera plucked one shoe, then the other, from the floor and padded over to Emmy. She held them out at arm's length. "Sorry, Emmy. I just can't wear these."

Taking the shoes, Emmy curtsied. "Yes, my lady."

"Okay, Emmy," Kiera said as she collapsed in a chair, "that's another thing. Please, please, stop with the curtseying, or ducking down, or whatever you call it here. And I'm not your lady. I'm just Kiera," she pointed behind her, "this is just Alex, and while I do appreciate your help, you do not need to bow and scrape."

The whites showed all around Emmy's eyes.

"Could we have something to eat?" Kiera asked with a sigh.

SOMEONE KNOCKED at the door a couple hours later. When Kiera opened it a young man in blue livery stood outside. From somewhere behind him, Emmy rushed up and pushed past.

Kiera's eyes flicked to Emmy, who stood just inside the door.

"Greetings, uh, sir. Am I to go with you?"

He nodded, bowed and held out his arm. Kiera turned to Emmy. "And you are staying here with Alex, I presume?"

Emmy started to curtsey. Stopped. "Yes, Lady Kiera."

Alex streaked to her and wrapped his hands around her leg. "Don't go, Keer!" he wailed.

Kiera unhooked his hands, then squatted down and hugged him. "I have to go, sweetheart. I'll be back as soon as I can."

"No!" he whimpered, "no, no!"

Emmy took one hand and pried him away.

"I promise I'll be back as soon as I can. Play with Emmy, okay?"

Alex pulled free of Emmy, grabbed Kiera's skirt with one hand and clung to her leg. Again disentangling his hands, Kiera knelt before him and pulled him into her arms. She held him close until he calmed down. "Alex, I can't get us home until I learn how to do it," she whispered into his hair. "That's where I'm going. Please try to understand."

He sniffled, and hugged her tight. After a time he nodded, and let Kiera pull free.

Kiera closed the door and took the man's arm. He led her down the stairs and into the main hall where Vayu had held court. Empty now, the open space under the cavernous ceiling made her feel small. Sharp light from the rose window pierced the room, but the air tasted chilly. The young man— he wasn't eighteen—led her out one of the left doors and into a hardwood-floored hallway. Their footsteps seemed loud after the carpet of the hall.

The back of the russet dress she wore today dragged behind her. She had noted this morning, and to her delight, that her dressers and closet were stuffed with clothes, and that all looked like they would fit. To her chagrin, most all were dresses.

At the end of the hall the man opened the door, then bowed her inside. Kiera entered and he shut the door behind her.

She turned and stared. The hundred-foot room was laid out like a church, benches and all, stark white walls embellished in a way she could only call rococo. A center hallway led down to an altar and the lectern behind it.

A woman, perhaps five feet tall, stood in front of the altar. A mass of curly red hair flamed above her head. Her grass-green gown looked luxurious, but she needed a comb.

Kiera stepped slowly down the aisle and stopped a few paces before the altar. "Greetings, ma'am. I am Kiera."

A surprising lot of wrinkles lined the woman's face. Green eyes set amongst them assessed, then narrowed. "I am pleased to know you, Lady Kiera. I am Lady Agni. I will be instructing you in magic."

"I am pleased to know you as well, Lady Agni."

Lady Agni nodded, then motioned to a bench in the front. Kiera sat. Lady Agni turned and lifted a book from the altar.

"Do you come from a deconn?"

"No, Lady Agni."

"What element do you claim?"

"I apparently have some power with fire."

Unsurprised, Agni nodded. "You have called it since what age?"

Kiera smiled. "Since a few days, turns, ago."

"Let us find where we must begin." Agni folded her hands. "Do you know the two laws?"

"No, Lady Agni. I am afraid I don't know anything about magic."

Lady Agni lifted her head. "We start from the beginning, then."

She walked over and handed Kiera the book. "You will read this by nex-turn. Thisturn I will explain the basics and then we will assess your strength."

Agni clasped her hands together. "In magic, there are two laws. One. All is power." She looked down at Kiera. "What is the first law?"

Kiera hid a smile. "'All is power'?"

"Correct. All is power. Power is everything. Power infuses all things that you see, and all that you do not. It is never still, but is ever moving, flowing, and twining. It cannot be stilled. Power is made up of four elements, and this you should know. Fire, air, water and earth. These are the foundations of all things."

Kiera cocked a brow. "Where does power come from?"

"It comes from the goddess, child." Agni looked over Kiera's head. "In the beginning, She-Who-is-Fire created air, then water, then earth. She fused them together, in her, creating all things, both real and in potentia, and the world was born. She uses them still to keep the world in motion. I see your next question on your face: What causes the motion? And that answer to that is the stars.

"The stars, the Earth, the sun and moon, push and pull on the forces. This motion alters the essences and the flows of the elements, creating life, and substance, and change, and taking all away.

"The forces are like waves in the sea, or wind in the sky. They are flowing from every direction at every minute. Think of the sun shining on the snow. Light flashes everywhere. A drift here sends a glimmer to the right, while the stone over there traps rays in its lee. Do you understand?"

Kiera looked downward, then nodded. Shrugged.

"The second law is this: Vessels of glass. What is the first law?"

"Uh, 'all is power.'"

"Correct. What is the second law?"

"'Vessels of glass.'"

"Lady Kiera, our bodies are fragile things. Power is strong. Pull it into you," Agni fisted her hand, "and it will crush you. The lesson of the second law is to never make that mistake. Make this mistake once with a strong calling and you will die."

Kiera flushed.

Agni sat down next to Kiera. "You have learned this lesson already."

"Yes, Lady Agni."

"Tell me."

"I made lightning fall and when I was finished I didn't know what to do with the rest of the power. It nearly crushed me."

"You are not dead."

"I sent what was left into a mountain."

Agni nodded her head. "Good. Remember: Power is strong but your body is weak. The magic inside you calls to the power, but your wish should not be to pull its strands into you, but to change their flow. To do so, you must become as smooth as glass."

Kiera leaned back and stared at the ceiling. She hadn't noticed before the dozens of flying people—angels?—painted inside the blues. She traced them with her eyes as her mind raced, trying to fit this new information, to force it past her disbelief. She had seen it. She knew something made all this work.

Agni patted her hand. "To call lightning names you a sunwyr child, but an untrained mage is a threat to all." Agni shook her head. "Do you know the ranks?"

"Not really," Kiera said, turning to face Agni on the bench.

"Skani born without the ability to call energy, or who sense it weakly and may sometimes move it, are called nuwyr. If their element is manifest, most can change its flow. Of course, even the strongest can only do so during one of their six marks each turn."

Kiera pursed her lips. "By 'manifest' you mean present, right? Physically present? Like a burning candle? Emmy, the woman who comes to my room, can send the flame from a candle to the fireplace."

Agni nodded. "Yes. If the element is already present in the physical world, and if she is a fire nuwyr, then yes, she can change its flow. But understand that you will not be able to do much more inside the manse. The stones that form the manse are cast with gold so that only the smallest of magics can be done inside, which is why we meet here."

"Okay. Gold inhibits the flow of magic, which the manse contains, and I can understand why. I think. But a nuwyr, and any mage, can call the magic that remains?"

"For a nuwyr, only during one of the six marks each turn."

"So which are which marks, and why only then?" Kiera asked.

"We will begin with fire, your element. The marks in which the energies of fire run strongest are nighttide to one and noontide to one, four to five of both morning and after noontide, and eight to nine of both morning and night.

"Why it is so is the bigger question, of course, and understanding it requires that you understand the first rule, which is what?"

"'All is power.'"

"Yes. And power is always flowing. Remember that the stars, most of all, are pulling on all the elements' strands, bending them, mixing them, exposing pieces otherwise covered." Agni paused. "You cook, yes?"

"Yes."

"You know how to make a bean soup, do you not? You add water and beans and carrots, and a slice of meat, and cook it until it is ready to eat."

Kiera smiled. "I don't do much cooking."

Agni ignored that. "You can create it because you know how to prepare it, what to add in, and how long to boil it over the fire. You can make the same dish again and again because you know these things. In the world everything is moving and changing all the time, but there are only so many strands, and so much heat, and the world moves in cycles, big and small. At nighttide all the ingredients for bean soup are present in your kitchen, and you mix it together and cook it just so, and it's ready to eat for that time. Every night. And then the world moves, and the stars turn, and it's suddenly much harder to make your soup."

Kiera was nodding. "And that's why the sunsigns are important, because the earth, for a moon each year—cycle, I mean—sits in a place where things mix just so."

Agni smiled. "Yes, child."

"So during the times that it's harder to detect fire, those without the ability to call it cannot even feel it."

"Yes, but during fire moons, the entire thirty turns of each, it is much easier."

Kiera nodded again. "Well, then my next question is this: How do I make bean soup when it's a breadmaking hour—ah, mark?"

Agni smiled. "The ingredients for your soup are always there, Lady Kiera, for a mage such as you. They are simply harder to find, and more dear."

"So how then do I find these strands? I have tried and tried, and I cannot make the fire come. It has come when I needed it, but not when I want it to."

"Be thankful, child. Without knowing how to send it back out you would burn to a husk." Agni stood up again and walked back to the altar. "What is the second law?"

"'Vessels of glass.'"

"Yes. And that is what you must learn to become. Now, the second level of mage is called awyr. Most children are nuwyr, but most mages are awyr. These mages—"

"Wait, Lady Agni. I beg your pardon for interrupting, but are shifters mages as well?"

"No, child." Agni shook her head. "To be mage you have to be human."

Kiera's jaw dropped. "What?"

"Shifters are but half-human, child. Like the rest of the beasts of the land and sea, they cannot even sense magic."

"Is that why they're enslaved?" she asked.

Agni pursed her mouth. "Child, can you enslave cattle? Of course not. The goddess put them here to serve, and in their places in the deconn they thrive and are happy. Much happier, and safer, than they would be out in the wild."

"And when they run away?"

Agni grimaced. "Shifters do not run away. The few who have tried were ill, raving sick in their mind, and had to be put down."

Agni stood up, holding the book close to her chest, and walked back to the altar, where she laid it. "I think that spending time with the army has misled you, Lady Kiera. The shifters can talk, but many animals are just as smart as the smartest of them. I know that my dog understands everything I tell him, but I wouldn't think of letting him take a room of his own." She smiled without looking at Kiera. "He would poo all over the floor and starve to death if I did.

"Now, awyrs—"

"I'm sorry again, Lady Agni," Kiera stood and laid a hand on her stomach, "but I'm feeling unwell. May we resume nexturn?"

Agni narrowed her eyes, but nodded. "I'll call for a boy."

LASZLO CAME TO HER ROOM after Alex was asleep. He kissed her, but she smiled and pushed him away, instead leading him to one of the couches.

She laid a tray of bread, cheese and fruit on the table nearest his arm. "Do you want something to eat?"

Smiling warmly, he took the bread from the tray. She brought wine and two glasses and poured for them both. She sat beside him, watching him eat, and found tears stinging her eyes.

He set the bread aside and took her hand. "What is so wrong, *a'kala?*"

She wiped her eyes. "What does *a'kala* mean, Laszlo?"

He looked at her for a long moment. "My lover. My woman."

Her heart thumped in her chest, but she smiled a little sadly.

Laszlo held her eyes and stroked the back of her hand with his thumb. "Why are you crying?"

"I had my first magic lesson today. I learned many things, but the lesson I remember best is that you were right."

He leaned forward and tapped her nose. "That is a lesson you should remember, as it is so often true."

Smiling, though unwilling to be swayed, she captured his fingers and pulled his hand into her lap. "They revile the slaves." She picked up the bread he had set aside and handed it back to his free hand. "Lady Agni, my teacher, told me that shifters can't be mages. That they don't feel the energy." She leaned back, smoothed her dress.

He took a bite. Chewed it. "Yes. They say it's because we are animals." He ate the rest of the bread, then reached for an apple.

Kiera stood up and stalked to the fire. She picked up the poker. Tapped the fireplace. "Laszlo, that's crazy. We're all animals." She shrugged. "All animals or all people. We're just all different species, types, I mean, like fish and birds and cats. Where I come from, most everyone knows that." She turned to face him. "Is it true? Shifters can't sense energy? Be mages?"

Laszlo shrugged. Drank the wine down.

"I'm sorry, Laszlo. I don't speak Laszlo's body language. Is that a 'yes' or a 'no,' or is it an 'I don't know'?"

"I don't have an answer for you, *a'kala*. I have not met all the shifters. It seems to be true in this deconn."

She replaced the poker and turned to plunk down on the couch across from her lover. "Laszlo, why do you leave me every day before morning?" Kiera asked as she pulled her feet up beside her, avoiding his eyes. "Are you trying to protect me, or are you embarrassed of me, or is it something else?"

Laszlo stood abruptly and crossed the space between them. He pulled her to her feet and into a crushing embrace. His voice, when he spoke, rumbled through his chest. "Never say such things, Kiera, even in jest. I leave early, *a'kala*, because I have much to do and because I would spare you the scorn of your peers if I can."

Kiera closed her eyes and wrapped her arms around him. "What if I need you during the day, Laszlo?" she said into his shirt. "How do I find you?"

He led her back to the couch and covered them both with a blanket. "Send for me. Anyone can tell you where I am."

They sat watching the fire lick the wood on the grate. "So tell me what you did today, Thisturn," Kiera asked.

He leaned his head back against the top of the couch and shut his eyes. "We took in another batch of recruits, so we're back in training. I put them to staffs and swords all morning. After noontide we did field work on horseback. The new batch of boys need to train, but the veterans need their time, too." He grunted and slid further back.

"Soldier work."

He smiled grimly. "Solider work."

"Are you tired? Can I get you more wine?"

"No more wine. I would like to hear what your teacher told you, if you are willing to share it with me." Without opening his eyes he lifted his arm in invitation, and she slid in and laid her head on his chest. He locked his arms around her and squeezed her closer.

"Why? Won't it bore you?"

"Slaves are not schooled in magic, and I would like to hear it."

Kiera nestled in, then told him all her teacher had said.

When she was finished, he sat up and stretched. "You shouldn't have left, Kiera. It doesn't matter."

"Laszlo, I can't just sit there and listen to that!"

Laszlo grunted and leaned back again. *"A'kala,* you will hear worse." He sounded resigned, and it hurt her heart. "If you will take my advice, you will keep your thoughts close." A moment passed, and he laughed, then sat up and rubbed his face. "I am more tired than I realized. Asking you to hold your thoughts is like asking the snow not to fall."

She gasped and shoved him, and he laughed again. She stood, then reached out a hand to him. "Let's go to bed."

THE NEXT MORNING a man in livery came to take Alex to school. Alex cried and clung to her, so Kiera, after permitting herself one melodramatic sigh, decided to go with them. They walked through the great hall but exited through a door on the right this time, and into the building on that side. It opened into a large room as lovely as the great hall, all lacquered wood and marble. An indigo runner bisected the room. They walked through the hall and the man opened the doors on the far side. He left them there, at the edge of another room. Another palatial room.

The entryway in which they stood opened into an airy and slightly convex sitting area. The ceiling peaked abruptly above the pale yellow walls and led the eye toward the dozen windows that pocked the east wall and into the morning sunlight spilling across the room. Two sections of carved wood benches filled each half of the front half of the schoolroom, all facing a large, presidential desk placed at the room's apex.

At least fifty elementary school-aged children, most fair-haired, inhabited sections of the benches. Each had what looked like a notepad in their hands. Some scribbled fiercely on paper while others looked bored. All were quiet. Perhaps twenty other children sat empty handed on the floor behind the benches.

A man and a woman stood in front of the desk, writing on separate ends of a piece of paper laid on top of it. Kiera took Alex's hand and marched them down the aisle between rows of benches. She stopped when they reached the desk and waited for them to finish.

The two, both in their 30s, she guessed, were almost ethereally beautiful, and Kiera couldn't help but stare. Even in profile the woman was stunning. Her tousled strawberry blonde hair draped seductively over her shoulders. When she heard Kiera's steps she lifted her head, revealing startling blue eyes.

The man straightened to study Kiera with icy blue eyes and the merest hint of a sneer on his aristocratic face. Kiera didn't take it personally; he looked like he wore that look a lot. He stood a full foot taller than the woman, well over six feet, and had a strong, lithe body. His platinum hair, his most beautiful feature, fell like water past his shoulders.

He was Marco—Marco in twenty years, but with paler hair and colder eyes.

The man continued to study her, taking in her hair, her face, her gown, and apparently found her wanting. He held her eyes long enough for a small smirk to slide across his face, then went back to work.

And Kiera hated him.

The woman, watching Kiera, stepped away from the desk to take both of Kiera's hands in her own. "Welcome, Lady Kiera," she said earnestly. "I sent a boy for your son, but I am so pleased that you joined him."

Kiera smiled back. "Thank you, Lady—"

The woman laughed. The sound tinkled like wind chimes. "Oh, forgive my manners. I am Lady Naga, the children's instructor, and this is Lord Valen, my paramour."

Lord Valen bowed his head and kept it lowered humbly for a long second. Kiera wanted to roll her eyes.

Lady Naga kept one of Kiera's hands and led her behind the desk. Kiera watched Valen hand Alex a flat wood panel and some other supplies. He knelt down in front of Alex for a moment, spoke to him, then led him to one of the benches. Alex sat, then smiled up at Valen. Kiera relaxed.

"I had hoped to meet you at brooding—" Naga seemed oblivious to the fact that Kiera's attention remained on Alex—"but I am so pleased to know you even sooner. Lady Kiera, forgive me for being forward, but I have to tell you how much I admired your courage at court. My goodness." Kiera felt her brows raise as Naga put a hand to her heart. "Everyone is saying how brave you are."

Kiera hid a smile. "Um, well, thank you, Lady Naga."

"And is it true that you are a sunwyr of fire? You know, true fire magicians are so rare!"

"Uh, yes, Lady Naga, I am." Kiera let the smile rise. "And now I must get back. I have my own lessons to attend."

"Oh, of course, of course. I'm just so glad to finally know you."

"And I am happy to meet you, too, Lady Naga."

Kiera made her way to Alex, then squatted down in front of him. She explained that he was here for school, and after only a single long look, he agreed to stay.

Kiera nodded to Lady Naga and turned to go, but Lord Valen held up a hand. She stopped to wait as he glided up.

When he offered his arm, she shook her head. "Lord Valen, I thank you, but I am not returning to my room."

"I would be honored to escort you to Lady Agni. It is time for me to return to her lessons as well."

Instead of sighing, Kiera laid a hand on his arm. "Then I thank you, Lord Valen."

After they exited the room, Valen stopped her. She lifted her gaze to his, curious, and he smiled at her. "Lady Kiera, I owe you a debt of thanks for the life of Marco. My brother. Twice, if I understand."

Eyes narrowed, Kiera stared at him for a heartbeat. "No thanks are necessary, Lord Valen, and, forgive me, but please don't tell me you owe me recompense or a debt of honor or anything else. I did it because he's my friend."

Valen laughed. "Oh, you really are every bit as spirited as Marco tells.

What a charming girl you are, Lady Kiera." He patted her hand and resumed their walk.

"Are you a mage, a sunwyr?" Kiera asked, trying to be polite.

"Oh yes, Lady Kiera, I am. I was fortunate that my gift came early, in childhood. I have been training in magic for twenty-eight cycles." He smiled down at her.

Kiera wanted to slap the smug look from his face, but forced herself to concentrate on the tap-tap of their footsteps on the wood of the hallway floor.

When they entered the church Lady Agni was speaking with another woman in front of the altar, but she looked up when they came in. She smiled fondly at Lord Valen, picked up a book from the altar and came forward to take Valen's hand. He pulled her hand up and kissed it.

"Welcome, both of you. Lord Valen, the ring room is readied for you thisturn. Luck, my boy." Agni turned to Kiera. "You left the book, Lady Kiera, and so for some time thisturn I want you to read it. We will discuss what you have read in a mark."

Kiera nodded, taking the book, and found a seat on a bench. She sat sideways and laid the book down beside her. The ornate letters used for the title made it impossible to read, but she found she could read the handwritten words splashed across the pages, though not well.

Within an hour Lady Agni came to sit beside her. Kiera lifted her eyes from the page, leaned back and yawned.

"Oh, surely it is not so bad," Agni chided.

"No, Lady Agni. I'm sorry."

"Have you questions about what you have read?"

"Not so far. It mostly says the same things you told me yesterday, uh, yesturn. I would like to know about the other levels of mages, though."

"Very well." Lady Agni sat back and laid her hands on her thighs. "Yesturn we discussed nuwyr. There are three higher levels of mage. Awyr is the next level. He is a mage who can sense an element, and sometimes two, and can call one of them, though he can handle only a little energy at one time. Which element, of course, depends on his sun- and moonsign. Awyr are not powerful in their own right, but are plentiful, thank the gods. Their magic, while not strong, is very useful.

"A skilled nuwyr can manipulate his element during his sun mark. An awyr can do the same, but at any time. They can also call their element, though most readily during their sun mark. They support a sunwyr's spells, and provide ballast and fuel to all big workings. This deconn alone employs well over a hundred. They help regulate the weather and water spells, and oversee the farming slaves."

"Pardon me, Lady Agni, but what do you mean by 'call'?"

"To call one's element is to locate its strand outside its manifestation and divert it."

Kiera frowned. "So I called fire when I made walls of flames? Because there was no fire around and already burning for me to borrow from, so to speak? And when I sent lightning?"

"Yes, child." She nodded. "Be patient. I will next explain what sunwyrs can do." Agni paused, looking thoughtful. "Sunwyrs are third level mages. They are rare, perhaps one in five thousand, and fewer than half survive their first calling." She rolled back her head and looked into Kiera's eyes. "Tell me why."

Kiera smiled. "Because they don't know not to pull the energy into themselves without it having a way out."

Agni nodded. "Crudely put, but correct. Remember: 'vessels of glass.' Now, sunwyrs are naturally strong mages, but extensive training is required before these mages can learn to create intricate workings. Yes, they can call lightning, or tidal waves, or make earthquakes or tornadoes—brute force workings—but spells that last in time or that are more complicated require a blending of elements and a finessing touch that only training and practice can endow.

"As you have discovered, sunwyrs can sense and call their own element, not just in strands, but can also tap the lakes and streams that the stars leave puddled, such as what is in storms and other bodies. What you may not realize is that almost all sunwyrs can also learn to sense and even call at least one other element as well, usually the complimentary, so air, in your case.

"Further, it is not unusual for a well-trained sunwyr to manufacture a spell that uses three elements, Kiera. A few very powerful sunwyrs use all four. In fact, the spell that keeps most of the frigid air off of this city is an exceedingly well-designed, fifty-cycle-old sunwyr spell that incorporates all four elements to varying degrees. The awyrs continue to fuel and regulate it and to this turn it shows no signs of weakening."

Kiera's heart thudded. "What other spells might a sunwyr do?"

"The possibilities are only limited by the mage's training and talent, my dear."

Kiera's lips felt frozen. "Travel between—long distances?"

"Oh most certainly, although that would be a very difficult undertaking. I know of only one who is reputed to have created such a spell."

"Who?" Kiera whispered.

"Lord Asana."

Asana? Kiera tried to moisten her mouth with her tongue. That name could not be a coincidence. Could it? "How can I meet him? Will you introduce me to him?"

Lady Agni laughed. "Oh no, my dear. He is the governor of Bethel." She looked down her nose at Kiera. "We do not fraternize with that barbarian or his dogs."

Asana. Asana and dogs. Shunakah? Governor Asana and the Shunakah. Kiera rocked back, but then nodded her head to cover it. Swallowed. She filed these tidbits away for later. For the day she would go to Bethel. Of course it was Bethel. "Lady Agni, you said there were four levels of mages."

Lady Agni cocked a brow at Kiera. "You are most impatient. Yes, Lady Kiera, there are four levels. Above sunwyrs are the helfarch. Technically, I suppose the helfarch are not more than an elite branch of the sunwyr. They have no abilities a sunwyr does not possess, but they have learned to blend the elements in such a way that they can create." She paused, and Kiera leaned forward, anxious to hear what she meant.

"You eyes ask what do they create? And I can only give you examples of the few things I know. They are very few, my dear, very, very few. They do very great magics, and they are reputed to be able to make living mass out of energy. One helfarch is believed to have created the shifters, though the truth of that is not known." Agni sat back and patted Kiera's hand. "And now I want to gauge your ability to sense and to call. Are you ready?"

Kiera blinked. "All right."

Agni stood and motioned for Kiera, who stood and followed Agni through the hall and into a back, stone-walled room. Four white sconces, one at each corner, provided the sole decorations in what was little more than a glorified cell.

Agni walked to the center of the floor. She turned and faced Kiera, then closed her eyes, bowed her head and clasped her hands as if in prayer. After a moment she loosened one and traced a triangle in the air, which she slashed with a finger. The air suddenly hummed with power, sending ripples down Kiera's back. She shuddered and rubbed her arms.

Agni smiled. "Very good. You sense air energy, child." She made a small waving motion with her right hand and the buzzing stopped. Agni bowed her head again, then lifted it, eyes again closed, and raised fisted hands above her shoulders. Her left hand dropped, then her right, and with both fists she waved circles, or maybe squares, Kiera couldn't tell which, at thigh-height.

Kiera suddenly felt heavy. Her thoughts became surreal. She lifted a hand and looked at it. It seemed to undulate. She blinked her eyes and her mind was suddenly clear. Dizziness washed though her and she staggered back.

Agni looked triumphant. "Earth magic. You sense that as well."

"Lady Agni, that magic made me feel the same way that calling my fire did the first, uh, one or two times. Did I call earth magic as well?"

Agni frowned and stared over Kiera's shoulder. Kiera turned to see what Agni was looking at and found Valen staring at her through the open door. *Didn't we close that?* she thought, annoyed.

Valen smiled and bowed slightly. "I beg your forgiveness, Lady Agni. I did not mean to interrupt, but I admit to being curious about our newest mage. If it will not distract you, please continue."

Kiera shot him a glare, which he ignored, then turned back to Agni, who looked a question at her. Kiera shrugged. What could she say? Agni held her eyes for a moment, then nodded at Valen. He came in and shut the door behind him.

"Lady Kiera, please tell me your question again."

Kiera tried to ignore Valen. "Just Kiera, please. When you sent out that earth magic, it felt the same way that I felt the first couple of times I called fire. Does that mean that I called earth, too?"

Lady Agni looked surprised. "Are you certain, Kiera? The very same way?"

"I'm positive."

Lady Agni looked thoughtful. "Yes," she finally said, "it is possible. But you stopped feeling it when?"

"When I called lightning. The last time I did not feel that feeling at all."

Agni nodded. "That is not surprising. It is unlikely that you would pull that fire from a pool—a storm, I think you said—and yet catch up other strands in it." She nodded again.

"Think of it like this, child. When a child learns to grasp, his fingers are weak and his motor skills poor. He reaches for a stone, which like a strand is small, but his fingers clasp dirt, too, which he did not intend. Compare: If the same child reaches a hand into his feeding bowl, which is like a pool of energy, his hand comes out covered with the carrots that his mother filled it with. His hand is not soiled with fish because the bowl has nothing but carrots in it.

"With time and practice, my child, you will be able to pluck the finest threads without pulling others in as well. Now, let us try water. Do not fret if you do not feel it. It is fire's counter and it is very uncommon for a mage, even a sunwyr, to sense his sign's opposite."

Kiera nodded, then let out a breath.

Lady Agni closed her eyes and bowed her head. She fisted her right hand

and placed it over her heart. With her left, she drew a sideways crescent moon in front of her chest.

Kiera blinked. The air had turned sparkly, like it was snowing inside, but with tiny, tiny flakes. They blew as if in a storm, swirling around her. She pushed an arm into the stream. She felt nothing when they landed on her. Instead they seemed to spark out and disappear when they touched her skin. She stepped into the swirl and turned her face into the flow. At first she felt nothing, but then it felt soft, like a sweet breeze. In moments it seemed heavier somehow, and then it was hard to pull a breath. She stepped out of the flow, coughing, and cleared her throat a few times.

She looked up and into Lady Agni's astonished face. She coughed again.

"Well done, Lady Kiera," Agni nodded, and Kiera smiled and ducked her head. She glanced over at Valen. He was leaning against the doorway, one foot up. He stared back through slotted eyes.

"I have one more test, and then I will send you back to your apartments with homework. Are you ready?"

Kiera nodded, then stood straight.

"I want you to call fire. Make it manifest. To do so, first choose where you want it to go. How about the middle of the floor?" Kiera nodded. "Then close your eyes and search for a strand. Just find a small one, child." She smiled. "No need to try and burn down the house. Pull the strand into you and send it out to where you want it to go. After it appears, I want you to stop pulling, but first tell me the two laws."

"'All is power.' 'Vessels of glass.'"

"Good. You have shown that you can find fire. What you need practice doing is spinning, reflecting, sending the flow where you want it. Now are you ready?"

Kiera grimaced, then nodded.

"Begin."

Kiera closed her eyes. She wasn't sure how to search, so she let her thoughts go, just a little. She remembered how touching the fire had felt, like electricity, but smoother.

Nothing.

Minutes passed.

In the silence, she heard Valen shifting.

She opened her eyes. Agni watched her curiously.

"I'm sorry, Lady Agni, but I'm not sure exactly how to sense it. Would you give me a hint?"

Agni smiled encouragingly and then nodded. She took a step away from the wall, bowed her head, and opened her hands in what looked like supplication. With the first finger of her right hand, she drew a point-up triangle.

Electricity buzzed across her arms, up her neck. Instead of unsettling her, it felt comforting, like an old blanket, and she shivered as a wave of pleasure slid down her back. She closed her eyes and drew it in like a breath, letting it fill a hollow spot that opened up inside her, in the middle of her chest, where it seemed to fit. When she thought she had enough, she forced it into a cyclone flow, then sent it out and to the middle of the floor. A fire appeared, smallish, and burned.

Kiera gasped and the flow of power inward stopped. She pushed the last of the energy into the fire and watched it flicker out a moment later.

"Okay," Kiera said, breathing out. "Now let me try." She looked at Agni. "What did you do with your hands again?"

"Lady Kiera, I used sigils, which are shortcuts to summoning. I do not want you to call elements that way yet. Seek and call what you want using only your own magic. You must first learn to master elements before calling them without the means to control them. When you have mastered calling, I will begin to teach you the sigils."

Kiera nodded and closed her eyes.

She slowed her breathing. Tried to feel it.

Nothing. Impatience sparked, but she let it drift away.

She took a deep breath. Quieted her thoughts. She remembered the flow, the feeling.

She reached out with her mind, lifted a hand, and felt—something.

No. That was air. They feel so similar in some ways, she thought, then pushed that away. She reached out again. And could, well, see. After a fashion.

She shifted her mind up.

She found the air flow again, but pushed past it.

A knot of green earth wound across her feet, hugging the ground. Using only her—what would she call it? Her mind? Her magic?—she picked it up, held it, wondered briefly why it was the only flow that had color, but let it flow away from her without pulling any in.

There! A large flow, wrist-sized, flowing quickly northward just below the ceiling. She reached up and into it and plucked out a small thread, pulled it into her. Inside her chest it wound circles before she sent it spinning to the floor. The flame whuffed out just as she opened her eyes.

She bounced on the balls of her feet, clapped once, and grinned at Agni.

"Very good, Lady Kiera." Agni said. Her face looked a little pale.

Kiera turned to gauge Valen's face, but he had gone.

Agni gave Kiera some homework to do, and Kiera turned to leave, but turned back. "Lady Agni, I have a question I hope you can answer."

"You may ask."

"How can someone defeat my fire? No, wait. That's not the right question. How can someone get inside my fire but remain unburned?"

Agni drew her brows together. "Well, an air mage might push through a flamewall. A water mage might try to douse the flames. A fire mage would not be burned, so he could push through it, were the flow weak enough."

"No. Not a mage. Someone without magic."

Agni looked at Kiera for a long, puzzled moment. "Anyone with less magic than a sunwyr could not withstand a sunwyr spell, Kiera. Not in any way that I can imagine. Perhaps it just appeared to be so?"

Kiera grimaced. "I think I'm not saying this right. Every time I call fire there have been people, children, who were touched by it but not harmed by it at all. And every time I call it it has healed me, I think, at least a little. Oh and once Alex, too. Why? Why to both, I guess."

Agni paused, considering. At last she said, "I do not care to admit that I do not know for certain the answers to those questions, but that is the truth. I can only speculate, Kiera. Do you wish to know my thoughts?"

Kiera nodded. "I think your guesses are the best ones I'll get."

"I would guess that you have woven spells." Agni smiled and shook her head. "It is nearly beyond reason to imagine it as truth, but I cannot think of any other explanation." She paused. "That would mean that you wove spells of protection and spells of healing while calling and sending fire, although spinning and holding three spells in one casting is nearly impossible for any mage." She leaned forward and clasped her hands in front of her. "Are you certain, Kiera? Are you certain that the children were not outside the fire's reach, or that you were simply less harmed that you had thought?"

"No. I mean yes. Yes, I am certain."

Agni nodded, pursing her lips.

"Thank you, Lady Agni. I'll see you nexturn."

CHAPTER 11

ALEX WAS ALREADY BACK WHEN KIERA RETURNED to her room. A short school day, for some reason he didn't know. He chattered for a while, described the new friends he'd made, and asked to go outside to play.

What an excellent idea, she thought.

She rang for Emmy, who brought food. To her great surprise Kiera was able to convince Emmy to take lunch with them. While they ate, Alex told Emmy about school and his new friends. Emmy teased him, and Kiera smiled at their banter.

After they'd eaten the last bite, Kiera told Emmy that she wanted to take Alex outside and asked for suggestions. "The other nobles ride horses," Emmy said, and Alex jumped off the couch.

"Please, Keer, please!" he begged.

Emmy put a hand on Alex's shoulder and cast a pleading look at Kiera. "How do we arrange to go riding?" she relented.

"I will go and find out," Emmy told her, and scurried out.

Kiera dressed Alex warmly, then put on her old clothes. Her benefactor, Lord Vayu she assumed, had provided her with many things, but neither pants nor a new, warmer coat were among them. She dug out her old blue coat and put it on, then slid on her boots.

Emmy returned with a young, dark-haired man, who smiled when he met them. He offered his arm and Kiera took it. "I'm Kiera. What's your name?" she asked him as they walked down the hall.

He looked surprised. "Hullis, my lady."

"Hullis, are you taking us to the horses?" Alex asked.

"Yes, young lord," he answered gravely.

Kiera hid a smile.

Once outside they crossed a snowy field north of the manse and headed toward buildings set back a half mile. When they were a hundred yards out

Hullis spoke without turning his head. "Lady, forgive me, but may I ask you a question?"

"My name is Kiera, and of course you may," she answered.

"Did you really use fire to save the army from a brigade of Shunakah?" he asked.

Kiera stopped. "Where did you hear that?"

Shrugging, he stood facing the great mountains behind the gate.

"How many is in a brigade, or is that just a fancy word for 'group'?"

"A thousand."

Was this common knowledge? What were people saying about her? About what happened? "I'll answer you if you answer me one. Fair?"

He shrugged again.

"Hullis, fair is fair."

"Yes, my lady," he answered.

"Yes. It's true. Now tell me why that matters enough to you that you would broach etiquette to ask."

He blushed crimson.

"Hullis," she warned. "Tell me."

He darted a glance at her.

"Hullis."

He ducked his head. "No noble ever saved an army before, is all." His voice fell lower. "I did not believe it and wanted to know."

Unlikely, Kiera thought, feeling a blush creep up her neck, but realized that he probably wouldn't be told very much, and so how would he know what went on outside the city? No television, no radio, no media whatsoever, and she knew how gossip grew the stories it carried. "Oh, I bet lots of things happen that not everyone hears about. And maybe they just don't want to brag, Hullis."

Without further ado he left them at a stable that lay north of the church building. "Have someone send for me when you want to return, my lady," he said with a bow, and walked away.

Men's voices, their laughter, rang out as Kiera took Alex's hand and stepped into the stable. Through a second doorway she found an office, and around a table inside it milled several soldiers, including Mosha.

"Mosha!" Kiera cried, and he turned and stood up. His face broke out in a smile when he saw her, and he walked over and took her hand.

"My lady, ye are looking well," he said.

She pulled him into a hug. "It's so good to see you," she said.

"What can I help ye with?" he asked.

"Alex and I would like to go riding," she said. "Can you help us?"

"For certain, my lady," he told her. "Please have a seat here and I will saddle you two horses."

"Gentle ones, Mosha," she called as he walked off, then turned to thetable. Four men stood by their chairs. They scattered when she walked toward the table.

She stopped and held up her hands. "No, please. Don't let us disturb whatever you were doing."

Not one of them met her eyes, but all slid by her, one by one, to exit through the doorway she partially blocked.

She sighed.

Mosha ambled back in a few minutes later and motioned for her to follow. He led them outside to two shaggy horses. One, a tall and sorrel mare, lifted her head when they walked over, while the other, a smaller gray gelding, eyed them while he lipped the snow on the top of the post to which Mosha had tied him. Mosha helped Alex onto the smaller horse and offered to help Kiera onto the larger.

"I think I'll try to get on myself." Eyes narrowed, she stepped forward to gauge the logistics required to get her behind into that saddle. More important, she thought, would be staying in it; that little leather cup looked pretty slick. Swallowing, she wondered briefly if her pride wouldn't lead her to a very literal fall today.

With a small shake of her head she grabbed the knob atop the saddle and slid one foot into the left stirrup. With a little grunt, she pushed up. The horse took a step back and she balanced a little precariously for a second, but she managed to swing her leg over and sit down. It took more than a moment to find the stirrup on the other side, and half a minute more to get her boot inside it.

Mosha grinned, showing his teeth. "Never sat a horse before, my lady?"

Now how did one hold these reins? "Shut up, Mosha, or I'll climb back down and punch your nose."

He laughed. "But then ye'd have ta climb back up again after."

"You're right, damn you," she said with a smile. "Now tell me where we should go, and what to do if the horse tries to run away."

He grinned. "Stay inside this area—" he pointed to a large clearing behind them. "Do not go out the gate—" he pointed to the northwest, "or ye will get lost, or too far that way—" he pointed east, "or ye'll run inta the river, and the horses might break through the ice if ye take them out on it."

"That sounds grim. And what do I do if they run away?"

He shook his head. "They wilna run 'nless you want 'em to. If they try, just pull their heads down with the reins." He mimed the motion and Kiera nodded her understanding.

"Did you see that, Alex?" she asked.

"Yeah," he answered. "Let's go."

They got the horses turned around and walked them toward the trees. The snow was new here, but not deep, and it popped when the horses' feet broke through. Kiera took a deep breath. The air tasted so clean here. The mountains loomed behind the wall, thrusting their blackened peaks to the sky. A line of fog lay like a fuzzy stole just below the summit. Ravens stared down from their perches in the trees, and Kiera wondered why they never seemed cold.

She also wondered if Alex was a mage like her.

"Hey, Alex," she called. "I wanna try something and I need your help. It's like a game. Do you wanna play?"

"Sure," he answered. "What do you want me to do?"

"I'm going to do something, and I want you to tell me if you feel anything, okay?"

His pony tossed its head and he laughed. "Like what? Feel what, Keer?"

"Just tell me if you do, okay? Anything weird."

"O-kay."

Kiera grabbed the—wasn't this called a saddlehorn?—in one hand to keep her balance before closing her eyes. It was easier this time to find strands. She sensed them as soon as she shut out the distractions. Kiera reached out to air, flowing strongly now, several strands, thick and thin, stretching several directions. *What time is it?* she wondered. *Must be an air hour.*

Kiera pinched off a thread and shredded it, doing what she thought Agni had done, and sent it spinning around Alex. Even here she could feel the vibrations, the tingling.

He was busy whistling a Christmas song and didn't pause.

"Do you feel anything, Alex?" she asked.

The song died. "What?'

"Never mind."

Kiera reached out again, this time searching for fire. She found it, thin strands weaving through air, some smaller ones pulsing awkwardly. She squeezed off a piece from a crooked thread, pinched it into droplets, then flung them to Alex.

Nothing. He was talking to the horse.

She found water, but felt reluctant to touch it. She skittered around it, looking for earth, but couldn't find any. She kept her eyes closed and parsed through the threads until she caught a smidge of green flowing just below her. She reached in, peeling the air from around it, and broke off a piece. It felt heavy and swollen, and she worked harder to shred it before sending pieces to Alex.

The horse nickered and shook its head—Kiera felt her brows raise—but Alex didn't seem to notice at all.

I need to ask Agni how old kids are when their magic comes, she thought. *And how to tell what they're going to become.*

Oh yeah, she remembered, faintly embarrassed. *His birthday is June 15. A Gemini. Air. And sheesh! I have no idea what time he was born.*

They had reached the treeline. They turned the horses and headed east, toward the river. She was sure it would be beautiful; maybe they could build a snowman along the bank.

She looked over in time to see Alex bump his horse's sides with his heels. It started to trot.

"Alex," she called. "Don't. Slow down. That's the river up there, remember?"

He acted like he didn't hear her, and he was getting farther away. "Alex!" she shouted, but he kept going. "Alex, you need to stop! Right now!"

His laughter drifted back on the wind.

Damn him! He hadn't acted up the whole time they'd been here. He would have to pick today when they went out on these damned horses.

"Alex! Stop!" She knew he could hear her. She could hear the occasional bellow from the stables, and it was three-quarters of a mile behind them.

A trickle of something cold slid down her back as she realized he was headed toward the river. Thinking of television shows she'd seen, she kicked the horse's sides with her heels. Startled, the horse jumped sideways. Kiera nudged her again, this time more gently. It seemed to work; she started to trot, but then broke into a frightening gallop. Kiera grabbed the horn with both hands and gritted her teeth.

The world bobbed up and down, but Alex had apparently kicked his horse, too, because she wasn't gaining any ground on them. She dug her boots into her horse's sides and the mare leapt ahead into what must be a run.

She opened her mouth to yell again but forced her jaws closed before any sound could erupt. She knew it wouldn't do any good at all.

Another horse shot across her path, a white horse, barely missing her mare's head, and Kiera flinched back and dropped the reins. Time seemed to slow. She felt her horse leap sideways, trying to avoid the collision. She tried to find the saddlehorn, anything, with her hands, but the horse was stumbling, and she missed. The horse slid, tried to catch herself, and started to fall. Kiera's balance was off, and she couldn't find it.

With a *whuff* they crashed down together into the snow. The mare landed on her left leg and her hips with bone-jarring force, and Kiera heard herself scream as her head hit the ground. The horse squirmed, and Kiera pushed at its back with both hands and tried to pull her leg out from under it. She had to stop Alex, had to find Alex, but she couldn't get her damned leg out.

Her horse shifted and pulled herself abruptly to her feet, then shook her head and whinnied. She lifted a leg, then put it back down.

Kiera tried to sit up, but agony seared her left leg. After a quick breath she clenched her jaw and pushed herself onto on her right side so she could see. She had to find Alex. Some distant part of her noted that she was breathing too quickly, so she tried to slow it. Ignoring the shaking in the arm she leaned on, she arched up and tried to look toward the river, but a drift blocked her view.

"Goddamnit!" she screamed, then screeched again and pounded the snow twice with her fist. She turned over as slowly as she dared and maneuvered until her left leg rested on her right. She hooked a hand in the snow above her hair and slid herself toward the dune.

Kiera didn't hear the other horse until it was almost on her. She tried to jump back, thinking the white horse had returned, but this one, a black one, stopped far enough away she needn't have bothered. Big feet hit the ground, a hand grabbed her shoulder and Laszlo's face was suddenly in view.

He was white with rage.

Eyes wide, she flinched back from the hand he held out.

"*A'kala,*" he growled, breathing hard, then softened his voice. "Are you hurt?"

"Alex," she tried to say, but it mostly came out as a hiss.

He stood, face stony, and mounted his horse. Kiera lay back in the snow and watched him turn the horse toward the river and kick it into a run.

The horse's hooves kicked snow into her mouth.

Kiera tried to lift her arm to wipe her face, but it shook and refused to leave the soft ground. It was as if all her strength had flowed away. She shifted, then heard herself gasping too quickly as pain seared through her, throbbing in time with her heart. She struggled to turn back over but—couldn't. She focused on her breathing, trying to slow it, willing the pain to lessen.

The sun seemed to dim and a feeling of stillness spilled over her. As she relaxed the pain faded, and she realized that the snow next to her face wasn't really white. It was more variegated, peppered with shades of something darker than white. Did smoke do that? Maybe because they burned so much wood?

Even polluted, still the snow sparkled. Fragile crystals crowned a layer of crushed pack, and the spots that weren't smashed by Laszlo's feet still held snowflakes, some with fuzzy arms, some with spikes, and all with symmetrical patterns. Hadn't she read someplace that all snowflakes had six arms?

She heard voices, then someone's hands took her shoulders and lifted. Her head fell to one side. She tried to lift it but it stuck stubbornly to her shoulder. Fuzzy faces loomed above her. Someone else grabbed hold of her legs, shooting spears of agony into her hips, and she screamed and kicked out, knocking the hands loose.

The hands laid her back in the snow.

Something black crowded her view of the ground. As it dropped in the snow it mushed the crystals, and she wanted to tell them to take it away, but she was just too tired. Many hands on her this time. They lifted her gently, dragging her legs. They pulled and pushed until she was lying on the black thing.

She wasn't even cold anymore, not really. Someone covered her with a blanket. Her eyes felt heavy, so she closed them.

KIERA WOKE in her room. She tried to sit up, but a hand dropped on her chest. Someone else's.

She pushed it away, sat up, and found herself staring into the face of a strange, fiftyish man who happened to be sitting on the foot of her bed.

"Where is Alex?" she demanded. Her words felt rough against her sore throat.

The man smiled kindly. "He is fine, Lady Kiera. Just fine."

Another hand found her shoulder. Squeezed. She looked up and into Laszlo's face. Relief washed through her. He sat down on the edge of the bed near her waist and took her into his arms. She rested her head against his chest and let out her breath.

"Thank the gods that Lord Valen happened to be out riding, Lady Kiera," the man said, and Kiera felt Laszlo tense. "He got Alex's runaway horse stopped just short of the river." He leaned forward and patted her hand. "It is such a tragedy that your own horse fell."

Kiera leaned back. Laszlo kept his arms around her. "I'm sorry. Who are you?" she asked.

He bowed his head. "I am Lord Saman, your healer."

Kiera nodded in return. "Well I thank you, Lord Saman. How badly was I hurt?"

Saman smiled broadly, evidently pleased that she had asked. "A small bone in your left leg was thoroughly broken. You also cracked the large bone in the same leg. Oh, and you were in a progressed state of shock when the men brought you in."

Laszlo's arms tightened, and she let him pull her back to him, but she rested her head on the edge of his shoulder so that she could still see Saman. "How long until I can walk again?"

"Oh, you should be up and running," he grinned, inviting her to share in his corny humor, "within ten turns, I should say."

Ten days to heal? Her eyes opened wide. "How long was I out?"

Saman flicked puzzled eyes to Laszlo.

"She wishes to know for how long she lay unconscious," Laszlo translated.

Saman nodded at Laszlo and smiled, chagrined, at Kiera. "For an extended time, my dear. You came to me during fifth air yesturn and it's now third earth."

Kiera looked at Laszlo, too tired to do the math.

"More than half a turn," he told her. "You fell a mark before sunset and it is now the morning of the following turn."

Kiera turned an astonished face to Saman. "And no cast? No other treatment? You're one hell of a healer, Lord Saman!"

He dropped his eyes and actually blushed. "I thank you, Lady Kiera."

"No, Lord Saman. I thank you."

He smiled again. "And now I will leave you to your rest," he said, getting up. "Rest, Lady Kiera. Do not put any weight on that leg during the next two or three turns. After that time, you may walk with aid providing it does not pain you too badly. You will know when you are able to walk without it. I have left you something to lessen the pain," he indicated a small packet lying atop a table. "Send for me if you need anything else."

"I will," Kiera said. "And again, I thank you."

After Saman left, Laszlo tried to lay her back down, but Kiera balked, pushing his hands away. "Where is Alex?" she asked.

"He is at school," Laszlo answered.

"When he gets back, I am going to beat seven kinds of hell out of him," she said, pushing herself back against the headboard for support.

Laszlo raised his eyebrows.

"His damned horse did not run away. He disobeyed me, then ignored me over and over when I told him to stop."

A soothing voice. "I know."

"What?"

"Mosha."

"He saw it all, didn't he?"

"Yes."

She pulled in a ragged breath. "And Valen tried to kill me, didn't he?"

He clenched his jaw. "I—yes."

Saying it out loud, hearing it confirmed, felt like a fist to the gut. "How did you know to come?"

"Mosha."

"He sent for you?"

"Yes."

Kiera stared at her hands. "Laszlo, I do think he would have killed me if you hadn't come. And it's not like Vayu would believe me over his own son if I told him. That son of a bitch."

He leaned closer, put both arms around her shoulders and pressed her against his enormous chest. "I know."

"Would he have let Alex get hurt?" she asked with her face in his shirt.

"I don't know, Kiera. I saw him grab the reins of Alex's horse, but then he saw me."

They sat there, quietly, for a few minutes.

"That son of a bitch is jealous of me," Kiera finally said.

He pushed her back so that he could look at her face. "Tell me."

She told him all that had happened in her magic lessons, and what she had tried to do out on the horses.

He stared at the headboard, face hard. When Kiera reached up a hand and cupped his cheek, he looked down at her expressionlessly.

"Laszlo, I know that you're really pissed off, but please don't do anything to him. Promise me you will let me take care of this. I am all right, and I don't want you to get hurt."

He jerked his face out of her hand. She reached up and gently turned his face back to hers. "I am not saying that I think he could kick your ass, nor in any way am I trying to insult your masculinity. We both know how that match would come out. I am saying that I am very sure the penalties for your beating seven kinds of hell out of him would be very severe, and I prefer you in my bed rather than rotting in jail, or the dungeon, or dead."

She laid her head on his chest and listened to his heart beating. "Laszlo."

"Kiera, I cannot."

She made a sound of protest, and he wrapped his arms around her. "Shhhh. I will promise not to do anything now. We will talk about this more later, when you have healed."

She shrugged, remembering his face when he had found her. Although it was less than she hoped, it was in truth more than she had expected.

Laszlo laid her back on the bed, pulled the covers up around her, and then lay down beside her on his side, facing her, one hand under his head.

Kiera turned on her right side, snaked one arm around his neck and pulled his face close. She nipped his lips, then kissed him.

He grunted and kissed her back hard. He reached beneath the covers and found the peak of her breast. She leaned into his hand as he tugged and kneaded, moaning softly into his mouth.

"Shall I bar the door?" he whispered huskily, kissing her jaw.

"What?"

Chills skittered across her back when he laughed against her throat. "Beautiful *a'kala,* Alex will be home soon, and your maid will be back before that."

"Damn it," she swore, and he laughed again, dark and sexy.

God, she loved that laugh. She sighed heavily and scooted back a little.

He brushed a lock of hair from her face. "Tell me more about what Agni told you," he said.

"Do you really think I'm beautiful?" she asked.

He leaned in and kissed her hair, apparently undaunted by her non sequitur. "Yes. You are the most beautiful woman I have ever seen." Laszlo kissed her still-open mouth, just a soft pressing of lips against lips.

"Thank you," she whispered.

He released her, stood up and walked to a table. The mixture he made from Saman's packet smelled foul. "Drink this, then tell me about your magic lesson with Lady Agni," he said, his back to her.

EMMY BROUGHT a chattering Alex back a half hour later. She shut the door and helped him out of his coat. Kiera waited until Alex looked over and saw that she was awake.

His words died in mid-sentence.

Kiera pulled back the blankets, holding his eyes. "Emmy, Laszlo, please excuse us," Kiera said. "Laszlo, please give Mosha my most heartfelt thanks."

Emmy scurried to the door and let herself out.

Kiera pushed to a sitting position and let her feet slide to rest on the ground. Her left leg began throbbing fiercely. She put her head down, then took a breath and held it, waiting for the worst of the pain to subside.

Laszlo walked toward the fireplace and dropped down onto one of the couches, his back to her.

"Laszlo, will you please give Alex and me a minute?"

"No," Laszlo answered, voice bland.

Alex looked back and forth between them, eyes wide. He hadn't moved from his spot just inside the door.

Kiera fumed at both males, but decided not to pursue the less urgent argument with Laszlo. Instead, she turned back to the wayward child.

"Alex come over here," Kiera commanded. "And sit in that chair."

Alex came, dragging his feet. Looking sullen, he plopped into the chair.

"Alex, you disobeyed me yesterday. Not once, not even twice, but many times. Your misbehavior put both of us in danger."

Alex sat for a moment. He looked angry, so Kiera stayed silent while he digested what she'd said. Suddenly he looked up at her. "Is it my fault you got hurt?" he asked quietly.

"No, it's not," she reassured him. "But it made accidents like that more likely. I know it's hard to understand when I tell you not to do something that you really want to do, Alex. And I know you sometimes still feel mad about—well, about things. But you have to understand that when I tell you not to do something, I am trying to make sure you stay safe." She paused. "And so you're grounded for two weeks."

He jumped up. "No, Keer. Please. Please! I'm really sorry!"

"I am glad to hear that you're sorry," Kiera said. She pulled her legs back into bed and laid back. She felt incredibly tired. "I think two weeks is just enough time to make sure the lesson sticks."

"Keer!" Alex whined.

"Two weeks, Alex," she said. "Now go fetch someone to find Emmy. You need something to eat."

"Keer," Alex said, "if I tell you I felt funny when we played that game, can it be one week?"

Kiera shot up, wrenching her leg, and she fell forward, gasping with pain. Suddenly Laszlo was there, his hands on her head and back, easing her down on the bed. She breathed raggedly through her mouth and tried not to curl up because she knew it would hurt like hell.

Laszlo brought her a cup and helped her take a drink. It was that bitter mix from Saman's powder, and she choked, trying to keep it down. She closed her eyes, focused on breathing, just in and out.

When her ache had eased a little, she turned her head and looked at Alex. "Are you okay, Keer?" he asked, face pale.

"I'm fine, Alex. Honest." She sounded a little breathy, so she focused on evening her tone. "I just hurt my leg some."

He nodded uncertainly.

"Tell me what you meant when you said you 'felt funny,' Alex." Kiera said.

Someone knocked on the door, and Kiera sighed heavily.

Laszlo opened it, then stood aside. Lord Valen strolled in, with Lady Naga in tow. Naga turned and closed the door behind them, then turned back and smiled sweetly at Kiera.

"Lady Kiera, my Lord Valen told me about your accident. I thank the gods that you are all right," she said, then came forward and stood behind Alex's chair. Alex looked up at her and smiled hesitantly, and she bestowed him a benevolent look.

Ignoring her, Kiera's glance slid to Laszlo, who had gone completely still. Only his mouth betrayed that he felt any emotion. It was one flat line.

Oh, shit. Well, the best defense was a good offense, and it might keep Laszlo from killing him.

"So, Valen, did you come to gloat?"

Valen moved forward. He stopped behind Naga and dropped one hand on her shoulder. She reached up and laid her hand atop his.

"My lady Kiera," Valen said, voice even, "I would never stoop to laughing at a girl who cannot sit a horse. No. I came to offer my condolences. And I expected to receive your gratitude for saving your delinquent boy from the river."

Perhaps he didn't know the word, but the tone was clear, and Alex blushed crimson. Kiera stopped just short of rolling her eyes at the arrogant bastard. Ignoring his volley, she needled, "Never put anything off until the last minute, eh, Valen? If the competition looks like it might turn out to be a little too stiff somewhere down the road, don't bother waiting to see. Better to get rid of it now and make sure that time never comes."

Valen raised perfect brows. "Lady Kiera, if you are suggesting that I in any fashion contributed to your accident yesturn, I fear that you overrate both of our abilities. I have no control over animals, or weather, or footing, or—" he paused for emphasis, "the lack of riders' judgment or competence, and I am afraid taking some harm from a fall such as yours is to be expected."

"Get out," Kiera said through her teeth. "Get out of here, Valen, and stay the hell away from me. We both know what happened yesterday, and I am not going to play these stupid games with you."

Perhaps feigning bewilderment, Valen shook his head, dismissing her, then turned and looked at Laszlo. "And Captain. What are you doing here, I wonder."

"Playing maid," Naga giggled. She walked over to Laszlo and looked up into his face.

A muscle in Laszlo's face ticked, then stilled. "Leave," he commanded, staring over her head at Valen.

Valen's features twisted with contempt. "Do not speak to me, slave."

Laszlo flashed and was suddenly in front of Valen. Without taking a breath, Laszlo leaned in to Valen until their faces were almost touching. Valen was taller by an inch, but Laszlo was twice as broad and outweighed him by eighty pounds. To Valen's credit, he did not flinch. "I have told you once to leave." His voice sounded glacial, frightening. "I will not ask again."

One heartbeat. Two. Valen went pale with rage. He turned suddenly, threw open the door—it banged on the wall—and stalked out. Naga followed him, looking back once over her shoulder at Laszlo. He closed the door behind them, then barred it.

Tension still thickened the air. Kiera peeled back the covers and started to bring her legs down. She needed something to drink.

"No," Laszlo said, walking over. She stopped and shot him a look. He ignored her, instead lifting her legs, helping her back under the covers and tucking her in. "Kiera, you must rest."

"Laszlo, are you going to get into trouble?"

He pulled the top blanket up higher.

"Laszlo."

"What did you want?"

"Something to drink."

He nodded, then brought her a cup of cold water. "Alex," he said, "go fetch Emmy." He helped Kiera sit up and drink, then sat the cup on the table beside her bed. He paced back and stood behind the chair. "I have to get back," he told her. "I will send Mosha if you want him."

"Are you avoiding my question, or just me?" Kiera asked.

He looked at her then, and amusement touched just the corners of his mouth. "Neither, a'kala. I have left my duties for a full turn and must return to them. I will come back tonight."

She nodded, and yawned. Thank God the medicine was finally starting to work. "Well, Valen and I are officially enemies now," she told him, a trifle unhappily.

Laszlo pulled on his coat. "He was already your enemy."

"Yeah." She looked up at him. "Will he get you in trouble?"

His voice was calm. "Do not waste your worry. All will be well."

"Why are you being so enigmatic?" she asked, more than a little annoyed.

"I do not believe he will wish to draw attention to this," he said with the ghost of a smile. "Better?"

She smiled. "I'm sorry, Laszlo, but it annoys the hell out of me when you try to protect me."

He came over and kissed her forehead. "I know," he whispered. A laugh escaped her.

The door popped open and Emmy bustled in, carrying a tray of something. She had loaded Alex with bottles of wine. Laszlo helped Kiera sit up, propped some pillows behind her, then kissed her mouth. "I must go. Eat, rest. I will see you tonight."

CHAPTER 12

O N THE NINTH MORNING AFTER HER "ACCIDENT," Kiera woke when Emmy came bustling in with breakfast.

"Oh, my lady!" she exclaimed as she set the tray on the table. "There will be a tournament thisturn." She smiled brightly, then made her way over to the windows to pull back the curtains. Overbright sun-spears shot through the room, forcing Kiera's eyes to narrow. "We should go. All of us. It will do you such good to get out, and young Alex as well."

Alex woke, yawning, and got up to use the toilet. He flashed Emmy a grin, which she returned with a sweet smile.

Little monster has her wrapped around his finger, she noted drily. "As you know, Emmy, except for school, Alex is restricted to this room for five more turns." Kiera answered, pushing back the covers.

"Oh, my lady," Emmy pleaded, wringing her hands. "Will you relent just for thisturn? You could tack another turn on to the end!"

Kiera grinned when Alex's groan echoed from the bathroom. "So what is a 'tournament'?" Kiera asked as she got out of bed, gingerly shifting weight to her left leg. It felt nearly healed this morning.

Emmy set three plates out and starting dishing their portions onto them. "It is a whole bunch of fighting. Man to man and shifter to shifter to start. At the end of the turn the two best ones, a man and a shifter, meet."

Alex came out of the bathroom and Kiera went in. When she was finished, Kiera made her way to the couches, snagging her plate on the way. She pointed to the fire with her right hand, and it roared to life.

"My lady!" Emmy gasped, and Kiera grinned.

"Sorry. I was showing off. I've watched you do that so many times and I've always been jealous. I have had nothing better to do for the last week than lie in bed and search out strands. Strands and strands and strands."

"But you dint use the candle!" Emmy exclaimed.

"I don't need a candle. What do you think all those magic lessons are for?" Kiera grinned again, then bit into her bread. "I can show you, if you want. It takes someone to explain it, well, explain and demonstrate it. Or at least it did for me."

"Oh no, my lady, I could not," Emmy said, shaking her head. "That training is for mages."

"Don't be ridiculous, Emmy," Kiera snapped. Emmy flinched and looked down, and Kiera felt ashamed. "I'm sorry, Emmy. I didn't mean it. I have a nasty temper sometimes, but please don't take it personally. I am just sick and tired of the entire slave-nobility mindset. It is such stupid bullshit." She stood, limped over to the table and put some more bread and cheese on her plate.

"Are there no nobles, then, back home?"

The walking didn't tire her as much as it had the past week. Kiera tottered back and perched on the edge of one of the couches, close to the fire. "Nope. The people I come from escaped all that. They built ships and crossed a great ocean to get away from them. When the nobles followed them over, they rebelled. They drove the nobles out, then established a government and laws that said that no one could ever be noble again, or rule them that way. For more than two hundred cycles we have elected our leaders, Emmy. We vote, and the person who garners the most votes wins." Well, that was a gross oversimplification, and glossed over some pretty nasty details, but the point was a good one, she thought.

Emmy's eyes were wide. "Do you have slaves, then?" she asked.

"No. I should be honest, though. We did in the beginning."

The serving spoon lay forgotten on the table. "What happened?"

"It's a long story. The short version is that a little over a century ago we had a civil war. One half of our country fought to free the slaves and the other half fought to keep them. Needless to say, the side that fought to free them eventually won. We made new laws after that that no one could ever be enslaved again, not for any reason."

Emmy stood up, took Alex's and her plate and walked to the table. "How many died?" Emmy asked softly.

"What?"

"How many people died during your war?"

Kiera looked over at Emmy, who was busy cleaning the table. "I don't know for sure." Emmy looked up and Kiera smiled lopsidedly. "I'm not an historian and it's been a long time since I was in school. Far too many, I'm sure. I'm not one who revels in war, but I think that was one that had to be fought. Those soldiers fought and gave their lives for a very noble purpose."

Emmy left the table and began picking up Alex's dirty clothes, which he had left on the floor the previous night. "What happens when men do bad things, then?" she asked.

"I wish you'd let Alex do that. I have told him," Kiera glared at Alex, who looked abashed, "that it's his responsibility to clean up after himself."

"Aw, I don't mind, my lady."

Kiera leveled another look at Alex and he got up to help. "To answer your question, we built jails and prisons to house our criminals, the people who break our laws."

"The evil men are not beaten? Beaten as punishment, I mean."

"No, Emmy. We do not hurt each other. Well, mostly." She threw up her hands. "We're not supposed to."

"Oh, my lady," Emmy said, shaking her head. "I cannot imagine why you would leave there to come here."

"I didn't mean to," Kiera sighed though her nose. "I still don't know how it happened or how to get home." Her leg started to cramp, so she stood and stretched. "Yet, anyway. There has to be a way, and I will eventually find it." She walked over and opened the closet, searching for something to wear. "One thing I will miss when I go is the magic. We don't have any there, or at least any I know of." She turned back to Emmy. "Now, what should I wear to a tournament?"

Alex whooped and Emmy covered her ears, grinning.

THE FOURTH HOUR OF AIR, sometime after 2 P.M., a young man rapped on the door and offered to escort them to the tournament.

Kiera felt proud of herself. She had been reading her books, and during her downtime she had gotten really good at telling when the hours changed. Fire to earth, earth to air, air to water, then back to fire. The strands changed at each hour, and the dominant sign became, well, dominant. She wondered how it would differ when the stars changed as the earth made its course into the next sunsign.

Their young escort, Dondun, led Kiera, Emmy and Alex to a coliseum behind the school. Perhaps a hundred feet high and three hundred across, it was cast with tan stone, all fitted together in a symmetrical pattern. The structure reminded Kiera of the famous one the Romans had made, but there were subtle differences from what she remembered the pantheon to be. This building was oblong, like a football stadium. Arrow-shaped doorways led inside, bas-relief carved into the spaces above them. When they passed through the doors Kiera noted with a grimace that the carvings all contained scenes featuring winged persons fighting overlarge animals.

Dondun escorted them in and up a flight of stairs, which they ascended until they reached a landing. He led them across it, through an archway and to the edge of the arena. From here Kiera could see out into the field. They climbed a second flight, and then another, and from this floor Kiera could see that nearly the entire inside of the coliseum contained seats. The field lay at the lowest floor. The second, the one with the landing, contained benches for open seating. On the third floor, and the fourth and the fifth, sections had been cordoned off into large, stone-walled rooms with windows cut low and facing the field below. Each room had real chairs and couches, and braziers that steamed in the cold. Above the fifth floor rose a final level of more benches. Flat stone lined the top, unfinished level.

The coliseum already held three-quarters of its capacity. Perhaps five thousand sat in groups or alone in the benches along the second floor. Another two thousand milled in over half of the little stone rooms.

Dondun led them to an unoccupied room on the fourth floor. A brazier nestled close to the wall, and Emmy and Alex made their way over and huddled together on the couch in front of it. Kiera remained standing, willing the ache the long walk incited to ease in her leg. She limped to the front of their room and stared out at the field below.

Where would the fighters stage? The field contained only bare ground, so the fighters must have to wait underneath the coliseum for their turn. The ground floor was for fighting and waiting, then.

She turned and took a seat on the couch next to Emmy. Her stomach felt uneasy, though she didn't know why. Alex babbled happily, asking Emmy about past tournaments, and Emmy, in turn, regaled him with stories of uncanny bravery and skill. Kiera tried to remember to smile at all the right spots.

It was cold. She scooted as close to the brazier as she dared and let her thoughts wander.

Emmy abruptly stopped talking. She stood up and curtseyed, then stayed standing, head down. Kiera turned her head to see what had happened.

Lady Naga and Lord Valen stood just inside the entry to their room, apparently awaiting her acknowledgement. A laugh bubbled up and out before she could stop herself. She stood up and opened her mouth to tell them to get out when Leith, Lady Vayu, emerged from behind Lord Valen. She nodded her head to Kiera.

Kiera blew out a breath, but nodded in return.

Valen wore his standard haughty look, but Naga smiled sweetly.

"Welcome, Lady Leith," Kiera managed through gritted teeth. "How may I help you?" She ignored the others. Nothing in this world could make her pretend to like Valen.

"I have wanted to know you better, Lady Kiera," Leith told her, though her tone was as disdainful as her son's expression. "We would join you."

She saw Emmy stiffen out of the corner of her eye, but had no polite solution to end this uneasiness. Leith was her benefactor and, until she and Alex had found a way home—or she became desperate enough to break her oath—she had better play nice.

So instead of rolling her eyes Kiera ground out, "I welcome you, Lady Leith. Please come in."

Leith inclined her head, then led the way inside. She found a seat close to Alex on one of the couches, taking the spot that Emmy had just vacated. Valen sat in a chair on the other side of the brazier and Naga stood beside him. Kiera's choices were to sit next to Leith or Valen.

She remained standing.

"Lady Leith, how is Marco?" Kiera asked, rubbing her hands together.

Leith eyed Kiera's coat a tad disdainfully. "Lord Marco is recovering."

Kiera pushed her hands into her pockets and smiled. "I'm glad. May I visit him?"

Leith shook her head. "His healers have forbidden visitors until he is better improved."

"Oh. Well, please give him my best wishes."

Other people filtered into the stands. Some came to rooms, but most filled the open seats. Within thirty minutes there had to be nearly ten thousand people seated in the coliseum. She wondered what percentage of the city they reflected, and if any of the attendants were slaves. If they were permitted to come. She shivered in her inadequate coat.

Suddenly a horn sounded. Everyone stood, and Kiera walked over to the edge of the box. Alex rose and stood beside her. Naga claimed her other side.

A large, shaggy horse pranced out on the field, topped by a man in blue livery. The man led his horse through a series of figure-8s and other graceful moves, blowing his horn off and on in the skeleton of a song as he rode. He stopped in midfield and bowed low from his saddle. The crowd roared. He turned to the other side of the field, Kiera's side, and repeated the bow. The roar from this half nearly deafened her.

He waited until the crowd had quieted, then stood in the stirrups. His horse, apparently taking a cue, began circling slowly. The man began to chant. The sound of his voice carried, rather unnaturally, Kiera thought. She closed her eyes and focused on the man, doing what one of her books called "opening her sight," and noted that he was pulling strands of air into him and then sending them out in broad waves that spilled over the crowd. She opened her eyes and, somewhat to her surprise, he looked normal again, just a man on a horse.

Kiera could feel the level of excitement increasing, and she wondered if people were just anxious for the games to begin or if there was a magic being worked that helped make them so. She closed her eyes again, but saw nothing untoward. Not that she'd know what to look for, she supposed.

The man turned toward her, and when he faced them his chant washed over their group like water from a hose, then abruptly cut off.

The man continued to turn, apparently planning to make yet another circuit, and Kiera decided to try an experiment. She closed her eyes and pulled up several strands of air, then held them. When the furthest edge of the rider's magic began to again fall upon the section of audience she stood in, she spun the air inside her and sent it out into a narrow wall that shielded the front of her body. She had to work to keep the sides tight to avoid covering anyone else, but it seemed to hold.

She opened her eyes as the horseman's voice fell. The sound drew closer, she heard it coming, but when it would have washed over her it broke into warbles, at least until it passed her, and she flinched hard and lost the air when it suddenly blared again.

"Very good," Valen whispered from behind her. She spun around to find him standing too closely. He smiled politely, belying the contempt in his eyes.

Kiera called herself seven kind of idiot as she turned back. She hadn't really considered that Valen, and every other mage in this coliseum, would be able to watch her working. From here out, she promised herself, she'd be more careful.

But that made her wonder if mages could see magic being worked through buildings, through trees, and across distances. It seemed fair to think that a mage could detect another mage just by noting changes in flows, like disruptions and such. What would that look like, she wondered, and just how far away could they be before you noticed it? Another horn from somewhere below drew her attention back. Kiera leaned forward, trying to see, but the man on the horse had gone.

A thin blond man ran onto the field, wearing nothing but brown pants. From where she sat it was hard to be certain, but it looked like he was barefoot as well. He had a pole arm of some kind. Maybe a spear.

The crowd cheered when he lifted it over his head.

Another man burst onto the field from the opposite direction. He was shorter, sandy haired, and bigger chested. He, too, was shirtless, and bore a huge, misshapen ax.

The crowd roared again as the men began circling each other, each step bringing them closer to each other.

Alex climbed up and sat on the ledge. He grinned up at her, legs dangling over the far side.

Kiera flashed a look at his back before letting her gaze drop back to the field. The axman had caught the spear under his ax blade and was doing his best to pull it out of the spearman's hands. In a deft move the spearman stepped in and swept the axman's feet from under him, and the axman fell. The spearman brought his spear down to pin the axman, but the axman brought his ax up as he rolled out of the way. The ax ripped into the spearman's midsection, and a ruby red flower blossomed on the spearman's belly as he staggered back.

Kiera gasped and gripped the railing.

She heard Valen snort from somewhere behind her.

The cut was apparently less than deadly. The spearman rushed the axman, the two weapons crashed together, axman high and spearman low, but this time the spearman managed to twist the ax up and out, opening the axman's right side. The spearman made a quick swipe with the tip of his spear and slashed into the axman's face. A red line raised on the axman's cheek.

The spearman moved in, using his spear like a staff, and disarmed the axman, though Kiera couldn't see how he did it. The spearman danced back a step, then back in, and swiped crosswise with the spear. Blood sprayed from the axman's neck, drenching the spearman's jaw and chest. The spearman lifted his spear above his head as he leapt back, and the axman fell to his knees.

The crowd went wild. From where she stood, everyone she could see had jumped up. They waved their hands, mouths locked open as they screamed their approval.

As if invoking the sun, the axman lifted a tremulous hand, then fell forward, face down.

The whole spectacle had taken less than five minutes. Kiera turned away, her stomach roiling. She marched back to the couches and fell back into one, not caring if the seams of her dress tore out. She leaned forward, put her elbows on her knees and her head in her hands and then closed her eyes.

Kiera's weight tipped to the left as someone else sat on the couch. It was too heavy to be Alex, so she cracked open her eyes and turned to look. Lady Leith looked back with a spark of what might have been compassion in her eyes. She patted Kiera once, then stood and returned to the wall.

A young man in livery entered their room with a tray of steaming refreshments then, and Kiera almost laughed at the ludicrousness of serving fine drinks to observers while men fought and died below. Another young man followed, bearing a tray laden with a large ceramic pot and a half-dozen small bowls.

Valen approached one of them. He said something Kiera couldn't hear and handed the young man some small metal disks. Coins?

Kiera shook her head. Screw this. As soon as she felt better she was taking Alex home. The men turned to go. *Oh*, she thought, *I'd better ask for an escort now or who knows how long we'll be stuck here.* She stood and walked over, touching one on the arm. He turned to her and bowed slightly. "Did you wish to place a bet as well, my lady?"

Kiera rocked back. "I beg your pardon?"

He smiled at her, a young, brunet man with very nice teeth. She wondered briefly if the governor only allowed young, attractive men to serve as runners, since that was all she had ever seen. "The next match is Hallond the farmer, a shifter, against Eloni, also a shifter, and a church slave. The odds are four to one against Eloni, and the minimum bet is four vayans."

Kiera started to laugh, then slapped her hand over her mouth to cover it. "You bet on these fights?" she said through her hand, then shook her head. "I'm sorry," she said. "I'm sorry. Never mind. Just please send an escort for me, my maid and my son. We wish to return to our rooms as soon as possible."

The boy bowed and retreated.

They were also apparently chosen for their ability not to show shock at crazy women's behavior, she thought, and almost started laughing again.

She returned to the couch and sat down. A horn blew. She stared at the ground, trying to tune out the sounds below. A smiling Naga sat beside her. Kiera wondered if Naga ever got tired of smiling. "What can I do for you, Naga?"

"You have such a kind heart," Naga said, still smiling. "A kind and courageous heart."

Kiera raised a brow.

"It was hard for me to watch in the beginning," Naga confided.

Kiera sighed. This whole "we're so alike" thing just wasn't working. "Naga, again, what can I do for you?"

"Lady Kiera, these slaves choose to fight," Naga said earnestly. "If they win, they can enroll in the army! They are permitted to travel outside the city, and earn glory. They all want to do it, Lady Kiera, and Lord Vayu is most compassionate to give them this chance."

"And if they lose, they die. Talk about a Catch-22. Die here or die later.

Out there."

Naga leaned back and looked puzzled.

Kiera sighed. "Naga, I don't like this and no matter what you say I am not going to stay. In fact, I am going to go back to my room just as soon as an escort gets here."

"Oh, Lady Kiera," Naga chided. "Please stay. We have barely had the chance to know you." Naga smiled and took Kiera's hand. "I just know that we will be friends, given time."

Kiera returned the smile but pulled her hand away. "Naga, the only thing you'll see here if I stay is me being sick. Let's work on being friends another time, okay?"

"All right, Lady Kiera." Naga looked over at Alex, and Kiera followed her gaze. He stood tucked up against Emmy at the corner of the ledge, both of them staring into the ring in apparent fascination. When had he gotten down? "But please let the boy stay. His maid is here with him, and we will make sure he gets back all right when the festivities are over."

Kiera absolutely did not want to leave Alex with Naga, and especially not Valen, but if she was honest she had to admit that neither had posed a threat to him thus far. After all, if Valen had ill intentions toward Alex, he would have let him go into the river that day, and Alex was with Naga every day at school. And Lady Leith was here. Kiera didn't know exactly why, but she trusted her to make sure Alex stayed safe.

Not for the first time, she wondered if they were stuck here. If they were, would leaving Alex here be wrong? This was reality. And was it worse than TV? Besides, Alex would scream like the devil if she tried to pry him away, and Emmy would be deeply disappointed to miss this event.

Kiera looked up at Naga and nodded, once. Naga clapped her hands together and beamed, looking entirely too much like a peppy cheerleader.

"Would you like a glass of mulled wine while you wait, Lady Kiera?" Naga offered, overflowing with goodwill at Kiera's apparent capitulation.

Kiera accepted a steaming mug and walked over to Alex. She told Alex and Emmy that she was feeling unwell and was going to return to her apartments. Emmy looked taken aback, but nodded. Alex, on the other hand, seemed simply thrilled that she was allowing him to stay.

Her escort arrived before she could finish her wine, and she followed him back across the snow. As they passed the school a small movement in the direction of the river caught her eye, and she looked up. Laszlo sat atop his horse, which was pawing the snow, thirty yards away, watching her. Their collective darkness—Laszlo in his long, black uniform coat sitting atop a shaggy black horse—stood beautifully incongruous against the soft white of the snow.

A sharp pang of joy snaked through her. She smiled broadly and lifted a hand, and the white of his smile broke across his face. Seeing him, seeing him smile, was just what she needed.

The young man left her outside her room. She thanked him, then went inside, closed the door behind her and slid the bar down.

Big hands grabbed her, spun her around and pinned her against the wall. She struggled, but before she could scream a hard mouth pressed against hers. She opened her eyes wide—and stared into Laszlo's.

She surrendered with a sigh.

Laszlo licked her lips, nipped her jaw. He lifted her skirt and tried to pull down her underwear. They bunched up around one leg, so he tore them away. He lifted her up, pushed her legs apart and slid inside her. When had he opened his pants? she wondered faintly. He held her there against the wall, pumping fiercely, urgently. He bit her neck and her shoulder, groaning, as the heat built in her. And then it washed over her, suddenly, unexpectedly, and she cried out, arching and thrusting her hips forward, urging him on. *"A'kala,"* he moaned, thrust up hard, and spilled into her.

She fell against him, still suspended, and gasping like she'd just run a race. He let her down gently, smoothed down her skirt, then led her over to the bed. They lay down together. She looked up at him. His face was relaxed, unshuttered. His eyes were clear.

She scooted back so that she could lean on the headboard and stared at him. She realized, with a little wrench of her heart, that she had never seen that look on his face before.

He looked slightly puzzled. "What?" he asked, and smiled.

"You're just very beautiful," she answered.

He laughed and touched her face with his hand. "I have to get back, *a'kala.*" He stood up and leaned down to kiss her. Just a feather-light touch of the lips, but it made her shiver. "Your early return might convince me that you did not enjoy the tournament," he teased as he tied up his pants. "Are you feeling any better now?"

She grimaced. "It was horrible."

"Yes," he agreed. "It is."

SOMETIME DURING THE NIGHT Kiera's eyes opened to the dark. Someone was shaking her. She turned her head. Laszlo was leaning over her. "Are you all right?" he whispered.

She felt muzzy, confused. She took a breath. He smelled musky and sweet. "I think so," she finally answered. "Why?"

"Who is Julia?" he asked instead.

She scooted out from under him and sat up. "What?"

"Shhh. You spoke her name in your sleep."

"You must have misheard me."

Laszlo reached out and took hold of her forearm. He tugged, and she gave, and she ended up lying on her side. He snuggled in behind her, cradling her back to his chest, his knees under hers, and wrapped an arm around her chest.

"You spoke her name many times," he said.

She struggled to pull away. He held her fast.

"You did that on purpose," she accused.

"Yes," he answered unrepentantly. "Who is Julia?"

"Am I not permitted to choose what I want to talk about?"

He snuggled up closer, pressing his hips suggestively into her backside.

"That's cheating," she said.

They lay quietly for a while. Laszlo brushed her hair with his fingers.

"Julia was my sister," she whispered into the darkness.

His fingers kept combing.

"She died."

"Tell me," he whispered. Still combing.

Kiera closed her eyes. Pushed everything away. Focused on his fingers in her hair. "Her husband beat her to death," she said, voice expressionless.

His fingers stopped, then started again.

"He had been beating her for years."

She breathed in. Breathed out. Saw Julia's face in her mind.

"She was very pretty," Kiera said, a smile in her voice. "Long, dark hair. Big brown eyes. Smart." She laughed. "The bitch."

She took another breath. "No. She was so sweet. The kindest heart. She even cried when my mom killed spiders. No one could stay mad at her for anything. But she loved Hunter. He was a boy in her class. I mean, they went to school together. They got married right after high school."

She took a breath. Held it. Let it out.

"The first Christmas after, she showed up at Mom's with a black eye."

She felt tears spilling down her face, but she wasn't really crying. They were just tears.

"She told me that she had fallen off her bike. She said, 'Oh, you know what a klutz I am sometimes.' But she was never a klutz. She was graceful. She loved to dance. She had had lessons. I never saw her fall in her life.

"But I didn't say that. I said, 'yeah.'"

She was silent again for a while.

"It went on for years. Even when Mom died, God, four years ago now, after the funeral we stayed at a hotel. She stayed in my room. She had a big bruise on her neck. We were pretty broken up, and we drank a bottle of wine. I asked her, right out, if Hunter was hurting her.

"I said, 'Julia, you look like Mom used to. You're telling the same lies that she used to tell, the same lies I used to tell when I had marks that showed.' But she denied it. She smiled and she lied. But I knew. She never went out of the house anymore. I knew something was going on. Jesus God, I knew exactly what it was but she wouldn't tell me."

Kiera took a breath, then another, letting her anger carry her. Hoping it would wash away the pain. "On Alex's birthday last June we had a party. At Julia's house. It was lovely. The house was decorated so nice. We had chocolate cake, both of our favorite. Alex got a bicycle and we took him outside to ride it. He got going real fast and fell a couple times, but he was such a good sport.

"Something went wrong. I don't know what it was. But Hunter had gotten mad at Julia. I was in the driveway with Alex, but I heard him shouting. Julia came out the front door.

Kiera closed her eyes. "She was wearing this red dress. She looked so pretty in red." She blew out a breath. She could feel her heart pounding. "Well, Hunter came charging out behind her. He grabbed her arm and she tried to pull away. She was embarrassed. I could tell. He called her a 'bitch.' He said it real loud. Even Alex heard him.

"He hit her in the mouth, Laszlo. He punched her with his fist. It sounded like an ax hitting wood. And she fell. She just fell.

"There was blood on her mouth. Red blood. It just ran down her face and got all over her dress.

"I screamed at him. I screamed and ran over. He was scared of me, that son of a bitch. He knew I would kill him. So you know what? He ran. He fucking ran. I called the police. I don't know if you know what that means, but I called for some people to take him away. They locked him in jail and I took Julia home with me.

"But do you know what? Do you know what she did? The next day she went back!" Kiera rasped, and Laszlo turned her over and pulled her face to his chest. "He beat her to death," she whispered, unable to stop talking now. "He beat her and beat her until she died. I found her, Laszlo. I found her lying on the floor of her house. The decorations were still up. But her face was—it was broken."

Laszlo rocked her, whispering things she couldn't understand. He held her until she stopped crying.

He got up and brought her a towel.

"I'm sorry," she finally said, wiping her face.

"Where is your father?" he asked, confusing her.

"Back home. Far away. Why?"

Laszlo was silent. He finally sighed, then got up and poured a cup of water. He brought it back and sat down on the bed. Offered it to her, but she shook her head.

She pushed a smile up. "Now aren't you sorry you asked?"

His voice was tired. "No, *a'kala*. I am not sorry I asked." He took a drink of water. "It explains a great deal."

"What does that mean?"

He sat the cup on a table.

"Do you want to go back to bed?" Kiera asked.

"Not yet."

"Let's go to the couch then so we don't wake Alex."

They walked to the couch and sat down. Laszlo offered a hand and Kiera scooted over and laid her head on his chest. She waved a hand at the fire and it lit.

Laszlo jumped.

Kiera looked up at him. "I'm getting better. I've been practicing."

He smiled. "You are magnificent."

That startled a laugh out of her. "So how did you end up being such an amazing guy, Laszlo?" she asked. "I mean that. Not to be too crass, but this isn't a terribly great environment for boys to grow up to become great men."

He looked down at her, eyes unreadable, and held her gaze. When he spoke, he surprised her. "Unlike most slaves, *a'kala,* I lived with my mother for twelve cycles." One side of his mouth turned up, but his eyes looked elsewhere. After a handful of seconds, he grinned down at her. "She would have beat seven kinds of hell out of me if I mistreated a woman."

"She was very kind," Kiera guessed, fascinated. She sat back so she could watch his face.

He nodded. "She was a loving mother. I was fortunate."

"Can you tell me what happened?"

His face lost its mirth. "I was found and taken away."

"I'm so sorry, Laszlo," she said, squeezing his hand.

He shrugged, a world of pain in one small movement. "What happened to your husband?" he asked.

She raised her eyebrows. "Well, since this seems to be a bare-your-soul kind of night, I suppose I'll tell you." She made a face. "All right." She took a breath, looked down at their hands. "We met in law school." She looked up. "A school for learning about the law. Well, obviously." She laughed. Looked away. "He was very handsome, very smart." Her voice grew soft. "I thought he was the most wonderful man I had ever known. He asked me to marry him the day we graduated—finished school. I was so happy."

She blew out a breath. "The first couple years were good, I think. After that we had, well, an issue arose that couldn't be fixed. Not something that was anyone's fault, or anything we could do anything about, but it was there, casting a shadow on everything else. I thought we'd get through it. I really did. I thought, 'Well this is just one of those "for worse" times, those times when you're supposed to cling together and weather the storm,' so to speak. 'Come out stronger afterward' and so on.

"The first time I really doubted happened the night before our five-year anniversary. I'd been out of town for a couple of days. I came home and found these earrings in my bathroom. I knew they weren't mine, but I made excuses. I didn't even ask him about it. Denial is a beautiful thing sometimes.

"Things got pretty cool between us during the year after that. I won't bore you with the details, but the short version is that I eventually found out that he was, uh, seeking his physical comforts elsewhere. Three years ago, on the day after Christmas, that's a really big holiday back home, he told me he wanted a divorce. He got remarried half a year later. The bastard."

Laszlo got up and poured some more water. Drank it. "What does that mean?"

"'Divorce'? It means to, um, nullify the marriage. Undo it, so to speak. It's a legal procedure."

"Put aside," he said.

"I suppose."

He set the cup down. "What was the 'issue'?"

"No, Laszlo. I don't want to talk about it."

The ghost of a smile drifted across his lips.

"If you're thinking up ways to get me to talk, I'll tell you right now they won't work." She stretched. "Now unless you have other deep dark secrets you want me to excavate, I'm tired. Let's go back to bed."

He walked over, pulled her up and kissed her mouth. "Only if you take that nightshirt off first."

Chapter 13

KIERA'S DAYS TOOK ON A RHYTHM. Breakfast, magic, practice, play with Alex, dinner, bed. The days grew longer, and passed smoothly, one after another. Her nights were better—wonderful—and she found herself content.

One afternoon, while Alex was still at school, Kiera answered a knock to find Lady Leith at her door. "Please come in, Lady Leith," Kiera said, hiding her surprise.

Leith inclined her head and walked inside.

"Would you like to sit, Lady Leith? I can send for Emmy if you would like something to eat."

Leith walked over and perched on a couch, then motioned for Kiera to sit. Choosing her best wine, Kiera poured for both of them, and sat.

"How is Marco?" Kiera asked.

"He is much improved," Leith answered. "If you would like to visit him, he would be pleased."

"Oh, that's wonderful!" Kiera smiled. "When?"

Leith considered. "Nexturn after noontide."

"Thank you for the invitation, Lady Leith. I have missed Marco very much."

Leith looked at her for a long minute. "I did not come to invite you to visit my son, Lady Kiera, nor for your thanks. I came to give you a gift and to explain its use."

Kiera sat back. "All right," she said, and sipped her wine.

Leith reached out a hand. It took Kiera a moment to understand that Leith held something in it, and one more for her to reach out a hand. Four golden rings fell into her palm.

"They're beautiful, Lady Leith," Kiera said. "Thank you."

"They are favoring rings, Lady Kiera," she explained coldly. "Wear them to parties and give them to the men you would dance with."

Kiera inclined her head. "Is this a tradition? Is there anything I need to know?"

Ignoring her, Leith stood, her wine untouched. "There is a party tonight. Your attendance is mandatory. You will be summoned a mark after dinner. Please dress appropriately. If you need advice, ask your maid." With that, she turned and let herself out.

When Emmy brought Alex home, Kiera told her what Leith had said.

"Oh, my lady! You've been invited to a brooding party! How exciting!" she gushed.

"Is that unusual? Wait. What is a 'brooding party'?"

Emmy walked to Alex's bed, which he had unsurprisingly neglected, and pulled up the sheets. "Oh, you know it's brooding moon." Kiera didn't, but something about this seemed familiar. Hadn't Marco said something about brooding? "And the nobles have parties. It is a sign of great favor to be invited! Oh Kiera, everybody wants to go to those. You will meet the most handsome men." Emmy positively beamed.

So the nobility divided itself up as well. She should have expected it, Kiera thought with a sigh. "So they're just parties? Parties where people go to meet each other and dance?"

Emmy nodded, smoothing out the blankets. "I will find you a dress."

Thirty minutes and two dozen rejected dresses later, Kiera plopped on the bed. Emmy seemed to want Kiera to leave as little to any looker's imagination as possible. "Emmy," Kiera grimaced, "isn't there anything less revealing? I want to look a little less like I'm advertising wares!"

Emmy giggled and pulled down another. It was long and cast in a deep indigo. Silver threads wove through it, and they sparkled in the light. Kiera tried it on and decided to wear it despite that it was a little too tight and the bodice a little too low.

"So exactly what do I do with these rings?" she asked.

Emmy pursed her lips, but helped Kiera slip them on to her two first fingers, two on each hand. "Well, you give them to the men you favor, of course," she explained. "Or you can give them all to one man, if you prefer him above the others."

Kiera laughed. "Okay, okay," she said, giving up. Emmy sat Kiera in a chair, then helped her brush out her hair. She plaited and arranged it into a complicated twist, set high on the back of her head, but left curling tendrils hanging down. It looked very floral, Kiera thought, amused. Kiera did her own makeup, but Emmy added more lipstick.

When the knock came, Kiera felt ready. She hugged Alex and went with the man standing outside. Kiera could hear orchestral music before they reached the door. The young man opened the door and bowed her in.

A young woman took her wrap, and Kiera looked around. The cavernous room should have been as intimidating as a cathedral, but the careful designer had worked hard to make it both regal and appealing. A bathroom-sized chandelier hung from the ceiling. A thick rug clung to the floor. Fluffy navy and yellow couches, arranged in circles and interspersed at intervals, invited participants to sink deep and forget their cares. What looked like a dance floor lay on the far side of the room, with an attendant band poised above it on a raised platform.

Although no one yet danced, at least a hundred people sat on couches or stood between them, talking and laughing, though she wondered how they could hear above the music. Everyone she saw looked to be in formal wear.

Several sets of eyes had lifted when she entered, and she felt a little shy. She ignored them and walked deeper into the room. She caught sight of Lady Leith and Lord Vayu, who sat together toward the back of the room. Instead of couches they each had a luxurious chair. Around them sat about a dozen young women, none over twenty.

Kiera walked over to them, wanting to be polite. One of the young women stood up and curtsied to the couple before she walked away. When she turned toward Kiera, Kiera saw tears on her face. Kiera frowned and watched her go, then turned and curtsied. Vayu inclined his head. Lady Leith sat motionless.

"I wanted to say 'thank you' for the invitation, Lord Vayu, Lady Leith," she said, nodded, then walked away. She made her way to an empty couch toward the back of the room, not quite ready to begin talking to people. A lovely young woman in a short blue dress brought her a glass of wine. Kiera stared at her; it was the first time she'd seen a woman in a short dress here.

A man sat down beside her. She looked over at his handsome, smiling face. Blond hair curled around his ears. Kiera smiled back.

"Lady Kiera?"

She nodded.

"I am Lord Thesin, and I would be very pleased to know you."

"It's nice to meet you, too, Lord Thesin."

He took her hand and kissed it. "So what do you think of our city, Lady Kiera? Are you enjoying your stay?"

She grimaced a little, trying to think of a tactful way to remove her hand. "I haven't been out much in it, I'm afraid," she admitted. "But I'm sure it's lovely."

"Lovelier with you in it, for certain," he said, and leaned closer. "I had heard that you were lovely," he confided, then slipped a ring from her finger. "Will you dance with me?"

She pulled her hand back, shocked. "Uh, Lord Thesin, I'm afraid I don't know how to waltz."

He laughed, rolling her ring in his fingers. "Do not worry, my lady. I will be most honored to teach you." He looked at her slyly. "I've taught many to dance, and as yet had no complaints."

Some bizarre message wove through his words that Kiera wished she understood. She cocked her head a little, trying to puzzle it out.

Before she could answer a second man, younger, stockier, and darker haired, came up behind Thesin and looked down at Kiera. Thesin had to twist to look up, but the second man ignored him, keeping his eyes on Kiera. "Lady Kiera?" he asked.

"Yes."

"I am Lord Gethor, and I would be pleased to know you," he told her before walking around the side of the couch to face her. He leaned down, took her hand, and kissed it softly.

"It's nice to meet you, Lord Gethor," she said, feeling a little uneasy.

He looked up. "May I have the honor of a dance, my lady?"

Kiera looked from Gethor to Thesin. The silence felt charged. "So what do you two do?" she asked, using small talk to carve out some distance.

They traded a look.

"I mean, do you have a certain profession, or some special responsibilities?"

Thesin smiled. "I am a weather mage," he said.

"May I sit?" asked Gethor, and Kiera scooted toward the middle. He sat down between her and the arm. Put a hand on her knee.

She flinched, and flashed him a glare.

He laughed and squeezed her knee.

Thesin leaned out so that he could see Gethor. "Lady Kiera has told me that she has not waltzed before," he said.

Gethor smiled broadly. "Oh my dear, you must let me teach you."

"No, she has accepted me," Thesin said, and held up the ring.

Gethor smirked and held up another. Kiera looked down at her hands. Her right was bare. She hadn't even felt him take it.

Kiera stood up. "Gentlemen, I have enjoyed meeting you both, but I believe I am going to go look for my friends."

Thesin stood up and took her arm. "No, Lady Kiera. Please stay." He gripped her firmly.

She tried to pull her arm free, but he squeezed, and it hurt. "Sit down," he commanded.

People were staring.

"Let go of my arm," she said in a low voice, not wanting to make a scene. Not at her first party, for God's sake.

Gethor stood. He put a hand on her shoulder and spoke quietly. "Lady Kiera, let us have a pleasant night. Please sit down."

She gritted her teeth. "Let. Go. Of. My. Arm."

Gethor nodded at Thesin, then pulled her out of his grip. He put an arm around her shoulders and led her toward an alcove at the side of the room. "You are new here, Lady Kiera. It's a brooding moon. Perhaps someone neglected to tell you that women are given the right to choose, but you mayn't refuse tonight, not tonight or any night of this moon. Come with me now, and I promise you that Thesin and I will be careful with you."

Kiera pulled out from his arm and turned to look at him. "What the hell are you saying? That I have to have sex with you?"

He spread his hands wide. "I am saying that you have to choose someone."

She gaped. "Someone here, at this party?" she asked, and he nodded, not unkindly.

"And the rings. The rings are for choosing with whom?"

He took her hand and patted it. "Shall we dance first?"

KIERA DANCED BECAUSE she didn't know what else to do. Other men asked her to dance, but she declined politely and let Thesin and Gethor take turns leading her around the floor. She refused food and wine. Her heart wouldn't stop pounding. As they danced the men tried to talk to her, but she ignored them.

She wondered what would happen if she tried to leave. She looked around the room and saw that a pair of uniformed guards stood next to each door. Were they for women who balked? She wondered what would happen if she had to fight. Would Vayu imprison her? Take Alex? Could she get back to her room and get Alex out before the guards arrived? Would Vayu kill Marco if she ran? Did the guards obey Laszlo? If she got caught, would he make them let her go?

Her stomach clenched as she thought about Laszlo. She knew he would hate her for this, and who could blame him? "I'm not Skani," he'd said when she accused him of philandering. Well, Jesus Christ, she understood now what he'd been saying. She shut her eyes and for a moment she let herself wish he would come and rescue her, but she knew he would not, probably could not. Had he known?

Why hadn't anyone told her? Remembering Emmy's dress choices, Kiera realized she'd known. But had not been upset. In fact, she'd seemed excited.

Was this just a cultural thing? People looking forward to this?

If there was no Laszlo, would she feel differently?

No. Definitely no.

Oh God, she thought, *I can't do this. Please get me out of this. Please.*

A hand tapped her shoulder, and Thesin passed her to Gethor. She opened her eyes and saw Leith staring at her. What might have been a flicker of understanding passed over her face.

A handful of girls still knelt on the floor in front of Vayu. From this angle she could see that they were posing, moving in ways that showed off their bodies, acting coy. She wondered if Vayu was selecting another mistress. Did he force his wife to sit there while he chose a new lover? Or was this just a partner for the night?

She looked again at Leith. Leith must have felt her gaze, because she raised her eyes and stared at Kiera. She blinked slowly and looked down, and Kiera felt Leith's shame roil through her. She staggered, almost fell. Thesin, or was it Gethor, caught her and pulled her close. She pushed back, angry, but another hand grabbed her shoulder and she spun around to find Valen standing behind her.

She gaped. "May I have this dance?" he asked. She shrank back a little, and he made a face, obviously as displeased by the thought as she was. "I do not want a ring, Kiera," he grimaced, showing his teeth. "Just a dance."

He reached out a hand and she went unresisting into his arms.

He danced her away from Gethor and across the floor. *I never thought I'd be glad to see Valen,* she thought.

"Are you enjoying the party?" he asked, and she couldn't read his tone. She shook her head once, not trusting her voice.

He was silent for a minute. "Naga wants to talk to you. Will you come?"

She nodded without looking up.

When the song ended he bowed politely and offered his arm. She took it and let him lead her across the floor.

She looked around, but where was Naga?

Valen led her to one of the guarded doors. He raised a hand and one of the guards stepped over and opened the door. Valen escorted her though it and Kiera sagged with relief as it closed behind them.

She knew she shouldn't. She would have to go back.

Valen released her hand, abandoning any pretense of politeness now that no one was watching, and walked ahead of her down a hallway. She followed. She would have gone to see Satan to get out of that room.

He stopped in front of a doorway, then opened the door. He held it for her, and she walked inside. It was a square, smallish room, maybe twenty feet across. It had a fireplace, with two green couches and two chairs arranged facing it. There was an oak table, which held the room's only light.

Naga was sitting in one of the chairs. She rose, smiling, and took Kiera's hands in hers. "I'm so glad you came, Lady Kiera."

"Thank you," Kiera said helplessly. Naga smiled indulgently and led her to one of the couches. "Sit, sit," she said, and poured Kiera a glass of wine. "Drink this," she said, handing it to her, and poured herself one.

The door thumped when Valen let himself out.

Kiera took a drink of the sweet wine. "Am I a prisoner here, too?"

"Lady Kiera, you mustn't think of it like that." Naga frowned. "This is a time of hope. We celebrate life and joy in these moons."

Kiera sighed heavily. "Naga, what did you want to see me for?"

"My lord told me that you seemed unhappy." She leaned forward. "I thought it might be because you were thinking of Laszlo and how he will feel."

Kiera flinched. "What?"

"Oh, Lady Kiera, I saw how he looked at you. And you at him," she added. "And tonight you are sad, and I know it isn't my affair, but my heart aches for you." She reached for Kiera's hand, but Kiera ignored her. A log broke inside the fireplace and Kiera turned to watch it burn. Naga sighed. "Lady Kiera, I have to tell you the truth. We may not be friends, but you're a sunwyr, Kiera, and he is a slave. A shifter slave." Her mouth twisted in a moue. "And I will not let that slave mock a Skani this way."

Kiera crossed her arms. "What are you trying to tell me, Naga?"

Naga leaned back, pulling her legs up beneath her. "Laszlo was my lover, Lady Kiera, for many cycles."

Kiera felt her eyes widen.

"No, no. We had affection, but there was no love." Naga leaned forward and took Kiera's hand before she could pull it back. She smiled sweetly. "I kept him until he married, Lady Kiera, or as near to married as slaves can get."

"What happened to his wife?"

Naga shrugged. "Nothing. She is a farmer. Here." She picked up her wine and took a drink. "I believe he thinks becoming captain of Lord Vayu's army entitles him to take a mistress as many Skani husbands do, which is why I asked my lord to bring you here." She looked up at Kiera, willing her to understand. "I saw how you looked at him, and I knew I had to tell you, Lady Kiera. If word gets out, you will look very foolish."

It felt like a fist slammed into Kiera's chest. She lifted herself off the couch and stared at Naga. "No," she said, shaking her head. "This is just some mean trick of Valen's. I don't believe you."

"Ask him, Kiera." Naga sounded tired.

I loved him, I loved him, I loved him. Oh God. I loved him and he betrayed me.

The fire crackled, then exploded out, sending sparks flying across the room. Naga jumped back but Kiera lifted a hand, stilling the flames. But she couldn't slow her breath. And she was going to throw up.

A blank moment, and then Naga had a hold of her arm and was helping her to the couch. She handed Kiera a glass of wine.

Kiera's hands shook, but she drank it all, then stood up again. She turned toward the door, but it opened before she could reach it. Valen came in, looking grim.

Thesin and Gethor followed him in.

CHAPTER 14

THESIN WALKED IN TO THE ROOM, grabbed one of Kiera's arms and backhanded her. She lifted a hand to her mouth and it came away bloody. He smiled, teeth wolfish in the thin light.

"Let go of me!" she ground out, and jerked her arm out of his.

The sour smell of alcohol wafted in the space between them. Thesin grabbed a handful of her hair and pulled her face to his chest.

She went limp and he stumbled and let go of her hair. She surged up, grabbed his head with both hands and smashed her forehead into the middle of his face as hard as she could. He screamed his pain and let go, stumbling back, blood gushing from his nose.

Sweet adrenalin washed through her, burning the pain away, leaving nothing but rage. She turned around. "Who's next?"

Gethor reached for her but she stepped out of the way. She set her feet in "L" stance and lifted her hands, palms out, to the space in front of her chest. He snarled and swept his arm in a wide arc, aiming for her head.

She blocked his clumsy attempt with her left arm, then popped him in the jaw open-handed, putting everything she had into it. He stumbled back, mouth open.

Someone opened the door. She turned.

Marco.

"Come with me," he commanded, and held out a hand.

Kiera took it. Without a word he pulled her out of the room and shut the door. He led her swiftly down the hall, in the opposite direction from the party. The unmistakable sounds of people having sex exuded from the doors of every room they passed.

They turned a corner. Marco stopped, opened a door on his right and shoved her inside. Near darkness enveloped her. He followed her in, waved at a lamp, which lit, and shut the door behind him. He leaned his back against it and shut his eyes.

Kiera was still breathing hard. Still shaking.

"Sit down," he commanded.

Something banged against the wall of the room next to theirs. Kiera jumped, but crossed her arms and stood fast.

He opened his eyes. "Gods all damn it, Kiera, sit down."

"What the hell is going on, Marco?"

He stalked over to her and grabbed her arms. "I think I just saved you from what was looking to be an exciting night, but you have to do exactly what I say. Do you hear me?"

His eyes blazed, and he stared at her until she nodded. With one hand, he reached up and grabbed the neckline of her dress, then tore it down, baring one breast.

Her mouth fell open.

From some nearby room a woman cried out her pleasure. Grimacing, Marco took Kiera's hand and led her to the couch, then pushed her down and fell on top of her. He kissed her inartfully, but firmly, and she went stiff and pushed him back. "No, Marco. Absolutely not!"

"Kiera," he urged, and the door crashed open.

They sat up. Gethor stood at the doorway and Thesin pushed past him, blood and fury on his face. Valen leaned against the wall behind Gethor.

"Get out," Marco ordered.

"I have her ring!" Thesin bellowed, stalking toward the couch. "That bitch belongs to me tonight!"

Marco stood, then helped Kiera sit up. She grabbed the remnants of her bodice and tried to cover herself with it.

Marco clucked. "I'm sorry, lover," he murmured, just loud enough to be heard. He took off his jacket and draped it over her shoulders, then stood, wiping lipstick from his face before turning to the doorway. He used a reasonable tone. "Lady Kiera had promised herself to me, Thesin, long before she arrived at the party. She was given rings, but no instructions, as you well know." He shrugged. "By her own oath, she is mine tonight."

"You are just a boy!" Thesin spat, rage twisting his mouth and carving his eyes to slits.

Marco smiled coldly, looking much like his father, Kiera thought. "I've been a man for some time, Thesin. Lady Kiera is far from my first lover."

Gethor walked around Thesin and came to the couch. He eyed her torn dress. "Is this true, Lady Kiera?" he asked. "I find it hard to believe that you would say nothing."

Kiera looked up at him. She did not have to fake the tremor in her voice or the tears in her eyes. "I didn't think it would make any difference," she said. "And Marco—wasn't there. The way you explained it, I thought I had no choice."

"Enough," Valen barked, pushing off the wall. He turned to Marco. "I, too, find this hard to believe, brother." He picked up a vase from a table and pretended to examine it before deigning to meet Marco's heated gaze. "She is not the type you usually prefer." His mouth twisted as he laughed, an ugly sound. "I did not know your tastes ran to old and ugly."

Kiera dropped her head to hide her eyes and the shock and hatred she knew they would show. *I will see you die,* she promised Valen silently.

"And until recently I did not know your tastes ran to torturing slave girls, Valen, or to vipers like Naga," Marco shot back.

Valen snorted. "Each has its purpose, brother."

"Yes. My point exactly. And if we were not lovers, why by the gods would she offer for me at court?"

Valen set the vase down. Smiled. "I confess it confused me."

"Leave us, all of you," Marco commanded, but kept his eyes on Valen.

Valen shrugged and walked out. After a moment, the other two followed. Kiera did not watch.

MARCO SHUT THE DOOR, then barred it. He let out a sigh, then turned around. "Are you all right?"

"No." She dropped her head to her hands. "No."

Marco came and sat down beside her. She lifted her head. "Marco, thank you. God. You saved my life."

He snorted. "No, I saved theirs. You forget I've seen you fight."

She smiled, but tears came, and she hung her head and let them.

He hugged her, just one arm around her shoulders. She should have been comforted, but she just ached.

"It's all right, Kiera," he said, squeezing her once and letting her go. "We will stay together during brooding moons. This won't happen again."

"You are a very good man, Marco," she whispered.

Marco knelt down in front of her. "Kiera, what's so wrong? This isn't about that," he waved his hand toward the door. "Is it? You would be yelling. What happened?"

There was a fireplace. Kiera stood and walked to it, then waved a hand and the wood inside lit. She squatted down and stared at the flames.

"He's married," she whispered.

"Who's married? Valen? What are you talking about?"

"Laszlo."

"Laszlo is married?"

"Naga told me that—" she blew out a breath, "Naga said that she was his lover until he got 'as near to married as slaves can get.'" She leaned toward the fire. "She said his—his wife is still living. Here. She's—a farmer."

"Did he think to take a mistress?" he wondered.

Kiera nodded. "That's what Naga said."

"Did he tell you he was married? That there was another woman?"

"No," she whispered.

"Naga is a snake," he spat.

"I believe her." She wrapped her arms around herself.

"Oh, Kiera," he said, and knelt down beside her. He pulled her into a tight hug. "I am so sorry."

"I loved him."

"I know," he told her, voice kind. Kiera closed her eyes and leaned into him.

When her tears finally stopped, Kiera made her way to the floor in front of the fire. She plopped down and rubbed a hand across her aching forehead. Marco followed her over and leaned his shoulder into hers.

BOOM.

They jumped. Marco scrambled to his feet. "What is that?"

The door crashed inward, shards flying across the room. Laszlo followed them, landing on his feet. His eyes blazed.

Kiera sat up.

Marco leapt in front of Kiera. "Get out!"

In two steps Laszlo was there. With one hand he grabbed Marco by the shirt and lifted him until they were face to face. "Get away from her," he growled, then hurled Marco onto the couch, which flipped over and slid into the far wall. Laszlo leaned down to Kiera, took her arms, and lifted her to her feet.

Kiera's heart lurched. She closed her eyes.

Gentle fingers touched her mouth.

Oh, God. Oh, God. Oh, God.

She wanted to wrap herself in his arms. Wanted it more than she wanted to breathe. To tell him what had happened. To feel his fingers in her hair.

To give in. Pretend she didn't know. For just one more night.

A sob escaped her. *I can't do this.* She pulled away and turned her back.

"What has happened?" he asked her, voice quiet.

His voice. God, how she loved his voice.

But he had lied to her. Betrayed her.

She spun around. "You don't have any right to ask me anything," she spat, and shock rolled across his face.

She started to cry again. He laid a hand on her arm. Squeezed once.

Kiera jerked it away, then slapped him as hard as she could. "Why did you come, Laszlo?" she yelled, letting the tears roll down her face. "Why did you bother? How could you do this to me?" she wailed, and doubled over, sobbing.

He grabbed her shoulders and pulled her up and into his arms. She pushed away and stumbled back, then fell. "Why aren't you home with your wife!" she screamed.

He flinched.

"Deny it," she sobbed as she climbed back to her feet. "Tell me it isn't true. Please, Laszlo, God, please tell me it isn't true!"

He closed his eyes.

She wailed. "Get out! Get out!"

Laszlo turned. He screamed wordlessly, then sprang forward and grabbed the oak table in front of the couch with one hand and catapulted it against a wall, where it shattered into dozens of pieces. He was gone before they stilled.

Kiera dropped to her knees and covered her face with her hands.

MARCO HELPED KIERA back to her room. Her head was pounding, but she lay awake in bed for a long while. She had spent all her emotion. Only hollowness remained, leaving her feeling numb and dead. She wondered how much of what she felt was real. Had she really loved Laszlo? Or had his betrayal, so much like her husband's philandering, opened an old wound? Had she clung to him because he was her only rock in this crazy world? Had the tenderness he'd shown her been real, or was it just sex for him? Was her reaction so violent because of the fear she'd felt all night?

She finally slept.

When she woke, the sun was shining. It was quiet. *Alex must be at school,* she thought, and sat up. *I wonder why Emmy didn't wake me.*

Her mouth felt parched, so she reached for the pitcher sitting on the table next to her bed.

Her heart lurched. All four rings were lying on top of the table, eighteen inches from where her head had laid.

She jerked her hand back. Memories flooded her, and with them came pain. Pain and grief, like stones on her chest.

She moaned, then lay back on the bed. She pulled the covers up over her head and curled up in a ball in the darkness beneath them. Tears washed hotly down her face.

She pulled tighter, closed her eyes, and willed the world away.

KIERA SLEPT FITFULLY, but did not rise from bed that day. She told Emmy and Alex she was sick. The next morning she pled sick again, and Emmy closed the curtains.

She woke during the day to knocking. She turned over and tried to go back to sleep, but the knocking continued. She hissed through her teeth and pushed back the blankets. She stalked to the door and pulled it open, uncaring that she stood there in a dirty shirt, hair tangled.

Marco. He looked her up and down, then walked in. Kiera moved aside and shut the door behind him. He strode to the window and peeled open the curtains. Kiera put up a hand to block the light.

"What do you want, Marco?" she asked tiredly, then made her way to the bathroom.

He called out, "Kiera, you can't stay in here forever."

"Yes, I can," she shot back. When she finished, she crawled back into bed and pulled the covers up over her.

Marco came and sat on the bed. "Kiera, I know that you're hurting. But you came here to learn magic, and you can't learn anything from bed."

"Go away, Marco."

"Kiera, if you don't want to learn magic anymore, my father will marry you off. If you want to escape, I'll go with you, but I can't do it yet. He's got guards watching me all the time now. I have to wait for a while. So you have to at least act like you're learning, just for a while, okay?"

She sat up, arranged the pillows, and lay back against the headboard. "How did you know to come?" she finally asked.

"A servant fetched me." He grimaced. "I am sorry I didn't get there earlier."

"Who sent a servant?"

"I panicked and didn't think to ask," he answered. "I should have."

So she had a friend at court, too. She wished she knew who it was.

"What did they tell you?"

"He said that his master said I must come immediately because Lady Kiera needed my assistance. Valen hates you, so I guessed what that meant."

She sat up. "What do you mean?"

He ran his hand across the blanket. "I didn't know who it would be, but I figured Valen would use someone at brooding to hurt you. I bet he put Thesin and Gethor up to it. They're his friends, and I'm sure they thought it was a chance to have fun." His mouth was a hard line.

"How do you know that Valen hates me?"

"I can tell," he said darkly.

Kiera shook her head. "Why did you run away, Marco?"

He looked at her. "Allie came to stay here from Barrow, a city up north, and at the next brooding my father chose her for his mistress. Did you see him last night? He is choosing his next." He made a face. "He and Valen. They like the shy ones." He looked down. "She was so scared of him, Kiera, and he hurt her. She begged me to help her, so I took her away."

"Bless your heart," she said, then saw his face. "You love her," she teased.

He shrugged, and then nodded.

"Does she love you?"

He shrugged again, face pink.

"She doesn't know," Kiera guessed. She lay back on the bed.

He stood up. "Kiera, please. Get out of bed and go take a bath. You smell like a horse."

She sighed and got out of bed. "Did you bring back the rings?" she asked, pulling on her robe. "I should say 'thank you.'"

"What do you mean?"

"My rings, all four of them, were back here, on this table," she pointed, "when I woke up yesterday. Yesturn. Thank you."

Marco avoided her eyes. "Uh—no."

"What? What is it?"

He grimaced. "I don't want to tell you."

"Just say it, Marco," she said tiredly.

"Someone found Gethor and Thesin outside the wall yesturn. They had been lying there for a long time and they were nearly frozen to death." He paused to look up at her. "They had been beaten. It was—bad."

Her jaw dropped. "How would anyone know what happened, Marco? Valen wouldn't tell, and I don't think Naga would either."

He raised his eyebrows.

"How would he know, Marco?" she said gently. "I didn't tell him. And neither did you."

He shook his head. "Your lip was bleeding. Maybe one of the servants told him who you danced with. Maybe he smelled them on you. I don't know."

"He can smell people on me?"

"Shifters have a really good sense of smell. I'm pretty sure that's how he knew I was me in the wagon."

She nodded. Tears came. They fell. She blew out a breath. "I miss him so much, Marco."

He patted her hand, eyes sympathetic.

"How can I love him like that? Marco, I keep asking myself why the hell I feel like—like my heart has been ripped from my chest." She lifted her head. "It wasn't like we were married for ten years." She shuddered. "But I feel like a part of me is dying."

Marco squeezed her hand. "It's time to get back up, Kiera." He smiled, but his eyes looked sad. Sad and old. "We have to keep standing up because we have things to do. People to save. Isn't that what you said?"

Kiera glared at him.

AFTER MARCO LEFT, Kiera took a bath. It was early afternoon, and she had a few hours before Alex came home. She rubbed her hair dry, then dressed. She put on her coat and drifted out the door.

She wandered down the hall, then down the stairs. She avoided the people who ambled around and slipped out a door. The air outside felt cold and crisp. She walked around the perimeter of the building and then around the far side of the church. As she got colder, she put her hands in her pockets. She kept walking.

After a while she came to the river. It was smooth and flat, and frozen solid. She stood in front of it. She wished that she could make her heart that cold and smooth.

She thought of the day she'd been thrown from the horse, and her heart wrenched. The way Laszlo had looked when he found her. She had never seen a man so angry, angry because someone had tried to hurt her.

She took a deep breath.

She remembered seeing him silhouetted by the sun the day of the tournament. She closed her eyes and saw him there. Beauty in black. The flash of his teeth when he smiled at her.

She remembered how he'd looked that first night in the tent. How beautiful he was, how gently he had touched her.

How fiercely he made love. How tenderly he held her.

She imagined him holding another woman. Making love to her. Touching her hair.

She wrapped her arms around herself, willing the pictures to stop.

She straightened and opened herself to the fire. All of it, all she could hold. It came immediately, wrapping itself around her like the lover she'd lost. She thrust out a hand and sent it out to the ice.

The ice popped, and then cracked. The top faded from white to blue, then became clear. She kept her hand out, the fire flowing. Water broke through, roughly, the current fast underneath.

She released the fire, letting the last of it fall in the water.

A hand touched her shoulder.

She spun around and found Mosha. He lifted his hands, smiling slightly.

"I am sorry, my lady," he said. "I dinna mean to startle ye."

She let out a breath. "Mosha," she said.

"How fare ye, Lady Kiera?" he asked, eyes kind.

She turned back toward the river. "I am fine."

He moved to stand next to her. "Thinking of going inta that river is 'fine'?"

"I was not!" she said hotly.

"Lady Kiera, I could feel yer grief from the stable," he chastened.

She opened her mouth. Shut it. "Fine. I am hurting. God, I am hurting. But Mosha, I'm not about to jump in the river."

"Glad ta hear it," he said mildly.

"Did you know?" she finally asked.

"Know what, Lady Kiera?"

"Just Kiera."

"Know what, Kiera?"

She closed her eyes. "That he has a wife."

He shifted. "I dinna."

She nodded. "Me either."

"Do ye love him?"

"Are you asking for you or asking for him?"

He smiled. "I wunna tell him if ye dunna want me to."

"I don't want you to."

"So ye do."

She sighed. "The son of a bitch. He never deserved me."

"I wilna disagree."

They stared silently at the river for a while. A raven called from a tree.

"I hate ta say it, but maybe you should think on this, Kiera. What would ye have done once ye learned how ta go home? And dunna ye think he thought of that too?" Mosha asked gently.

"Laszlo?"

"Yeah."

She turned to him, furious. "I offered myself for Marco, Mosha, in front of God and everyone. I gave my oath to stay. I admit that I have often wished, fervently, that I could go home, and I freely admit that right now is one of those times." She spread her hands in surrender. "But I gave my word, Mosha! I wouldn't go back on it. With Laszlo, I guess I thought—well, I guess it doesn't matter," she lied.

He wrapped an arm around her shoulders. "Come have something ta drink and warm up."

CHAPTER 15

KIERA CLAMPED DOWN HER FEELINGS and returned to her magic lessons the next day. Marco went with her. Agni took Kiera aside when she got there and led her back to the room where Agni had tested her.

"Thisturn, Lady Kiera, you learn to cast your first spell. You will pull and blend strands of two energies together into something new, and send them out here—" she pointed to the center of the floor—"to manifest. To begin, first pull strands of fire—" she opened her hand—"and set them to spin inside. That is called storing. Without letting the fire go out, call air and set it to whirl, melding the strands together—" she put her hand on her chest.

"Next, you imagine the working, what it should look like and how big it should be. You will feed the streams out, sending them to manifest here—" she again pointed to the center of the room. "Thisturn, Lady Kiera, the manifestation will be small, no bigger than a man, and I want you to keep pulling both fire and air to feed and maintain your working's size. Do not let it escape its bounds!" Agni clapped her hands together, obviously pleased. "Thisturn, Lady Kiera, we make a firestorm."

She nodded to Kiera. "Do not be discouraged if the mix is off, or if it is hard to maintain. I will be here if it gets away from you. It takes time and practice, but when you can do this, you may wish to learn to add earth, and the storm will be stronger."

Agni stepped back and nodded to Kiera, who swallowed. *Am I ready for this?* she wondered.

Kiera closed her eyes and called to the fire. She pulled it into her, where it behaved perfectly.

"Excellent," Agni whispered.

She reached for air, taking her time, and found a thick stream. She peeled off the strands and pulled them into herself, where they spun softly.

186

She tried to blend them into the fire, but they wanted to spread, so she pressed down on them. The strands burst and pieces flowed away. Gritting her teeth, she reached out again, pulling more strands from the stream she had used before, calling them into her. This time she clamped down before wrapping them around the fire as it whirled inside her.

It was hard to keep track of both elements, so she kept her eyes closed. She concentrated on how they felt, memorizing, and opened herself further, pulling another feed from the fire, then another few strands of air, letting them trickle inside her, where she slowly mixed them together.

Kiera pictured a storm, and nearly lost the air again. She squeezed her eyes harder and made herself breathe. Picturing the storm again, she pushed the fire flows toward where she thought was the spot on the floor.

"No," Agni called. "You have to direct where it goes."

Kiera's eyes popped open and she lost the air. She closed her eyes again and pulled it, faster this time, and rapidly blended the flows. She sent a stream out and heard the working pop to life. Without severing the flow she cut it back, tightened the strands, then opened the flow again. She sent more, then all of it, letting the spinning air suck in the fire, which had started to glow orange as it manifested. She eased the strands so the working lifted off the floor and raised the top until it was taller than she was.

Agni clapped once.

Sweat poured off Kiera. The hardest part was keeping the strands of the two mixing inside her, so she decided to try pulling then guiding them so they fed directly into her storm. She unhooked the fire and shaped the strands so they flowed from the stream directly into her storm. She unhooked the air, almost losing it, then held the flow away from her chest.

Kiera felt herself fly backwards as the room exploded. She slammed into the wall, then stumbled down. Her dress was on fire. She closed her eyes and plucked away the tiny threads feeding the fire, sending them down to the floor, where they hissed as they went out.

Kiera stood up and found Agni, who had knelt on the floor by the door to pat a small fire from the hem of her dress.

Kiera smiled apologetically when Agni looked up. "I am so sorry, Lady Agni," she said, chagrined. "I wanted to try something new. I thought it would work."

"Girl, I saw what you did," Agni said, standing up. "But as you see you cannot control elements without the reflection. You have to pull the strands into you, Kiera, use your own magic, the magic that lives inside you, to shape the elements, or the results are unpredictable. Obviously—"

Kiera leaned forward. "Obviously?"

Agni's mouth was open. She stared at Kiera's arm.

"What?" Kiera said. "Shit! Am I still on fire?" She patted the sleeve of her dress. Spots had burned off. "Am I burning?" she asked frantically. "I can't feel it!"

Agni took a step and grabbed Kiera's hand. Kiera stilled when she saw the look on Agni's face.

"Where did you get that?" Agni asked softly, reaching out to touch Kiera's upper left arm with a finger.

Kiera turned her head. "It's a tattoo," she said, confused. "I got it —back home. Right before I came here, in fact."

"You let someone do this?" Agni asked, incredulous.

Kiera shrugged. "Yes. It's just ink. An artist uses a tool to puncture your skin and they inject ink in to make the design."

Agni pulled Kiera's right hand across her chest and laid it on the tattoo. "Close your eyes," she hissed.

Kiera did.

"Open your sight. Sense it."

Kiera tried, strained, but it just felt like skin. She shook her head. "I don't feel anything," she finally said, opening her eyes.

Agni looked thoughtful as she dropped Kiera's hand. "It is a very powerful spell, Kiera. A spell bound in this ink."

"What do you mean?" Kiera gaped. "What is it?"

Agni took a step back. She closed her eyes and lifted her hands. After a moment, she let her hands fall. She lifted her right hand again, and then opened her eyes.

"It may be some kind of curse," she said matter-of-factly.

"What? What did you say?"

"It is a powerful spell, Lady Kiera." Agni pursed her lips. "I have seen this type of binding before. It's something an enemy does to an enemy he has captured before setting him free, though I've never seen this large a mark." She rubbed her arms briskly and paced toward the door. "Sometimes it is done to track an enemy, but in other cases a spell is set to do some thing when certain conditions are met. This one pulls earth and water. A veil-piercing spell, and perhaps more." She turned back. "We need to determine its trigger first of all, Lady Kiera, and then how to remove it, if that is possible."

Kiera's knees buckled. "I need to sit down," she said, and dropped to the floor.

Agni lifted a brow but continued to pace. "Try not to fret, Lady Kiera. If it has not been triggered by this time, it may be that it will not. We can be

certain that the trigger is nothing ordinary. It is not fire, or air elementals."
Agni continued to pace. "It may be something—no; even this working
would require a touch, I am sure of it." She turned to Kiera. "Perhaps a
cut, then, across the ink." She came over and reached a hand out to help
Kiera up.

Kiera reluctantly took it.

Agni clasped her left hand, then pulled a small knife from her belt with
the other. Kiera jerked back, out of her grasp.

"Do not be silly, girl," Agni chided.

Kiera hesitated for another moment, but finally nodded. The knife rose
as Agni took a step in. Kiera watched as it pierced the lowest border of the
ink. A drop of blood rose on her skin.

She was suddenly flying though fire-tinged air. She landed on the floor,
retching. It felt like she had swallowed an anvil.

"Oh, God," she moaned.

"Yes," Agni said from someplace on the floor. "Returning your blood to
the ink is the key to this spell."

Kiera ground out, "I'm so pleased that you're pleased."

Agni laughed a little and pulled herself to her feet. "Can you get up,
Lady Kiera?"

Kiera managed to stand, but her stomach still roiled. "How do I get
it off?"

"I do not yet know."

Kiera hissed a breath.

"Do not worry, Lady Kiera. I may be able to find a way, and now that
you know its key, you can avoid the trigger."

"Have you done that before? And what is it supposed to do, Agni? What
happens if I get a cut all the way across it?"

Agni grimaced, but before she could answer the door flew open, and
Kiera turned to find Valen and Marco framing the entry. Valen's face was
white, but for what reason Kiera didn't know.

"What was that magic?" he demanded.

Kiera covered her tattoo with her hand and turned her back on the door.
She faced Lady Agni, pleading with her eyes.

Lady Agni flickered a glance to Kiera before meeting Valen's eyes. She
cleared her throat. "Lady Kiera had an accident with her magic, Lord Valen.
I am sorry if we disturbed your working."

Kiera closed her eyes and breathed.

"Kiera, your clothes are burned," Marco told her as he walked into
the room.

She turned to him. "I lost control of a fire storm," she admitted sheepishly.

His back to Valen, he mouthed, "Wow!"

Kiera hid a smile. "Would you mind taking me back to my room, Marco?"

"Not at all, Lady Keer."

"What happened to your arm?" Valen asked, motioning with his head to the hand covering her tattoo.

"I burned myself," she muttered as she swept past.

"That was a stupid excuse," Marco whispered as he whisked Kiera down the hallway. "Fire mages don't get burned."

Kiera pressed her lips together. "Oh, well."

"What happened?"

She opened her mouth to tell Marco the truth, but she couldn't. *I don't want to add another worry to his shoulders,* she thought. *And I don't want to think about it right now.* "Agni cut me."

"She cut you!"

"Shhh! We were trying a spell."

They went around a corner and Marco stopped abruptly. Kiera ran into his back, then looked up, prepared to be annoyed.

Laszlo was standing there, arms crossed across his chest. He looked angry. He was also blocking the hall. "What happened to your dress?"

Kiera's heart jumped to her throat. She swallowed it down, then forced herself to pull her hand from Marco's and push past him. Her breath caught as her shoulder brushed his arm.

"A'kala," he called from behind her, but she did not stop.

DURING THE NEXT WEEK Kiera saw Laszlo three times. Once outside on her way to the school. Twice in the great hall as she made her way to her magic lessons. He did not try to approach her.

Marco came every night and stayed for an hour, sometimes two.

Agni did not find a way to remove her tattoo curse, but Kiera did learn to twine earth into her fire storm without blowing anything up.

On the eighth day after the discovery of her curse, Kiera returned to her room from magic lessons to find Alex and Emmy already there. Alex lay curled up on his bed, crying, and Emmy sat on the edge of the bed, rubbing his back.

"What happened?" she asked, appalled. She pulled off her coat, then walked over and sat on his bed. He sat up, crawled into her lap and buried his face in her chest.

"Alex, what happened?"

He just snuggled closer.

"Emmy?" she asked.

"Alex got into a scuffle, I think, my lady."

Kiera pushed him back so she could see his face. Someone had blackened one eye and bruised his cheek. "Alex, what happened?" she gasped and brushed his eye with a finger. "Did you get in a fight?"

He nodded.

"What happened?"

"Jaken pushed Nista down and she cried," he told her solemnly. "He kicked her in her mouth and it was bleeding. I tried to make him stop and Jaken and his friends pushed me down and they kicked me in my face."

Kiera shut her eyes. "Is Nista a slave?"

Alex stuck out his bottom lip as he considered. "I don't know, Keer. Jaken said she was a 'fucking animal,' but she's a girl in my class."

Kiera flinched. "No, Alex. She isn't an animal. She is probably a shifter, though, like Laszlo."

She'd said it without thinking, and just saying his name dredged up the stones in her guts. She took a breath, held her face still and patted Alex's shoulder. "And you did the right thing. Standing up to bullies is always the right thing to do, and I'm very proud of you."

Alex grinned, further wrenching Kiera's heart.

She turned to Emmy. "Will you please send for a healer?"

Emmy got up.

"Wait, Emmy," Kiera said. "How about instead have someone call Mosha, okay?"

Emmy nodded, but couldn't hide her surprise.

Alex squirmed, so Kiera combed her fingers through his hair. "Did you use your *tai kwon do*, Alex? How did he get you on the ground?"

Alex looked affronted. "He got his friends to gang up on me, Keer. They pushed me down and kicked my face and I couldn't get my hands up. But I kicked a good hook kick and an ax kick! I kicked Jaken in the nose."

Kiera pulled him close.

In fewer than twenty minutes Mosha bounded in without knocking. "What is it, Kier—Oh, I see." Mosha lifted Alex's face from Kiera's dress. "Lost a fight, I see," he chuckled.

Kiera glared at him. He almost hid a smile.

"Lay back, my brave lad," he said, and motioned for Kiera to get up.

Kiera stood. She poured herself a glass of wine with trembling hands, then sat on the couch next to Emmy. She tried not to listen to Mosha.

She started to wave at the fire, but stopped. Kiera closed her eyes and pulled a strand of fire, then spun it and sent it out. The fire lit, softly, perfectly.

Emmy jumped back. "Lady Kiera, did you do that?"

"Yeah." Kiera smiled wanly.

"Bless me, Lady Kiera, but you scared me."

"Sorry, Emmy. Sorry."

A short while later, Mosha came and dropped on the other couch.

"How is he?" Kiera asked.

"Oh, he will be fine. He just needs ta rest now."

Emmy smiled and Kiera breathed a sigh of relief.

"Lady Kiera," he said, eyes serious, "Will ye take a walk with me?" He winked at Emmy as he stood up, and she blushed like a schoolgirl.

Kiera raised an eyebrow, and he grinned. She picked up her coat and looked at him—*do I need this?* —and he nodded. After she shut the door, Kiera turned to Mosha. "What do you want to talk to me about? Is Alex really okay?"

"Alex is fine, but I want ta talk to ye about some other things. It is a beautiful turn and I would rather be out than in."

To Kiera's surprise, Mosha took her down the gravel drive toward the city.

"I've never been this way before. Well, not since we came here."

"That is a shame." He patted her hand and smiled. "I will take you ta get a hot drink you wilna forget."

Ashen clouds blanketed the sky, and the frigid air stung Kiera's nose. She snorted, blowing out steam. "This is a beautiful day?"

Mosha smiled but kept his eyes on the road.

Below Lord Vayu's keep, the city crept up like a stone dog. Small, granite-blocked and haphazardly constructed wooden buildings crowded the streets, and each other. Black smoke drifted from every chimney. Accumulated snow covered the worst of it, but inky stains streaked most walls. People of every age scurried from place to place, seemingly oblivious to the poverty of their lives compared to how others lived just up the hill. All wore thick, drab-colored coats, and Kiera couldn't tell women from men. No one met their eyes.

"Why won't they look at us?" Kiera asked.

"Because yer a lady."

"I am not!"

"Well, ye are, and ye have a lady's garb besides."

Kiera's brows drew together in a frown. "So why won't they look at a lady?"

"B'cause no one wants yer attention on them, Kiera."

Kiera rolled her eyes. "What? Like I'd say, 'You displease me' and have them whipped?"

"That is closer to the truth than you know," he said darkly.

Her stomach clenched. To change the subject, Kiera asked, "Are you waiting to talk to me until we get wherever it is we're going?'

"Yup."

A few roads later, Mosha led her into an alley and then right into a door she would have missed from the street. It was dark inside and she stopped to let her eyes adjust. She waited in a small room, an entry, and someone had lit four candles and anchored them in a bowl set on a small wooden table set to her right. Their flames cast an eerie flicker on the stone wall.

Mosha took her hand and led her through a door on the far side, which opened into a restaurant of some kind. People sat in ones and twos, eating at the tables. Glances slid their way.

Mosha led her around the perimeter of the diner and through another door, which he closed behind them. A large table dominated the window-less room, and a sconce of candles perched atop it. Mosha sat near the head and motioned for Kiera to sit, too. A woman about her own age came in, brunette and very pretty, and set down two steaming mugs. She winked at Mosha and left without a word.

"Did you take me back here so I won't frighten the people out there?" Kiera asked.

Mosha grinned as he sipped. "No, Kiera. Just wanted some privacy."

Kiera slipped off her coat and folded her hands around the drink. It felt deliciously hot. "So what do you want to talk to me about?" she asked.

Mosha leaned back in his chair and regarded her for a moment. His eyes glittered in the candlelight. "Many things, Lady Kiera." He sighed and crossed his arms over his chest.

His gesture reminded her of Laszlo, who did that so often.

"I wanna'd to wait ta tell ye these things, but I am forced ta do it now. I hope that ye'll keep that in mind."

"Well, that's really cryptic," Kiera said, and took a drink. A hot, bitter tea sweetened with cream. Yum.

"Kiera, I am going ta begin by asking ye to tell me the truth, all right? No matter the question. Even if it seems odd." He held up a hand. "And I promise ta keep yer secrets close."

"That means you won't tell?"

"I willna tell a soul. On my honor."

"All right, but the reverse has to be true then, too. You have to be honest with me, and I of course give my word to keep what you tell me secret. Deal?"

He nodded. "Done."

"First, how are ye, Kiera?"

She made a face. "What kind of question is that?"

"Ye promised," he reminded her.

She forced a smile. "Um. Well, I'm all right."

"The truth."

"If you're asking about Laszlo, I really am all right, Mosha."

He made a disbelieving face.

"Yes. I am sad, and yes, I dream about him and it hurts like hell to see him. But I am getting through it. Alex helps. My magic helps. Emmy helps. Marco helps." She shrugged, then looked up at him. "And you help."

Mosha reached over and took her hand. "I was hopin' ta be on that list." He smiled warmly. He kept her hand but drank his tea with the other. "So if ye still want him, why dunna ye agree to be his mistress then? He cares for you. You know he does. Is it such a terrible thing if he really cares for you?"

Kiera pulled her hand away and covered it with the other. "I can't do that, Mosha." She shook her head. "I see how things are here, and you may think it's selfish of me, or whatever, but I can't do that. I will not share a man with another woman. And Mosha, if you're asking for him, I will say that I thought I'd made that plain to him. If I hadn't, let me be clear now. No. I will not." She lifted her hands and spread them apart. "Imagine sharing your woman with another man, Mosha! I know none of you will do that, and it's bullshit for him to ask me to."

Mosha grinned at her. "He did not ask, understand me, but I will admit ta ye now that I'd'a thought a great deal less of ye if ye'd agreed." He drank the last of his tea. "Now that ye have been there some time, what do you think of the Skani?"

Kiera blinked at the change of subject, but then scoffed. "I hate them."

Genuine amusement lit Mosha's face.

Kiera warmed to her subject. "I hate everything about them. They're selfish. The men are pigs. They're cruel. They're thoughtless and ignorant. Should I go on?"

He considered. "So will ye go home when ye learn how?"

Kiera shifted back in her chair. Mosha leaned forward and again took hold of her hand. She sat up, then lifted their joined hands from the table. "You need to tell me right now why you're holding my hand."

Mosha sat back in his chair. "Yes, Kiera, that is a good question." He leaned forward and extended his right hand—not the hand he had been holding hers with, she noted. She looked at his hand, then his face. He held his hand out until she took it. "Now clear your mind, Kiera, and pull just a little water from me. The thinnest thread."

"Pull water?"

"People have elements, too, as I am sure ye know."

Kiera closed her eyes and sank in to the tempest that was Mosha. Unlike the streams she was used to finding scooting across the ground or soaring through the sky, the energy in Mosha pooled or streamed, and sometimes both, like rivers and lakes, the pools slowly spinning, the streams flowing. There were small fire storms in his heart and his brain. "This is amazing," she whispered.

"Find water and pull a strand," he said, equally quiet. "A small strand. Pull it inta you."

Kiera pulled a thread from a pool in his middle and threaded it out his right arm, out his hand, then into her left hand.

She gasped. Warmth, affection. Amusement. A slip of fear, buried deep. Determination. Kiera let go and opened her eyes.

"I was feeling you, wasn't I? What you're feeling."

He nodded once, wiping his hand. He extended it to her again. "Try once more," he said. She took his hand, then closed her eyes and concentrated. To her surprise, she found nothing. She concentrated again, straining outward, sending her sight out through her hand. And into nothing. It was like he wasn't there.

She let go of his hand. "Is that some kind of shielding?"

He nodded approvingly. "A good guess."

"Will you show me?"

"I will. Now tell me if ye will be going home once ye learn how."

"Mosha, I already told you that I won't. I can't leave Marco here to die, which is exactly what would happen, even if I hid him first. He's not so great at staying out of trouble, as you may have noticed. I gave my word."

"But if ye hate it so much, what will ye do?"

Kiera tried to be matter of fact. "Learn as much magic as I can. Wait until Marco is older and then maybe he'll want to go someplace else. I pray so. Maybe someday it will be safe for Marco, for me, to go home, but that won't be for some time."

"But Kiera, it is not going ta be easy. Ye could go. Get some protection for Marco. Go home."

"Mosha, this is you testing me again. I can tell. My answer isn't going to change." She held out her right hand. "I assume you held my hand so you could tell if I lied. Take it. I'm not lying." Mosha ignored her hand, so she dropped it and sat back. Then she sat up. "Wait a minute. The other day you told me you felt my grief from the river. That's big power, sensing emotions, isn't it? Especially from that far. And you shouldn't be able to do something as complicated as a shield must be." She pointed a finger at him. "You're a mage, aren't you?"

Mosha flashed his teeth, but the smile didn't reach his eyes. "Mayhap. But if you tell anyone, I will see you dead."

Kiera held up her hands in surrender. "Whoa, whoa. If you don't trust me, you shouldn't have shown me that." She rolled her head back and stared at the ceiling. "I won't tell anybody. Jesus Christ." She lifted her head and looked at him. "Do you want to see if I'm lying?"

"I dunna need ta hold yer hand ta tell if ye lie, Kiera," Mosha said tiredly.

"Then why this hand-holding charade?"

"I s'pose it's because I thought it would be better if you guessed than I told ye."

"Why are you telling me?" she demanded.

"I will answer yer questions when mine are finished." He sounded a tad annoyed.

Kiera was, too. She crossed her arms. "All right, Mosha. What else?'

"Who is Alex's father?"

"What?"

"Alex's father."

Kiera shook her head. "No."

He looked puzzled. "Why not tell me?"

"No."

Mosha sighed, then pushed away from the table and stood up. He went to the door, opened it, and called out. A moment later, he asked for more tea before closing the door. The same woman brought two more steaming cups and whisked the empties away. She smiled at Mosha on her way out.

"Kiera. How old is Marco?"

"I don't know. Sixteen?"

"Then three cycles until he is grown." He leaned back. "Ye dunna have the time, Kiera."

"What does that mean?"

"What do ye know about the Alak? The shifters?"

"Very little, I'm embarrassed to say."

"Well, they are not animals, not like the Skani say. Ye need ta know that, Kiera. They are just as smart as Skani. They dunna run and hunt animals, though they could if they wanna. But then so can Skani." He leaned up, laid his hands on the table. "They can be born of shifters or they might

196

have one full-Skani parent. Either way, they come ta their shifting at puberty." He sat up and made sure she was looking at him. "And sometimes as young as nine or ten."

Kiera was puzzled. She lifted her hands in a "so" gesture.

"Who is Alex's father?"

Kiera's jaw dropped. "No," she shook her head. "He wasn't a shifter. He was born in, I don't know, Idaho or something. He moved to, uh, my hometown in high school."

Mosha took her hand. "How do ye know?"

"Well, wouldn't someone see him? Shifting, I mean?"

"Kiera, I have lived fifty-six cycles. I have lived in this deconn for forty-eight of those. Not one Skani guessed I was a mage in that time."

"But—" Kiera folded her arms on the table and dropped her head down. After a minute, or two, Kiera sat up. She heaved a sigh, then made herself smile at Mosha. He had been under no obligation to tell her a damned thing. "How can you tell?" she asked weakly.

Mosha's eyes held understanding. "The way he heals," he answered. "By the time ye get back, he'll be completely healed up."

Kiera stood up. "Emmy!"

Mosha motioned for her to sit back. "Emmy wunna say a thing."

"How can you be sure?"

"Her love for that boy fills the room, Kiera, and she wunna see him hurt for any reason. The two of ye must keep him home nexturn and the turn after so no one will know."

Kiera nodded, then shook her head.

"Has he always healed fast?"

Kiera dropped her eyes. "Not noticeably."

Mosha sounded chagrined. "And here ye are lying and ye promised ye wunna."

Kiera looked up, trying to push down the panic. "Mosha. I can't tell you."

Mosha laughed harshly. "What? Is it bigger than Alex being a shifter? Or do ye wanna me to tell ye that I know he's not yern? Or maybe, maybe it's that ye canna have children?"

Kiera rocked back. She grabbed her coat, hands shaking, and turned her back to put it on. She felt Mosha's hand on her shoulder and jerked away. Fear and pain bunched hard in her belly. She dropped her coat and put her head in her hands.

Mosha's voice was gentle. "Kiera, I'm a healer. I had to heal ye, remember, the turn we found ye." He patted her shoulder. "And stop worrying. I told ye, girl, that yer secrets are safe with me."

"What do you want?" she asked from under her hands. Her head was pounding, so she sat down and rested her elbows on the table. She refused to look at him. "What is it you want me to do?"

Mosha made a sound of irritation and slapped his hand on the table. "Gods all damn it, Kiera!"

She looked up at his angry face.

"Now yer thinking like the whoreson Skani and I dunna appreciate being held as one either. Gods, girl! I dinna bring ye hear ta blackmail ye! I brought ye here ta tell ye the truth, and to ask ye ta help!"

Kiera sniffled, and wiped her nose on her sleeve. Mosha whuffed and tossed her a cloth napkin. "And I wanna ye ta know ye can trust me." He leaned back and put his feet on the table. "I will tell ye the truth, Kiera. I wanna use ye. Yer already a very strong mage. Ye have showed that yer a good woman, and a brave one, and that yer loyal and wunna be swayed.

"I asked ye about Laszlo because when I tell ye what I want, gods know I dunna want ye to do it for him. Girl, I dunna wanna ye to do it for me, either, or even for Alex, though I will accept that if that's all there is. I know yer heart is hurt for the slaves, Kiera." He took a deep breath and looked her in the eye. "What we are is planning a rebellion."

Kiera sat up. "Against the Skani?" she asked blankly. "But how will I be able to help? That keep is filled with mages! There have to be hundreds! I'm not trained! I can't take them all on!"

Mosha shook his head. "How many mages have ye met, Kiera?"

She considered. "Valen, and Leith. Um. Marco, of course. Those two men I met at the brooding party were mages. One of them told me he did weather stuff. I haven't met very many people, Mosha. I just don't know."

"Hmmmm. How many mages go ta magic lessoning?"

"Just Valen and Marco, but the others could just be finished with their training."

He sat up. "Mayhap. We need ta find out," he said firmly.

She took a deep breath. A part of her wished she needed time to consider. "All right. I'll help. Like you knew I would. I don't know how helpful I'll turn out to be, but I have to do something. Now show me how to shield. And tell me how many mages we have on our side."

Mosha sat back.

"Wait a minute. Wait a minute. Mosha, Alex told me that he can feel magic. I did the same thing my teacher did to me. That day Valen made me fall. I pulled small strands of each element, one at a time, and shredded them, and then sent them out over him. That was when he took off on that horse, but he told me later he felt them. I have two questions. First, when does a mage come into their magic, and two, how can a shifter be a mage too? Isn't that impossible?"

"Do ye think he told the truth?"

"He could have lied. He wanted to get out of punishment. What with this and that, I didn't test him again. But I will. Nexturn." She looked up at Mosha. "Is it possible? Or could it be that he is a mage, and that's why he heals fast?"

Mosha sighed. "Kiera, he is a shifter. Mages dunna heal fast. But it is possible that he is a mage, too. It is rare, but it can happen. Ye need ta test him again. As ta when the magic comes, it is like the shifters. Mainly at puberty, though sometimes younger and sometimes older. Ye canna tell the strength by the age, either, as ye yerself showed."

"Well, I have time to figure out how to deal with this." She looked at her hands, still pressed flat on the table. "And who are you, Mosha, in this big rebellion?"

She heard him smile. "The leader."

PART II

Chapter 16

Dark had fallen by the time Kiera made her way up the gravel drive to Vayu's keep. Home. Ha. She hurried into the manse, stripped off her coat, and padded up the stairs. Thoughts tumbled through her mind. Could they pull this off? What kind of chance did they have, really? And she still needed Mosha to show her how to shield. Maybe tomorrow? She shuddered at the thought of anyone being able to read her feelings.

She wondered why she had been so quick to agree to help. But what else could she have done? She couldn't stand by and let the horrors of this place go on, not when she knew she could do something to help. Did Mosha have more mages than just her? Her and himself? She prayed that Vayu had fewer than she feared, or at least that most of them wouldn't, or couldn't fight. Why would he want her, a woman, to be a war mage if he had others who could do it? Right?

She wondered what would happen to Alex if she were killed, and that stopped her in her tracks. She would have to make sure she didn't take those kinds of risks.

Why don't I just leave? a small voice inside her asked as she started to walk again. *Why don't I just take Alex and run away? Surely we would be able to find someplace safe to live until I could find out how to go home. I could take Marco, too.*

But where would that be? And she knew that Vayu would pronounce her a traitor, and Marco, too, if he came, which he'd have to, because Vayu would certainly kill him if she left and he stayed.

And if she did, surely Vayu would send his army after her. She was a powerful fire mage, not just a recalcitrant boy and a teenaged mistress. Since everyone was at war with everyone else, he would probably suspect she was defecting to some other side. He would probably send the army, or at least give them orders if they found her.

202

And that would mean that Laszlo would be under orders to capture, and maybe even kill her.

The voice replied, *You'd burn them up.*

She stopped again. Even if she could turn her fire on Laszlo, and she wasn't sure she could, the fire hadn't burned him. He had walked right through it.

She turned the corner and entered the hall leading to her room.

How in the hell had he done that?

She shook her head. There had to be an explanation. Were shifters resistant to fire? No; the dogs had fallen when she burned them, even before she called lightning. Well maybe just some of them had that resistance, like some mages were born to fire.

She needed to find out his birthday. Maybe it was related? Were shifters born during fire months resistant to fire? Maybe some of the mages were resistant to fire, too?

I wonder who I can ask—

A hand grabbed Kiera and pulled her into a doorway she hadn't seen. She didn't even have time to scream. From behind, arms wrapped around her and yanked her tight against a chest, pulling her into a semi-darkened room, someone's bedroom. She wriggled an arm free and elbowed the attacker in the stomach, but she didn't have good leverage and the blow didn't phase him. She cocked a leg and stomped down on one of his feet as hard as she could. The attacker grunted—she could tell that one hurt—but did not let go. Using her whole body, she tried to twist away.

"*A'kala!* Stop!" A commanding voice.

Kiera went still and let out an exasperated sigh. "Let go of me. Now."

Laszlo released her and she turned to face him. "What. The. Fuck. Are. You. Doing?" she spat. "I do not want to hear anything you have to say." She turned to go out the door but his hand grabbed her shoulder and spun her around. He reached behind her and slammed the door shut.

She clenched her hands and thought really, really hard about popping him one.

"*A'kala,*" he began, but Kiera interrupted.

"Do not," she pointed her finger at him, "call me that."

Laszlo put his hands on her shoulders. "You left with Mosha. Where did he take you?" he asked.

Kiera pushed his hands off. "Don't spy on me, Laszlo. It's none of your business. I want to go home. Alex was hurt today and I need to go see him."

"Apparently not badly enough for you to stay." For the very first time, she heard pleading in his voice. "Give me a moment."

"Go home to your wife," she shot back.

His face hardened. "Where were you?"

"I told you it's none of your business. That means that I'm not going to tell you." She lifted her hands in an exasperated gesture. "Laszlo, there's nothing between us anymore, okay? That means that you don't get to ambush me in halls, or follow me around," she closed her eyes briefly, "or anything else. Nothing. Okay? I am going on with my life here, Laszlo, and I want you to go on with yours. You have your wife, and you need to do the right thing by her." She tried to breathe around the knot in her chest, but she couldn't bring herself to look at his face. "And please don't beat up the men around me." She frowned. "Even if they deserve it."

He grabbed her shoulder and squeezed. Her breath caught. It hurt, a little. So much like everything else that was Laszlo. Without raising her eyes she lifted her hand across her chest and let it drop over his fingers. For a moment, just long enough to ease the ache.

She made herself pull out from under his hand and turned to leave, but a thought made her stop at the door. She had to ask this favor. She had to ask this favor of *him*. "I beg one promise, Laszlo. If you ever loved me at all, swear to me, give me your oath, that you will protect Alex if something happens to me." The rest came out in a whisper. "No matter what happens."

She heard him come up behind her. He leaned down and kissed the top of her head. "I swear it," he said, and she let herself out.

WHEN KIERA OPENED the door to her rooms, she found Alex sleeping. And healed. Completely. Emmy was sitting on his bed, sewing or embroidering. Or something domestic. Kiera couldn't tell, but when Emmy looked up, she put it aside and stood.

Kiera looked at Emmy. For the first time, Emmy looked back without a ghost of a flinch. Instead she looked defiant. *Hmmm, and perhaps protective,* Kiera thought.

Kiera smiled wryly. She strode to Emmy and, without ceremony, pulled her into a hug. Emmy stiffened a little, but after only the briefest pause she hugged Kiera back. "It's going to be all right," Kiera told her, meaning it. "We'll keep him home and out of sight for the next couple of days. And pray this doesn't happen again."

Emmy pulled away and nodded, then sat down and picked up her sewing. Kiera went to pour herself a glass of wine.

Someone knocked on the door.

Emmy shot up.

"Cover him up," Kiera whispered, and went to open the door.

It was Marco. Kiera smiled but stood blocking the door.

Marco frowned and pushed past her, then dropped down on the couch. He put his feet up and lay back.

"Marco, what do you want?" she asked.

He looked at her oddly. "Kiera, it's a brooding moon and we're supposed to be lovers," he reminded her. "If I miss a night here, people will talk, and others will approach you."

"Not even one night?" she asked.

He shook his head. "Why is Alex in bed?"

She barred the door and poured herself a glass of wine. She held up the carafe to him and then Emmy. Marco nodded, so she poured him one, too. "Alex got in a fight today at school. I think the healing tired him out." She sat down their glasses on the table and perched on the opposite couch.

"Is he all right?"

"Yeah."

"Something is strange, Kiera. What's wrong?"

She smiled. "I'm just tired, Marco."

"Kiera, you are such a terrible liar. Has anyone told you that? If they haven't, they should have." He leaned forward. "You need to think about what you're going to say ahead of time. Choose all of the details, from before it happened to afterward. Think what you would feel and practice feeling it. Don't tell anyone anything until you have done that, and even then sometimes it doesn't work." He stopped a moment, considering. "Denial works best, then. Don't ever admit that you're lying. One time confirmed and none will believe you again." He sat back and drank his wine.

Kiera laughed. "I can't believe that you're lessoning me in lying, Marco."

He closed his eyes. "You haven't lived here as long as I have."

She scooted back and pulled her legs up on the couch, then laid back. "Marco, I want to meet some of the mages here. How can I do that?"

"Are you changing the subject?"

"Yes. But I really want to know."

"Tell me about Alex."

"There's nothing to tell. He got hit, he cried, he came home. I called for a healer. He is sleeping."

Marco got up and walked toward Alex's bed. Emmy dropped her sewing and jumped up to stand in front of Alex's bed. Marco stopped. He looked back at Kiera, puzzled, and turned back to Emmy.

Because there was nothing else she could say, Kiera said, "It's all right, Emmy. Marco isn't going to hurt him."

After a moment, and what might have been a glare, Emmy stood aside. Marco pulled back the covers and looked at Alex, who grunted and turned over in his sleep.

Marco looked for a long moment, then covered him back up. Concern radiated from him. "Where did he get hit?" he asked Emmy.

Kiera held her hands in her lap. "He was kicked, he said, but he was too upset to talk much about it. The healer said he would be fine. He just needs some rest, I think."

Marco paced back out to the couch. Emmy flashed a relieved look from behind his back, then sat gently back down on Alex's bed.

Marco picked up his wine and took a long drink. "So why do you want to meet the other mages?" He grinned. "Are you tired of me already?"

Kiera suppressed her sigh of relief. Marco was right. She needed to think these things through a lot more thoroughly than she had been doing. Living with the Skani was certainly an education. Why did she feel so stupid? Had she sheltered herself from the truth before this? Certainly people could be deceptive, but it just had never seemed to be to this degree, with this many layers. Maybe because circumstances differed here so drastically, or because the stakes seemed so much higher. Or maybe the truth was that she had spent her life willfully, luxuriously ignorant, focusing on herself at the expense of the rest of the world. Well, she could not afford either selfishness or ignorance anymore.

"How many mages are there, Marco? I guess I'm wondering how many others are like me. Are there other fire mages, even ones who can work with fire just a little? There are so many things that I want to know how to do, if I can, and I'm sure there are lots of things I wouldn't think of unless someone suggested it." Most of that was the truth, she thought. That probably made it more believable. "And you know that Agni makes me go so slow. I hate it sometimes."

Marco cocked his head to the side and held a small smile. "Better," he said, and they both laughed.

"I'm serious," she said, still laughing, and took the last drink. She got up to pour more, and Marco held out his glass.

"Kiera, you don't want to know the other mages. There are some that are all right, I guess, but most of them are devious snakes who will do almost anything to gain favor from my father."

Kiera twisted her glass in her hands. "And if that's true, then why are you so different?"

"I don't know." He looked a little sullen, or something, so Kiera changed the subject.

She sat up. "I want to meet some mages, Marco" she said. "Will you help me?"

"We could go to another brooding party," he suggested jokingly.

"Are there other events like that, where mages get together, I mean?"

He shook his head. "Not really."

She breathed out. "Then that will be fine. How many mages are there, Marco?"

He looked at her sharply. "You have been here for what, three moons, Kiera? Why are you only now interested?"

"Marco, honestly, up until now I have been trying to get used to the idea that I'm stuck here. You mentioned denial before. Well, that is exactly what I have been doing. Hiding my head in the sand, asking no questions and looking no further than my own nose. But I have to live here, and I am expected to be a mage. A skilled one. If you father makes me a war mage, then I would really like to be able to come back from wherever he sends me.

"In my life back home I learned that I can't really expect to win if I don't learn as much as I can about everything I can, because sometimes you win for the strangest reasons, ones you never saw coming. But if you hadn't done that little extra you simply wouldn't have known and you would have lost. Most people are lazy, Marco, and so you have to know more and spend time practicing so you can be better. And you have to take chances."

Marco raised his eyebrows. "You made your point," he said. "And it's a good one."

She smiled. "Where can I learn about shifters?" she asked. Her head was feeling a little light. She sat her glass down. No more wine.

"Why about shifters?"

"Well, that's who I'll be working with, right? And I know I'll be fighting them."

"Kiera, I don't know much about them. Not really." Marco slotted his eyes. "And I don't think many people do. Maybe Mosha or someone like that would help you."

Kiera took another drink and nodded. "Do you know why they can't be mages?"

He considered a moment. "No. I don't. In fact, I don't understand why they're not."

"Me either," she said over the top of her glass. When had she picked it back up? "Do they have to change? I mean, like at full moon or is there some certain thing that makes them shift against their will?"

"I don't think so. No, wait. I think they have to change at first. Like when they first learn to do it. It happens when they're pretty young, I think.

Ten or twelve. But I think they learn how to control it and then they just do it when they want to."

"Why are they so strong? And why do they heal so fast?"

Marco looked up at her sharply.

Kiera stared back. Inside she roiled and called herself a hundred kinds of fool. *Stupid, stupid, stupid. I should have just let it drop.*

"No one knows, Kiera, and if they do, they're not telling."

Inside she sighed with relief.

Marco downed the rest of his wine and got up to pour another glass. She held out hers and he filled it. She took a long drink.

"I won't tell," he said, and she choked, shooting liquid strings across the fabric of the couch. He came over and slapped her back until she stopped coughing.

"What?" she finally croaked out. He handed her a cloth and she started blotting the crimson droplets from her dress. Emmy had come to stand behind her. Her fists were clenched, and Kiera tried to catch her eye. She fervently hoped that Emmy wasn't planning to pummel Marco. For one, she wasn't sure which side she'd take.

He sat down, glass in his hand, with a face more serious than Kiera had ever seen him wear. "Kiera, you idiot, you saved my life. Twice. And not just saved it, like giving me food when I'm hungry. No. You faced an army for me, and for Allie." He stopped, looked down. Then up and held her eyes. "And then, Kiera, you gave up everything, including your freedom, for me."

Kiera opened her hands. "I couldn't let him kill you, Marco! Jesus Christ! Don't make it sound like I was a hero or something."

A tinge of sadness wove through Marco's words. "And how many others did you have to push aside?"

She looked away because she had to.

He knelt down in front of her, and took her hand.

Startled, she looked at his earnest face.

She set her glass down with her free hand and tried to gently pull her other away. "No, Marco, don't—"

"Kiera, listen," he interrupted. "All right?"

She looked at their hands. Both of his hands were wrapped round her left. After a shockingly short moment of ambivalence, and without closing her eyes, she pulled a thread of water from him.

Affection. A lot of warm affection. Pride. Determination. All bound together with a wisp of shame.

She dropped her free hand on his and squeezed.

"Well Kiera, what that means is—well, it means that I owe you more than I can ever repay." Unflinching fervor. "What it means is that I'm your man for life. I may not have majority yet, but in three cycles I will, and when I do, all I have is yours. Yours and Alex's."

Kiera made a strangled noise. "No, Marco." She shook her head. "You do not need to hitch yourself to me, or marry me, or—whatever. Your friendship, and your loyalty, and your discretion," she added as an afterthought, "is more than enough."

Surprise. Amusement. Affection. He barked out a laugh. He let go of her hand and stood, then plopped down on the couch next to her, acting like the teenage boy he really was. "I wasn't offering to marry you!" he laughed, then grew sober. He looked at her. "But I will if I need to."

"Thank you, Marco," was all she could think of to say to that. "But that will not be necessary." She prayed. "Here's my biggest fear for the present: how will I keep Alex from being enslaved? What if he starts, uh, you know, before you are old enough to protect him? And what will happen even after you are?" Saying it out loud made it more real. And more scary. Her next words were scarier, even to her. "I won't let it happen, Marco. I'll burn this city to the ground first."

Out of the corner of her eye she saw Emmy flinch.

Marco grimaced and looked thoughtful, apparently unperturbed by her apocalyptic threat. "I don't know yet."

SOMETIME DURING THE NIGHT Kiera woke, gasping, from a nightmare. She sat up and pulled the pillow to her chest. She rocked back and forth, unable to wash Julia's broken face from her eyes. Or Alex's. Or Laszlo's. But they'd been yoked first.

She lay back, but sleep wouldn't come. Kiera stood, pulled on her robe, then took it back off.

Her bladder led her to the bathroom. She shuffled out and crawled on the bed. Rubbed her eyes.

Her heart wouldn't stop pounding.

She got up and pulled on her old pants and coat, then went out into the hall and let herself walk.

It was late. Early. Air dominated the flows, twin streams overhead, each wider than a bus, flowing silently eastward. Two hours past midnight, nighttide, then.

She glided down the stairs, then ghosted through the deserted great hall. Only a fraction of the candles burned, just enough to jaundice the walls. She slipped out the door toward the school.

The wind drew the fire from her face as she crunched the path to the river. The white moon stared haughtily through lazy clouds. Icy mold grew on her hood where her breath billowed.

When she reached the frozen water, she dropped to her knees in the snow. Almost touching it. Just inches from her knees. She lay on her back with one hand on the ice until Orion slid below the horizon.

KIERA WOKE to a pounding headache the next morning. She groaned and turned to look at Alex, who was lying awake, tucked deep in the covers. He grinned when she smiled at him. She held up her arms and he hopped out of bed and crawled in beside her. She looked around, but Emmy wasn't here yet. Or maybe—Kiera hoped—she was getting breakfast.

When he started to squirm, Kiera sent Alex to bathe. When he finished, she took her own. Emmy came in while she was dressing. She had food.

They ate in silence. Neither Emmy nor Kiera seemed to want to bring up yesterday.

When they were finished, Kiera went to the couches and lit the fire, then sank back. "Alex," she called, "I want you to come over here." He looked up at her curiously. "I want to play that game again."

After he plopped down beside her, Kiera asked, "Were you telling me the truth when you told me you could feel something that day on the horses? I promise I won't get mad if you weren't."

Emmy sat down beside Alex and squeezed his hand. He looked up at her and smiled.

Kiera looked at her hands.

"I wasn't lying, Keer," Alex said.

Kiera forced a smile. "I want to try again, okay? I want you to tell me if you feel anything, and if so, what it feels like." She gave him a look she hoped seemed sincere. "It is fine if you don't. Okay?"

He nodded.

Kiera tried all four, and Kiera's heart sank lower the further they went. Alex claimed to feel "something" when she sent out the air, which she did last, but he couldn't articulate what, and Kiera found herself doubting him. Doubting everything but what Mosha had said.

Someone knocked at the door and Kiera sprang off the couch. "Into the bathroom," she hissed at Alex, who looked startled, but he went. "Stay in there. Take a bath."

"I already took a bath," he whined.

"Take another one!"

Her hair was still wet, but she was dressed, so she answered the door.

It was Mosha.

A bruise blossomed like a rose on his cheek, and his lower lip had been split, but he smiled. "Can I come in?" he asked.

Kiera blinked, then stood back and motioned him in. "Alex," she called after she shut the door, "you can come out."

Alex marched out of the bathroom and flung himself down on his bed.

Mosha walked over to Alex and knelt down in front of him. "Son, how are ye?" he asked him.

"I'm okay," he answered, sitting up, and Mosha nodded.

"Ye look better thisturn. Any aching? Do ye see funny?"

Alex shook his head and Mosha nodded again. He put a hand on Alex's head. "Good. I asked Kiera ta keep ye home thisturn and nexturn just ta be sure." He stood up. "Ye stay in these rooms and rest all ye can."

"All right," Alex answered. Mosha walked to the dining table. He picked up a piece of bread and took a bite.

Emmy sat down on Alex's bed. "How 'bout a game of filken?" she asked, and he grinned. Emmy went to the closet to fetch the game and Kiera motioned Mosha to the couch.

When he'd sat down, Kiera asked him, "What happened to you?"

He snickered, an odd response to getting smacked in the face, Kiera thought. "Aw, I got in the middle of a disagreement," he grinned. "Don't worry yer head about it one bit."

"Someone hit you at least twice," Kiera accused.

"Mayhap. But I sent him ass first through one of th'walls, so we're even," he countered, still grinning.

Kiera rolled her eyes at his bravado, then laughed. She couldn't help it. "What can I do for you today, Mosha?"

"I want ye ta skip magickin' thisturn and come take lunch with me."

Kiera looked to Alex, who played the domino game with Emmy. "Will you be okay if I go out for a while?"

He shrugged. "Yeah."

Kiera frowned. She got up and walked over, then sat down on his bed and, pointedly not looking at Mosha, picked up Alex's right hand and held it in her own.

Annoyance. Resentment. She almost let go.

"Do you want me to stay?" she asked quietly.

Surprise. Annoyance. "No," he said, and she was quite certain he meant it.

She let go and stood up, wiping her hands on her dress. She looked at him for a moment before she nodded and turned away.

Kiera dried her hair as much as she could with a cloth, then braided it and twisted it up in a roll. She secured it with a couple of thin sticks that had been painted yellow.

She pulled on her coat, still avoiding looking at Mosha, and slipped out into the hall.

They didn't speak until they were outside.

"Do ye wanna talk about it?" he asked gently.

"No."

They strolled into the city. The sun shone, and the snow had crept back as it melted, revealing a layer of grime beneath the cracking facades of the buildings they passed. They turned a corner into an alley and Mosha abruptly thrust Kiera into a deep doorway on the left. He piled in next to her and pressed her against the wall with his body. She looked at him, puzzled, and he motioned her to be quiet.

Footsteps entered the alley. Mosha held a hand over his face and whispered through his fingers, too softly for Kiera to make out the words. A man, huge, dark, bulky, and dressed in a parka, walked right past them, not two feet away. He couldn't have missed them—Kiera in her bright yellow dress and blue coat pasted against a stone gray entry—but he never turned his head.

After he passed, Mosha pulled her out of the doorway. Without looking at her, he again motioned for her to stay quiet. After a half a minute he grabbed her hand and pulled her down the alley at a jog. They seemed to follow the man, but he had gone.

Mosha took her to the right at the next corner, then right again at the next. She was breathing hard, but tried to keep up. He turned left into the next alley and pulled her into a doorway about halfway down. She leaned over, hands on thighs, and gulped in as much air as she could take.

Mosha grinned at her, then knocked. Two fast, three slow. The door opened and he pulled her quickly inside, then dropped the bar.

Kiera turned to look at the woman who had opened the door. To her great surprise, it was the same woman who had served their tea yesterday. She had braided her dark brown hair, though, and her long blue dress showed off her more than generous curves. She flashed a smile at Kiera.

Kiera smiled back, but an unpleasant frisson raced down Kiera's back as she pulled off her coat. The woman lifted it from her hands and draped it across a chair by the door. Mosha slid out of his heavy jacket and dropped it over Kiera's.

Kiera followed the woman through a well-lit, narrow hall into a dingy, but wide-open, room that smelled stale like unwashed bodies. Only one window, cut too high in the far wall, let in the sunlight. Someone had pushed back the tables and pulled a couple dozen chairs together, but three at the other end of the room had been tucked next to the wall and turned toward the audience. The three sat empty, but people occupied most of the others. At least twenty, some blonde, some dark, mostly all men, and they all looked like slaves. Some turned, and Kiera smiled politely.

When they reached the three front-facing chairs, Mosha motioned for her to sit. With a raised eyebrow, she did. He dropped down beside her.

She felt completely ridiculous sitting there facing the audience. What in the world was this about? "Why am I here?" she murmured. "I thought we were going to have lunch."

"Shhhh," he chastened. "Just listen."

Blinking, she leaned back and looked out at the audience.

Mosha stood and took two steps. "My friends, I am pleased to introduce the lady I tole ye about. For her sake, and yers, we will call her Jaya, our victory, for that's what she is." He turned and bowed a little to Kiera, who nodded back, not quite sure of her role in this charade.

"I want ye ta tell her yer stories," he continued, addressing the entire room. "But I don't wanna ye ta tell her yer names." He pointed at a man in the front. "Ye start," he said, then returned to his seat next to Kiera.

She wanted to glare at him, but all thoughts of Mosha fell away as the light hit the face of the man in the front as he stood up. The left half of his face had been torn and crushed and it caverned grotesquely. Not recently; the scars were old and whitened. The web-shaped scars started at his mouth and spread upward, like a cancer, pulling his eyelid tight and ending at the base of his forehead. He wore his stringy blond hair long to hide it.

He walked hesitantly to the front of the room and stared down at Kiera. She could not begin to decipher the look on his face. His fervent blue eyes held hers, perhaps challenging her to flinch. Or look away. Instead she summoned a small smile and tried to pour her heart into it.

Seeming satisfied, he looked down at his feet and then back at her face. He took a deep breath. "My name is Lorgda," he began, his voice strong, and Mosha lifted a hand to stop him. The man looked over at Mosha. "I will say what I will or I will say nothing," he challenged, tone hot, then turned back to Kiera.

"My name is Lorgda," he began again. "And I am a farmer. I have lived here," he spread his arms wide, "for all of my life." Kiera nodded encouragingly. "I have been a slave since before I could walk, lady." He paused, took a breath. "I am one of the ones who takes care of the pigs. Always have."

Kiera didn't know there were pigs, but she should have, she thought.

"When I was one and twenty cycles, five cycles past, Andra came to help us. She had come from the church because she had trouble remembering things. They put her to watching the pigs and some of the other animals. She was frightened of them, so I helped her." He paused. "We worked there together for over a cycle." He paused again. Swallowed.

"One morning, early, she came to the stables. Her face was bruised. Her face and one of her arms. I asked her what had happened but she would not tell me. Well, long and short, she came to my bed that night, and I loved her. For many turns of the stars, we loved each other." He stopped and brushed his face, angrily, as if his feelings offended him.

"One night before supper she disappeared, so I set out to find her. I looked everywhere I could think she might go but she was nowhere to be found. I kept searching, all the night, until close to dawn I thought I heard her crying from far away. It was in the stables back behind of the cows. I guess now she'd gone to get milk for our supper."

He plowed on, emotionlessly, his eyes reliving another time. "Some mage had her pinned in a stable. She was beaten as bad as I ever saw a person beat, but she was still crying." He spoke quietly, evenly. "Her face was smashed bad, and I could see her arm was broken. There was blood on her face, and her dress, and the hay." He drew a breath. "He was sleeping beside her, there in the hay, his hands bloody."

He looked up at Kiera then, eyes feverish. "She saw me then. She saw me and she tried to tell me to go with her eyes. Even then, she dint ask me to help her. She dint want him to hurt me. But he woke and he saw me, and before I could say one word, he jumped up and he threw me on the ground and he kicked me and kicked me and he beat in my face." His hand lifted partway, as if to touch it, but then stopped. He let it drop.

"She died, lady. She died while I lay there on the floor. I heard her breath stop." He looked down and Kiera saw the tears fall, painting wet dots on the cold stone floor. When he spoke, his voice was thick with grief. "I could not help her, lady. And I loved her. I loved her and I never told her that I did."

He started to say more, but shook his head. He turned and went back to his seat.

Hot tears slid down Kiera's face. "Who was he?" she asked. When he didn't answer, she stood. "Who was he?" she shouted, but Lorgda made a gesture that said *does it matter?* and stared at the floor.

Mosha put a hand on one arm to encourage her to sit back down.

The woman who had let her in rose and came to stand in the front. She curtsied. "Lady, my story is not so brutal, but, to me, as important." She wrapped her hands in the folds of her dress. "I was brought here as a child and I went right into the church. I was always real pretty, and when I went to school the boys would smile at me. When I got some older, maybe 12 cycles, the noble boys started to notice me, too. Some would wait for me after school and walk with me back to my bedhouse. I liked it at first, at least until they started touching me. When I tried to say 'no' they would slap me or push me down. It got real bad and so I tried staying in the bedhouse, pretending sick, but after a handful of turns the overseer made me go to school. Even though I begged. She told me she did not believe me." Her eyes did not waver. "Those boys, they hurt me. They did—some very bad things. Sometimes people heard them hurt me there, there in the house of our lord and lady, but nobody ever made them stop.

"When I got older, I asked to be a farmer. They sent me to till the fields and it's very hard work, but no one sees me out there. In the winters I run an eating house. I never go to the house or the church or anywhere near there. But every single turn I fear that one of those boys will see me again, or some other noble will." She stopped, nodded her head and went back to her seat.

"Mosha," Kiera whispered, "Make this stop."

He squeezed her hand.

Another came forward, then another and another. For hours they told her of their beatings, their rapes, their losses, their horror and their shame. None seemed hopeless, or broken, but their words carved holes into Kiera's chest.

It had fallen dark sometime before the last speaker finished. The slaves drifted out in ones and twos. No one stopped to say "goodbye."

Mosha helped her to her feet. She turned to him. "If you weren't already hurt," she rasped, "I would break your goddamned nose." He handed her a glass of water and she drank it all. She slammed the cup down and stared at the table. "Why, Mosha? Why? I already said I would help you."

He took her hand. His voice was strong. "Because I want ye to know what ye fight for. Ye've had a hard life, Kiera, I can tell, and ye have seen some of the sadness here. But ye dunna see so much, Kiera. Most folks up there dunna. It is one thing ta fight for ideas and another ta fight to right the wrong ye have seen. For the people who have been hurt." He gripped her harder. "These folks come in the good and the bad, but nunna them deserved what they got. I have been building this movement for near twenty cycles, Kiera, and for many reasons, including you, now is the time to finish it."

Kiera squeezed her eyes shut. "Take me home."

"WHAT HAPPENED?" Marco cried when Kiera turned from shutting the door.

All she could manage was, "I need to lie down," so he led her to bed and helped her slip under the covers.

Sleep pulled her down like a lover.

CHAPTER 17

AGNI ROSE FROM HER SEAT WITH RAISED BROWS when Kiera arrived early for lessons the next morning, but put her right to work. After less than an hour, Kiera padded back out to the altar room and dropped down onto a bench. "Lady Agni, something is wrong. I'm already exhausted and my head is pounding, but I swear I'm not doing anything different."

Agni clucked. "Lady Kiera, you must actually read the books I have given you. Which marks are these?"

Kiera grimaced, hating having to admit the truth. "I don't know."

"Lady Kiera, how do you think you shape the strands you pull?" Agni pursed her lips. "Think of building a house for a moment. All of your supplies come from outside your body. But in order to fit them into the right shape, you have to use your muscles and your mind. Creating spells is the same, but instead of muscles you use the elements in your body to shape the strands you pull through you, and you draw from them again to send your working out. Every breath you take is a spell, Kiera, and learning to do more than just breathe takes even more energy.

"But there is another aspect to this equation, an external one that affects how difficult it is to do these additional tasks. You know that elements peak and ebb during the turns, and wax and wane during different moons. But during each turn the manner in which elements flow differs as well."

"What do you mean?"

Agni lifted a hand. "When you read *Rotgar's Elementation*, the book I gave you two yesterns to read, you will discover that the cardinals make up the first four marks after nighttide and the first four after noontide. During these times the elements flow strongest of any other time during the turn. What you have noted this morn is how much harder it has been to build storms than during your past lessons here, which has always been in the first four marks after noontide."

Kiera smiled. "Ah. I thought I was just tired."

Agni nodded. "The next four marks, four to eight, both after nighttide and after noontide, are fixed marks. During those times the elements are the most stable. Most general spells work best then, but it is much harder to do powerful workings than during the cardinals. Now, I should tell you that one must be careful during cardinals as they are at no other time, which is why I start mages then. You must learn to control the strongest flows first because I have learned that once a mage begins pulling, he will invariably pull too much—" she flashed Kiera a look—"and after cardinal mastery he no longer poses a risk to himself or others. But during the fixed time the risk is much smaller. It almost like the elements want to balance during that time, and your spells are most stable. It is a reliable time.

"The last four marks, twentieth to nighttide and the eighth to twelfth, the time now upon us, are termed mutables, and during those marks the elements are thinnest and weakest, but fastest flowing, like the last sands out of a glass. It is the best time to work change spells, or creations, but trying to build storms out of those flows will leave your head aching."

Kiera nodded, the relief evident on her face. "That makes a lot of sense. Thank you, Lady Agni. May I ask another question?"

Agni nodded.

"Is it possible to feel another's feelings?"

Agni drew back and slotted her eyes. "What do you mean?"

Kiera struggled for the right words. "I mean, like touch them and know what they're feeling?"

"Has this happened?" Agni asked sharply.

Kiera felt childishly pleased with herself for thinking this through ahead of time. "Well, I thought I felt something when someone grabbed my hand once, and I'm pretty sure it wasn't what I was feeling, if that makes sense. I took their hand afterward, but I couldn't make it happen again."

Agni gauged her for a moment, and then nodded, almost reluctantly. "Lady Kiera, you are forever surprising me," she said. "Yes. It is possible. A powerful water mage can do as you suggest."

Agni paused, as if considering whether to go on. "But I should say that I imagine that such a mage would be most unwelcome here. There have not been any water mages in this deconn for the ten cycles I have been here."

Well, that was pointed enough. Kiera wondered briefly if Agni knew that at least two apparently very powerful water mages, Leith and Mosha, had been living in the deconn longer than she had, but she took the hint, smiled and let the matter drop. "Would you mind taking me through a fire/water storm after lunch?"

AFTER NOON, Marco turned up for his lessons. Unfortunately, so did Valen. Anxious to question Marco about the manse's mages, Kiera slipped away and tried to find Marco after they settled in. There weren't that many doors, she reasoned, and she should be able to hear him, or something.

At the third door she heard someone crying. A woman. No; maybe a man. She put her hand on the latch and lifted it up as quietly as she could. She pushed the door open and peered inside.

It was exactly like the room she used. The same size, the same stone, the same coldness seeping in from every wall. What differed was the dark-haired man crouched in the middle. He was naked, he had tucked his head, and he had wrapped his arms around his knees.

Kiera could feel the magic in the room. It was heavy, thick, winding in sluggish circles. Earth.

The magic surged and the man jerked back, losing his balance and falling on his bare bottom onto the cold stone floor. One of his legs shot out, and he writhed on the ground in some kind of seizure.

Kiera stepped in and snicked the door closed.

Valen was standing against the wall on her right, where she couldn't have seen him until she was in the room. She marched over to him, but he held his eyes closed in apparent concentration.

She waited until she was right in front of him. Leaned forward. "Stop!" she screamed into his face.

Valen slid open cold blue eyes. Anger seeped up from his mouth and across his face.

The magic died. The sounds from behind her did, too, and the man cried out again.

Valen slapped her hard, knocking her back a step. She raised a hand to touch her burning face.

"You filthy, evil son of a bitch," she snarled. "You monster."

He raised his hand to strike her again.

Kiera held his eyes. "Touch me again, you piece of shit, and I swear to God I will burn you alive."

The moment stretched. His eyes glittered.

She didn't need to touch him to know what he wanted, and for the first time in her life she wanted to murder. She let herself imagine him burning, writhing in her flames. She hoped he saw it in her eyes.

The door burst open. He lowered his hand but his eyes never left hers. Kiera did not turn around.

"What happened?" Agni asked, rushing across the room to put a hand on Kiera's shoulder. Kiera turned to her, then past her to the shuddering man lying curled upon the floor.

"Lord Valen, what are you doing?" Agni asked Valen, her voice a shade from shrill.

He shrugged. "I was trying to make this shifter change form," he said with a sigh, then pushed past them. He paused at the door, then went through.

Kiera knelt next to the man on the floor. His eyes were shut tight. "It's all right," she whispered, wishing it were.

"Marco!" she called over her shoulder. "Lady Agni," she said, "do you have a blanket? Anything I could use to cover him up?"

Lady Agni shook her head. "That boy," she muttered as she wandered out.

Kiera gritted her teeth, shut it out and focused on the man. "It's all right now," she told him again. She raised her hand to touch his shoulder, but let it drop to her knee. She wouldn't want some stranger to touch her in such degrading circumstances. Especially not naked.

Marco rushed in, eyes blazing. In moments he took in the scene. "I'll get a blanket," he said, and flew out the door.

Kiera sat down on the stone.

Agni came back in with a couple of drying cloths. Kiera grabbed them from her hands and covered him as well as she could. "Is he all right?" Agni asked. Kiera shrugged and pulled her knees up off the cold of the floor.

Marco, trailed by a woman, rushed back in ten minutes later. Marco handed Kiera a blanket, which she wrapped around the still-shivering man.

He held his eyes closed.

The woman knelt down and began examining him with brusque hands. "I am Gilna," she told him. "Do not be frightened. I am a healer."

"I'm so sorry," Kiera whispered before climbing off the floor.

NEITHER SHE NOR MARCO SPOKE on the way back to her room. Once inside, he barred the door and rounded on her.

"What were you doing?" he shouted.

She rubbed her forehead with one hand. "I heard him crying," she said weakly, and plunked down on the couch.

Emmy glanced up from the game she and Alex were playing, but looked away when Kiera turned her head.

Alex stood up and went to sit beside Kiera. He took her hand and glared at Marco. Touched, Kiera kissed his cheek.

Marco turned to the door and put one hand on it. A minute passed, and then another. When he turned, he looked exasperated.

Kiera laughed. She couldn't help it.

"Kiera, this is not funny."

"Sorry," she said, and made herself stop. She patted Alex's hand.

"Kiera, I know you can't help it. The gods know I owe you my own life for acting just as impetuously as you did thisturn. But next time, please, Kiera, find me or Agni or someone before you go barging into a room where Valen is working magic, no matter how horrible. Promise me you will stay away from him, especially alone."

Kiera nodded mendaciously. "I promise."

Marco came and sat down beside her. He wrapped an arm around her shoulders and squeezed for a second. "You are such an idiot," he said, and she made a face at him.

"How many mages are there, Marco, in total? How many sunwyr?"

Marco shot her a look. "What have you gotten into now?" he asked, and she laughed again.

"I have already explained this, Marco. And I want to go to a party."

Marco sat back and stared at her. "There are a handful of sunwyr. You. Me. Father. Mother. Agni. Chanda. And Valen, of course."

"Who's Chanda?" she asked, hiding her surprise. She'd expected so many more.

"He's my cousin. In fact, he just got back from a trip through the nadeconn. He's tall, about as tall as Father. Dark hair. Blue eyes." He waggled his eyebrows. "The same age but about two stone heavier than Valen."

Kiera ignored his volley. "He? Huh. No; I don't remember him. How much is a stone?"

"In what?" He smiled.

Kiera waved it away. "So how many awyr?"

He shrugged. "A hundred, I'd guess. Maybe more."

"And they all live in this, uh, keep?"

"Are you doing reconnaissance?"

She grinned at his teasing. "Please."

He gave her a long, thoughtful look. "Yes. And some of the slaves. Two hundred, maybe." He looked at Emmy, perhaps for confirmation, but she didn't look up. He crossed his arms. "Any more questions?"

"Are there any water mages here?"

"Oh no. Father hates water mages. Water and earth. All our sunwyr are air mages, except you, of course."

"Okay. One more. How many slaves total live in this city?"

He looked up, considering. "Kiera, I don't know for sure. Ten thousand? Maybe more. It's something like that."

Kiera's jaw dropped. "That many?"

Marco shrugged.

She sat back, considering. "Why does he hate water and earth mages?"

"It's really hard to lie around water mages, and there is a lot of lying in this court," he laughed without amusement, "but I don't know for sure. Earth cancels air, and Father will not abide them."

Kiera nodded.

"Is it my turn?" he asked mischievously.

"Later," she promised. "Let's eat and then get ready to go to a party."

Marco had a funny look on his face, but he didn't press her, though she knew he would eventually. She needed to think about what she was going to tell him. She got up and poured them some wine as Emmy rushed out to get dinner, she said, though it was a bit early.

Kiera splashed red wine into her glass, feeling completely flummoxed. She absolutely did not want to involve Marco in her agreement with Mosha, but she just didn't see how she couldn't. She did not want to gamble with his life, and that's exactly what he would be risking if he got involved with this. And if he was found out, there was nothing she would be able to do to save him since she'd likely be executed right along with him.

AFTER DINNER, Kiera asked Marco to take a walk with her. He flashed her an amused look and hopped off the couch.

After they closed the door, Kiera began searching for an open room—an easy task, since no one lived this far down her wing. Marco laughed at her clumsy attempts to pry open locked doors, but she eventually found one open, and empty, and a lot like hers. She motioned him inside and shut the door after making sure no one was around to see them.

There was wood laid for a fire, so she lit it, and gestured to the couch.

He plopped down and sat back with a funny look on his face.

"What?" she said, smiling, but he just shook his head.

She sat on the opposite couch and pulled her feet up. The fire had not yet warmed the room. "Marco," she began hesitantly, "is there any way someone could listen in here?"

He considered, then got up and walked to the door. He opened it, and looked around, then turned back and shrugged. He walked through the room and looked anyplace a person could conceivably hide, but found nothing. When he was finished, he returned to the couch.

"Is there any spell you know that would allow someone to listen in on another person's conversation?" she asked.

"Not that I know of," he said, "although I would love to know it if one existed."

Kiera got up and sat beside him anyway. The quieter the better.

Marco leaned so that his shoulder was resting against hers. "Okay, Kiera, now tell me."

She sighed, then looked into his face. Kiera marveled at how boyish he seemed at times, while at others he seemed almost ancient. He was kind and authoritative, she mused, and moody and sweet, and smart as a whip. She felt honored to have him as her friend.

And frightened to death to put him at risk.

"Marco," she whispered, "I—" she faltered and looked at the floor.

Marco slid off the couch and sat down on the floor in front of her. He reached up and took her hand. He looked so earnest.

She smiled ruefully at him. "Marco," she whispered, "I may need your help. No. I want your help," she clarified, "and I want you to know that you are free to refuse. In fact, if you don't consider all that I have to say very carefully, I won't let you help."

His face was unreadable, but she had the feeling nothing she was about to say would surprise him.

"I have—" she started, and he lifted a hand to stop her.

"Let me guess," he said evenly, and his tone made her heart sink. "You've gotten involved in some kind of rebellion. You were recruited by, oh, probably Mosha. You have committed your magic to help free the slaves. You need to find out how many mages you have to face, and what other defenses the keep has." He looked up at her. "Did I leave anything out?"

She was gaping. "How did you know?"

"Kiera, I have lived in this manse my whole life. This place runs on intrigue and deception. You, on the other hand, are maybe the least deceptive person I've ever met. And that's saying it nicely. I could have said that you're the most terrible liar I can imagine. You changed completely, one turn after meeting with Mosha, from wanting to stay as far away from the rest of the Skani as possible to wanting to become best friends with them all. You asked me about mages, and wouldn't be put off. Anyone, and I mean anyone, who lived here would guess what had happened before the second sentence left your lips."

He paused to take a breath. "I know that you're worried for me, Kiera. I do, and I love you for it. But if you try and remember what I was doing when you met me, I think you'll realize that not only am I going to agree, I'm going to do it no matter the risk, and whether you want me to or not. I hate the things that happen here as much as you do. I have never been able to do anything about it, and the ones who are moving this rebellion would probably never think to ask me because they never get to see me.

Or even if they did they'd probably think I would be a bad choice because Vayu's my father.

"Because I do love and respect you, I waited to see if you'd tell me, if you'd ask me to join you. But I'll tell you the truth, Kiera. Even if you didn't, I would go to Mosha myself."

He stood up and pulled her to her feet and then into a hug.

"God. I'm so bad at this," she whispered, heart pounding. "I am going to get us killed."

"Yes, you're pretty bad at this. Just stick with me, okay? We'll be all right."

"Okay. But don't get killed, either," she begged.

He laughed. "I won't." He let go and stepped back. "Now you need to let me plan how to do this without arousing suspicion, all right?"

Fear warred with panic, but she nodded.

"And you need to take my advice, all right? You have to trust me."

"I do," she said, and kissed his cheek.

CHAPTER 18

"WEAR THIS," MARCO SAID, AND TOSSED Kiera a dress. She held it up and started shaking her head. "Marco, the whole top is practically missing," she complained.

He laughed. "That, my friend, is exactly the point." He walked over and poured some wine. "Emmy," he called, "would you mind getting us some more wine, and maybe something else to eat?" He grinned and put a hand to his chest. "I feel faint."

"Of course, Lord Marco," she said, and scurried out the door.

Kiera rubbed powder into her face in front of the mirror. She frowned after Emmy. "That reminds me, Marco," Kiera said. "Would you be willing to help me train Alex in some basic magic? I tested him, and I think he can feel at least air." She looked at him meaningfully.

Marco set his glass down and came to stand in back of Kiera. He looked at her in the mirror. "He can?"

"I think he can," she corrected. "I don't know what it means," she murmured, "but Mosha is sure about the—the other thing. But I want to help him develop this."

Marco looked thoughtful. "That doesn't make sense. Hmmm. But sure. I'll help."

Kiera dabbed on some colored powder over her eyes.

"More, Kiera." Marco pointed. "Use the gold and the blue ones."

She looked at him, sponge halfway up. "Do you want me to look like a whore?" she said quietly, and more than a touch sullenly.

He winked at her. "No, but I want you to look like you want to look like a whore."

She couldn't help it. She laughed.

He picked up a tube of lip color and tossed it up. Caught it. "That's better," he said between tosses.

"You're sure in a good mood," she remarked, dabbing on lipstick.

"I am happier than I have been in a long time, Kiera." His smile warmed into a grin. "And I'm about to have a lot of fun."

She raised her brows, but he ignored her, tossing the tube. He moved to stand with his back to Alex and spoke quietly.

"I want you to meet my cousin, Chanda," he said, "because I want to know how he thinks. Now. We have been fighting, you and me, although we've gone to the party together. You are really mad at me, Kiera, but you're too ladylike," he flashed a wicked grin, "to show it. I've been looking at other women, you see, and you suspect I've been doing more than that. You're new here, so you haven't settled for the fact that some men just do that."

"And I'm supposed to disclose this to—uh, Chanda?"

"Oh, just let little pieces slip through. I'll be eyeing the ladies while you're dancing with him, and you make a frustrated noise or something. He'll notice, but let him sew the story together himself. Try to pretend you're a little embarrassed about it and if he guesses, minimize it."

"God you're devious. And so what am I trying to do tonight?"

"Just let him think you're vulnerable," he said. "And let Chanda do the rest. He loves the ladies, Kiera, and he won't be able to resist you. You're wearing this outfit to try and make me jealous, you see, but I don't notice. Chanda will. Tonight you just need to earn a little trust. He'll talk to you a bit at a time as he comes to trust you. Just act impressed with whatever he says and later you might ask his advice."

He took a breath. "Remember that at least ten people will be watching everything you do. Don't give me meaningful glances, Kiera, or do anything secretive.

"And Kiera, don't punch him. Or anyone. If anyone offends you, run to me. Don't try and save anyone. I mean that. And try and be demure." He laughed. "I can't even say that without laughing. Okay. Try to be more demure than usual, all right?"

AFTER THEY ATE, Marco went back to his rooms to change and Kiera cleaned up again. Emmy helped her don her dress, and she almost shrieked.

She'd known it was the deep red of blood. What she hadn't known is that if she breathed heavily her breasts would come tumbling out, or that it was tight enough to show every wrinkle, every roll, and every curve.

It belled out just above her knees, and the fabric was a little stretchy, God knew how, so she would be able to sit down. But it was the sluttiest dress Kiera could even imagine.

Emmy pulled up her hair, then let it down again. She compromised by pulling the center bit up and knotting it on top and letting an inch or two of the edges hang down. Emmy curled the tendrils with an iron bar she'd warmed over the fire. Kiera put on even more makeup, and when she was finished, she stood in front of the mirror and thought that that she had never, ever looked like this in her life, and it looked like what she should be was for sale.

Emmy thought she looked beautiful. Or at least that's what she said.

Alex gaped at her.

A young man came for her a half-hour later. He took her back to the same room the last party had been in.

As soon as she entered, she felt a hundred eyes on her. She took a deep breath, then took off her wrap.

It was the hardest thing she had ever done. She felt stiff and awkward, and tried to relax. That was hard, too.

She handed the wrap to the young woman who waited by her side to take it, then turned to the room. She spotted Marco standing in a group of men, not including Valen, thank God, and wandered over. On her way, a server offered her a glass of wine. She took it.

She tried to remember everything he had said, and she stopped. Took a drink. Looked at the room. How was this different than trying a case, she thought. *It's not. I just have to put on this perspective. Make my case. Make everyone feel what I feel. What I want them to feel.*

She relaxed a little.

She pulled her chin up a bit and waltzed over to Marco, slowly, trying to look sexy.

He looked up, met her eyes, looked away.

She frowned, then continued.

When she got to his group, she slid her hand over his arm. He was laughing about something. He leaned over, pecked her cheek, and kept talking.

She moved a little, like her dress was uncomfortable, and showed off her breasts.

Marco patted her arm. "Just a second, Kiera, all right." He sounded like someone trying to conceal annoyance.

She lowered her eyes.

A hand on her arm made her startle. She looked up to the man who must be Chanda.

He was big. Not as big as Laszlo, she thought with a pang, but a big man. Tall, over six feet, with almost black hair and dark blue eyes. A strong face. A proud nose.

A real looker, she thought, and smiled sweetly.

"I don't believe we have met, Lady Kiera," he said. He lifted her hand and kissed it, then lowered it gently to his arm.

She looked back over her shoulder at Marco, who didn't look back. She lowered her eyes again.

"My cousin is just happy to see his friends again," he said as he turned her slightly away from the group.

She looked up at him. "Oh, I know. He just looks so handsome to-night," she said wistfully.

Chanda smiled at her. "Well, my cousin may be a lout, but I am pleased to know you, Lady Kiera. My name is Chanda."

She laughed, then lifted a hand to cover it. He had a really nice smile. "I am pleased to know you, too, Lord Chanda."

He was staring at her intently, like he was trying to gauge her measure. "Would you like to dance?" he finally asked, and she panicked, a little. He must have seen it, because he smiled again and leaned close. "Just a dance, Lady Kiera."

She breathed out. "All right," she said. "But I'm not very good at this."

He smiled indulgently and led her out to the floor.

To her surprise, she remembered the steps to the minuet from the last party, and Chanda was a good partner, gracefully leading her through the moves when she hesitated. When the music ended, he walked her back to the group.

A man moved, and she saw Marco. He was standing toward the back of the room, and far too close to a young woman in a dress nearly as revealing as Kiera's. He was making no attempt to hide his attraction. She let out her breath and looked at the floor.

Chanda stopped. "Are you all right, Lady Kiera?" he asked.

She looked up and pasted on a smile. "Oh, yes. I'm fine. Uh, do you know where I might get something to drink?"

Something flashed in his eyes. "Let me call someone." He raised a hand and a woman rushed over. "A glass of red for the lady. Make it two." He led her to an unoccupied table. "Do you wish to sit?" he asked. "You look a little tired."

"Thank you," she said gratefully. And sat. And was terrified her breast was going to fall out. She leaned back a little and prayed that gravity pushed things back in. She tried to look forlorn. Just a little. And less worried about her breast.

He sat beside her and they watched the dancers for a moment.

Marco came over and took her hand. She stood but kept her face even, then smiled brittlely. Her eyes flicked to the young woman he had been talking to and back. "Are you having a nice time?" she asked.

"Dance with me, Kiera," he evaded and led her to the dance floor. He pulled her so close that their chests were touching.

The ridiculousness of the situation hit her and she almost laughed, right then. Instead, she lowered her face and pressed her lips into a frown.

Marco put his mouth in her hair. "Darling Kiera," he whispered, and she almost laughed again. She could feel his heart pounding. "I have to tell you that either you feel very uncomfortable in that dress, or that you are a far better actor than I had thought."

"It's a little of both," she whispered back, and sniggered.

He laughed outright, like she had said something funny, which maybe she had.

"Oh, gods," he said as he nuzzled her hair. "Kiera, I have to tell you something, but you have to promise me that you won't do anything rash. Don't change anything about what you're doing, okay?"

"Okay," she whispered, wondering if she could.

"Laszlo is here," he whispered back, then laughed again and rubbed his face against her head to hide her flinch. "Ignore him, Kiera. Just go along with this for a while. You can ask to be taken back to your rooms in a mark, all right? Plead a headache or something." He pulled back and smiled at her fondly, but his eyes were a little panicked. "Just hold on," he said, and kissed her nose.

The music was over, so Marco led her back to the table. And to Chanda, who was watching them with interest.

"Cousin," Marco, said, shaking his hand. "Please don't get up. You met Kiera, I saw."

"You're a lucky man, Marco," Chanda said, his eyes on Kiera. She looked at the floor.

"Yes, I am." He flashed a smile. "Could I impose on you to entertain my lovely lady for a while? She has a slight headache and I don't want to tire her further by dragging her around to see all my old friends." He looked at Kiera. "Is that all right, Kiera?"

She smiled hesitantly. "Yes, of course."

"Good. Chanda?"

He smiled. "It would be my pleasure."

"Thank you." Marco walked away.

Kiera turned to Chanda. "My apologies, Lord Chanda. Please do not feel at all obligated to sit with me. Marco was right when he said I have a headache and I may just head back to my rooms in just a bit."

He looked faintly amused. "Obligation is not what I feel, Lady Kiera.

Do you feel well enough to dance with me?"

She smiled gratefully. "I would love to," she said.

He led her out to the dance floor and held her just as gently as the last time. As she whirled around the floor, her eyes came to rest on Laszlo.

She had almost forgotten.

He was standing at one of the doors, acting as one of the guards, and he watched her. His face was hard and unreadable. And yet she wanted him. She wanted to feel his arms around her so much it hurt, hurt right in her chest, squeezing right below her breastbone. She wanted to lie naked with him, his big hands on her body. His lips in her hair.

She closed her eyes and turned her head to hide the ache that wrapped around her heart. She breathed out, then in.

She was not going to make it for an hour.

When the music was over, Chanda held her on the floor. "Another?" he asked. "Since you're going home soon?"

She smiled at him. "You are such a kind man, Lord Chanda. Thank you for making this night so—nice."

He smiled back, desire in his eyes, but he looked away, perhaps to hide it.

And looked right at Laszlo.

Shit.

Her heart was pounding, so she kept her eyes down and pretended not to notice. She prayed that Chanda wouldn't notice either. After an eternity, the music restarted and Chanda began to lead her in another dance. She smiled up at him, trying to look attracted, and grateful, and charmed.

Chanda was buying. He smiled back, holding her gaze, and let his attraction fill his eyes.

When the music stopped, she asked to return to her table. He led her back and sat beside her again. Someone brought more wine.

"I have heard so many things, Lady Kiera, and it's hard to know what to think of you. Where are you really from, and how do you like it here?"

Kiera smiled her first genuine smile of the night. "Well, I'm adjusting, thank you, but my home is far from here, and things are really different there, so I feel like I have so much yet to learn, especially about magic. How about you? I know you're Marco's cousin, but that's about it."

He seemed pleased she'd asked. "My mother is Leith's sister. She has gone to the gods now, as has my father. I have traveled outside the deconn many times, and in fact I have just returned, but I have lived in Fairbanks my entire life and so it's here I always return after my wanderings."

He sat back, considering. "So. What would a lady like to know?" He tapped his lip in mock concentration, then slid his gaze to hers. He tried to press a smile away, then let it come. Kiera couldn't help but smile back. "I am not married. I have no children. I spend my lonely winter turns managing the weather here, and helping the farmers in the summer when I am about. I like the way the earth feels in my hands, and the way it smells." He leaned closer, as if imparting a secret. "In fact, during the long winters I sometimes dream about it."

She laughed. "Really? A man who dreams about dirt?"

"You wound me, Lady Kiera." He put a hand to his heart. "What else would a man dream of?"

"Oh, I wouldn't know," she laughed. "Are you an earth mage, then?"

He looked at her oddly, all mirth gone from his face. "No, Lady Kiera. Not an earth mage."

"Oh. I'm sorry if that wasn't the right thing to say," she said, eyebrows drawn together. "Marco keeps trying to explain things to me, but I don't always understand the nuances, I'm afraid. I beg your pardon."

He patted her knee. "No, no, Lady Kiera. It's fine. Do you feel up to dancing again?"

"I am flattered by your attention tonight, Lord Chanda, but I really should go back to my rooms."

"Is your headache worse?" he asked, genuinely concerned.

"A bit. I think I'm mostly tired."

"Will you be coming back nexturn?" he asked, and he didn't try to hide the hope in his eyes.

"Yes," she said, and didn't look away.

She stood, then walked to the main doorway. And nearly into Laszlo.

Her heart lurched. He had apparently changed his assignment.

She accepted her wrap, eyes down, slipped it over her shoulders, then turned back to look at the room. Marco was hip-deep in young women, and she raised her eyebrows and turned back. Laszlo held the door for her as she left.

She did not look up.

KIERA WOKE to voices. She'd drunk far too much wine the night before, and her head was pounding. She lay and listened for a moment. She heard Marco's voice. Then Mosha's. They were both raised. "Stop!" she said, head in her pillow. "Stop arguing."

Both men came and stood by her bed. Mosha glared at Marco, who glared back.

"What?" she said, pushing back the covers so that she could sit up, then groaned.

Mosha turned his ire on her. "Why did ye tell him?"

She gaped. "I didn't! He guessed, Mosha!" She lay back down. "And he wants to help. You should let him. He's very smart." She closed her eyes. "Now go away."

They didn't, but they did retreat to the couches. Kiera fell back to sleep listening to their voices.

WHEN KIERA WOKE, it was midday. Her body ached. It felt as if she had been sleeping in the same position for ages.

She turned over and realized that she had to go to the bathroom. Now. She eased up and slid out of the bed.

A hand grabbed her arm, and she turned to see Marco standing beside her bed. She smiled and batted his hand away. She sighed. "You know, you were right. I am really, really bad at this spying stuff."

"Why do you say that?"

"Oh, Chanda didn't say one significant thing to me."

Marco grinned. "You're a woman, you twit. He isn't ever going to discuss his important business with you." He waggled his eyebrows. "Well, not unless you bed him."

Kiera gaped, then slapped his arm. "I'm not going to have sex with him just for information! Besides, I just met him! I don't even know what kind of man he is!"

"He likes you," Marco told her, still smiling, and Kiera pushed past him. "And would taking a lover be such a trial? You don't have to bear his children!"

"I have to go to the bathroom. Hold on."

"He's handsome," Marco called to her. "And all the ladies say he's charming. I saw you smiling at him."

Kiera finished then came out of the bathroom, grinning and shaking her head. The day was overcast, so even with the curtains open it wasn't as light as she liked. She sent fire into the lamps and they flared and caught, casting a warm glow over the carpets. She made her way to her dresser and sat down, then reached for her comb. Her hand brushed something rough, and she looked down to find her fingers resting on the little wooden comb Laszlo had made her.

The smile died on her face.

"He didn't even look at any other women the whole night," Marco went on. "I am sure he would take you to bed, and maybe to mistress."

Kiera stared at the comb, then picked it up in her fingers. A sharp sting of grief pierced and flowed into her, leaving a hollowness in her chest.

She looked at herself in the mirror. She looked bedraggled, her hair in a tangle and dark circles under her eyes. She looked herself in the eye and wondered if Laszlo ever thought about her. Ever ached to hold her. Ached so much it hurt.

Marco walked over. "Kiera, are you listening to me?" he asked. "If you can get him to fall for you, maybe you can persuade him to—I don't know. Maybe not join, but at least not fight. He would be a good ally."

Kiera closed her fingers around the comb and lowered her eyes to her hands on the dresser. "I can't, Marco," she said, and was surprised that her voice sounded taut. "I can't have sex with him."

Marco pulled up a chair and sat down. "Why not?" He looked honestly puzzled.

"Because." She blew out a breath, then put the comb back on the dresser, pushed it into a mess of silk ribbon at the back of the dresser and folded a piece across it.

Marco watched her with a jaundiced eye and a little twist to his mouth. He waited until she was finished, then told her, "Kiera, you do whatever you want." His eyes were sympathetic.

She nodded. "Is your mother a water mage?"

Marco sat up straight and stared into her face. "Why do you ask?"

Kiera closed her eyes. "The first night I went to the party, the night those two guys—well, you know. That night you mother sent—well, her feelings to me. Just to me, I think. It was while your father was picking out his next mistress from those little girls."

Marco looked grim. "How did she feel?"

Kiera looked at him. Shrugged. "Ashamed."

He gritted his teeth. "Why did she 'send' that to you?"

"I don't know. It was a terrible night for us both. Maybe camaraderie. Who fucking knows."

Marco stalked to the couch and flung himself backward. He put his arms behind his head.

"I'm sorry, Marco," Kiera said.

He looked at her. "Why should you be sorry?"

"Because I know it hurts to know that someone you care about is hurting."

He turned his head.

After a minute, he turned back, eyes slitted. "Is that something you can do? Can you tell what I'm feeling?" he asked.

Kiera stood and walked to him. She knelt down and took his right hand. Pulled a thread of water. "Anger. Frustration."

"You could have guessed that. Try again."

She closed her eyes. After a moment she jerked her hand back and stared at him, eyes wide. "No, Marco. No."

He looked thoughtful. "You really can do it." He shot her a grin. "I was thinking of—uh—someone else. No offense meant."

She smiled in relief. "None taken."

He sat up. "So how do you do it?"

"Just pull a strand of water from them. A small strand. Send it out through your other hand. Take their right with your left."

"Let me try." After a minute, he shook his head. "I can't make it work. The strand slips away from me every time."

"All right. Tell me how many mages can fight. And what they can do."

"It depends on what you mean."

"Marco," she warned, and he grinned.

"Only the sunwyr can really do anything major, although if someone set out some fires, the few fire awyr could probably send it to whoever was attacking." He paused. "The air awyr could throw out some small surges, but I don't think they would stop anyone determined. The water awyr could probably push snow around, but again, they're not trained to think like that and I don't think they could do much harm. If someone attacked, I think they would run."

"So the obstacles are Valen, your father, Chanda," she paused, afraid to go on.

"And my mother, yes."

"All air sunwyr?"

"Well, it sounds like my mother may be water," he smiled wryly. "I've never seen her use her magic, Kiera. I don't know what she can, or would do."

Kiera's heart thudded. She had one more option, though it would be her very last choice.

"Is there ever a time when the three men are together?" she asked.

He turned to look at her. "I don't think you can beat Valen, Kiera, not right now," he said. "Or my father. Chanda, I don't know. I've never seen him manifest a big spell. Maybe. But definitely not when they are all in one place. No matter the spell, even as strong as you are, they could probably work together and defeat it."

Kiera sighed. "Is there ever a time, a regular time, when they are all together?"

"Tell me what you would do."

"Answer me first."

"Maybe. I might be able to get them together."

"No. Not with you there."

He narrowed his eyes. "No more until you tell me."

"No."

"Then no." His face was mulish.

She grunted. She'd get it out of him later. If she needed to. Which she prayed she wouldn't.

"Do you think Mosha lied to me about Alex to make me want to join him? What do you think it means if Alex really is a shifter and can do magic?"

"I don't know the answer to either of those questions, Kiera." He shook his head. "But I hope Mosha didn't lie about anything because if he did we're in very serious trouble. Can't you tell if he is?"

"No," she replied, flipping her hair behind her shoulder. "He can shield."

Marco looked thoughtful. "I will say that if shifters can do magic, the world is much different than I have always thought."

"Marco," Kiera began, then faltered.

"What?"

"Can one mage give another mage power?"

He sat up on his elbow. "What do you mean?"

"Like say you were calling air and it was—I don't know. A lot, a really big stream, and you were having trouble controlling it. Could I take your hand and feed you some energy? Help you?"

He sat up. "Let's try it."

"Marco, no. I'm too tired right now."

"Not a big one. Just try."

She rolled her eyes. "All right."

She took his left hand with her right. Closed her eyes. Found a stream of fire. Pulled some threads. Not a lot, but enough to be sure he would feel it. Pulled them into her. Spun them. Sent them out into his hand. Pushed hard enough to push the flow into him.

Marco gasped and jumped up, breaking her hold on his hand.

Kiera opened her eyes. His hair was standing straight up, like he was in the middle of an electrical storm.

He smiled a huge smile. "Gods," he breathed as his hair drifted down.

She looked at him for a long moment. "Regardless of whether Alex is a shifter or not, shifters can do magic," she finally said.

He made a face. "What?"

"They can. Or some can."

An annoyed face. "Kiera."

She shook her head. "It isn't my secret to tell, Marco. But I want you to know that because someone should teach them to do it better."

She stood up and stretched. "And now I need to take a bath."

Marco lay back on the couch. "I'm going to stay here for a while, all right?"

"Sure," she said, and walked into the bathroom.

CHAPTER 19

KIERA LET MARCO PICK OUT HER DRESS again. This time he chose a close-fitting plum gown that shimmered to black when she turned in the light. It was smooth and soft, made of silk, and there was a black, sleeveless overjacket that tied at her waist to complete the ensemble. The outfit wasn't as revealing as the one she'd worn the night before, but it still left precious little to the imagination, both above and below the so-called neckline. "Curl your hair, but leave it down," he told her as Emmy helped her get ready. "And add more color to your eyes."

Kiera looked at him in the mirror. "Marco, where are all the pregnant women? Do they stay home after they get pregnant?"

Marco looked puzzled. "What do you mean?"

"Well, with all of this, uh, mandated sex going on, I would think every woman in this city would be pregnant. Every cycle. Constantly."

"No," he told her, pulling up a chair. He reached out and used a finger to push the ruby-colored lip stain in front of her. "There aren't many babies."

Kiera turned and faced him. "Why not? Is there something wrong?"

Marco grimaced, then leaned back. "Maybe."

She picked up the lip stain and pointed it at him. "Don't be evasive," she chided.

He smiled. "I don't know, Kiera."

Kiera tapped her lip with the tube. "Maybe that's why someone started that stupid brooding custom. Trying to increase fertility rates. I wonder if it's the men or the women. Or both." She narrowed her eyes. "Do the Alaks have this problem?"

Marco shrugged, then stood up. "I need to go get ready, my pumpkin. I'll send an escort for you."

"Pumpkin?"

He grinned, then let himself out.

KIERA ATE A LIGHT SUPPER and played a game with Alex. She rose when the knock came and wrapped herself in the black, lacy overjacket.

It was chilly enough in the ballroom that Kiera felt reluctant to part with her shawl, but since no one else seemed to be wearing one she handed hers over and crossed her arms in front of her, then let them drop when she realized how much cleavage that created.

It was just after the sixth fire hour, 8 P.M., which was better than two hours earlier than when she had come last night, and as she looked around the room, she realized that there were far fewer souls than had been there when she arrived last night, maybe a tenth of the people, although the band was already playing and some brave couples were dancing. One couple danced too closely, and too slowly to the music, caught up in each other's eyes and seeming oblivious to the rest of the world. As she breathed in, an unexpected twinge of sadness wafted through her, and she looked away and smiled a tad sourly to herself.

Over three-quarters of the couches were unoccupied, so she walked to an empty one set fairly close to the main doors and sat down on an over-stuffed azure loveseat with a view of the dance floor. She sat far enough back that she could rest completely against the back, then had to lean forward and pull her hair out from behind her shoulders.

As soon as she was comfortable a young man in livery brought a tray with several glasses of wine. Smiling, she chose a sweet-smelling red and plinked it down on the table in front of her.

As she looked around, Kiera lifted her glass and took a drink. There was no one here yet that she knew. The wine was strong and smooth and it warmed her. She held it under her nose, enjoying the scent, and watched the dancers make their way around the floor in time to a minuet. They moved smoothly. Step, pause, step, pause, step.

It was three songs since her arrival, yet, to her annoyance, the couple she had noticed earlier, a handsome young couple, were still dancing. She tipped her glass toward her and looked down at the garnet liquid, then took a long drink, finishing it. The server came over with another before she set the glass down.

She took two.

The song changed to something with a faster tempo, and many couples left the floor. Some wafted over to her, nonchalantly, watching her with varying degrees of interest, and then passed or went another way. Some held her eyes.

Many of the men and some of the women took in her dress, or her, and the men let their attraction shine coldly in their eyes. Some smiled when they saw her looking back, but for many the smile didn't reach their eyes.

Kiera drank her glass of wine a little stiffly and watched the dance floor, where couples had come to cling together for the minutes the concerto played. She drank the glass in her hand and then another before the crescendo. More people filtered in as the music played, and the couches began to fill up. Her server brought her another glass and set it down on the table.

Marco plopped down next to her as she sipped from her fourth glass. Or maybe it was her fifth. He wore a sleeveless gold and midnight blue overcoat over a nearly orange long-sleeved undershirt and navy pants that fit tight to his legs. She leaned back and smiled broadly, genuinely happy to see him. He leaned forward, resting his elbows on his knees, and tried to hide a smile. "You're drunk!" he accused softly.

She shook her head. "I'm not!" she said, a little too loudly, and Marco snorted.

"Let's take a turn around the floor." He stood up. "But leave the glass here."

He pulled her up and led her out to the dance floor. The band was playing a slow-tempoed waltz, and she fell into the pavan-based steps effortlessly. Marco was an agile dancer, and she let herself relax. After she had the rhythm down, she lifted her eyes from Marco to watch the other dancers.

With a start she found herself staring at Chanda, who was smiling at her instead of his partner. Before she could stop it she felt her lips lifting in return, but she tried to quash it, thinking it might seem rather wanton to smile at Chanda while dancing with her supposed paramour.

His eyes crinkled as he turned to answer some question his partner asked.

She caught him staring at her a half dozen times.

She wasn't sure how she felt. About anything.

After the song ended Marco, who was either oblivious to or apathetic about the attention Chanda had been paying Kiera, led her off the floor and to a different set of couches. A server hurried up as they sat but Marco waved him away, and Kiera shot him a glare. "I'm going off in a minute," he warned, "and I want you to hitch off the wine."

She pursed her lips but decided to ignore that. "Where are you off to?"

He shrugged absently, then leaned back and stretched out his legs. "I'll be back a bit later." He arched his back in a stretch, then turned his head so that he could see the main doors. Kiera followed his gaze.

A young woman, blonde and buxom and dressed in a rich, full garnet gown, was handing a black shawl to an attendant. Perhaps feeling the weight of their stares, she looked up and at Marco, and started to smile, but then her gaze slid to Kiera and it died on her face.

Kiera had to turn away so the girl wouldn't see her expression, which Kiera tried to force under control, since she was about to laugh. She put one hand over her mouth and looked at the floor. She wished Marco would hurry up and leave so that she could have another glass of wine.

A set of fine black boots under black pants invaded her perusal of the carpets, and she looked up, ready to smile at Chanda, and up. He was wearing all black, black pants, a long black cloak that hit him mid-thigh covering a black shirt that fit a little too tightly across his chest.

A very large chest.

Her eyes slid up. It was Laszlo.

He was looking at her with a bland expression, but it was belied by his eyes, which were tight with some emotion she couldn't identify.

Marco stood up and Laszlo turned to him. They said some words to each other—she could hear their voices—but Kiera tuned them out. *Goddamn it. Goddamn him.* They shook hands, and she felt her face heat and wasn't sure why. She took a deep breath and sat back on the couch. She ignored them both, and instead stared out at the dancers.

Kiera didn't see Chanda walk up until he was there, and when she did, she stood before he could sit down. She turned to Marco, ignoring the others. "Excuse me. I'll be right back," she told him a little breathlessly.

He nodded once, suppressing a smile, and she fled to the recess in the back of the chamber, feeling the heat of their gazes on her back.

When she finished in the restroom, she slunk out and looked around. Marco was sitting with the blonde girl on the couch she had taken when she first entered the room. The other two men were nowhere in sight, so she walked out and looked for a server. A young man in livery, carrying a tray, was coming her way, so she stepped toward him. She saw that all of his glasses were empty so she walked past him, then stopped.

Kiera stood for a moment and wondered why she didn't just go back to her room. Her heart was still pounding and, she admitted, she did feel a little tipsy. What did she think she was going to accomplish, anyway? It was going to take weeks to earn Chanda's trust. *What do I really want from him?* she asked herself. *Am I willing to have sex with him to earn it? Could I? And is that the kind of person I want to be?*

Kiera made her way to the closest empty couch and took a seat tiredly. The music was slow and the couples clung to each other tightly as they slid across the floor. She knew she should go to Marco, and she would, she really would, in just a damned minute. A young man brought her wine and she took a glass, smiling up at him. She startled a return smile from him before he turned away.

It made her heart hurt.

Everything looked so serene here in this room. So civilized. Watching the finely dressed women and men hold each other so primly, speak so carefully, in this almost obscenely beautiful room while heartbreakingly lovely music played on and on all night, a stranger might never guess that one of these men beat a woman to death and maimed her lover for nothing more than his own pleasure, or that no one would care if she told them. The stranger would never think that the servers were slaves whose bodies and lives could be maimed and exploited in every conceivable way and that no one, not one cursed person in this room, would raise a brow.

She drank the wine down and wanted another.

Laszlo walked past her and her heart clenched. He did not look at her, so she let her eyes follow him, appreciating the unthinking, and fluid, grace with which he carried himself. Unlike all of the Skani men, he looked incredibly powerful, like a crouching lion, and just as ready to spring. She wondered if people found him frightening, and then why she never had feared him. He had the most amazing hands, big and strong, but they had never given her anything but more passion and pleasure than she would have ever before imagined a man could, or would, give to a woman. It had always seemed like he had loved her with his hands. He had held her too tightly, and for too long, like he was afraid she would slip away if he let go and couldn't bear it if she did.

That's crazy, she chastised herself harshly. *He couldn't have loved me. We just had great sex and—*

She let the thought waft away because she couldn't bear to finish it.

Her eyes were burning and her chest felt tight, so she turned and motioned for a server. One hurried over with a glass of wine and she took it, though she felt a little dizzy when she turned back. *Okay,* she told herself, *this is the last one.*

The music played on, this time a haunting concerto. She sipped from her glass and watched the dancers. A couple walked lazily past her. The woman, a reed-thin blonde with her hair tied back, wore a belled yellow gown, while her fair-haired male partner sported a dark green overcoat. He looked at Kiera with heat in his eyes, and she turned away, pretending to look over her shoulder into the room.

Chanda was standing in a group of men about twenty feet behind her, a glass in his hand, eyes appraising her. He lifted his glass a little and she nodded just as slightly in return. Her gaze slid to his companions, and she lost her breath. He was standing with Valen, Thesin, Gethor and another 30-something, platinum-haired man she didn't know. The men were talking animatedly about something and none met her gaze except Chanda, but she felt her eyes grow wide and she turned away as quickly as she dared, trying to stifle it.

She got up and walked to Marco, leaving her half-filled glass on the table. He looked up as she approached, and flashed a smile. "Kiera, this is Bandel, my friend for many cycles. Bandel, this is Kiera, my paramour."

Bandel looked up at Kiera and smiled, but it was strained. Kiera smiled back, equally falsely, then looked back at Marco. "I am going to go back to my room," she told him.

He lowered his brows. "I'd rather you stayed," he said pointedly and lifted his head. "Why don't you ask Chanda to dance with you?"

"I don't want to dance," she said tiredly, and Bandel's eyes widened. Uh-oh. Was it a faux pas to say "no" to a man? Or just to your paramour? She smiled. "But of course I'll do as you ask, Marco," she added, and turned so that she could see Chanda. He was still watching her, so she smiled a little, and he smiled back. She turned back to Marco and found that Laszlo had walked up.

Without preamble he asked her, "May I have the honor of a dance, Lady Kiera?"

Heart pounding, her gaze slid to Marco, who shrugged very slightly, as if saying *it's all right; do what you want.* There was no polite way to say "no" with everyone watching, and so she nodded and took his arm.

And a treacherous part of her really, really wanted to touch him.

He led her out to the dance floor and took her hand gently, letting the other settle on her waist. She took a deep breath and put her hand on his shoulder. She shuddered a little, and took a step to hide it, but he didn't seem to notice, or hid it well. He led her through the first steps and she looked up at his face. He was staring at her, her eyes, her mouth, face impassive.

"I thought you didn't like dancing," she said softly.

"I like holding you," he murmured, and she started. She expected anger, betrayal, to rise, but instead a thread of longing clenched her heart.

She looked down.

"You're drunk," he told her.

"A little," she admitted without looking up.

"Why?" he asked as he turned her.

She shrugged.

"Do you wish you could go home?" That surprised her.

"Not anymore," she answered honestly, perhaps more vehemently than she would have liked, and looked into his face.

He gazed at her appraisingly but didn't reply.

As they turned again, he pulled her a little closer and spoke into her hair. "Are you going to lie with Chanda?"

She took a moment to consider how to reply, but abandoned everything she thought of. "Laszlo, that's none of your business anymore," she finally said, voice as tired as her heart.

He squeezed her waist tightly, but the music was over, so he led her off the floor and back to Marco. Chanda was standing there, watching her over the top of his glass as he sipped.

Laszlo bowed and turned away, and it felt like her insides unraveled with each step farther away he got. She forced herself to keep her eyes on Marco, who held her gaze and tried, unsuccessfully, to hide his pity.

After a moment, she forced a smile and took a seat on the couch opposite Marco and whatever the hell her name was. Chanda walked around and sat on her couch, though at the opposite end.

"How are you faring, Lady Kiera?" Chanda asked her.

She turned to him. "I am fine," she lied. "How are you tonight, Lord Chanda?"

His smile was genuine. "All the better for seeing you," he answered, pointedly not looking at Marco.

She smiled back. "Would you consider me too wanton if I asked you to dance?" she asked.

His smile broadened. "Not at all," he told her, and stood. She stood as well, and he walked her out to the floor. He led her and turned her and she let herself get lost in the dance.

"You look beautiful," Chanda told her, and she looked up at him.

"Thank you," she said, surprised. "And so do you," she blurted, then wished she hadn't.

He snorted, and she looked up into his amused face. "I've never been told that I looked beautiful," he said with a grin.

"Who are you, Chanda?" Kiera wondered aloud, and the tiny, remaining rational part of her wished she'd drunk a great deal less.

To her great surprise, he smiled at her. He seemed far less guarded when she asked personal questions. Maybe because it was more of a woman thing to want to discuss relationships?

"I am, I believe you said, a man who dreams of dirt." His face shifted a little as he looked at her and became serious. "What is there between you and the—Laszlo?" he asked her.

Kiera held his gaze. "Absolutely nothing," she told him, willing him to believe her. Willing her to believe herself.

After a moment, he nodded, and led her across the floor.

The music was ending, so she started to leave, but he held her fast. She looked up, curiosity on her face, and he smiled. "One more?"

"Sure," she said. The dancing, and time since her last drink, were clearing her head a little, and the look on his face as he watched her made her increasingly sure that he was going to ask her to come to his bed before the song ended. Her heart pattered a little as she wondered whether she would go.

He didn't wait long.

"Are you still bedding Marco?" Chanda asked her during one of the turns.

That startled a laugh out of her. "Is that appropriate to ask about?" she countered, more than a little embarrassed.

He smiled at her. "I don't know, Kiera, but I want to know the answer."

"No," she admitted sheepishly. "I'm not."

"Will you consider me?" he asked, holding her eyes.

"For bedding?"

"Yes," he answered, and squeezed her hand. His eyes looked warm, and hopeful.

She found herself wanting him. Her body had suffered since Laszlo had gone, and he was very handsome.

She opened her mouth to reply, but caught sight of the liveried man who had breached the dance floor and was walking purposefully toward her. She stopped dancing to wait, and Chanda turned to see what she was looking at. He kept her hand.

The young man bowed. "I beg your pardon, Lady Kiera," he told her, "but your son is ill and your maid requests your presence."

Her stomach clenched. "Oh my God. What's wrong with him?"

He shook his head. "I do not know, my lady," he told her apologetically.

Kiera looked up at Chanda. "I have to go."

He squeezed her hand again. "Of course. I hope your son is all right."

She fled, not even stopping to get her wrap or ask for an escort. After the big doors closed behind her, she picked up her skirt and ran, then walked when she faltered, then ran again.

When she got to her rooms, she was panting and queasy, but she threw open the door and charged in, leaving it open.

The room was dark.

Maybe they took him someplace, she thought wildly, and turned to go back out.

"Is that you, Lady Kiera?" Emmy called, coming out of the bathroom.

"Where is Alex?" she demanded. "What's wrong with him?"

Emmy stopped. Kiera sent fire into the lamps, lighting the entire room. Alex was asleep in his bed.

"Alex is here," Emmy said, a little hesitantly. "He is—well. Did you hear differently?" When Kiera didn't reply, she added, "If you're back for the night I'll take myself off."

Kiera shook her head, then sat down on the couch and laughed breathlessly.

LATE THE NEXT MORNING, and to her surprise, Kiera felt well enough to go to magic lessons.

Agni greeted her with an affectionate pat on the arm, then told her she was changing things today.

"What are we going to do?" Kiera asked, alarmed.

"It is time to make a bigger storm, child, and for that we must go outside," Agni told her.

Marco popped out of one of the rooms and gave her a peck on the cheek. "I'm going to try, too," he told her.

They went out past the altar, which exited into a room Kiera had not seen before. It was large and lined with grey, unadorned stone. Cold seeped from the walls. They went swiftly through the room and out through a door in the back. Snow had fallen sometime during the night, and it lay sparkling and unbroken before them.

Their crunching steps were the only sounds Kiera heard as they walked past the stables and toward the back city gate. Marco kept her hand. After they exited the city walls they tromped another quarter mile toward a blackened circular football field-sized clearing set a half-mile or so from the feet of the mountains. The river was a silver line a mile to the east, and the treeline had been pushed back another quarter mile behind that.

"All right. Here," Agni told them as they reached the black circle. This close Kiera could see that the snow had been cleared away and that the ground was carpeted with pea-sized black rocks. "Go on."

Kiera stepped in the circle and then leaned down and rested her hands on her thighs, which were a little sore from the walk.

"There is a storm in the west." Agni told her, pointing. "I want you to pull fire and air from it. Wrap them tightly together, then spin them and manifest them there—" she pointed to a flat spot about fifty yards away. "Hold the storm there. I want you to build it until it is the height of the walls—" about 30 feet, Kiera thought—"and the same width. Hold it until I say release it."

Kiera nodded. *That's a big storm to hold.*

Agni must have read her face. "Don't worry, child. I am certain you can do this. Are you ready?"

Kiera smiled. "Sure."

"Begin."

Kiera closed her eyes, sending her sight out and westward. She found the storm immediately. It was warm. Warm and soft, and it beckoned her in. No lightning in this one; maybe it was too young? *Can I make lightning come anyway?* she wondered. *Did the other storm feel like this?* She shook her head. *I can't tell. I just didn't think of things the same way then.*

Reluctantly she pulled out of the storm. Fingers of fire, strands, followed her out. She gathered some of them up, both fire and air, then called more to her. Water, wrapped tight in the threads, wanted to come, too, but she pulled it free and let it drift back.

She pulled the threads down, down, and into her. She ended up holding more than she'd thought, and they tangled and tried to unravel. *Glass,* she told herself, *glass,* and set them to spin. She raised her right hand, opened her eyes, and sent the first threads out. She tightened the spiral, and sent more.

She could see the stream of molten energy, sparkling flame, flowing from her hand.

Manifest, she said in her mind, and the firestorm roared to life.

She heard Marco gasp, and she almost lost hold.

"Focus!" Agni yelled. Kiera closed her eyes and took hold of the torrent of energy inside her. She pulled a deep breath. The fire was spinning, but the air had slowed, and had tangled again, so she took a minute to unthread them as they spun and wove them back together. When they were beating as one heart again, she extended her right hand, sending the torrent into her firestorm, which was starting to flicker out.

When the new stream hit it, it exploded upward and out.

"Control it!" Agni yelled.

Kiera extended her other hand and sent a strand of air to the fire, cutting off the top.

She pulled more from the storm, leaving herself open and pulling, so it would continue to flow. She spun it as it reached her, weaving strands together, and sent them out and into the fire.

She opened her eyes. The fire storm was larger than Agni had wanted, perhaps fifty feet tall, but too narrow at the bottom, so it looked like a tornado. She adjusted the air, let the storm gain girth, with a hard spin in the middle and a slower turn on the outside.

Tornado is right, she thought as she sent her sight out into it to keep it spinning.

She brought the top down a little, to about thirty feet, and loosened her hold so that the border expanded. When she could feel the heat she stopped pushing it, and just conduited the flow to let it settle in and burn. She held it, and fed, and found she loved it, after a fashion, like a child. Her child.

She grinned at her foolishness.

"Focus!" Agni yelled again.

Once it was established, Kiera found it was easy to keep going. She was less maker than conduit. More manager than creator, and she realized she understood how awyr could maintain a built working. It was the creation that took a sunwyr. Maintaining it was relatively easy. Trimming off the edges. Keeping the feed lines open.

The storm started to move away, so Kiera shifted her focus into it. She adjusted her pull, pulled a little too much, and her fire exploded up. She jerked back but kept her sight open, and parsed the flow into two streams. She sent half of it into the storm and the rest of the mixture she sent out into the ground below her. She felt her feet leave the ground, and she shrieked and almost lost control of the entire working. Agni was yelling, but Kiera ignored her and tried to concentrate. Tamping down hard, she pushed the stream back together, then sent it out, weaving it in and out of the firestorm, using a tendril of her stream to hold the edges of the working so that it wouldn't expand outward (to avoid killing Marco and Agni), but it took a full minute of careful work to spin out what was in her and get it pared back to size.

All right, she thought, and for the first time she felt herself shaking. *So it takes a skilled awyr to manage a making.*

"Let it go," Agni shouted.

Kiera severed the flow from the storm. Fingers of fire followed her, wanting her as much as she wanted them. She sent out the mix left in her and watched her storm begin to flicker. As the last strands fed it, it fell fast, sinking to the ground, and with a final *whoomp!* it went out.

She leaned over and rested her hands on her thighs. She had to fight to stay on her feet.

"Are you all right, Lady Kiera?" Agni asked her, resting a hand on her back.

"I'm just tired, Lady Agni," she said.

"You should have said!" Agni scolded, but Kiera waved it away.

"Did I do all right, overall?" she asked, and looked over at Agni.

"You did better than I had hoped," Agni admitted.

Kiera stood up. "Really?"

Agni smiled. "Yes. Now let Marco try."

Marco walked up and Agni stepped back. Kiera took Marco's hand. "Agni," she whispered. "We forgot about Agni."

He held her eyes for a moment, then looked away and nodded.

Kiera looked back at Agni. *She may be ignorant, but she isn't mean. The problem is that she is the most powerful mage in this manse. By far. And if I can't even beat Valen. Well.*

She shifted, her stomach tight.

She squatted, then sat down hard.

"Move back," Agni told her, so Kiera scooted back toward the edge, pushing her wicked thoughts away as she went.

Agni gave Marco the same instructions she'd given Kiera, then stood back.

Marco closed his eyes.

Kiera closed hers, and watched. To her surprise, a silvery, diaphanous Marco shot out of his body. What would you call that? His power? Or was that his sight? It shot up and into the storm, moving faster than anything she'd ever seen. It plunged into the middle of the storm, leaving a hole. In moments it emerged, with strands of air and fire wrapped around it. Unlike the fire's love for her, for him the air blossomed out, enveloping his essence, tendrils following him, thousands of strands, trying to slide down and around him. He kept hold of the strands he wanted and let the rest go, reluctantly it seemed, but he pulled air and fire into and around him.

She opened her eyes as the pearly double plunged back into his body.

His hair was standing up and he had started to glow, just a pale orange shine, reminding her of how her skin looked when she was a child and had held a flashlight beneath her hand.

Wow! Do I do that? She looked up at Agni, whose seemingly unsurprised gaze flicked to Marco then back to the field.

Kiera looked back at Marco. The energy spun around him, a tiny whirlwind, and he extended a hand toward the spot Kiera's storm had blackened.

"Tighter!" Agni yelled, and Kiera jumped.

His storm exploded, knocking Kiera back hard in the snow. She turned her head to find Agni lying next to her. Kiera sat up. Marco was still standing, arm extended. His storm had manifested. It wasn't as big as hers, but it was big.

He was spinning it like she had done.

It was beautiful. She stood.

Agni stood. Her hair was burned.

"Hold it!" Agni yelled.

Kiera closed her eyes. Marco's strands were faltering. He was having trouble concentrating, she saw, between pulling the threads and sending them out. His storm expanded and collapsed with a boom like a drum.

She sent her sight up and into the storm. She took a step, then another, as she basked in the warmth. She opened her eyes. She was next to Marco. On his left. With her right hand, she took his left.

She pulled. Hard.

She spun the threads from the storm and sent them into him.

He gasped but held it.

She could hear Agni speaking, but not what she said.

Marco sent out the spinning mix, into his fire, and it roared higher.

"Keep it narrow," Kiera said, and hoped he could hear her. "But let it go high."

She opened herself to the storm and let it fill her. The fire felt like a caress of a needy lover, urgent and wanting. She spun it all, wrapped it together, and sent it into Marco. He bent forward, then straightened, and sent it out.

The fire flashed. Higher. Kiera opened her eyes.

Their fire was sixty feet high. Spinning beautifully within its well-marked, to her eyes at least, bounds. It was perfect.

"Let it go!" Agni called.

Reluctantly, Kiera severed the stream from the storm. She spun and sent the last of it into Marco, who sent it out.

When it was gone, she let go of his hand.

He collapsed on the ground.

"Marco!" Kiera screamed, and dropped to her knees and leaned over him. Agni rushed up, looking grim.

Marco opened his eyes. "I'm fine," he croaked, then grinned.

Kiera sank back on her heels and let out her breath. "Good job, Marco," she told him, feeling her heart beat.

"Not bad for ten cycles' practice," he replied a shade sarcastically.

Kiera would have laughed, but Agni was staring at her. "How did you know the means to do that?"

Kiera shrugged, embarrassed. "I read in one of the books that you can, or should be able to, transfer energy to another mage. Marco and I tried it, though not like this of course."

"Of course," Agni agreed, brows up.

"I want to try something else," Kiera grinned, "if it's all right."

Agni nodded once and stepped back. Marco was still collecting himself, so she stepped around him and walked out on the black gravel, feeling it shift beneath her feet.

She stopped about fifty feet past Marco. Looking at the rocks, she muttered, "This won't work," and began pushing the rocks away with her boot. When she had bared the ground, which was also black, into a circle bigger around than she was, she stood in the middle of it and sent out her sight. Instead of the storm, she sought a steadier flow for this experiment. It was an air hour, so she quickly found a car-wide stream flowing southward directly above them, from which she pulled two-handfuls and brought them into her.

She set them to spin and then shot back up, seeking fire. There were no strong flows because the hour was shifting toward water, but she found twin creek-sized flows making their way east, and she pulled from both. She blended the strands together in her, then mixed them with air, then set a pull from her three source streams to keep them flowing into her.

When she had as much as she could hold, she sent them down to the ground as fast as she could.

She shot into the air.

She opened her eyes and found the world blurry, the air stinging her eyes, and she was shooting up thirty, then forty feet off the ground. She tried to slow it, but it stuttered and she fell forward and started to fall like a skydiver, so she closed her eyes and pushed more power into the ground. She didn't stop, but she slowed, so she sent more down, and the rebound flow hit her like a fist in the stomach, knocking the wind out of her.

She tried to gasp, and almost let go of the flows.

She struggled, trying to breathe, trying not to let go, trying not to panic. She could hear shouts from the ground but didn't dare open her eyes.

Her diaphragm spasmed painfully, then relaxed, and Kiera gasped, pulling exquisitely sweet oxygen into her lungs. She wasn't falling, so she set the flows and opened her eyes. She found herself staring at the sky and realized that she had turned over. She lay there, cradled in the flow of the small storm she had called, and let herself breathe for a minute, then two, until her panic subsided.

When she felt better, Kiera closed her eyes and adjusted the flow so that she was more upright. She opened her eyes. Her buttocks and back were being cradled by her storm. She looked out and realized she'd gone higher, too. She was more than twice the wall's height. She sat up on the flow and turned a little so that she could look over the city.

She ignored the shouts below.

The walls made an almost perfect circle, she realized with some surprise.

She could see the manse crouching majestically in its bed at this end of the city, with the twin church and school snuggled up to its haunches. The stables were there, and the barracks behind them, and what must be two other barracks buildings set south and up against the west wall. The river, a frozen silver thread, lay still and quiet in its bed on the east side of the city. It cut into the city near the top of the north wall—or did it flow underneath the wall?—and meandered down a few hundred yards, then cut west in a C before winding back to edge toward the bottom of the east wall. What looked like a garden and some sheds sat on the small space it bisected from the main city. Below the manse lay the bulk of the town, with its perfectly straight, criss-crossing streets and the buildings that lined them. The central road was a gash that cut from the front gate at the southeast edge of the city wall and led to the manse. All of the city roads crossed it.

The newfallen snow gave the city a pristine look, but she could see scurrying people profaning the white of the streets below.

Movement caught her eye and she looked down to see Marco waving frantically at her. Agni was standing beside him with her hands clasped in front of her. From this distance Kiera couldn't tell if her face held fear or pride or annoyance, and right now she just didn't care.

Using her hands, she turned herself so that she could see into the mountains north of the manse, the ones at whose feet she floated. Back home in the other Alaska these were named the White Mountains, but here she had heard someone call them the *Pi'tahs*, one of the few remaining words from the Alak the Skani here still used. They rose steep and snow-covered, with crags of black granite peeking through the new snow. The green of pines blanketed the mountains' ankles and feet, and the river ran between the toes of the one to her left—east—and the one east of that. A lake supposedly lay behind the three in front of her, but even from here she couldn't see it.

It was so much more than breathtaking.

She pulled more power and pushed it down, lifting herself higher. She stood on the flow, and pulled smaller strands up and wrapped them round her arms to secure her. At a hundred feet or so she stopped because she was cold and she was starting to feel tired, though she still couldn't see if there was a lake.

Kiera closed her eyes for a moment and wondered how to return slowly—and safely!—to the ground. She had never done anything except cut off a flow. *It's a little late for second thoughts,* she chided herself, and sank into her storm. She traced it back to the ground and then up to the air flow, where she snipped off a few of the strands. She paused, but didn't feel anything happening, so she pinched off a few more, and dropped a foot, then ten quickly, then stopped. A bead of sweat slipped down her face.

She left the air and followed the flow back down and then up to the fire, where she pulled off some of the strands. Instead of falling back into the flow, they sparked and dissolved. She felt herself sinking and opened her eyes. She was down to sixty feet and was falling a little too fast. She breathed out, then closed her eyes again and followed the flow back to the air. She pulled a few strands into her and pushed them into her storm.

She opened her eyes and started.

Movement. Many figures. In the trees at the foot of the mountain to the east. One of the giants couching the river. She was falling, not too fast, but she wanted to see, so she closed her eyes and sent her sight directly to the air flow. She pulled strands and tried to feed them directly into the flow she was already pulling, but they tangled and spun off.

Goddamnit, she thought desperately. She sunk back into herself—*seconds are ticking!*—then followed the flow below her down and back up to the air. From inside the flow, she pulled more and fed it into the stream, then down and into the storm.

It must have been enough because she felt her body shooting up.

She opened her eyes to find herself back up to eighty feet, and climbing.

She screamed her rage, but instead of adjusting, she tried to see.

Nothing. Nothing at the treeline.

She closed her eyes and sank into the flows. She tightened the bands around her arms and shifted the base, so that it began leaning eastward. *Not too far,* she counseled herself, *or I'll fall over.*

She kept her eyes open, fervently wishing she could stop the climb, but she looked into the trees as she reached forty, then fifty feet east of her base.

Nothing.

She closed her eyes and pulled the flow back, righting it, then sent her sight down the stream then up into air. She snipped off a handful of strands and felt herself falling. She opened her eyes. It wasn't as bad as she thought. She was losing a few feet a second; she should be able to survive that.

She lifted her eyes back to the trees, then looked past them at the mountain.

And screamed and pointed.

At least a hundred Shunakah were crawling at the foot of the mountain like lice on a coat. A little more than a mile away.

She lost the flow and fell.

It was less than thirty feet, but it hurt like hell when she hit on her back and her head bounced once. She lay on the rocks and gasped in pain, then rolled over to her side and pulled her legs in.

As soon as she was able, Kiera pushed up. Marco stood, mouth open, staring at the mountain. Agni was standing behind him, a hand on his shoulder, her face grim.

"We have to call for soldiers!" Kiera screamed at them, hands up, hoping to shake them out of their shock.

Agni shifted, then spoke softly, but her voice carried easily across the fifty feet of flattened ground between them. "They were called away early this morn." She sighed heavily. "A small contingent remains, and they will come soon. I heard the horn while you were descending." She gave Kiera a heavy look. "Let us go inside. Quickly. Can you walk?"

Called away? Why? Kiera nodded, but kept her questions to herself. *Why are they here?* she thought frantically. *What could they want? A hundred is a pretty small contingent to send to menace a city.* Her heart began to pound. *Are there more? Why did they let us see them?*

She had no intention of going in, not until she at least knew what they faced, but Marco would stay with her if he knew. "Go in, Marco," she told him, leaning over to exaggerate the pain in her back. "I'll follow in a minute."

His face was white—and no wonder, Kiera thought, remembering his broken body after they found him—but he nodded.

She turned to watch the dogs, but they had slunk back into the treeline. *You will not get into this city,* she swore to them silently.

CHAPTER 20

KIERA WAITED UNTIL MARCO AND AGNI disappeared through the back gate, which swung closed behind them, then jogged to a small alcove in the wall just a hundred feet west of the city's door.

Uniformed men charged out the gate in front of Kiera, forming lines two, then four, then ten or more deep. They were armed with spears. Bows.

They were young. Some were tall. Most had dark hair and the thick bodies she associated with shifters, but thinner blonds populated the ranks as well. They stood in their lines. Some looked back and forth, and many fidgeted. Kiera could feel their tension.

None turned back. None saw her, and they should have.

An older soldier, a dark-haired man with a confident mien, walked through the gate and up through a gap in the ranks to make his way to the front. Kiera slunk back into the alcove as he turned to face them. He said something, and the men straightened and began to walk forward.

They stopped a quarter mile out. They waited.

And waited.

Kiera leaned back against the wall.

Ten minutes. Fifteen.

Kiera wondered if Vayu would come, or Valen. Was it their job to provide magical protection, or did they leave these kinds of things in the hands of the soldiers? These were questions she should have thought of before.

She heard shouting on the other side of the wall, then sighed as she recognized Marco's voice. That would be a fence to mend.

She closed her eyes and put it out of her mind. She sent her sight up and searched for flows. The south-traveling airstream still flowed. Check. She left it and went up and out.

Shit. It was a full water hour now, and the fire streams she'd used had faded to almost nothing. She looked up, cast around, but besides a few trickling streams, fire was nearly gone from the skies. She shot out to the sunflow, from where she could always find something, but even its flows were brittle and tremulous, breaking apart when she tried to pull them.

Shouting startled her eyes open, and for a moment she saw double, then realized she hadn't waited to pull her sight back before trying to see.

Hundreds of Shunakah were running toward them, their feet silent in the snow.

Kiera gasped, then closed her eyes and shot her sight out as fast as she could, pulled a huge hank of air from the flow she had just left and yanked it back. Too quickly, and too much filled her, and she started to choke.

Kiera flung some of it out and into the ground ahead of her, where it sent snow flying. She held on to as much as she could, though the mass she held felt like an anvil in her stomach. She closed her eyes and shot her sight upward and into the flow from the sun, which stuttered under the oppressive masses of water plaguing the air. Teeth gritted, she pulled as much as she could from it, but most of it splintered off and wafted away, so she let what she had go and dove in again. She pulled strong pieces from here and there and tried to divert their flow to her, but too many weak strands tore.

She took what she could keep and fell back to herself. The fire didn't fill her the same way the other elements did, especially air, and though she added to the flow inside her, she felt no fuller.

Her thoughts bounced and jumbled. *Oh my God. Can I do this? Storm? Would that work? A firestorm. Should I try to make lightning? No. I don't think I can make it. And where is that storm?* She closed her eyes and shot out. The storm she had called from—it seemed like hours ago—had moved farther north from the manse, and was drifting away. She didn't think she could count on strands from a moving body, not with her focus on two other streams as well, so she left it and plunged back into herself.

The shouting sounded closer.

She opened her eyes.

The Shunakah poured into the men. Spears rose, arrows flew.

Men fell, dogs tearing at them.

Kiera lifted her eyes. More fed out of the mountain pass, too many to count, filling up the plain, while some ran round the group and filtered off to the west. They followed the river, Kiera realized.

She closed her eyes and spun fire and air into tight strands. More and then more, then sent the stream up and let it hang over the ranks. She set the flow, held it in place, and though the mass contained almost too much air to control, she opened her eyes. She had to see where to send it.

She lifted a hand and pointed at a spot where the dogs were thickest, running together as they made their way across the snow to join in the fray.

"Manifest," she whispered, and a hundred-foot sheet of sizzling fire dropped like a stone from the sky and into the dogs.

Dozens screamed as the fire consumed them, their blackened bodies jerking and twisting violently like paper tossed into a campfire. They were gone in a handful of seconds, leaving only charcoaled hulls and clouds of ashes to flit in the wind.

She pointed again, and fire fell behind the blackened hole to consume another clutch.

Kiera screamed when something whizzed past her head. Her hand flew of its own accord to slap her stinging face, but she held tight to the fire. She stepped back, eyes wide, but as she started into the sea of writhing bodies, she realized she would never be able to pinpoint a single shooter, probably not even one as odd as a dog with a bow.

Kiera shot a look backward and realized she was a good fifty yards from the wall, so she backed closer but kept her eyes to the front. She stopped when she bumped into a fallen soldier, and darted a glance behind her, still twenty yards from the wall, then raised a hand and pointed to a spot just in front of a clot of desperately fighting, and rapidly falling, soldiers, and sent the fire down.

The flames caught many dogs, but not before one pulled the older man she had seen leading the soldiers into the orange blanket, and Kiera screamed and leapt forward, willing it not to be true. *They're all going to die,* Kiera's mind shrieked.

Ten steps in front of her, a group of soldiers of apparently the same mind broke rank and ran, passing her like water flowing around a rock, each of their faces a rictus of terror. Breathing through her mouth, she inched backward toward the edge of the field. The dogs had deeply penetrated the dwindling ranks of soldiers, and she turned her head to find fights going on her left and her right.

She clamped her feelings back down and moved again, southward, and followed the wall. When she had a free spot she started to push the flow back out, but a soldier she hadn't seen jostled her from the left and she fell and lost the flow, which exploded in the snow front of her, sending two other soldiers flying.

She screamed in rage and pushed to her feet.

Screw air. She needed pure fire. Standing in the middle of the battle, she closed her eyes, fisted her hands, and sent her sight up. She flung herself into the stream from the sun, which still flowed tremulously. A hunk bigger than she was wound around her, and she shot back and spun it.

When she opened her eyes, men were screaming as they fell around her.

A dog for every man, tearing them apart. A soldier fell at her feet, his throat torn out. Everywhere she looked blood stained the snow that just a half an hour past had lain untainted.

Kiera's eyes lifted higher. And her heart stopped.

A naked man stood fifty yards from her, a strung bow in hand, an obscene smile on his face.

Hunter.

Rage flooded her, blinding her to anything else. Everything else. Nothing else mattered, not *why* or *how* or *what do you want?*

Kiera heard herself scream wordlessly.

She pointed and charged forward, pushing fire in a shaft a few feet ahead of her.

Hunter snarled and leapt over a row of dogs separating them, then dropped to all fours, changed into a Shunakah, and leapt toward her in the snow.

Insanely fast.

Not as fast as this, you son of a bitch, her thoughts screamed, and sent out her fire, a thin stream made just for him.

He leapt as the fire hit him, slammed up to his hind legs, then back on his back.

He writhed, but he didn't burn.

There wasn't time to panic. Kiera took a step forward, then another. She could hear herself breathe.

She kept hold of her fire, pushed it out, as she walked forward. As she got closer she could see that she had him pinned, but her fire stopped a few inches above him.

A shield. Oh my God. He was shielding.

Was it earth? It had to be earth.

Still holding the fire, she closed her eyes and took him in.

A thin layer of earth separated her fire from his body.

She sent her sight up. The airstream she had pulled from earlier was still pulsing above, though far weakened, but she didn't have time to search, so she pulled. She spun it, twining it with the fire in her belly.

She screamed as someone punched her in the shoulder, knocking her back, and she fell onto her bottom, losing hold of her streams, which flowed out, exploded ahead of her and knocked her flat on her back. She opened her eyes and raised trembling hands to her face, but she knew she was hurt. Pain flowed, weakened her. She panted, and reached trembling fingers to her aching shoulder.

Someone screamed, a distant, silken sound.

An arrow. There was an arrow in her shoulder, and blood had leaked all over her dress.

A shadow fell across her face, and she looked up and into Hunter's. He knelt down beside her, face grim, and took hold of the arrow.

"You motherfucker," she panted.

He pulled out the arrow and her body arched with agony, following the arrow's path out, but she did not scream.

Hunter watched her fall back with empty eyes. "Where is Alex?"

"Fuck you!" she spat, and he punched her in the temple, making stars dance across her vision. With a grunt, he straddled her and pushed her arms up above her head.

She bucked as her shoulder screamed with pain, but his weight on her pinned her to the snow.

His voice seemed calm. "Bring Alex to me and I'll tell you how to go home."

Kiera shook with rage and exhaustion. "I will never give Alex to you, you murdering bastard."

Insanely fast, he punched her twice, once in the mouth and once on the cheek, sending an arc of blood across the snow.

"Where is Alex?"

"If you kill me you'll never find him," she wheezed, praying he would believe her. "He's hidden and well protected."

"You are going to bring him to me. If you try and leave this city, I'll find you," he told her, then used the arrow to slit open the top of the left sleeve of her dress. He tapped her shoulder with the tip. "I know he's in Fairbanks, Kiera. He was with you in Talium and after."

My tattoo? He can track my tattoo?

"Tell me that you will bring Alex to me and I'll let you up."

Kiera opened her eyes and stared in Hunter's, which were a disconcertingly warm shade of green. "What happens to Alex once you get him?"

"That is not your concern." He showed his teeth. "Living past this moment is."

Kiera was breathing too quickly, and she tried to slow it. Her limbs felt weak, and though strength was returning, she needed more time. "You brought an army to die so that you could ask me to bring Alex to you?"

Hunter brought his brows down in a frown. "They didn't die."

"The ones I burned died," she whispered, anger and satisfaction threading through her words like twin flows of energy to a firestorm, then abruptly wished she had kept her mouth shut as she watched his face fill slowly with rage.

He released her arm and leaned back, fisting a hand, and Kiera bucked, lifting him up, then kneed him as hard as she could in the groin, hoping for good aim and enough power to hurt. She laid her arms flat, ignored the shearing pain in her shoulder as best she could and brought her leg down. She kicked up again, hit him between the thighs and lifted him over her. He flipped, landed above her head and grabbed her hair close to her head when he landed, but she slapped out at his arm and hit the nerve on the soft underside with a hammer fist as she yanked her head back. As she'd hoped, his grip opened some, but she lost some hair when she wrenched out of his hand.

Kiera pushed to her feet and took a horse stance while Hunter still crouched on the ground, one hand on the snow, the other wrapped around his testicles, his face tense with pain.

Kiera started to grin, but loud sounds erupted behind her. She snuck a glance behind her.

The soldiers were coming.

She turned back around, but Hunter had shifted. He stood on four legs, stared at her for a moment, then whipped around and galloped back into the packs of dogs still worrying soldiers both standing and fallen.

She lost him that quickly.

She closed her eyes and sent her sight up, but she was weak and it faltered, surged up again, then plunged back into her.

She breathed out forcefully and tried again, this time finding and sinking into a smallish, body-sized stream of air and yanking out strings. She pulled them into her and spun them, which made her chest tight. She began walking forward.

She had never really worked just air before, so she tried sending it out in balls.

It slammed dogs to the ground, but they got back up, though they ran from her afterward.

Where the hell was Agni? Vayu? Valen and Leith? Didn't they have a responsibility to protect this city? Or did they just let their soldiers do the dirty work? What the hell would they do if a mage attacked?

Kiera's mind was clouding and she couldn't seem to clear it, but she kept going and stumbled out onto the field. Northward, dogs still tore up the men.

Not just men. Men and other animals fought the dogs. Wolves and bears, screaming rage and fury. Blood stained the snow in patches and spread around the fallen.

How do I stop this? she shrieked inside her head. *I can't call fire because I'll kill my own men.* She started to run.

She heard hoof beats behind her and started to turn, but something hit her from behind, knocked out her breath, and her feet left the ground. She arched back, swinging. Tears streamed from the agony of her shoulder, and she landed a blow, then another, onto armor. She was lifted and crushed to a steel chest.

"Stop," a man's voice commanded harshly. "You are safe."

She twisted around to see but could not, so she struggled again, pushed away from the horse with her legs, and got one foot onto the horse's side. She bent her knee, then launched herself back, breaking his grip on her. She flew through the air and landed on her back in the snow, where she lay panting. She struggled to her feet and turned, and tried to call fire, but her eyes wouldn't focus and the throbbing in her shoulder sent her to her knees.

The man turned the horse—she could see its feet—and came trotting back.

Kiera pushed up with one leg, then another, and stood with her hands out in front of her, head spinning. She wondered where her knife was, and began patting her dress. She found the sheath and reached in, but her fingers wouldn't close over the handle.

Booted feet hit the ground. Kiera stumbled back. Big hands took her shoulders and she flinched and cried out.

Someone spoke—"Shima's tit! This blood is yours!"—and she was smashed into the armor again. She tried to fight, but coldness enveloped her in one sudden crush and her legs threatened to give out.

"I have to sit down," she said breathlessly, and collapsed in the snow.

"Wound shock," the voice told her, and she closed her eyes. "Kiera," the voice beckoned, and she opened her eyes.

"Laszlo," she sighed, then grimaced as pain washed through her. "It hurts."

He pulled off a glove and knelt down. He touched the sore spot next to her eye, traced the scratch on her face, then tried to peel the fabric away from the wound in her shoulder. "No, no!" she told him. "Don't touch it!"

"Are you injured anywhere else?" he asked briskly, running a hand down her arm, then the other, then across her stomach. His voice seemed very calm, almost gentle, but his eyes looked hard and bright.

"No," she said, and closed her eyes.

"Kiera," he called. "Stay with me."

She opened her eyes. "They're still fighting," she told him. "I should get up. Will you please help me?"

"Not for long," he told her grimly, and laid a hand on her chest. "Why were you out here?"

"Practicing magic," she answered.

He looked up and to the north. A muscle ticked in his jaw. He slanted her a glance. "And where is your teacher?"

"I sent her back inside," she said, and started to tremble.

"What happened to your shoulder?"

"An arrow."

"Did it go all the way through?"

Kiera looked up at the sky. The sun shone very brightly. The ice in the air danced and sparkled in the breeze. "No. It went in a long way, though."

Laszlo leaned over so that he blocked her line of sight. "Did you pull it out?"

"No," she answered, then wished she'd said yes. "It fell out," she lied, then shifted a little to try and ease her shoulder, which had started to throb. "When I fell, I think. Earlier."

For the smallest of moments a corner of Laszlo's mouth lifted, but he turned away and looked north. "You smell like Shunakah," he told her without turning his head.

"I bet this whole field smells like those stinking dogs," she said with some heat. "Laszlo, my shoulder really, really hurts. I don't think I can fight anymore. Will you help me up?"

"No."

"Why not?"

"Shhhh."

"Don't treat me like a child, Laszlo. I want to get up."

He turned back to her. "Kiera, lie still."

Kiera pulled her elbows up and tried to push herself up, but Laszlo pressed her back down.

"If you don't take your fucking hand off me I'm going to knock the shit out of you," Kiera growled, and turned sideways, trying to get out from under his hand. Her shaking became more pronounced when she exerted her muscles, and even she had to admit that it was a pitiful attempt.

He pushed her back again. "Kiera, you need to lie down until a wagon gets here to take you inside to the healers. Wound shock can become very bad." He leaned forward again, a strange look on his face. "Why are you lying about the arrow?"

"Why didn't Vayu come and protect this city?" she countered.

His tone was mild. "He would have come if there was magic."

"Asshole," she responded. "Lazy ass was probably sitting up on his throne with his hand on his dick while everybody out here was fighting."

A smile washed over his face and then was gone.

"They can shield," Kiera whispered, and Laszlo leaned in, close to her face.

"What do you mean?"

"They, the dogs, can shield from my fire. Or at least one of them can, and if one can, others can," she told him, holding his eyes, despair in her own. "Using earth magic." She shook her head. "I don't understand."

His brows were down. "Shielding? Using magic, like you do?"

Kiera shifted, then grimaced, but although the pain was bad, talking was keeping her head clear. Mostly clear. "I don't know if it's like I do it, Laszlo. I don't know how to shield, and I'm not very good with earth magic yet. But to be fair, all of the others I burned fell just like they did when we fought them before."

Laszlo stood, then bellowed a phrase in a language she had never heard. Within seconds, a large black bear loped up. Laszlo said something to it—him?—and the bear galloped back off. He leaned back down. "A wagon will be here shortly. How are you feeling?"

"It hurts. But I'm okay." She smiled a little. "I'm sure glad you came back when you did."

He looked at her eyes, but his face was hard to read.

"I'm sorry I couldn't save more of your soldiers," she told him quietly. "I tried as hard as I could, Laszlo, I swear to God, I stopped, I don't know, hundreds, but after—I just couldn't hold on to the strands anymore. I sent air and that punched into them and I pulled as much energy as I could hold, but I was just too tired and it was hard to make sense of things and I couldn't see very well and—" She knew she was babbling so she let the rest of her breath out in a rush and dropped her gaze to the field behind him.

He put a hand over hers. "Rest easy. You carry no blame, *a'kala,*" he said gently, then stood. An open wagon was trundling up, drawn by a pair of dark, shaggy horses. When it got to them, several men leapt off the back and hurried over. Laszlo looked southward as one leaned over and reached for her arm, but Laszlo turned back abruptly and barked, *"Sen'ikcha a'kala achubruk,"* and the man, all the men, took a step back, heads bowed.

Kiera's gaze flew to Laszlo's face, but he avoided her eyes as he knelt down and picked her up. "I can stand," she complained, but he ignored her, and as he lifted, she flinched hard from the pain.

He walked around the wagon and laid her in the back, next to an unconscious man with a mangled face, and pulled a blanket off a pile and covered her. She pushed herself up shakily to a sitting position. "What does that mean? What you said?"

Laszlo smiled at her, showing his teeth. "Lie back. Go see the healers." He turned and walked away.

She watched him walk as the wagon jumped and started toward the gate. He was always so kind to her, even when he didn't have to be. And he sure didn't have to be today, for chrissakes. She'd been as overexcited as a teenage boy on his first date and people had died because she hadn't been a better mage.

"I love you, Laszlo," Kiera whispered, throat tight.

He stiffened and stopped.

He couldn't have heard me. He's twenty yards away!

But then he started walking again.

SEVERAL HOURS LATER, after Lord Saman finished with her, a still-fuming Marco walked with Kiera back to her rooms. Saman had managed to seal the hole in her shoulder, and with pain medicine she was almost as good as new. She had a salve for her face that he promised would heal the scrape and her bruises to nothing by tomorrow.

She loved magical healing.

Marco was glaring, albeit at the floor, which was an improvement.

"I'm sorry, Marco," Kiera said for the twentieth time. "I won't do it again."

He said nothing, which was not an improvement.

"How can I make this right?"

He shook his head and looked at her. "There is nothing, you lout." He was stifling a grin, and Kiera felt herself relax.

She reached out and snagged his hand.

AFTER MAGIC LESSONS the next morning, which a somewhat distraught Agni had insisted they attend, and which contained a half hour lecture on the dangers of pushing magic too fast, Emmy brought them lunch and then left to go run some errands.

"You know, Marco," Kiera said as she ate, "I really think that all of the shifters use some kind of magic. I want to go watch some shift." She turned to him. "Where?"

He looked thoughtful as he chewed. "Well, the farmers change, you know, to pull or push the plows, but it isn't summer." He took another bite, then smiled at her.

"What?"

"You won't want to."

"What?"

"Well, the soldiers train both in human form and in their animal forms."

She looked at him with narrowed eyes. "Is there a way I could watch and they wouldn't see me?"

"Likely. But they would smell you when you got close."

She grunted.

Emmy came back in as they were finishing lunch. "Emmy," Kiera asked, "do you have access to stores of clothes, like for servants?"

Emmy was surprised. "Yes, my lady."

"Would you mind doing me a favor? Please? I need you to find me an outfit, or two, that would fit me. Clothes for a man, though. And I need a hat. Or two. Like the ones the farmers wear."

Marco was nodding. "That might work," he said, "but you'd have to be willing to—"

Kiera wrinkled her nose. "I know, Marco."

"Emmy," Marco said, "would you please get something that will fit me, too? Farmer as well."

"No, Marco!" Kiera said, setting down her glass. "I won't let you do that."

He looked very annoyed. "Kiera, I'm sure that it was just one turn ago you promised that you wouldn't go haring off without me."

"Then I'm not going to go, and next time I won't tell you," she snapped.

Marco heaved a sigh. "What are you afraid of, Kiera? That someone will hurt me?"

"Well, since you asked, yes. Among other things. And how the hell are you going to explain the way you're dressed if you're caught? I'm some weird foreigner, but you are the governor's son!"

"See, Kiera, this is exactly why you need me," he said haughtily.

"What?"

Marco nodded at Emmy. "Emmy, please?" Emmy bowed her head and slipped out of the room.

Marco got up and sat next to Kiera. "You were planning on just going out. Right? Just putting on your clothes, dirtying them up, and then scurrying around in your smelly clothes until you found wherever it is in this city the army trains—"

"I don't need a damn map. I'd find it."

"—and of course you'll be hoping that none of the mages see you, right? And what if they do? What were you planning on saying?"

Kiera made a face. "I'd think of something before I left."

Marco took her hand, all signs of teasing gone. "Kiera, listen to me." His face was solemn. "Wherever it is you're from, it's different from here. You're so different from anyone I have ever known." He squeezed her hand. "A good kind of different. But Kiera, just because you're a mage, or a woman, doesn't mean you won't get in trouble. Or hurt."

Kiera looked at him for a long time before she answered. "Marco, I agree that where I come from is very different. But where I come from, people get hurt all the time."

She looked down, trying to stomp her way through a surprising puddle of grief and anger. And the deep sadness that seemed to blanket her life. She looked up. "I have been hurt many times, Marco. And so have people I cared about."

She stood up and faced the fire. "My sister is dead, Marco. Most of a year, a cycle, ago." She turned back to him. "Before that, even, I learned how to fight. Before I had magic. I learned how to protect myself. I carry weapons." She pulled a knife from a fold in her dress. "I know how to hit." She sat down on the couch. "And I know I can kill if I need to." She leaned her head back and closed her eyes. "I never wanted a life like this. Even when I was little. I wanted laughing parents and trips to the zoo." She let out a breath. "And to not be afraid."

After a moment she continued. "And so I was whisked to this place where I thought things were so different, but they're really the same. Where I come from, violence is hidden behind closed doors, but it's still the powerless who suffer."

Her mouth twisted. "At home, I tried to help and I couldn't. Or I failed. I'm not sure. Maybe both. But here I have a second chance."

Kiera opened her eyes and sat up. "So while I admit that I'm still struggling to learn how to think like a rebel spy, and how to be a mage, I do appreciate the risks involved, and the advice that you give me. But Marco, I'm not going to stop because it's dangerous or because I might get hurt." She got up and poured herself a glass of water, then drank it down. "And I don't want you to get hurt just because I have to do these things."

Marco stood up and walked to Kiera. When she sat the glass down, he pulled her head to his shoulder.

CHAPTER 21

To make sure they fit, Kiera and Marco put on the clothes that Emmy brought before bundling them up and hiding the packs inside their coats. Emmy pinned Kiera's hair so that a hat would completely cover it. Kiera pulled the hood of her coat over her head so no one would notice.

Marco stood in front of the door. "If someone stops us, you say that we are going for a walk in the city. No particular destination."

They went out quickly, down the stairs and out the front. They strolled into the city, occasionally dodging in and out of alleys to shake anyone who might be tailing them.

"So Marco, why didn't you use magic that day I met you?" Kiera asked as they turned a corner. "You're a powerful mage."

"For two reasons," he answered as he pulled her inside a stable. It was empty, except for a few cows. And it stank. "This is perfect." He led her in and down to a stall at the back. "I didn't use magic because then any mage in the area would know I was there. Pulling elements disturbs the stream flows." He turned to grin at her. "And because magic won't stop arrows, Kiera. Well, not unless you use a lot of magic, like a windstorm, and even then it's chancy."

"Why did you try to heal Allie then? And speaking of which, how do you know how? Is that something air mages can do?"

Marco went inside a stall and pulled off his coat, then his shirt, and put the more worn farmer's shirt over it. Kiera turned her back as he pulled off his pants.

"No. Healing isn't an air spell. Water maybe, or some mix. I learned I could heal my own bruises when I was just a kid," he told her. "I can't do much. I use something from inside myself to do it, but don't ask me how. Since it's not pulling from outside, no one can see me do it."

That made sense. Kiera bet a lot of mages had some small, hidden talents. Maybe it depended on what exact minute they had been born. "So there's no way to use magic to turn away arrows?" she asked. "There has to be something."

"Go get changed."

Kiera went into a stall and pulled her coat off. She felt a little reluctant to take off her dress, but after a long look toward the door, she backed into the stall and pulled it over her head. She slipped into the clothes Emmy had given her as quickly as she could, then dropped the old coat on over the top. It was not nearly warm enough.

"You know, Marco, I am going to freeze in these clothes," she complained.

"We'll have to keep moving then," he answered.

"How the slaves are clothed is another thing that makes me mad," she grumbled.

"I know," he soothed.

When they had finished, they hid their clothes under the hay in the stalls, then came out for each other's inspection. Kiera pulled on her round hat, and Marco adjusted it. Marco put on a similar hat. *He's getting taller,* Kiera thought as she reached up to adjust it for him.

Marco grinned. "Ready?"

Kiera grimaced. "Sure."

They walked out to the stalls where the dirty hay had been shoveled. Marco grabbed a handful and smeared it on his stomach, then began rubbing it into the fabric in earnest. He rubbed it into his hands, and even rubbed a thin coating on his face. He then used some clean hay to wipe it off, leaving a grimy mess behind.

Then it was Kiera's turn. Marco helped a little too enthusiastically.

When they finished, Marco pulled her hat down lower and they went to the stable door. Marco turned to her and spoke softly. "If someone stops you, look at the ground. Do not look anyone in the eye. If they ask you what you're doing, tell them you're on your way to get some bread. Say that: 'I'm on my way to get bread, my lord.' I'm your brother, Roke. Your name is Jano. No matter what happens, Kiera, do not raise your voice, or take a noble tone, or talk back," he sighed. "And do not try to stop fights, or hit anyone, or anything else."

Kiera nodded, a trifle annoyed that he thought he'd had to add that last part.

Marco opened the door just a crack and looked outside, then motioned for her to wait. He stepped outside the door and disappeared.

In less than three minutes the door opened, and Marco motioned her out. "No talking," he whispered. "And keep your head down."

She followed him out, then followed his feet in front of her as he led her away from the stable. She prayed he'd be able to find their way back when they were finished, because she knew for a fact that she wouldn't.

They walked for almost an hour, during which one good thing and one bad thing happened. No one spoke to them, or even seemed to notice them, which was very good, but Kiera was feeling increasingly shaky and queasy. She was almost ready to sit down in the middle of the road when he stopped. He motioned her to follow him into a building. Once inside, she looked around. It was just an old wooden shed, and it had been empty for some time. She plopped on the ground without ceremony.

Marco leaned down. "Are you all right?"

She nodded and held up a finger.

After a few minutes, far sooner than she would have preferred, she got to her feet and motioned him to go on. He led her through the building, out the back, and into an open yard. It was deserted, but she could hear shouting ahead. Marco led her around the perimeter and through a tall gate. She looked up, then quickly back down. People filled the arena, all of whom were men. She peeked back up and noted that an area in the middle had been cleared, and that two or three people stood in it. They wore very little.

Marco led her behind the crowd and into a big open stable on the far side. Once inside, he waited a second, then walked to the left. He stood there for a minute, looked left and right, then scurried up the ladder and into the attic. From the top, he motioned for her to come up.

She felt a little scared to do it. If anyone came in while she was climbing, they were going to ask what the hell she was doing. Marco motioned again. *Well, they'll ask what you're doing standing here, too,* she chastened herself, and went up the ladder as quickly as she could.

Marco helped her hide under the hay just as a couple of men ambled into the stable. They walked right through, though, and didn't look up.

When they had gone, Marco wiggled through the scratchy mound to the front of the stable and peered through the window. The boards beneath them felt wiggly, so Kiera took her time. When she got close to the window, she motioned him down. As quietly as she could, she whispered, "If someone finds us, you say that you and your brother came to watch the men fight. I won't talk."

After Marco nodded, Kiera leaned forward until she could see out the window, then arranged the hay around her. She hoped that if anyone looked up, they'd just see a big lump of yellow.

She turned her eyes to the clearing below where two men sparred. One jumped the other, shoved him back, and down the two went. A third waited until they had locked arms around each other and then jumped into the fray. The three rolled around for a while, but none worked any magic.

As she watched, she compared these men's styles to her own *tai kwon-do*. Although not strictly sticking to any fighting style she had seen, these men packed a lot of power and some finesse into their moves. This wasn't just street fighting; they had been trained.

Kiera watched the next few sets, all with three fighters, but soon had to fight yawns. All were Skani, or maybe shifters who didn't shift, and none of them used any kind of magic at all.

For the fourth match, three wide, dark-haired men entered the ring. She sat up as carefully as she could so that she could see better.

Without warning, one attacked another. The third jumped the second as well, and the two pinned the one, then released him. Head down, he scuffled out of the ring. The last two squared off and circled each other, lithe muscles rippling under their skin.

Kiera closed her eyes and sent out her sight.

Shock rolled through her. Both—*both!*—pulled earth, but not in the way she knew how to call an element. Tiny strands, almost invisible tendrils, seeped up through the ground, snaked across their feet and ankles, spread out in a thin sheet, then disappeared inside their skin. When they crouched, green hairs wound round, then sunk into their midsections and arms.

And they didn't spin it out. She couldn't see where it went, and she had no understanding of internal magic so she couldn't just look inside them to see what happened once it entered their bodies. *But magic can't just go in and not come out,* she thought. *They'll die!*

Wondering what it would look like with her eyes, she opened them, but they had started to shift, so she squeezed her lids closed and opened her sight.

Earth exploded around them as they shifted. Hundreds of little clouds, like green mist, mushroomed off them, then broke apart and drifted away like smoke in a breeze.

Kiera had to stop herself from shaking her head. She had never seen magic done like this.

As they fought, they seemed to actually pull earth magic into them. In their animal form, the magic streamed up in clumps, not strings, into their feet, their bellies, even their faces, and it puffed out across their upper bodies in clouds as they fought.

They're mages! she thought, clenching her thumbs under her fingers to keep her hands still. *They use magic and don't even know it! I bet they can be taught how to use the other elements!* Her thoughts grew grim. *This must be how Hunter can shield.*

With a heartfelt sigh, she opened her eyes to find two large, iron-colored wolves stalking each other.

Kiera snaked out a hand and touched Marco, who jumped. She leaned back and motioned down to him, but he held up a finger. She lay back in the hay and stared up at the mismatched boards nailed together above her.

How will I teach them to use the other elements when I don't even know how they do this? Can they use magic the same way I do? Is there any part of this that's conscious?

She had so many questions she wanted to ask someone. Maybe Mosha would know. Besides, he still needed to show her how to shield, which might help her understand how Hunter did it. But she knew it would all have to wait until tomorrow. She had to go back to her rooms and get ready to go to the party tonight.

She sat up and crawled back to the ladder, then peered down at the stable below. Men shouted from beyond the shed, apparently engrossed in the fighting, but the space below them lay empty.

After the fight ended, Marco scooted up next to her. "Wait until the next match starts," he whispered.

Within minutes, the shouting started again. After one last look, Kiera put a foot on the ladder. At the same moment, someone walked into the stable. She froze. Her heart raced. She knew he'd see her if she moved.

He walked right through without looking up, and she let herself breathe out. With an eye on the door, she set her other foot on the ladder, then started down.

"Hey!" someone yelled. Startled, she turned her head the other direction, toward the fighting, to find a man, a tall, blond soldier, peeking in the stable. "What are you doing up there, boy?"

She froze. *Shit, shit, shit.*

"Come down here!"

She climbed down slowly. When her feet touched down, she looked at the floor and prayed Marco was smart enough to stay hidden in the hay.

He grabbed her arm. "What are you doing, I said?"

"I am sorry, sir," she whispered. His grip hurt but she didn't try to pull away. "I wanted to see the fight." *And it was damned cold out here.*

"So ye came to fight?" the man taunted. Without letting go, he pulled her to one side, and she stumbled. "Ye think yer good enough to be one of us?"

Goddamn it. "No, sir," she whispered.

He laughed once, just a "hah!," then dragged her out through the door. She dragged her feet, not sure how to handle this, and he flung her into the ring. She tripped, then fell, and her hat barely stayed on. She almost got up, then remembered Marco's admonition.

"Who will go against this terrifying farmboy?" the man called to the audience, scorn large in his voice.

Fury threatened to overwhelm anger, but she kept her head down. She thought calming thoughts, then turned so that she could sit tailor style and folded her hands in her lap. Out of the corner of her eye she saw Marco slide down the ladder, then disappear. She prayed he would wait and then find her after this joyous ordeal had ended.

A pole arm, a staff, lay on the ground next to her. The last match must have been an armed one.

Well, that was good. Just in case.

"Pick it up," the man said. He must have seen her looking.

"No," she said quietly, then shook her head. He kicked it toward her, and it bounced against her leg.

All of a sudden she was finished with this. She put her feet out and started to get up.

Maybe if she hadn't kept her head down she would have seen it coming, but when the man slapped her, she lost her footing on the slick ground and fell on her side. Her face hit the mud.

The man laughed. "Come on, boy. Get up!"

She blew out a breath, then pushed herself up to a sitting position. She knew that Marco was right: if she fought, she would attract attention. But would it be more attention than she was getting now? And maybe if she knocked this bullying bastard to the ground, she could get away before this got any worse.

She nodded once, then reached for the pole. The man laughed again, clearly enjoying himself, but the crowd had fallen silent. She looked up. The man stood back, enough to let her up. Not trusting him, she stood, using the pole to protect her front.

He crossed his arms. Smirked.

She stood and waited. She was not going to attack. No one would be able to say that she started this.

He launched himself at her, and she stood firm. He was sloppy, slow and overconfident. When he got close, she stepped aside and used the pole to trip him.

He went past her, and down. He fell hard on his stomach.

Someone laughed.

With a snarl, he got up and threw himself at her again. She used the pole in a low stroke to pull his feet out from under him, then took a follow-up step in as he was falling and used the pole—and her weight—to make sure he slammed to the ground.

The she turned, dropped the pole, and ran into the stable.

She turned the corner Marco had disappeared into. She was watching the ground and shock zinged through her when she smashed into someone. He had good reflexes; he didn't give an inch and, in fact, he pushed back just a little.

She stumbled and took a step back, and he took a step forward.

Shit.

She darted to the side, but he was faster.

She turned, then faked to one side and darted to the other.

Still faster.

He reached out and put a hand on her shoulder. She stopped, panting, and looked at the ground. *Shit, shit, shit.*

"There is no need to run, boy. Such a strong fighter should join the army," Laszlo said, voice amused.

Shit!

She took a step back and lifted her shoulder, trying to shrug off his hand. He stepped forward and didn't let go.

"Tell me your name."

"Jano," she whispered, then pulled back and dashed around him.

He laughed as he grabbed her coat.

He pulled her back around. "Where do you work?"

Oh, shit. "Cows," she whispered, trying to sound hoarse, and hoping he'd believe her. God knows she smelled like cows.

He paused. "Take off your hat," he commanded. He was not laughing now.

She backed up and shook her head.

She saw his hand coming to grab it, so she ducked back.

He grabbed the front of her coat and pulled her to him so fast her feet drug on the ground.

He pulled off her hat and tossed it aside.

She looked up.

His normally bland face looked so shocked that she almost laughed.

He suddenly roared with laughter.

Men filed in behind him, trying to see what the commotion was about. Laszlo watched her face, and without looking away, he shouted, "Leave us!"

Kiera flinched, and everyone rushed out the door.

Without letting go of her, he half-dragged her out the far side of the stable to an empty area where the snow lay untrodden. He pushed her back against the wall, not ungently.

He looked at her mouth, her face.

Before she could say one word, he kissed her. And though she knew she should pull away, she did not. Instead she opened her mouth to him and kissed him back, as hungry as he was. He groaned in her mouth and pulled her into him. He slipped a hand underneath her shirt. Heat rolled across her back.

A fire exploded in her chest, and the tendrils flickered lower. Oh God, how she wanted him. Wanted his hands on her, his mouth on her, him inside her.

She panicked. *I can't do this,* she thought desperately, and pushed him back.

He wiped a strand of hair from her face that had torn free and tucked it behind her ear. "What are you doing here?" he asked softly.

She looked up at him. "I'm on my way to get bread, my lord," she answered.

His smile faded. "*A'kala,* you have to go back to the manse. Where are your clothes?"

She stared up at him.

He crossed his arms and pressed his mouth into a flat line.

After five full minutes of silence she gave in. "Please let me go," she sighed. "I promise I'll go right back to the house."

But his eyes had lost focus. His head shot up and his nostrils flared as he pulled in a breath. "Come out here, Marco."

He looked down at her, face still hard. "Have you taken the boy to your bed?"

"What?" Shock passed and anger snaked through her. "That's none of your business!"

Laszlo leaned forward until his face nearly touched hers. When he spoke, his voice was calm and even, but his eyes were not. "Take him to your bed and I'll kill him."

Kiera gaped, furious. "You goddamned barbarian! Don't you touch him! You have no right!"

Marco stepped out from around a corner wearing a sheepish face. Laszlo turned his head, but stood blocking Kiera's way out. "Touch her and your life is mine. Be warned, boy." She knew he meant his voice to be frightening, and Kiera had to admit that it was, a little.

Marco kept his eyes on the ground as he nodded.

Kiera reached down and grabbed Laszlo's hand. He turned to her. "Laszlo, you high-handed jerk, you have no right to me," she ground through gritted teeth. She shook with what she hoped was anger. "You lied to me. You knew how I felt."

She paused. Shook her head. "You have a wife, Laszlo!" she shouted, then clenched her lips shut. She did not want everyone in the vicinity to hear this. "I will not be your mistress, Laszlo," she hissed. "I will not share you with another woman. It's over between us, and what I do with my life from this moment on is none of your business."

He leaned in and kissed her once on the mouth, then turned away. "Stay here," he said. "I'll have someone take you back to your clothes and the manse."

"No," she said.

A look of annoyance passed over his face. "Don't be foolish."

She knew she was being childish, but she was hurting and angry and she just didn't care. "Do you know what, Laszlo? My getting home safely is no longer your concern."

He raised his brows and looked—amused.

She lost her temper. "Let me go, you arrogant, self-righteous jerk. I am sick and tired of this paternalistic, condescending bullshit. And you know what? I don't need your goddamned help."

Marco was making a face from behind Laszlo's back, and she knew he wanted her to shut the hell up. She flashed him a glare and shut his face from her mind.

Laszlo looked far less amused. "This is not a game, *a'kala,*" he said quietly.

"You could have fooled me," she ground out, hoping the dagger in her words pierced his heart. "Now move."

Laszlo grabbed both of her arms. "You will yield to me in this, *a'kala.*"

Now she was shaking with anger. "Or what? You'll make me?"

A flurry of emotions passed over Laszlo's face. When his face stilled, he let go of her arms, then lifted a hand and tapped her cheek with a finger. "No," he told her. "I will not." He stepped away, and she took an uneven breath. From five feet away, he turned back to her. "Will you please allow someone to help you get safely back?"

After a long moment, she nodded.

"Wait here," he said as he walked to the stable. He paused at the door and turned back to her. *"Hyhi eeido, a'kala,"* he told her and disappeared through the door.

She refused to wonder what the hell that meant.

WHEN KIERA AND MARCO got back to her room, Kiera went right in the bathroom and ran a bath. She had her nice clothes on, but she stank. "Marco," she called, "go back to your room and take a bath."

"No," he answered back. "I'm not going through the halls smelling like this."

She realized he was right, so she jumped into the bath and started washing hurriedly, which made her feel a little grumpy. She felt sick, she was tired, and her emotions were just plain worn out. She wanted to soak.

"Take your time," Marco called, as if reading her mind.

She hesitated, then sank back and closed her eyes.

When the water had cooled, she got out, feeling virtuous. She came out wrapped in her towel and climbed into bed. "I'll just lie here until you're done," she said, more than a little groggily.

Marco came and sat on the bed. Kiera wrinkled her nose. "You want to go so you can see Chanda, right?" he asked.

She didn't open her eyes. "Yeah."

"Sleep, Kiera. We'll go nexturn. It'll be just as good then."

All the fight went out of her. "All right," she said.

He snorted. "I wish I had something else to ask of you right now. Do you want me to wake you when Emmy gets back with Alex so you can eat?"

"No," she said.

"All right. Hey, I'm going to sleep here, all right? It will look a lot less suspicious if Emmy comes calling for a change of my clothes in the morn."

"Sure," she said sleepily. A thought struck her and she peeled open an eye. "Aren't you worried about that?" she asked.

"No."

"Why not?"

"Because you won't smell like me."

"What? Oh," she said, a little embarrassed.

He got up and walked toward the bathroom.

"He wouldn't do it," she said. "He's just being a jerk."

Marco didn't reply.

CHAPTER 22

KIERA AND MARCO WENT TO MAGIC LESSONS the next morning. Marco strode off to his room with a wave, but Agni, practically humming with excitement, pulled Kiera aside before she could make her way down the hall.

Agni gestured to a bench. "Sit down, Lady Kiera."

Kiera sat and faced Agni expectantly.

"I have happy tidings, child. After witnessing the firestorm you called and the other magics you employed in defense of our city, my lord Vayu called me to provide my assessment of your progress."

Kiera's heart sank. She hadn't thought about everyone else seeing her magic, or what it might mean. She wasn't ready for this, but she tried to keep the fear off her face.

"He is calling a tournament, Lady Kiera, and during your performance you will call a firestorm, and perhaps do some other magic. Thisturn we will go over what I want you to do."

"When?" Kiera asked though numb lips.

Agni smiled and patted her hand. "In seven turns. Do not be nervous, Lady Kiera. You will do well. I will ask Lord Marco to stand with you while you wait, and I will be there."

"What will happen afterward?"

Agni smiled broadly. "I expect that he will name you war mage."

Kiera nodded because she had nothing to say.

KIERA LEFT AT LUNCH, though she had agreed to come back in an hour because she needed the practice.

To her surprise Marco waited in her room, already eating, of course.

"What happened?" he asked without preamble.

She told him.

"What does this mean, I mean really?" she asked. "Does it mean I'll have to start going out with the army? Or will I get to stay here?"

"I don't know, Kiera. We've never had a war mage before." He looked thoughtful. "Anchorage has one, though. I think he goes out with the army."

"Is she or he a fire mage?"

"He. No. An air mage. The two best elements for fighting are air and fire, though water would be better if you were out on the ocean, I guess."

Kiera sat back, tapping the arm of the couch with her fingers. "The shifters have magic, Marco. Hell, they use magic."

Marco's hand froze halfway to his mouth. "What do you mean?"

Kiera grabbed a roll off the tray and took a bite. "It's a lot different than what we do. It's like they pull magic from the ground, so it must be pure earth magic, which none of us can do much with. By the way, I want to ask you about where magic comes from—each element, I mean—but wait until I'm finished to answer, okay? Anyway, it looks to me like it's sucked up through their feet when they're human, and into the undersides of their bodies when they're in their animal forms. And it isn't—I don't know how to describe it." She took another bite. "It's not—conscious, I don't think, and it isn't regulated like we do it. They pull a bunch in, and I don't know how they store it, but they do, but then they spend it to move quickly and shift and for strength."

Marco looked stunned. "Don't you think somebody would notice, Kiera, if they were using magic?"

"Well, you have lived here your whole life and never noticed. I think because so many of you are air mages you can't see it. Remember? Agni told me that most mages can't even sense their element's opposite. Well, my opposite is not earth, so I sense it pretty easily, though it's harder than hell for even me to use. It's so sticky and heavy. I have to tell Mosha, though he may already know. I don't know. He doesn't act like he knows. But anyway, I'd love to start working with some of them to see if they can use magic like we can, and to see if we—well, not the air mages, but the rest of us—can use earth like they do."

Marco sat his food down. "Kiera, I have seen tens of mages in my life. I trained with most of them. You have a talent for magic like I have never seen. It takes most people ten cycles to learn to do what you learn in a tenturn." He shrugged. "I know you think Agni is powerful, but even she is nothing compared to you. She just has decades of experience developing skills and learning control." He shook his head. "What I'm trying to say is that I have never heard anything like what you're saying—" he held up a hand to block her protest. "I do believe you, Kiera, but I don't think anyone else will, and more importantly I don't think anyone else will be able to train shifters or learn how they do their magic. This will be something you have to do, at least until some of the rest of us catch up."

KIERA SPENT the rest of the afternoon learning how to move objects by manifesting air around them. Sometime during her efforts she remembered Marco had failed to explain the origins of the elements to her, so she went to find Agni.

She found Agni in the altar room reading a book. "Lady Agni, do you have a moment to answer a few questions?"

Agni put down the book and smiled at her. "I was sure you would have many, child." She gestured to a place on the bench next to where she sat.

Kiera sat. "Where do the elements come from? The main flows, I mean."

Agni looked surprised. "Not the question I expected. Nonetheless I will tell you, though I should once again refer you to the books you should have already read." She softened her words with a smile. "I do understand that you have been working very hard to learn a great deal in a very short time. But after we talk, I want you to take several back to your rooms and read them all. We will discuss them as you read them, Lady Kiera, but it is important that you take in as much information as you can. You have a sharp mind and you push forward so quickly that you get ahead of your lessons on almost every turn. But you must read and develop a deeper understanding of spellmaking, Kiera, or you will begin making mistakes. Is that clear?"

"Yes, Lady Agni."

"Because mistakes could cost you lives, including your own."

Kiera wanted to roll her eyes. "Yes, Lady Agni."

"Each element has a different origin. Air comes from the streams that circle the world. Smaller streams break off, or are diverted, by mountains and by other streams when they collide. The streams, large and small, wax and wane here, in this place, as the cycles of the stars pull them to and fro. The very large streams, the mother streams, are very high, and I do not permit most mages to pull from them for any reason, nor do I recommend they try it on their own," she said pointedly, and Kiera hid a smile. "Those streams are very, very powerful, Lady Kiera, and if they are diverted into a mage, they are nearly impossible to stop. You could die from even a small thread from a mother stream because you could not stop the flow. Do you understand?"

Okay. That was frightening. "Yes, Lady Agni."

"Fire comes directly from the sun and the stars. It flows in waves, and like air, it also breaks into smaller streams that are pulled back and forth by the cross-pull of the stars. If you close your eyes and send out your sight, you will see the streams flowing from each star, as well as the arcs and the streams that are pulled off them. They are easiest to see at night, when the sun's flow does not overwhelm the rest. Similar to air, I usually do not permit mages to pull threads from the mother streams, but I believe that you have the strength to break a main flow, and so I will permit you to try, although I insist that you allow me to be there the first time you try it."

Kiera decided not to tell her that she'd been pulling from the sun's flow for months.

"Air is attracted to itself, and it wants to stay together, which makes it very dangerous in ways the other elements are not. Fire, like all elements, will flow in a stream, but even a large flow can be broken or diverted. It is easier to scatter. As I am sure you realize, small threads of fire remain in the air, even during water's strongest marks. It is not as attracted to itself as air and the stars have a harder time pulling it, and even when it is pulled, it leaves pieces behind."

Kiera nodded. She had noticed the same.

"Water comes from the giant oceans and from all bodies where it pools, and its streams flow both under the world and above it, although the flows above the surface are much weaker. It is very sensitive to temperature and easily broken. If I trained water mages, I would allow them to pull from the largest streams deep inside the world because as soon as your call stops, water falls back. What that means is that water requires effort to pull, unlike air and fire, which just need a channel.

"Earth comes from the body of our world and all that live on it. The movement of the life pulsing in our mother planet and all that live on it are believed to make this energy. It has no large flows but is instead made up of many small flows. Sometimes those flows meld and become a larger flow, but those last for only a short time. As you know, earth magic is sluggish, but it is also perhaps the strongest element. Anything made with earth magic tends to last.

"Lady Kiera, I should tell you that there is one other place where you will find fire, but I must stress as firmly as I am able to you that you must never call it, not for any reason. That flow is the belly of the world, the great fire lake that lives in her center. If you call that fire, fire will come, but it will also rend a weakness in the shell of the world and the fire from our world's belly will spill forth. It has happened before, and many died. Understand that if that fire is called, it might kill far more than just this city. It could kill everyone in this country. Am I clear?"

Kiera felt a little faint. "Yes, Lady Angi, I understand," she said. "May I ask another question?"

"Yes, my child."

"How do bodies, human bodies, work? I mean with the elements. Do we pull them in? How do they get there? How are they regulated?"

Agni smiled. "I can only provide you with the most basic of answers to those questions, my child. The healers are far more skilled in such matters, and I am certain I can find one to speak with you if you wish."

"Thank you."

"Allow me to answer that yes, all bodies attract elemental energy, and all bodies use this energy. Every body requires a constant inflow of whatever element claimed you at birth. None of this is conscious, though healers learn to do it on purpose when they heal themselves or others. We humans are just pale reflections of our world, which also uses the energies to regulate herself. I have a book or two that might help provide the answers you wish," she said with a pointed glance. "Read those and if you have further questions I will send you to a healer."

"Again, thank you, Lady Agni."

Agni smiled expectantly. "Have you more questions, Lady Kiera?"

"What will I have to do as a war mage? Will I have to go out with the army?"

Agni nodded. "Those are the questions I expected. The answers are simple. Your position as war mage, should Lord Vayu name you such, will be to protect this deconn using your magic. You will swear an oath to do so. As to time in the field, at times you will have to march forth with the army and at other times you will remain in the manse. I suspect you will be gone for only a few moons each cycle."

"So my magic will be used to fight battles?"

"Yes, child."

Kiera tried not to look as sick as she felt, which reminded her of another question she didn't want to ask Marco. "Lady Agni," she asked tentatively, "why am I drawn to water? Especially when I'm sad?"

Agni was silent for a moment. "I think those with strong feelings are drawn to that which would quench them. Perhaps especially when those feelings are difficult." She paused, then spoke firmly. "I do not think it means more than that."

Kiera felt a knot in her chest loosen. "Which books do you want me to read?"

AFTER DINNER, Marco and Kiera worked with Alex for an hour or so, and tried, unsuccessfully, to determine whether he could really sense air. After they gave up for the night, Kiera retreated to the couch to read while Alex played games with Marco in front of the fire.

"Time for bed," Marco told a yawning Alex some time later. Alex made a face but got up. Marco stood, stretched, and turned to Kiera. "And I am leaving as well." He walked over and gave her a kiss on the cheek. "I'm tired."

Kiera closed the book, but marked her page with a finger. "Sleep well, my friend." She smiled warmly. "See you nexturn."

Marco smiled back, then let himself out. Emmy got up from her sewing and began fussing over Alex as she got him ready for bed.

He's lucky. No; we're both lucky that we three were thrown together, Kiera thought, then got up and changed into her night clothes. Not really tired, she snatched a blanket off the bed and sat on the couch with her book.

A knock startled her. She laid the open book on the couch, then got up, wrapped the blanket around her, and padded across the carpet to the door.

Not knowing who to expect, she opened the door just a crack. Chanda stood outside, her wrap in his hand.

Surprised, Kiera smiled a little and opened the door a little wider. When he saw what she wore, Chanda laughed. "I was hoping to escort you to the party," he told her. "I can see I'm just in time." He wore a midnight blue sleeveless overcloak that fell to his knees and covered a soft-looking yellow shirt that fitted nicely to his chest, and dark, close-fitting pants. He looked very handsome.

Kiera grinned, then took a step back and turned in a circle. "You like it?"

"It's the most becoming I have seen you look," he told her with a lop-sided smile that, for some reason, made her feel a little uneasy. "May I come in?"

Kiera paused. She didn't really want him to come inside her apartment. It was one thing to be attracted to someone, and even to consider, well, bedding them, but it was something entirely different to have them standing at your door with you in your nightclothes and no doubts between you what's on his mind.

And she didn't really know him at all.

God! She wished Marco hadn't gone.

She forced her thoughts to still. Really, Kiera, she told herself. Emmy and Alex were here. What could happen?

She summoned a smile, opened the door and beckoned him in. "May I offer wine? Water? Something to eat?" she asked.

As he stepped inside, he flashed a return smile that proclaimed that he was going to pretend he hadn't noticed her ambivalence. "Wine, please," he said, and made his way to the couch she had been sitting on. He dropped down and picked up her book.

"Don't lose my place," she called as she closed the door.

"Talik's *Mastering Manifestation*. Hmmm. Looks like you were in for an exciting night," he teased and laid her book back on the couch.

"Don't laugh," she said as she poured wine. "It's amazingly insightful."

"It is. How is your son?"

Kiera handed him a glass and sat down on the other side of the couch. "Alex is fine. Thank you for asking. And thank you for bringing back my shawl. I forgot all about it."

"Who is that?" Alex called from his bed, and Emmy tried to shush him.

Kiera stood and motioned Chanda up. "Chanda, this is Alex. Alex, this is my friend, Chanda."

"I am honored to make your acquaintance, Alex," Chanda said with a little bow of his head.

"Is he going to kiss you?" Alex asked, and Kiera closed her eyes.

"Not right now, so you can go to sleep."

Emmy scurried out from Alex's sleeping area and stood in front of Chanda, head bowed and eyes down. Kiera stared at her, trying to puzzle it out.

Chanda finally spoke. "The child just went to bed. There is no need for you and him to leave us, uh—"

"Emmy," Kiera supplied a little breathlessly, not quite believing how quickly things could have skidded out of control. One more ritual she didn't love.

Chanda nodded. "Emmy."

Emmy curtsied and returned to Alex's bed.

Kiera shook her head, then dropped down on the couch and picked up her book. "I apologize, Chanda, for not coming last night or tonight." She forced up a little smile. "But Agni told me that Vayu, Lord Vayu I mean, is calling a tournament in a handful of turns and I have to do some kind of act in it, call a firestorm, so I've been practicing and studying like crazy to try and get ready."

"No apologies are necessary," Chanda said smoothly, still standing. "But if you will spare me a mark, I would be honored if you would walk with me."

Kiera looked at him for a moment, unsure.

He spoke softly. "The man has found himself dreaming of something other than dirt."

Kiera's eyes widened in surprise, and she bent her head to hide her warring emotions. She felt flattered and charmed, but found herself wondering about his true motives. Was he a kind man? A hard one? And still, winding around everything else, she felt that pang that was the loss of Laszlo. But truly, he could have taken advantage, could have told Emmy to leave. And apparently to take Alex, too. And yet he hadn't hesitated to say "no." And he'd said he wanted to take a walk. For an hour. That didn't exactly leave much time for anything untoward.

She looked up. "All right."

Kiera stood, then walked to her closet. She sent fire to the light atop her dresser and began looking through clothes.

"Impressive," Chanda murmured.

Kiera shrugged, a little embarrassed, then pulled a green dress from a hanger. Not looking at Chanda, she crossed the room and went into the bathroom to change. When she came out, he held her blue jacket. "Don't you have a warmer coat?" he asked her.

"This one is fine," she told him as she took it from his hands.

He opened the door and they walked out and down the hall. Outside, the rocks cracked beneath their feet as they walked down the mostly deserted road, and Kiera shivered a little when the crisp breeze finally wormed its way through the lining of her coat. Without looking at her, Chanda reached out and grabbed her hand.

Kiera glanced up at the sky, then pulled Chanda to a stop. A glimmering emerald ribbon twisted and wound across the sky, its silky tendrils blurring as they tickled the horizon.

"The guardians. They're beautiful," Chanda said. After a few moments, they started walking again.

"Where are we going?" she asked.

A slash of white, then gone. "Nowhere. Just walking."

After a while, Chanda asked, "Will you marry Marco?"

Kiera stopped and Chanda turned to her. Her breath was a foggy, white mist between them. "If I say 'no' then I'll have to go back to those parties, Chanda," she shuddered, "and I won't."

He reached over and lifted her chin. "It isn't like this where you come from."

She stared into his eyes, feeling bold. "No, it isn't, and I can't say that I agree with things here all the time."

He gave her a half smile, then took her hand and pulled her down the road. Just before the city gates she tensed, ready to make excuses for not going outside the city, but he cut suddenly east along a little pathway that followed the wall instead of exiting.

After a hundred feet the shoveled path ended, and their feet crunched through unbroken snow. There were no buildings back here, and Kiera realized that they were approaching the dike where the river exited the city.

"Does water frighten you?" Chanda asked, his voice an echo in the silent night.

"No," she answered honestly. "Though it probably should."

He stopped just short of the flat promenade that marked the river bank and turned to her. A brilliant waxing moon hung above them. At this angle it frosted one side of his face but left the other dark, giving him a sinister look, but then he shifted and the feeling was gone.

He stared up at the sky. "Tell me about the place you came from."

"It's nothing like here," Kiera confessed, still watching his face. "I worked as a—" she sighed. "I don't know if I can explain, or rather if you want me to spend the next six marks explaining it all. Let's just say that I had a job, employment, and a life, and Alex, and it was all right."

"Not a resounding endorsement," he noted.

"No. There are things I like about it, but of course there are things I don't. I can say that one thing I like best about—about my hometown is that no one forces you to have sex." She regretted her words the moment they left her mouth, so she summoned what she hoped was a grin and changed the subject. "And running water. Inside. Everyone has it there."

One side of his mouth lifted, and he turned to her and nodded.

Kiera's legs felt both cold and tired, so she squatted down. "Sorry," she said, "but I have to rest for a minute."

Chanda dropped down beside her. "Slavery," he said, but then stopped, and Kiera looked up at him, alarmed.

"Do you have slaves there?"

Kiera searched his eyes but found no clues. "No," she finally admitted.

Chanda leaned closer. "Kiera, I've spent a third of my life outside this deconn. Slavery, as you know, is not something everyone does."

Kiera did not know, but she kept silent.

"I have spent moons in villages, helping farmers plant and harvest. I have walked through this land, learned customs and languages, and made friends." His voice grew grim. "And I have seen families torn apart by slaving parties." He sighed and leaned back, resting his weight on his hands. It had to be cold, but he didn't seem to mind. "Kiera, I wanted to know you precisely because you are so different from every other woman in this pox-rotted court." He held her eyes. "I wanted to know you because I know you not only bedded, but truly cared for Laszlo."

Kiera rocked back, then pushed to her feet. She turned and walked back down the path. She heard Chanda's footsteps behind her, but when he grabbed her shoulder, she pulled free and continued to walk.

What the hell? Does he think I'm stupid? Well, maybe I've acted stupid around him, but there is no goddamned way I am going to admit to being a slave sympathizer, not to one of the sunwyr mages of this court. She almost laughed, realizing how suspicious she had become in the few short months she had been here, how afraid of deception and betrayal. *And it's no wonder,* she thought, *since everyone here does nothing but lie.* She shuddered, thinking of what would happen to her if Vayu heard this tale, much less thought her a danger to him.

Chanda took her arm, forcing her to hit him or stop. She chose to stop and turned back to him. "I want to go home," she told him, and moistened her lips.

He leaned in and kissed her, a soft touching of lips. She flinched and pushed him away. "No, Chanda," she said, and pulled her arm out of his grasp. "I don't want to play games." She turned and continued down the path. By his footsteps, he followed, but he did not try to touch her.

After she reached the main road she stopped to catch her breath and he walked in front of her. "Please, Kiera," he said, and when she looked up at him there was nothing but gentleness in his expression. "I'm sorry. I didn't mean to frighten you."

She nodded, then stood straight and turned toward the manse. It was really quite cold, despite the walk, and she couldn't stop shivering. Down here by the gate, even the buildings looked cold, all bunched up tightly together with not even enough room for a person to squeeze though the few gaps between them.

After some minutes Kiera said over her shoulder, "You don't need to escort me back, Chanda. I know how to get there."

"I need to see you safely home, Kiera."

She shook her head but didn't reply. Stupid men here.

"How did you get that scar on your neck?" he asked, and perhaps meant to chide her.

"A—one of the Shunakah attacked me and Alex," she replied crisply, and kept walking.

"When they attacked?"

She presumed he meant the battle with the army. "Nope. Before that. One of them attacked us outside our home the day I, uh, came here. The home I lived in before."

Chanda grabbed her shoulder and spun her around. His face looked stark white, but whether it was a reflection of moonlight or his fear or something else entirely she just didn't know.

"Why?" he asked flatly.

"How the hell should I know?" Kiera shot back, and pulled free from his hand. *And what the hell kind of question is that?*

He frowned, disbelief on his face. "You did nothing? Not throw fire?"

"I was going to a goddamned Christmas play!" she yelled. "With Alex! At his school!" She was panting, furious with his insinuation that she had somehow deserved to be attacked. "I had never called magic, Chanda, before that happened! I had never even seen a Shunakah before! It fucking attacked me, and I almost died!"

He stepped forward and put a hand on her arm. "Why did you name your son Alex, Kiera?"

Kiera took another step back, shaking her head. "What?" Was he crazy?

He sighed heavily, exasperatedly. "Alex. Alaks. The shifters call themselves Alaks."

Oh my God. Several pieces fell together forming a larger, frightening whole. *Goddamn Hunter. I am so stupid. Oh my God. No matter where I would have taken him, all he had to do was ask. How many children have that name? None, I bet. Zero.*

And his name is his badge. Anyone else who realizes this will test him and know.

No wonder Hunter is scared. I bet he's been waiting for me to go outside the city.

If Hunter wasn't such a son of a bitch, Kiera would have felt a twinge of pity for him, but since he was, she only wanted him dead.

And she fervently wanted Alex to be safe.

She had to leave. Would the guards let her out of the gates? How far would she get? Shit. Shit. Shit! Even if she managed to escape, how would she get away from Hunter out there? Trapped in here and trapped out there. What the hell was she going to do?

Kiera turned and started to run, but her muscles were cold and stiff, so she soon had to walk.

Chanda was still with her.

"Kiera, listen to me. Will you stop and let me talk to you for a minute?"

She turned around. "Why?" she hissed, breathing hard. "So that you can take my words back to Valen, and Vayu?" She shook her head. "I think not."

He grabbed her arm. "I am not going to say anything to either of those sapskulls. Will you please just listen? You don't even have to answer."

"Let go of my arm," she ground out.

Chanda released her and held up his hands in silent apology. Kiera considered, then, and against her better judgment, she finally nodded. He walked ahead of her into an alley and, after a heartbeat, she followed.

He led her down a street and around a corner, then into a barn or a stable—or something. It lay empty, and the only inside light was that cast by the moon through a broken shutter that hung limply across the left half of a window. The smell of old feces hung heavy in the air.

He closed the door.

Kiera stood next to a wall, crossed her arms and buried her bare hands underneath her breasts. Her breath billowed in front of her.

Chanda walked down the hall in front of the stalls and disappeared into a darkened room at the end. In a minute he trotted back out, bearing two chairs. He sat them both in front of the window.

He sat, and Kiera sat. Her knees nearly bumped his, so she scooted the chair back a foot. Chanda leaned back against the back of the chair and stared at her.

"You need a warmer coat," he finally said.

"You're preaching to the choir," she sighed, then leaned forward a little to try and create a warmer space.

He got up and strode back down the hall. He returned with a blanket, which he draped over her.

She smiled a little as she wrapped it around her. "Thank you."

"You're welcome. Kiera, I know you've probably heard this many times, but you're a very beautiful woman."

Kiera raised her eyebrows. "I thank you, I guess, but I wonder why you had to drag me into a barn to tell me that."

He laughed. "You're right." He leaned back in his chair and crossed one leg over the other, watching her. "I told you before that I grew up here, and I did. But the most important times in my life were spent out in the nadeconn, as I told you. I learned a lot of things out there." He leaned his head back on his neck so that he looked down his face while he talked. It was an oddly intimate gesture, and it made Kiera vaguely uncomfortable.

He continued, apparently unaware of his effect on her. "Things are going to change someturn, Kiera. Slavery will not be tolerated for much longer in this city."

Kiera's insides clenched hard as ice. "Why do you say that?" she asked softly.

He lifted his head and shrugged, but she knew he was lying. "I think the primary reason I wanted to talk to you about this is that I think that all of the Skani mages will be killed when—" he waved a hand, "whatever happens, and I don't think you should be killed. You're not like them, Kiera. You see people, not animals, don't you?"

There was no sense denying it. Everyone knew she did, so she nodded.

"I think that you should consider allying yourself with a faction that can ensure your safety in such event, you and your son with the auspicious name."

Kiera paused before answering, trying to be careful. "Are you proposing yourself to be that protector?"

He leaned forward. "Maybe I am. Marry me, Kiera. Become my sons' mother."

Tension bunched in her middle. She knew this was perhaps the most dangerous ground over which she'd ever trod. Offend him and he could say anything to Vayu, tell any story, make any accusation, and Vayu would never believe her over him.

She should never have agreed to come into this alley.

She should never have gone to the party. What the hell had she been thinking? That she was so damned smart? That she would play all these people? Wrap them around her fingers and escape unscathed?

I am such an imbecile.

He watched her face, and she knew he was trying to gauge her reaction.

She took a deep breath. "Chanda, since you've been so honest with me, let me show the same trust in you. I don't want to offend you, and I don't want you to get the wrong idea about my attraction to you, but I just don't know if I'm ready to marry right now." She leaned forward and wrapped the blanket even more tightly around her. She prayed the revelation of her pain would be enough to elicit his pity and that he would give her some space, and time. "I am still in love with Laszlo," she confessed in a whisper, letting truth rise from the depths of her sorrow and color every word. "My heart is still hurting from his—betrayal, I guess, and though I'm trying as hard as I can to get on with my life, I'm not ready to give my whole heart yet to someone else." She looked at him. Willed him to understand. "It wouldn't be fair to you, Chanda, to marry you right now while my heart longs for another."

She let her gaze drop to the floor, and tried to stay still, to keep him from reading the rest of her thoughts. Or see her fear.

She heard him shift in his chair. "How did Laszlo betray you?" His voice was hard to read, but it was definitely colder than it had been.

She shrugged and smiled a little, trying to ease the strain. "He's married. I guess he wanted me to be his mistress. Paramour. Whatever it is that's called here."

To her great surprise he snorted, and she felt a spark of anger ignite in her chest, but she schooled her face as best she could and awaited his explanation.

288

"How is a man having a wife a betrayal?"

"I won't share a man," she said, a little more fiercely than she intended.

"Kiera," and now he sounded condescending, and she hated him for it, hated him for sounding just like Valen, "no one can expect a man to limit his affections to one woman."

Kiera breathed in, then breathed out. "Does this no one expect women to limit their physical affections to one man?"

He continued in that same matter-of-fact tone. "Women are different, Kiera. They attach their feelings to only one man. They want men to protect them. Keep them safe. They want a stable provider."

Screw you, you arrogant asshole! she yelled back, but only on the inside. She managed to say, "and so you see my problem," with barely a catch in her voice.

He ignored her words, but echoed her fears. "But if you remain alone, Kiera, you are vulnerable. That isn't a very wise choice. Anyone at court could lay a claim against you, baseless though it may be, and you would have no man to speak for you, to provide your alibi, to vouch for your integrity."

She looked up then, unable to keep her face down. "How can you lament the plight of the slaves in one breath and threaten me in the next, Chanda? Don't you find that the least bit ironic?"

He drew his lips from his teeth, but she'd never call that expression a smile. "Women and slaves are different kettles of fish, my dear." He stood, and stretched, then walked over to look out the window. He tried to look casual, but the intensity of his gaze made her think that he was looking for something. "Who is Alex's father?"

More than her next breath, Kiera wanted to leave. To run back to her rooms, but it was too late and she knew it. "You don't know him."

"What is his name?"

"Hunter Daniels. He's from the same place I'm from. Nowhere close to here."

"Is he an Alak?"

Kiera's breath caught. "He is from my city. Not from here."

"You're avoiding my question," he accused.

"There are no shifters where I come from, Chanda. No mages either. Alex—it's actually Alexander—is a common name where I come from. His nickname is a coincidence."

As he watched her, she wondered if he was trying to think of another angle, uncover another path by which he might excavate damaging information with which to blackmail her. Or worse.

Chanda, she thought, *you are not a nice man at all.* Had he only been nice to her because he'd been attracted to her?

Taking the next logical step made her shudder, but she had to take it. What would he do now that she had rejected him? What was this man capable of?

"Are you cold?" he asked, sounding genuinely concerned, and she nearly laughed at the ludicrousness of his worry over her comfort. But that didn't mean she wouldn't take an offered gift.

"Yes," she said earnestly. "I want to go back to my rooms and take a bath. I think I've caught a chill."

A sudden, horrible thought exploded behind her eyes. A thought accompanied by the image of a crushed face. "Do you ever sleep out in these barns?" she asked, working hard to keep her voice even and smooth, like she was asking an innocent question. "In the summers, I mean, when it's warm outside?"

He turned to take her measure, and she summoned her sweetest face. "It just seems like a nice idea for a man who dreams about dirt."

"I do," he admitted with a half smile, and her heart sank, and sank. "During the summers when I'm working all the turn in the fields. It's a nice place to sleep. Away from the manse and its drama."

Kiera felt bile rise in her throat. "Chanda, is it all right if we go back now? I am really, really cold, and I wasn't exaggerating when I said I've caught a chill. You were right. I need a new coat."

He walked over and stood in front of her. Too closely. He looked at her eyes, then leaned in and kissed her. Because she didn't know what else to do, she let him.

He reached up and took hold of her shoulders. He pulled her out of the chair and slammed her against the wall, but didn't break the kiss.

Tears streamed down her face. He lifted his lips from hers and looked at her face, her mouth, the tracks the tears made. He grabbed hold of the blanket still wrapped around her and slowly pulled the ends out of her hands. He peeled it back slowly and let it drop to the floor.

"No," she whispered. "Please, Chanda. No."

He nosed her hair and bit the edge of her jaw beneath her ear. "You wanted me before," he whispered. "You're not bedding Marco. Tell me why I should let you go."

"Because it's rape," she whispered, "and how could you enjoy taking me when I'm not willing?"

He laughed low and pushed his hips into hers. "Oh, Kiera, you don't have to play coy with me." He continued in a whisper. "You are so beautiful."

Disgusted, Kiera put her hands on his chest but didn't push away.

"Please, Chanda. Please. Don't do this."

How could she ever have considered having sex with this man?

He continued to nip and push against her, oblivious to or apathetic about her lack of response. Her revulsion. Should she fight? Continue to beg? Scream? But who would come? No Marco was going to come and give her a convenient out tonight.

She hated that in this world, only a noble man had the power to say no, and even worse, the power to force acquiescence on the unwilling.

And in that moment she knew that she would do whatever it took to overthrow the Skani. All the Chandas and the Valens and the Vayus. No matter the cost.

So fight it was.

Her voice sounded different this time. "I'll tell you one more time, Chanda. Stop. I'm going back to my room."

He shoved her shoulders against the wall and pinned her lower body with his own. "No, Kiera. You're going to stay with me for a while first."

"You think?" she asked, and pushed him back as hard as she could, surging up to add her weight to her strength.

He was stupid and had overbalanced against her, and he fell on his backside. To her surprise he smiled, but she couldn't read it. He sat there for a minute, watching her, then pushed to his feet.

Kiera stepped away from the wall and took a basic stance, hands at the ready.

She flinched when a man yelled outside the window. "Ya stupid lout! Whaddaya think yer doin'?"

"I lost my button!" another answered. "Igid'll clout me if'n I dunna find it!"

Chanda strode past Kiera to the door and pulled it open. Kiera reached down and grabbed the blanket, then pushed past him to outside. She took off at a jog down the alley, not seeing the arguers, who must have been farther away than they sounded, and turned onto the main road. She stopped, heart pounding, and looked back. She could see the guards at the gate, and she wondered if they would help her if Chanda jumped her.

Probably not.

She turned back and walked briskly up the road toward the manse, the blanket waving behind her like a cape.

No one followed her.

KIERA SPENT the next several days preparing for the tournament, fearing a summons from Vayu, and alternating feeling stunned by and heartrendingly thankful for Marco's loyalty. During the evenings she played games with Alex and read every book she could find. After she told Marco what happened, he refused to leave her side.

During those days Mosha was nowhere to be found. She and Marco looked for him once and she sent for him twice, but he either ignored her summons or could not come.

CHAPTER 23

THE SUN IGNITED THE MORNING, burning fiercely as it climbed the sky. The tension in Kiera's shoulders softened as streamlets poured through the window she stood before and splashed over her on their way across the room. The sun always cheered her, always had, and she took the cloudless sky as a sign that things would go well today.

She took a long, hot bath and ate well, then Emmy laid out a couple of potential dresses. Kiera let them lie; she would let Marco make the final decision. In fact, she was still wearing her robe when he barged in. "Kiera!" he cried and pulled her into a hug.

"What is it?" Kiera asked, hugging him back. "What happened?"

"They found Aliyah!"

Kiera sat down. "How? Who? And how is she? And where?"

Marco laughed and dropped down next to her on the couch. Emmy stood behind them, beaming, excited that Marco was excited.

"Thanks to Mayor Nickinum, you remember him, right? The mayor of Talium?" Kiera raised a brow. Like she would forget. "Well, anyway, he had been collecting information that he provided to our army that was still in the field. They were able to rescue Allie, Kiera! Lord Nick notified her father, of course, after the soldiers brought her to his manse and he, Lord Vrishka, I mean, traveled to Talium right away. They all arrived late last night and presented themselves to my father."

Kiera felt a little confused, and not just by his meandering monologue. "Um, Marco, didn't you run away from here with her? I don't mean to be insensitive, and I know you're happy she's okay, but aren't you even a little upset that she ended up back here?"

He leaned back and grinned. "No. My father has already chosen another mistress, and he sees Allie as tainted." His grin widened. "By me. He would never stoop to touch a woman his son had touched."

Kiera's face melted into a smile. "Oh, Marco! That's just wonderful! Will he let you court her, do you think?"

"I hope that he will, Kiera, because I plan to marry her if she will have me. We will have to wait at least one more cycle, but she can stay here if he agrees, and my mother told me this morning that she supports me, so there is a very good chance."

"Marco, that makes me happier than I can possibly tell you. Thank God this all worked out." She kissed his cheek. "So no more staying nights with me, then! I don't want her getting the wrong idea." She shrugged carelessly with one shoulder. "No one will bother me now, anyway."

He looked chagrined. "I know, and you're right, but I want you to come with me to see her nexturn."

Kiera pulled him into a quick hug. "Of course," she told him, hiding a smile, then sat up. "Now tell me which dress I should wear."

"That one," he said, pointing to the more formal of the two Emmy had picked. The gold and orange one, with a high neck and an excess of ruffles. So excessive, in fact, that she couldn't keep a moue of distaste from her face. Marco grinned again, then told her, "And you need to wear your hair up."

"Yeah, yeah. Is there anything else I should know? Do?"

"No. You'll be fine. Father is impressed with your progress and will be very pleased to show you off to the Barrow governor."

"But no pressure," she said as she rose off the couch.

He was still grinning. "None at all."

KIERA, ALEX AND MARCO took a leisurely lunch. Kiera hadn't been able to eat much, but she felt, well, great, because Emmy had painted and polished and plucked her until she looked, even to her own eyes, simply amazing. Despite the ruffles. Ringlets framed her face, while the bulk of her hair had been tied up in a fancy twist. She even wore gold on her lips. And Emmy had insisted on going along to touch up anything that needed fixing. Kiera had held Alex out of school, and he chattered happily to anyone who would listen as they descended to the main floor of the manse.

For the first time since her first full day in this castle, the hall swelled with people. With a painted-on smile, Kiera followed their escort slowly through the crowd. People stopped to stare at her, and some even smiled back.

A voice called, "Lady Kiera," and Kiera's smile fell. She turned to find Lady Naga nudging her way through the throngs.

Naga looked her up and down, then smiled admiringly and laid a hand on Kiera's arm. "You look radiant, Lady Kiera," Naga told her earnestly, and Kiera had to fight not to pull away.

"I wanted to wish you luck," Naga continued blithely, "and to tell you that our arrogant bear is going to be punished thisturn." Naga paused to let her words sink in. "Lord Vrishka brought his own bear to play, and since ours is the one who lost my Lord Vayu's mistress, Lord Vayu has decreed that he has to fight Vrishka's."

It took Kiera a moment to comprehend that Naga, whether trying to cheer or chill her, was saying that the entire deconn would soon be watching Laszlo as he fought, presumably to the death, in the arena. Laszlo. Out there. Fighting to the death. Her fingers tangled in the fabric of her dress as she struggled to hold her face still. Naga, apparently oblivious, continued on. "If ours loses, yet lives," Kiera finally caught the entendre, "he loses the captainship." She leaned forward conspiratorially. "And that would be a victory indeed, would it not?"

It felt like someone had punched her in the gut. She had to get out of there. She reached out for Marco and took his hand, and a thought struck. She grabbed a thread of water from the fire roiling in her middle and shoved it into his palm.

He gasped and doubled over.

"Marco!" Kiera yelped, both relieved and sorry, and leaned down to him. "Are you all right?"

"I need to sit down," he ground out.

"Someone bring Lord Marco a chair!" Kiera shouted, and clung to his hand.

A servant dashed over with a chair and Marco dropped into it, then doubled over again.

Shame washed through her. She knew she'd pushed pretty hard, and she really didn't know what pushing elements might do to someone, not physically. "Are you all right?" she asked, meaning it.

He looked up at her through his hair. "My chest hurts," he said meaningfully, and she breathed a sigh of relief.

"Are you going to be able to go to this tournament?"

"Yes. Give me a minute and I will be fine."

Kiera turned back to Naga and pasted the plastic smile back on. "Thank you for wishing me luck, Naga," she said mendaciously. "I hope you have a nice rest of the turn." She squatted down next to Marco and took his hands. He squeezed back so hard she squeaked.

"Are you ready to go?" he asked her quietly.

"Are you?" she countered, then mouthed, "I'm so sorry."

He squeezed her hands again and got up. "I am fine now. I think it was something I ate. Let us go on."

Kiera kept Marco's hand as they marched through the snow to the coliseum. Instead of going in the way she'd come last time, though, he led them around to the far side, toward the river, and underneath the dome. They ended up in a small, stone room on the ground floor with a large, low-set window that faced the field. To Alex's glee, and Kiera's secret horror, they would get to witness the day's events from very close up. Someone had already set a brazier burning, and Kiera sank into one of the chairs placed next to it.

"Would you have someone bring us something warm to drink?" she asked the young man in livery. He bowed, then retreated.

Kiera rubbed her hands together. She hadn't worn her coat, which she now realized had been a tremendous mistake.

She hated that she couldn't see the sun from in here.

She hated that she was going to have to watch Laszlo fight.

She took off one of her gloves and threw it. She hated that he had bedded Naga. But as much as she detested Naga, at least she hadn't lied. Kiera wondered if Laszlo called all of his women—his women!—by a pet name. Branding them as his. Making them feel special.

The bastard. The absolute bastard.

She clung to her anger because she didn't want to cry. Not today.

She rubbed her face with her hand, and Emmy rushed over with her bag.

"You messed up your lipstick, my lady. Here." Emmy reached forward with a gold-coated finger. "Let me fix it."

Kiera closed her eyes while Emmy repaired the damage. When she finished, Marco plopped down in the chair next to her, her glove in his hand.

He smiled at her. "I have to tell you that I'm truly awed that you can govern feelings that strong, Kiera."

She flashed him a look.

He spoke quietly. "No. I mean it." He looked at the floor. "I suppose I knew that you loved him, Kiera, but I didn't understand how you really felt, and I want you to know that I am sorry. Sorry for all that happened."

Kiera felt her face soften. "Thanks."

"And Naga is a viper," he told her as he leaned back into the chair. "She didn't have to tell you that thisturn."

"Well, I would have probably noticed," she replied drily. "And I hardly ever see her, so maybe she was just excited to see me," Kiera went on, then wondered why in the hell she was defending Naga. She snorted. "You're right," she told him, because she knew he was. "She's a viper. And she and Valen are well suited for each other."

He patted her knee. "I have often said the same thing."

SOON AFTER A MAN brought their mulled wine, the man in blue who had opened ceremonies last time came galloping out on his shaggy brown horse. He executed the same moves he did the last time she was here. He blew his horn, and he chanted, and the crowd roared. Kiera watched from her chair, both bored and nervous.

When the man finished, instead of riding off the field he called to the crowd, "Thisturn, lords and ladies, masters and mistresses, we witness a grand event. Two captains thisturn vie for leadership of my lord Vayu's great army." Kiera stood just as the man nodded toward the north. "From Barrow, on behalf of Lord Vrishka, Captain Abhi of the Nanuk, the great white bears." He nodded toward the east. "From Lord Vayu's own stables, Captain Laszlo of the Denaa, the great brown bears. Their fight is to the death, lords and ladies. Let us wish them both the luck of the gods."

The crowd roared. Kiera could hear people banging things on the ground. She covered her mouth with her fingers, closed her eyes and shook her head. She walked over to stand by the window and laid a hand on Alex's shoulder. He beamed up at her, clearly excited, and she wanted desperately to slap him.

Kiera shook her head again. How could she have avoided this? What could she have done differently to avoid putting Alex here, in the middle of this barbarian culture that had rendered him a shifter? Would he someday be fighting in this stadium, awaiting the cheer of the crowd? Could he ever go back home? She just didn't think he could, which meant she had to stay.

She knew she needed to find a shifter to help educate him. She prayed that no one would find out. If the rebellion didn't succeed, she would take Alex when Marco was of age and flee this place, and go somewhere where he could be taught how to be a shifter and what that meant, because God knew she sure didn't, and she didn't want him believing that he was somehow less than her or anyone else.

She wondered if all the deconns held slaves, and how she would go about finding out. Hadn't someone told her that the Alaks didn't have slaves? Did they have cities? Would they accept her as Alex's caretaker?

The horn blew. She squeezed her eyes shut and breathed a prayer for Laszlo. She didn't want to watch, but she couldn't bear not to.

She scanned the field. Nothing moved for a long, pregnant moment.

Suddenly a man appeared. Nude. Huge. One moment he wasn't, and then there he was. Kiera used her tongue to moisten her lips. The man raised his hands over his head, tensed his chest and roared.

The grandstander must be Abhi. A big man, as big as Laszlo, as big and muscular, and maybe bigger, but where Laszlo was dark, Abhi shone white, from his almost pasty skin to his ivory hair. He looked no more than thirty, but Kiera had a hard time telling shifters' ages. She could tell, however, by the way that he moved and carried himself that he was a very strong man. Strong and fast and undoubtedly vicious.

Kiera whipped her head around when a snarl echoed across the field, and Laszlo suddenly appeared there. He wore his hair loose and had nothing on but a small cloth. His face looked cold and ferocious, and it reminded Kiera of the way he had looked the day he had found her in the snow.

Neither carried any weapons.

The men circled each other. In the objective, their dance was beautiful to watch. Their bodies moved with almost catlike grace—or *would that be bearlike*, Kiera wondered.

Without warning Abhi leapt, inhumanly fast, and flew the twenty feet between them, but Laszlo stepped almost casually aside and Abhi landed hard, then stumbled.

Laszlo took another step, flashed a smile and beckoned to Abhi with the large gestures parents use with children. Abhi snarled, then charged low and fast. Laszlo didn't move, and Abhi swept Laszlo off his feet and then slammed him down to the ground.

Kiera reached for Marco's hand.

Before her hand closed around Marco's, Abhi flew through the air, limbs akimbo. And landed on his back with a *whump*. He flipped over, knelt up, and changed. Even with her eyes open Kiera could see the air ripple around him as he shifted.

In five beats of her heart the man was gone and only a giant white bear remained. A fifteen-foot-long, two-thousand-pound bear, whose rounded shoulders easily breached five feet.

He charged.

With a snarl Laszlo leaped into the air, up and toward the white bear, pulled himself into a ball, and changed.

With a shimmer the dark bear met the white. Abhi's jaws snapped as they collided, and ruby droplets spattered from Laszlo's face. Their arms and legs tangled as they fell to the earth. They landed and rolled on the ground, clawing and biting. Skin tore, blood flew as they screamed their rage like fighting dogs.

Abhi again soared through the air. He landed on his side, panting, then flipped over and lunged to his feet. His coat now showed crimson patches. An angry gash along his neck. A ruddy splotch on his shoulder through which the meat below shone a glossy pink. Blood streamed from several tears along his side, to stain the ground at his feet.

But Laszlo bled, too. It showed up as a glisten when he turned.

They circled again.

Laszlo charged, then stopped short. Abhi snarled, then stood on his hind legs. Laszlo stood, too, and flung himself at the white bear.

Laszlo hit him high and hard. Abhi's head jerked back, his feet flew forward, and he hit the ground on his back. Laszlo rode him down and used the force of the throw to roll him twice. When they stopped moving Abhi had his muzzle buried in Laszlo's chest, and his claws ripped at Laszlo's belly. They tumbled again. Laszlo's hands tore at Abhi, and he clamped his jaws down hard on Abhi's shoulder.

Laszlo suddenly screamed, an animal scream, and pushed back at Abhi with his feet and claws. Abhi slid back along the ground, but as soon as he stopped he scrambled to his feet, pounced on Laszlo, and, with a snakelike twist to his head, bit deep into Laszlo's neck.

Kiera sat down hard on the floor. She laid flat hands on the cold stone beneath her and closed her eyes.

She heard another scream, and soon another. She braced herself and opened her eyes.

Laszlo had Abhi pinned on the ground. Abhi struggled, wrestling, squirming, shrieking as he tried to dislodge Laszlo, whose head was buried in Abhi's neck.

Blood suddenly fountained like the spray from a hose, drenching Laszlo's face and chest and the field behind him, but Laszlo held fast, keeping hold as Abhi struggled, clinging until Abhi stopped moving. It took far, far too long.

When it was finished, Abhi shifted back to his crimson-painted human form. Deep gashes covered his torso and arms. His head lay on the ground at an odd angle, likely because he had almost no neck to support it.

Laszlo stood on his hind feet, surged forward, and roared. He dipped his head, then dropped down to all fours. The air seemed to condense around him and then there was just a bloody man kneeling on the frozen ground.

He stood and bowed regally, first to the right, then to the left as blood slid down his face. The crowd went wild, wave after wave after wave.

Kiera pushed off the floor and stumbled back to the chair. She lifted her cup and tried to take a drink, but Marco grabbed it from her shaking fingers before she spilled it all over her dress.

KIERA DID NOT WATCH the other fights. She sat quietly, closed her eyes, laid her head back and sent out her sight. She marked the change of flows as the hours changed. She decided she thought that the assignation of hours was arbitrary. After all, there was only a true dominance of an element for perhaps half an hour, in the middle of the hour, with the fifteen minutes on each side marked by shifting and change. *Maybe time units should be renamed,* she thought, then discarded the idea.

She sent her sight high in the sky, higher and higher, and found two of the giant air streams that Agni had warned her about. They were traveling together, one under the other like a mother and her daughter, from the northwest toward the southeast. As she traveled around them, she wondered if all air streams looked like this but just on a smaller scale. They reminded her of giant blood vessels, these rounded, smooth tubes, and the substance inside looked to be moving fast, like soup through a straw. The air vibrated around them, and she suddenly realized that for the first time she could hear an element, or at least its flow. These two together made the *huuh* of a Bunsen burner.

With a reckless abandon she dove into one, the larger of the two. It was a half mile in diameter, and more powerful than anything she had ever felt. It hit her like a truck, though it didn't hurt, but it catapulted her forward hundreds of feet, and she fought her way to the side and dove out rather than be pushed round the globe. If her sight had a mouth it would have been laughing. She dove in again, and again.

When the flow of the streams started to change to a more easterly flow— the hour was changing—she left them and fell downward, thousands and thousands of feet in ten blinks, then plunged into the earth.

She passed streams of water and earth but didn't slow for them. She needed to find the fire in the earth's belly.

It was farther away than the air had been from the earth, and it took minutes rather than seconds to feel the first tingles. She passed through some mixture of earth and fire, deeper and farther, to where the fire burned everything else away. A knot opened in her chest in her body, miles away, and if her sight had arms, they would have been open.

She was suddenly there, and was going too fast to stop, so she dove into the lake. It was glorious. Beautiful. And despite the roiling around her, it felt tranquil. The fire seemed nearly solid here, and it surrounded her on all sides, as if it needed to touch her, too. To her surprise fire moved more like water here, but thickly and more sluggishly. She felt like a babe in the womb, and the gentle rocking made her remember being held by her mother, held and rocked in that old wooden chair, when she'd been very small.

The thought should have brought pain, but here it didn't. Here she was just peaceful and still.

Kiera let go, let her sight drift in the gentle rocking of the fire.

SOME TIME LATER, and many miles away, a hand touched her arm. She felt herself start to move, and before it was finished she was back. She opened her eyes.

"Ouch!" Alex cried, flapping his hand.

"What's wrong?" she asked him, sitting up. She twisted, trying to ease the stiffness in her back.

"You were glowing," Alex told her with some asperity. "And your eyes were red. So I tried to wake you up but you're hot!"

Kiera neither understood nor knew what to say to that, so she said she was sorry. She touched her arm, and it felt normal to her.

She looked up, and Marco looked down at her. "It's time," he said, and he smiled, but she could see that he was hiding his worry.

"It will be all right," she said, rising, and strangely she knew it was true.

Emmy came and helped Kiera brush out her dress, then fussed with her hair for a moment. She rubbed more gold into Kiera's lips, then smiled at her. "Luck," she said softly, and Kiera smiled back.

A young man in livery stood at the door of their cell. He offered his arm and Kiera laid her right hand upon it.

He looks so calm, she thought. Suddenly she knew he wasn't. He felt nervous—of her?—and attracted.

She started, and he turned his head to look at her. She hadn't meant to pull water from him, but somehow she had.

She smiled encouragingly, and felt his attraction overtake the fear.

How do I make this stop? she thought, a little desperately.

She looked past him and through the windows on her left that opened into the arena. Her stomach clenched, and she felt his feelings fade.

During their walk, which seemed to take hours, she first tried to focus on the upcoming event, but that made her so tense she felt sick, so she thought instead of the air she had seen, and wondered how long a working powered by such a flow would last. She remembered Agni's words about the fire, and readily believed Agni's warning that calling that fire, which was element and manifest, all at once, would wreak horrible damage to the place it was called. Although, she admitted in her heart of hearts, it would be a glorious way to die.

The young man stopped at a doorway which opened into the edge of the arena. He bowed his head and beckoned for her to continue to the field.

A horn blew.

She removed her arm from his, bowed her head in thanks, then strode out and into the arena.

Directly ahead loomed a low stage of aged wood, about ten feet to a side, for her to mount. A skeleton handrail lined the stairs, but the stage lay bare. Nothing up here would block anyone's view of her from any angle. She stepped up and looked down the field.

A glass cauldron had been placed in front of her stage as she'd asked.

Behind that the field had been smoothed for a hundred feet. It was the place where she would manifest a firestorm.

About three-quarters down someone had set up five rows of barrels. Each row contained six bunches. Each bunch had been arranged in a set of four, so from the top it would look like a clover. Each clover was set perhaps ten feet apart from its mates, with fifteen feet between the rows.

She remembered the routine Agni had made her memorize, as well as the ceremony. She turned and faced the left side of the audience—Agni had said to always start with left—and curtsied.

She caught sight of the box on the lowest level of the stadium, the same level she stood on, that contained Lord Vayu and Lady Leith. He was wearing gold, like her, and it shimmered in the sunlight.

The crowd roared.

She stood and turned to the right. Curtsied.

The crowd roared again.

She wondered briefly where Alex and Emmy and Marco were.

She wondered if Laszlo watched her.

She stood and faced the barrels.

She drew a deep breath. Let it out. Rubbed her hands together.

She leaned her head back and spread her arms, putting on the show Agni told her Vayu wanted, and sent out her sight. It was a fire hour, almost half past four P.M., but she first found a strong stream of air flowing a thousand feet above the coliseum. She dove into it. It felt laughably weak compared to its mother flowing above.

She spun the threads she pulled and sent them into the cauldron, then set the flow so it would feed her cyclone. She sent her sight out and plunged into the wave from the sun, which flowed to the west of her. It had to be ten miles across. She basked in its glory for as long as she dared, then called a ream to her, a bunch of strands wider than her body. She dove with them into the cauldron, and wove them into the air. Before they could manifest—and it was getting hard to stop it—she sent the bulk into the clearing and set it to spin.

Up and up and up she urged it, checking its width so it stayed narrow and far enough away from the stands and the barrels.

The crowd gasped, and she peeled open her eyes to check how it looked. It stood fifty feet tall and thirty wide. She waved her arms, again for show, and pulled more fire and a little more air and sent the fire higher. In less than a breath the storm shot up to seventy feet, then a hundred.

She brought it down again, down to perhaps ten feet, then led it up again, up to forty, then sixty. She made tendrils leap from the top, circle wide like the handles on a pitcher, and feed back down to the fire.

The crowd cheered.

She felt an unexpected twinge of amusement. *These are circus tricks.*

She stabilized the storm at about seventy feet, anchored it inside the cauldron, and let it go to feed itself, but watched it carefully for several moments. A surge in air could send it into the stands, or into the barrels, and the former in particular would surely be a Very Bad Thing.

She closed her eyes briefly and opened herself to the fire. Instead of pulling it into her, she sent the threads she called slowly into a mass in the air above the coliseum until she had enough for what she wanted.

When she was satisfied, she pointed downrange with her right arm.

A ball of fire fell from the sky and exploded a bunch of barrels on the far edge of the farthest row.

Ignoring the screaming crowd, she sent another, then another, exploding the barrels from left to right. When the last row was exhausted, she switched to the next row. Between each fireball she took a breath, so it would seem more like a show and less like an accident.

When all of the barrels had burned she folded her arms palm down across her chest, something like an Egyptian mummy, and severed the flow to the firestorm.

She stayed with it, cutting it slowly, and it fell slowly, gracefully, like a curtain of water falling back to the sea.

When it sputtered out, the silence was deafening.

She turned to the left. Curtsied.

The crowd lunged to its feet and screamed. Some of the people stomped and beat the floor with large sticks. *Boom, boom, boom.*

She turned to the right. The people were already on their feet. She curtsied, and the crowd roared.

Sometime during this performance she had crushed her feelings tightly into a corner of her heart, but she could feel them beginning to stream out. She wanted nothing more than to go sit down and let herself shake.

She turned to the rear of the stage and began to walk off.

"Stop!" a voice boomed. Kiera froze. That voice came from the stands, a voice the entire stadium could hear, apparently aided by air.

She turned around.

She could see Vayu standing at the edge of his cell.

303

Surely this wasn't where he passed his judgment? Well, even if he did, she had done everything right. Her fire had minded, her storm had been good, and she hadn't missed a single target. She willed calm to her legs, and her stomach, and dropped her hands to her sides.

"An impressive fire, Lady Kiera, but We require one more performance." He shifted and sparkled, and she wondered desperately what the hell he was talking about. "You will wait there for instructions." He turned and sat.

Kiera curtsied. What else could she do?

She lifted her face and for a moment she stared up at the sun, then closed her eyes and let the light wash over her face. She wondered why this land didn't have any other fire mages.

She opened her eyes and turned when she heard movement on the field. Men marched out, prisoners by the look of them, prodded by other men wearing Vayu's blue livery. They stopped mid-field and turned to face Vayu's box.

Vayu stood and stalked to the edge. He put his hands on the stone ledge in front of him and leaned out to look. After a moment he straightened and began to speak. As his solemn words washed over her, Kiera's heart sank.

"We have judged each of you traitors. You," he spat, "on whom We had bestowed the privilege of serving Our deconn as soldiers. But you were soldiers who ran from danger. Ran like children from the Shunakah. Cowards who left others to face the enemy alone."

Kiera remembered them. These men who had run while she stood and fought the dogs. Should they have stayed? She didn't know, but she did know that if Vayu or one of his mages had come to help her, far fewer of the soldiers would have died, and none would have run. Had he seen how many soldiers died? How futile their efforts against the Shunakah were? Had he ever, ever had to face a real enemy before?

A clothed Laszlo, who appeared to be nearly completely healed, emerged from a side door and strode across the field until he stood in the space separating Vayu from the men. He turned toward Lord Vayu and knelt.

"Do you wish to address Us, Captain?" Vayu's voice boomed across the field with such an icy edge that Kiera shivered.

Laszlo lifted his head. "These are brave men, my lord, brave men who acted foolishly. I ask that you spare their lives. The fault is mine, my lord, and I offer recompense in their stead."

"How is their cowardice your fault, Captain?"

"I left too many undertrained men in the city, my lord, and when their leader fell, no one remained to guide them."

Vayu paused. "That is not your fault, Captain. Step aside."

"My lord—"

"Step aside, Captain," Vayu snarled, and for a long, ponderous moment, one in which Kiera and probably ten thousand others else held their breath, Laszlo hesitated.

With an audible intake of breath, he finally stood and took just enough steps to stand even with the far edge of the soldiers. He held his head up and his mouth closed.

Vayu ignored him. "You are traitors, and for your crime," he continued relentlessly, "you will die. Since the hells are your destination," he told them, "you die by fire thisturn."

He turned to face Kiera, and his voice washed over her, wrapped around her like a spider's web. "You, Lady Kiera, will perform the execution."

Kiera's ears roared. She tried to take a step back, but stumbled over the hem of her dress and nearly fell. Her eyes locked with Laszlo's for a moment and she felt her breath catch.

She looked up at the stands, filled with people. Some seemed to be smiling. Some laughed. A few looked somber. Most sat in groups. Women. Men. Children. The same people who watched slaves desperately butcher each other in the hope that they would earn a place in the army.

Kiera's gaze slid to Vayu, and she stared for a long, long minute. Thoughts jumbled in her head, one pushing another aside only to fade before the next. *I can't run. I can't call fire to kill these men. What the hell is he thinking? Vayu will kill me if I run away. How can this be happening? He'll kill Alex if I don't do this. Dear God, make this not be happening.*

She didn't need to pull water to feel the men's terror.

It was hard to breathe.

The horn blew.

Kiera closed her eyes and let the sun burn the fear from her. She wondered briefly how it would feel to swim in its depths. She wondered if her sight could go that far.

She kept her eyes closed and her face raised, and pressed all thoughts away.

She heard a shout, then another in a slightly higher pitch, and she opened her eyes.

A man in livery came running out the door she had exited and mounted the stage. His blond hair swung when he bowed to her. "My lord Vayu bids you begin," he told her breathlessly.

She looked into his very young face. "You may tell him I decline."

He blanched, but he bowed and retreated, and she turned and faced the men now rowed in front of her. Laszlo was gone. Gone or standing behind them.

She felt a spike in their tension, and wondered how she did.

She kept her hands at her sides. And waited.

The tension ebbed, little by little, like air leaking from a punctured balloon. She heard a yell, and a smile brushed her lips.

He was shouting, was Lord Vayu, but she couldn't make out his words. Then someone apparently reset the spell because she could suddenly hear every word that he said.

"Lady Kiera, you will do as We bid you!"

She turned to him, curtsied, then stood and said, "I cannot, my lord." She knew that he heard her. That everyone had. "We are not in the field. Or at war, and I will not kill the innocent."

"They are traitors," he roared, his voice so loud that she flinched. "Do your duty, Lady Kiera, or face your lord's wrath!"

Kiera stood straight. "My duty, Lord Vayu," she answered calmly, "does not include killing innocent men."

The silence thundered.

In less than a minute a man came through the door at her back and jumped onto the stage. Kiera turned to look at him.

It was Lord Thesin, his face ugly with triumph. He grabbed her arm and yanked her off the stage. She stumbled on the stairs and fell. He jerked her to her feet and dragged her downfield.

She did not try to fight.

Laszlo stepped out from behind the clot of men as she slid past. Their eyes met, and a flicker of something washed through his. "No," she whispered, and prayed he'd understand.

Another man entered the field from a side door pulling a stack of boards behind him. He carried it to the middle of the field and unfolded it. It looked like a stand for an awning.

Thesin dragged her to it, then pulled up one of her arms and cinched it above her head to one of the poles. He grabbed her other arm, too hard, and jerked it up to the other side. He forced her to face downfield, away from Vayu.

She stared into the stands, praying that Marco or Emmy would take Alex away from this before the bad things began.

People were standing. No one was talking. No one laughed.

Thesin came around so that she could see him. He slapped her, once, hard, then again. "Filthy whore," he called her, a sneer on his face.

She closed her eyes.

Then he was behind her, his hands on her dress, and water poured into her guts. *Is he going to fuck me? Here, in front of the crowd?*

He grabbed the back of the neckline and yanked it down, strangling her until it tore, baring a strip of her back.

Her heart felt like it was going to hammer out of her chest. And then something hit her on the back, tearing into her skin, digging a fiery groove down her ribs. She writhed and screamed, but the ties on her hands held her fast.

When it fell away she sobbed and wheezed, and the next blow fell.

Between screams she heard someone roar from the stands, but she couldn't tell whether they cheered or raged.

Kiera felt the whip hit her back again, but time and sound were lost after that. There was nothing left in the world but the pain.

SOMEONE WAS DRAGGING HER, and she struggled to walk, but her feet kept slipping from under her. Another man came and took her shoulder on the other side. She walked, mostly, but the journey went on and on.

She found herself dumped onto the floor of a small, stone room. The door closed and she heard a bar drop on the other side.

A jail, then.

A small, dirty mattress had been pushed against the far wall. She pulled herself over and crawled on top. She lay on her side, facing the wall, and fell into a delirious drowse. The fire in her back kept her from falling asleep.

She tried to send her sight out, but she was too exhausted. She couldn't even cry.

Sometime later the door opened and someone came in. She didn't bother to open her eyes. Either they would hurt her or not, and she could do nothing either way. She couldn't even care.

They sat down on the edge of the mattress. A hand touched her shoulder and she flinched.

Laszlo's voice poured over her, cool as a stream. "You are awake."

"Yes," she whispered.

"Let me help you," he said, and lifted her up a little.

She cried out when the skin on her back twisted.

He steadied her with one hand while he pulled the fragments of her dress out of the tears in her back with the other. She squeezed her mouth shut and held her eyes closed.

When he had bared her back, he pulled the remaining strips down her arms. He laid her back down on her stomach and pulled the hair that had escaped the pins off her shoulders. She gasped when a dot of coolness touched her back.

"Oh, God," she moaned.

Another dot, then his fingers smeared it down her spine, leaving blessed numbness behind.

She laid still until her back was covered with whatever magical cream he had brought her, her breath softening as the pain eased.

He stopped, finally, and she breathed, "Thank you."

His pants rasped against the floor as he laid down on the floor beside her. She opened her eyes and turned her head toward him.

His face looked hard and cold.

"Are you mad at me?" she asked, strangely calm.

He stared into her face. "No, *a'kala,* I am not angry with you."

She shut her eyes. "Please don't call me that, Laszlo."

He laid a hand over hers. "Why did you do this?" he asked gently.

She pushed up to her elbows, not bothering to try and cover her nakedness. "What should I have done? Killed them? Burned them alive?"

He sat up in one smooth movement, bringing his legs under him to squat by her side. "Tell me why, Kiera."

She let her head drop back down. Spoke into the mattress. "Why did you try to stop it? I imagine we did it for pretty much the same reason."

"They are my men," he told her gently. "They are nothing to you."

Kiera sighed. "If you have to ask, you'll never understand."

His voice held a tone she couldn't quite read. "You risked your life for a score of traitors, Kiera. Traitorous slaves."

Kiera made an annoyed noise, pushed up, then moved until she could sit. She tried to lean against the wall but touching her back against the stone sent zingers of pain skittering down her spine, so she leaned forward with a grimace and used one arm to cover her breasts as best she could. "If I wasn't hurting, I would probably slap you," she told him with some heat.

A smile ghosted across his face.

Kiera sighed. "If this doesn't make sense, you're an idiot," she told him without malice. "And don't spout that Skani bullshit to me. You know as well as I do that they were just scared boys. Scared, outnumbered, and destined for death. The Shunakah were killing them all. Shit, Laszlo, if I didn't have magic I would have run, too.

"And what the hell was Vayu doing while these boys had to decide whether to die out there or run and risk dying in here? Sitting on some plushy couch, I'm sure, or screwing his newest virgin mistress. You sure didn't see him fighting out there." Kiera shook her head. "Fuck him. How dare he sit in judgment?"

She turned so she could slide down, then shifted so she could lay facing the wall.

Laszlo leaned down and brushed a kiss on the top of her head, then left without saying goodbye.

THE NEXT MORNING a runner fetched her. The robe he gave her to wear over her tattered dress abraded the raw skin of her back. He led her back to her room.

When she closed the door Alex slammed into her and wrapped his arms around her waist. She gasped and tried to ease his arms off. Emmy scrambled over and managed to peel him off of her.

"Let me sit down," she rasped, "and you can come sit beside me."

Marco came barging in before she got comfortable. His eyes blazed.

Kiera held up a hand. "Please don't yell at me in front of Alex," she warned him. "I desperately need to take a bath, but I'll ask Emmy to take Alex outside for a bit and you can say your piece before I do."

"Keer," Alex whined, and Kiera pulled him close.

"Marco has a right to yell at me," she told him, "and it will only upset you to listen to it." She looked down at him. "I'm fine. I promise. Just a little sore."

Marco poured himself a cup of wine as Emmy bundled Alex up.

When they were gone, Marco flopped down on the couch, nearly spilling his wine. He looked at the cup disdainfully, then drank it all down and slammed the cup on the table.

Kiera waited, but no torrent ensued. She lifted her eyes and realized Marco's face was tight with pain.

"Oh, Marco," she said, and got up, bit by bit, to go sit next to him. She reached one arm around his neck.

He pulled back out of her reach. "You are summoned to court. You have a mark to prepare."

She felt her heart lurch. "All right."

He stood stiffly and paced toward the bed before turning back. "Don't you want to know what he is going to do?" he yelled.

Kiera flinched. "I'm sorry, Marco," she told him without looking up. "I'm sorry I put you through this, and in this position. The only thing I ask, and I will beg on my knees if you want me to, is that you give me your word that no matter what happens you will do all that you can to keep Alex safe."

His voice was harsh. "You should know without asking that I will."

"Thank you."

Marco grabbed her arm. "Are you going to lie down for this?"

She looked over at him. "Of course not," she said, and pulled her arm free. "But from now on, I'm going to fight when I should, instead of when

I want to. Fighting right now would be stupid."

She looked at his face, still fused with anger, and tried to make him understand. "As long as he doesn't decide to have me killed, and I don't think he will over this, I can fight later." She pulled herself to her feet and turned to look at him. "I am sorry, Marco, if I put your life at risk. I really, really am."

He gave her a sullen face. "Don't be a fool."

She turned and walked toward the bathroom. "I have to take a bath, Marco. If you want to yell at me, you're going to have to come with me."

His posture changed to one of concern. "Do you need help?"

She grimaced. "Probably, but I don't want you to do it."

He heaved a melodramatic sigh, then took her arm and led her into the bathroom. He sat her down on the toilet and knelt down to turn on the water.

"You have to plug it down there," she told him, and he flashed her a glare.

"Why are you so—serene?" he asked her.

"I think I'm still in shock," she replied honestly.

That startled a laugh out of him, and he reached to help her out of her robe.

"No, Marco," she said. "I can do this."

"Hush up, you impertinent woman," he chided. "I've seen plenty of naked women."

"Plenty?"

"Well, a couple," he admitted, and she laughed like he wanted her to.

He gasped when he saw her back. "Gods, Kiera." He leaned closer. "Who tended you?"

"Turn around, Marco!"

Once he had, she let the robe drop to the floor.

"Laszlo came and put something on my back. I think he only did it so he could question me," she said sullenly, and stepped into the tub. She slid down into the water, which barely covered her thighs. She held an arm over her breasts and didn't look up.

Marco eased her embarrassment by walking out, and although she couldn't lie back, the water felt glorious. When she'd scrubbed until she felt clean, she pulled herself out of the tub. She let out a groan when she discovered there were no towels.

"Marco?" she called. "Would you throw me a couple drying cloths?"

He walked right in and she hunched over a little, using her hands to hide as much as she could.

"Let me help you," he said, and dropped a towel on her head. A corner brushed her back, and she flinched, so he yanked it back off. "Well, this should be interesting," he said cheerfully.

She grabbed the towels from him. "Out," she ordered. He flashed a smile, but he went.

KIERA SENT MARCO back to his rooms before her escort showed up. She refused to permit him to share in her punishment, not even by association. She also left Alex behind, praying that Vayu wouldn't punish her further for doing so.

But his summons had been only for her, and she could claim misunderstanding if he pressed.

She wore the simplest dress in the closet, and left her hair down. She wanted to look plain and powerless, and she prayed it worked.

A man escorted her into the large hall and directly to the area in front of Vayu's stage. Kiera did not turn her head to look at anyone, but she could feel their gazes pressing her down.

Even before her escort released her arm, she dropped into a curtsy and remained there, eyes on the floor.

Vayu's voice boomed from above her. "We are pleased to see that you have remembered your place, Lady Kiera," he said coldly. "Albeit later than sooner."

His voice became stronger. "You have been summoned, Lady Kiera, to hear Our judgment concerning your future in this deconn."

She stared at the design inside the squares in the carpet as she breathed. In. Out. In. Out. Little diamonds, yellow against a blue background.

"It is apparent that you are unsuited for war. As part of Our judgment, you are henceforth forbidden from calling fire for any reason other than lighting the hearth except in defense of your own body, or those of your husband and children. The penalty for disobedience in this is death. But before you grow disheartened, We are certain that you will be pleased to hear that We have seriously considered two requests for your hand."

Kiera's heart pounded in her throat.

"Both Governor Vrishka and Mayor Nickinum have asked for your troth, and after much consideration, We have discerned that the governor is being far too kind. Further, since Mayor Nickinum seems clearly besotted with you, though I admit that it strains the imagination to understand his reasons, and because he has done Us a great service by returning the maid that was lost, We have chosen to bequeath you to him."

She felt sickened, but not surprised. Further, she no longer wondered where Valen had gotten his soft heart and charming personality.

"Have you nothing to say, Lady Kiera? No pleadings, or deals you might wish Us to consider?"

Kiera kept her head bowed.

"Remove her," Vayu snarled, and she stood when a hand gripped her arm.

CHAPTER 24

STICKY SILENCE ENVELOPED KIERA when she closed the door to her apartment. Midday sun cascaded through the open curtains, casting artificial cheer throughout the room like a forced smile. She didn't wonder where Alex and Emmy had gone. Emmy, who knew the ways of this deconn far better than she did, would keep him safe and away long enough.

She shushed across the carpet in her slippers and perched gently on the edge of the couch to wait. Emmy had left a plate of food out for her, but the greasy cheese looked as appetizing as mud. She poured herself some water and tried to keep her heart in her chest.

She rose when the knock came. Nick, of course, stood outside.

"Lady Kiera, you look radiant, my darling" he told her, and kissed her cheek. She motioned him to the couch.

"May I offer you something to drink?" she asked.

"Why, of course. Some wine would not go amiss."

She gave him the glass and sat down on the opposite couch. "What can I do for you, Mayor Nickinum?"

"Please, Lady Kiera, let us do away with formality. As you husband-to-be, you must call me Nick, and I will call you Kiera. Sit here, my luscious sweet, for we have much to discuss."

"Thank you, Nick, but I prefer to sit here. And please also allow me to tell you that if you came to bed me, I am in no condition to do so thisturn. I'm sure you remember that I was whipped yesturn and I cannot bear to be touched yet."

"So bold," Nick smiled coyly, "and so fiery. Mmmmm. What a wife you will be, my darling. But no. I have not come to claim you. Not yet."

Kiera sipped her water. "Then why have you come?"

"To tell you the terms of our marriage, my darling, of course." He sat back. "It begins next eve. We will attend the brooding party. You, my darling, will behave as a blushing bride-to-be should, and will hang on my every word."

"Will I?"

His face froze. "Don't mock me, Kiera," he said menacingly. He let the look go, and a charming smile metamorphosed his show of teeth into something else entirely. It was such a seamless, frightening change.

"Certainly you must know that I am the governor's spymaster, my dear. As such, I have collected a great deal of information. Some of it may even interest you, my darling. May I tell you what I think it might be?"

Kiera struggled to keep her voice calm. "Yes, of course."

He held her eyes as he lifted the wine to his lips and took a long drink. "I can't tell you how delighted I was, lovely Kiera, to learn all these amusing tidbits about you. And what a busy little girl you've been," he laughed, and then winked. "Consorting with rebels and traipsing the town in shit-covered farmer's clothes. Mmmm. Goodness."

The bile rose in her throat.

"No, my darling. No. I didn't mean to distress you. Instead I applaud your vivacity." He flashed a dazzling smile. "In truth, darling, I owe precious little to Vayu and will be well pleased when he falls. And as my wife, your secrets are of course safe with me."

"What do you want, Nick?" she asked, voice bleak.

"Why, just what I told you, my dear." He got up and sat beside her, then took her hand and raised it to his lips. He held it there for a moment, watching her eyes, then put it back on her lap. His lips curved in a smile, but his voice, when it came, was hard. "In exchange for keeping your secrets, little Kiera, you will do as you're bid. You will be my blushing bride, my willing whore," he laughed, "and even my slave if I should desire you to be so."

Kiera's gaze dropped to the floor, but she managed to nod. "I understand," she whispered.

With his fingers Nick lifted her chin. All trace of humor was gone from his face. "Understand this, Kiera. If you betray me in even the smallest of things, I will get word to Vayu of this rebellion and your participation in it. He will name you traitor and enslave both you and your son. If you displease me, I will make certain that your son is sold off and sent far away. Betray me, Kiera, and I will see you suffer more than you can begin to imagine."

Kiera pulled her face out of his hand. *And I will see you die screaming, you son of a bitch.* "You made your point, Nick. Now get out."

Nick stood, then touched her head. His fingers parted her hair and slid down until they spanned the back of her neck. He squeezed gently, for just a moment, then let go. "Heal quickly, my lovely Kiera," he told her, then took himself out the door.

NO ESCORT OTHER THAN Nick himself came for Kiera late the next afternoon. Emmy had dressed her in a beautiful gown. It was purple, royal purple, and embroidered with gold. Nick's colors. Floor length, a delicate silk, it cut low and fit close to her body. Emmy had left her hair down to cover the few welts on her back that would otherwise show, but had curled it into ringlets to fancy it up.

"Oh, my darling, mmm. You look scrumptious," Nick told her, then put a hand to his heart. "And the colors! My goodness! You flatter me."

Kiera smiled, though it hurt, and took his arm.

"You are looking much better thisturn, my darling," he told her as they walked. "Oh, I will be the envy of everyone." He laughed, then turned serious. "How are you, my dear? Is your back any better?"

Kiera stared at the carpet ahead of her. "I have healed some. Thank you for asking."

"But not well enough to welcome me to your bed?"

"Not quite. May I have another turn or two? It still hurts very much."

He patted her hand. "Of course, my darling, of course." He looked down at her. "But we leave in three, and since I don't want our first night together to be in a wagon, you must take care to heal as quickly as possible."

"I'll do my best," she said through gritted teeth.

People filled the dance hall, far more than the few nights Kiera had previously visited. And everyone stared at her as they walked its length.

Vayu and Valen sat leisurely on a couch in the back of the room, but they stood when Nick approached.

"Welcome, Mayor Nickinum. You are welcome indeed," Valen told him warmly, pointedly ignoring Kiera. They all did.

Kiera tuned them out as they discussed planting and weather and running the deconn. She smiled when she thought it appropriate. She smiled when Nick patted her hand. She smiled when he spoke to her. She smiled at each of the people, including the yellow-haired, cold-eyed Lord Vrishka, who came up to congratulate them. She smiled and smiled and smiled.

Kiera's smile slid from her face when Laszlo walked over.

Nick beamed like the sun when Laszlo shook his hand. "Well, I thank you, dear captain. I am a lucky man indeed."

Laszlo turned to Kiera. "And you, Lady Kiera, you are happy?"

She stared into his face. "Unbelievably."

After the barest pause, he lifted her hand to kiss her fingers.

She closed her eyes to the sight.

Still holding her hand, he took a step back. *"Hyhi eeido, a'kala."*

"You keep saying that," she told him, exasperation threading her words. "What does it mean?"

He smiled ambiguously and kissed her hand again before letting it go.

"Is is a curse?" she asked suspiciously.

To her surprise he laughed, then tried to look solemn. "Some would say that it is," he told her, and strode away.

AN HOUR PASSED, and then another. Marco didn't come. Kiera desperately wished she could see him, but knew she wouldn't be able to talk to him anyway, so instead she hoped he was with Allie. But the time wore on her, her back stung fiercely, and an extra large headache beat a staccato inside her temples.

Enough. "My lord Nick," she said sweetly, "I am sorry to tell you that I think I must go back to my rooms. I have a headache and I need to rest."

"Oh, my darling, the room will dim when you leave."

Kiera barely restrained herself from rolling her eyes. "I know I will miss you," she lied, "but I must rest or I cannot heal." She cast what she hoped was a meaningful look.

He sighed dramatically. "I will miss you, my darling, but of course you are right." He patted her hand. "I will come nexturn for lunch. Do you need me to find you an escort?"

"No, thank you." After bestowing him with a smile he didn't deserve, she eased through the crowd to the main doors of the room. "Please find me an escort," she said to one of the guards. A young woman brought Kiera her wrap.

Alex lay snoring when she got back to her rooms. After Emmy left she took off her dress and flung it across the floor. She pulled her night shirt carefully over her head, poured herself a glass of water, and dropped down on the couch. Barely a thought lit the fire, but she found her eyes drawn to the wagging tongues the flames made.

The tears came softly at first. She curled up on the couch and let them. She cried for Alex, fast asleep in his bed, and for Julia, whom she had failed. She cried for Laszlo, and for all of the slaves in Fairbanks, whose lives no one held dear. Mostly, though, she cried for herself. Cried because she was powerless, because she was enslaved, and because she knew she would never be safe again.

Her door opened, and she didn't bother to sit up, or to wonder who could get in after she had barred it. She just didn't care.

Someone sat down. Large hands lifted her head up and laid it on a lap. She smelled Laszlo and started to sob. He said nothing, but just stroked her hair with his hand.

When the tears stopped, he lifted her up so he could stand. He returned with a towel, and she sat up and wiped her face.

"How'd you get in here?" she asked.

"I opened the door."

She was too tired to press him. And did it really matter? Instead, she turned her aching face so that she could look at him. "Do you remember the first night we stayed together?"

His eyes warmed. "Yes."

"That night you told me I asked you more questions than anyone had asked you in your whole life. Well, lately it seems like every time I see you, some terrible thing has happened. It kind of seems like some bad thing happens, and then *poof!* you show up."

"Not every time," he said, and his eyes were still warm.

"You should go," she said lamely, wishing he wouldn't.

He brushed her hair with his fingers. "Will you marry him?"

She looked at him and tried to summon a smile. "I don't have any choice."

Laszlo leaned over and took her hand. "If you do, I will kill him." His voice was so mild that it took a second for his words to sink in. When they did, she laughed.

"You would lose everything, Laszlo."

"I won't lose you."

Kiera stood up and walked to the fire. "I was never yours to lose, Laszlo." She turned. "And what of your wife? I can't begin to imagine the pain it would cause her to know that her husband was sitting on his former mistress' couch, telling her how he didn't want to lose her."

Laszlo got up and took her hands. He drew one to his mouth and kissed her palm. "You could leave. Take Alex and go."

She shook her head. "I can't leave Marco, Laszlo. I can't renege. The price is too high. And even if I did, even if I thought Marco would be safe, what would happen? Vayu would name me a traitor and hunt me forever. I would endanger anyone who helped me. We would never be safe. Never. I can't do that, either. I won't."

When she looked up from the floor, he reached out with a finger and traced the tear stains. Heat shone from his eyes, flowed from his hands.

She knew there were a hundred reasons she shouldn't, but she leaned into him and let her forehead rest against his chest. She loved the way he smelled. And here in his arms she felt so safe. Safe and cherished. She knew it was an illusion, and maybe a sin, but his heartbeat softened her pain.

And, her heart whispered, *you will never get to hear it again.*

She lifted her face from his chest and stared into his eyes.

He kissed her softly at first, pressing sweet lips to hers.

She led him to her bed. He was very gentle, and he held her all night.

KIERA TOOK LUNCH with Nick. Emmy bustled around, filled his cup, added bits to his plate. She suspected that something more than the food had made her feel queasy.

"Are you all right, my dear?" Nick asked her as he finished his lunch. "You have hardly eaten a thing."

"I'm not feeling well," she confessed.

He stood. "You need to rest, my darling," he told her. "Now why don't you get back in bed and take a little nap."

"I think I will," she agreed.

"I will come for lunch nexturn, my dear, and perhaps I'll stay for a while after."

Kiera lowered her eyes. "I'll see you nexturn then, Nick."

He pulled her hand up and kissed it. "Yes. Nexturn."

After he'd gone, Kiera closed the door and leaned a shoulder against it. Then she stood and stalked to the closet, where she began pulling out dresses that she tossed on the floor.

Emmy hurried over. "Do you want me to help you pack, Lady Kiera?"

"Sure," Kiera agreed, still tossing out clothes.

Emmy picked up the strewn clothes, wound each into a roll, and stuffed them into bags.

"Keep Alex's separate from mine, please." She stopped, then turned to Emmy. "Do you want to come with us?" she asked.

Emmy kept her eyes on her task. "Of course I do," she said brusquely. "You didn't need to ask."

Kiera nodded, touched. "And how much time will you need to get your things together?"

Emmy looked up, revealing a pinked face. "Mine are already packed," she confessed.

Kiera couldn't restrain a smile. "Good. Now, will you pass me one of those bags?"

Someone knocked on the door.

Kiera's brows drew together.

When she opened the door, Lady Leith stood outside. Kiera took a step back, and Leith strode in.

Leith walked to the couch, then turned to face Emmy. "Leave us," she ordered. Emmy dropped the bag she was holding, curtsied, and fled.

Kiera felt more than a little confused. "Will you sit, Lady Leith? May I pour you some wine?"

Leith sat and motioned for Kiera to pour. Kiera brought her a glass, then sat down on the other couch.

"Let us say, if you are asked, that I came to wish you the best," Leith told her, and took a long drink. "And I cannot stay long, so listen well."

Kiera nodded. "All right."

"Kiera, you saved my son twice, yet I have recompensed you but once, and not nearly as well as I should. Therefore, to discharge my debt, I will impart some facts and assistance that I pray will be useful to you in the saving of your own.

"I know that a revolution is fomenting, Kiera, and that you have played a role in it."

Kiera's jaw dropped. Did every goddamned person in the deconn know?

Leith ignored her. "I cannot openly condone a revolt in my own deconn, Kiera, but I can well understand the motivation, as can you, and there, in part, lies my conflict.

"To resolve that conflict, I have provided certain assistances to members of the revolt. What, I will not share with you, but I will continue that assistance by sending someone to take you from the manse this evening. The boy I send will deposit you in a safe location and alert the members of the revolt where they can find you. You must not use magic, Kiera, not for any reason, past thisturn, or someone will find you. Nick, as you know, is an especially able spymaster."

Leith shifted and rested one hand on the arm of the couch. "Another conflict, Kiera, involves my son Valen, whose jealousies have perverted him past reckoning. It was he who set spies in the army and tasked them to skewer his brother with arrows in that bedraggled little town where you found him, and it was he who tried to ride you down. There is more, but you need not hear it. You know his nature as well as I."

Leith looked at the fire. "Further, you should know that it was Valen who suggested quite firmly to his father that not only were you ready to be tested, but that a demonstration involving slaves would best impress the governor of Barrow, knowing full well that you would refuse."

Leith sat back, face pinched. "I cannot condone the removal of my husband and my son, Lady Kiera, openly or non, though again I well understand why it must be done. I tell you this because I want you to assure me that when this revolution comes that you will do what has to be done. I will see Marco rule, but Valen must not."

Kiera asked the only questions that mattered. "Will Marco be safe if I go? And will Alex be named a traitor if I take him?"

Leith held her eyes. "If you leave, the only life you forfeit is your own."

Kiera broke her gaze to stare at her hands as she considered. Should she trust Leith? "Why now, Lady Leith? Why not wait until some later time?"

Leith paused, perhaps considering how much more to say. "Because, Kiera, my husband has reached an accord with Lord Vrishka." She paused to sip her wine. "Vrishka has agreed to provide Fairbanks with another mage in exchange for one thousand Alak slaves. This morn Vrishka left for Barrow. My lord sent Chanda with him to make his selection, and Chanda will not return for at least a moon. The manse is protected only by my lord and Valen for that time. If the slaves rise while Chanda is gone, I will ensure that Lady Agni will not fight."

Kiera's head reeled. She wished she had graceful words, and maybe the sense to hesitate, but she knew she had neither, so she settled for honesty. "I thank you, Lady Leith. What you offer me is a tremendous gift. It's beyond price."

"It is no more precious than Marco's life, Kiera."

"You have my oath," Kiera said, and then grimaced. "I would ask one favor in return, Lady Leith."

Leith's eyes grew hard. "And what would that be?"

"I ask that you permit Marco to marry Allie. Aliyah. After all this is over. Please don't force him to marry someone he doesn't love."

Leith gave Kiera a long, thoughtful look. "Done," she told Kiera, then stood and walked to the door.

"Wait," Kiera called. "Is Nick a sunwyr?"

"No," Leith answered, and let herself out.

CHAPTER 25

NO MATTER HOW MUCH KIERA PLED, begged and cajoled, Emmy refused to leave them. So when a man knocked sometime after midnight, he had three to escort. Using a circuitous route, their young guide led them through moonlight-dappled alleys, finally depositing them inside a darkened room where every breath frosted and the candle their silent escort lit revealed hoarfrost climbing a third of the way up one wall. Someone had pushed the one tiny bed, the room's sole furnishing, against that wall, so before the young man left Kiera pulled it into the middle of the floor and made Alex and Emmy lay atop it. After she covered them both with two of the room's three blankets and about half of the clothes they had carried, she used the last blanket to make a nest next to the bed and tried to force sleep to come.

It didn't.

First it was her tumbling thoughts that kept Kiera awake, but as time passed and the cold seeped up from the ground, she realized that she might as well get up. She rose and paced the three steps to the door. She pulled it open and stared for a moment into the grimy darkness outside, but she knew she couldn't dare leave the room. With a sigh, she pushed closed the door and spent a few minutes digging clothes of out her pack and then pulling them on.

One window had been cut into the wall, though someone had nailed boards across it. Kiera ran her fingers across the rough timber, lingering in the niches where the thin spikes held each to the frame. Maybe they had boarded the window to discourage the cold, or to keep secrets hidden. Steel through wood, binding pieces of unwilling trees in order to stop the light from shining in.

Alex made a sound and stirred in his sleep. Kiera turned, but the gloom hid his face. She wondered when he would start shifting. What he would think of himself when he found out. If he would see himself the way most everyone here saw the shifters. What would she have done with him if it had happened at Nick's?

Something between a laugh and a sob escaped her, a tinny sound that perforated the darkness. Why didn't she just leave this God-forsaken place? Take Alex and hide him away? Try to figure out how to go home? Surely she could hide them from Vayu!

Kiera leaned back and rested her head against the wall. She couldn't do that and she knew it, and not just because Hunter waited for them someplace outside the city walls. She simply could not wipe Lorgda's face from her memory any more than she could Julia's. She couldn't let Alex grow up in a place where his very essence beckoned slavery. Where children were ripped from their parents so fields could be tilled. No; she had known what she was going to do for a long time, but her thoughts skittered away when she tried to imagine it. Her own boards over the window of what she had to do.

But they had been so remote, those thoughts, and now that the time had come she felt more afraid than she'd thought she would. Yes; she was afraid something might go wrong and she would die. Not reluctant, though, and not horrified at her callousness. The deep sorrow that she might not get to see Alex grow up did not surprise her, though how deeply it pierced her did. The pang of losing Laszlo had dug a deep furrow, yet she felt surprised that here, now, it mattered so much. That she could lose Marco felt the same, and maybe for the same reason. How often did you really love someone? Never, for her. Never like she loved her three men.

But mostly, mostly, she wished that for a time any one of them would have loved her best, better than they loved anyone else, and her selfishness shamed her.

SOMEONE WAS SHAKING her shoulder. Kiera opened her eyes to find it was daytime. She sat up, then turned.

"Mosha!" Kiera pushed to her feet and wrapped him in a hug. She flinched when his hands touched her back, and he pushed her away, face taut. He stared at her for a second, then told her, "I am sorry, Kiera."

Alex got out of bed. "I need to go pee," he announced, breaking the spell, and Kiera let her embarrassment out in a laugh.

"Right under yer bed there is a pisspot," Mosha told him.

"I can't go here," Alex told him.

"Well yer gonna half ta," Mosha replied with a twinkle. "But we shall turn our backs, shan't we, Kiera?"

"Oh. Of course," Kiera said, and dutifully turned toward the door.

"So ye got engaged and then run away, did ye?" Mosha said with a smile in his voice.

"Yeah. Seems so. Poor Nick. But I'm confident he'll get over it."

"I dunna that he will," Mosha told her seriously. "Ye will haveta be careful."

"I plan to be. By the way, Mosha, I need to talk to you."

Alex finished and pushed the pot back under the bed.

"And I ta ye. Is now all right or did ye have plans?" he said.

Was he joking? "Right now is fine. Alex," Kiera said, turning toward the bed. "Stay here with Emmy—" whom Kiera noted was awake—"and I'll be back in just a bit."

Mosha led her out the door, then pulled it shut. He walked ahead of her down the hall and into a room only slightly larger than the one she had slept in, but this one held only table and a few chairs. He motioned her to a chair and took the one closest to the window.

"How did ye sleep?" he asked her.

"Oh," she lied, "fine."

"Why did ye sleep on the floor?"

"Oh, I gave Alex and Emmy the bed," she explained. "There wasn't room for three of us."

He nodded. "And how do ye feel about being on the run then?"

She considered. "I am doing the right thing."

"Not fearful, then?"

"Yeah. I am. Especially right after you prodded me about it. And that reminds me. How about teaching me thisturn how to shield my feelings?"

Mosha nodded. "I will."

"Good. Like in a few minutes would be just great for me." She smiled. "Now do you want to go first or should I?"

Mosha inclined his head.

"All right. First: The shifters are mages."

He didn't look nearly as surprised as she expected. Maybe he had known.

"Well," she corrected, "not intentionally. But they pull earth magic all the time, and they use it to fight and to change. And they don't spin it like we do." Kiera sat up, excited. "I think that they can be taught how to call magic, Mosha. I honestly do."

Mosha leaned back in his chair. "There are many ways ta use magic, Kiera. Not just the ways ye been taught."

"What do you mean?"

"The shifters are native ta here, and the Skani are not, and it stands ta reason that they have been using the magic here for a lot longer than we have, though mayhap in other ways."

Kiera leaned forward. "Are you telling me that the Skani couldn't use magic before they came to this place?"

"I dunna for certain, but I do not believe that we could."

Kiera looked thoughtful. "Well, it could be this place," she conceded, "though it could be that someone just learned and taught the others, too. I don't know that I can believe that it's just this place. I used fire back where I came from one time."

Mosha sat up. "Ye did?"

Kiera nodded. "It's how I got here, I think. And that's part of what I need to explain. I have an idea."

AFTER MOSHA LED HER back to her room, Kiera realized that once again he had not shown her how to shield. Annoyed, she paced the room while Alex and Emmy sat on the bed and played games.

Remembering a task she wanted to complete, she went to her coat and searched the pockets until she found the comb that Laszlo had made her. Next, she dug in her bag until she found her old silk shirt. Using her knife, she cut it into strips.

"What are you doing?" Alex asked her.

"Nothing," she answered absently. She picked up the comb in her right hand and closed her eyes. She pulled a tendril of water and pushed it through the wood to cleanse it, then sent her sight down, but not deeply, into the earth, and pulled a few small strands. It took longer than she was used to; earth always acted so sluggish. She spun the strands, and as she did, she evoked images.

She remembered the first night she made love to Laszlo. The way that his hands felt, the way that he held her, and how he had looked in the moonlight. She remembered the joy of their pairing, and the sweetness of his embrace as she sang to him after.

She remembered how he had looked in the meadow the next morning when the sun had hit him. She remembered how his smile had transformed his face, and how beautiful he'd been when he laughed.

She remembered how he had looked at her after he rolled her in the snow, and how her heart had turned over when she saw affection lighting his eyes.

She remembered how tender he was when he held her as she cried. How fervently she ached for his kisses, and how gently he had held her night after night. How passionately they had made love, and how it touched her. She remembered how the knots she carried every day in her chest opened every single time he held her, and how peaceful she felt while he slept beside her.

She filled the strands circling inside her with all of these things, and all of the love in her heart. When she was finished she sent the threads into the comb, little by little, knotting them tightly to the pieces of wood, coaxing them to sink in. She sent the last strand out and used it to coat the entire working. In that she poured the essence of Laszlo. His raspy voice, his gentle hands, his musky scent. It was the key, and when she was finished, she was sure that no one would be able to trigger this spell but him.

She opened her eyes and looked at the comb. It didn't seem any different, but when she put her hand over it she could sense a small pulse of power inside it. Pleased, she wrapped it in the pieces of her shirt and tied them fast so that no other hands could touch it. She put it inside her bag of clothes and made a mental note to give it to Mosha to give to Laszlo in case she didn't come back.

EMMY WOKE KIERA from a nap to tell her that someone was here who wanted her to go with him. Kiera got up, painfully, and followed the man out of the room. She could hear shouting from the hall, and hurried past him to find out what was going on.

What she found was Marco and Mosha, almost at blows.

"Ye get yer sorry ass out of this place Marco, and if anyone finds us, it's yer hide I'll be stringing!" Mosha bellowed, pointing at the door.

"Do you think me a fool?" Marco shot back. Kiera noted that he was wearing the farmer's disguise again. "Of course no one followed me!"

Kiera walked in to the room. "Gentlemen, please. Calm yourselves." Both turned to glare at her. "Mosha, if Marco was followed, his leaving now won't fix it, and Marco, you are an idiot to come here." She sat in one of the chairs. "I'm not going to ask how you found me, Marco, but I will hear what you came to say."

Marco pulled a chair just inches from Kiera and flung himself in it, eyes blazing. "I came here to tell you that my father issued your death warrant at noontide, Kiera." He stood up, knocking the chair back, then turned and stalked away. "How could you do this?" he shouted, then hit the wall with the flat of his hand. "Did you stop to think what he would do?" He turned back. "We could have waited until you were away from here, Kiera, away from the manse! Nick is no sunwyr and it would have been easy to take you away from there," he fumed. "There is no way you will get out of the city now, Kiera, and—" Marco leaned against the door, rapped his forehead against it, and his voice broke. "And I don't know what I can do to stop this."

Kiera went to him and pulled his head to her shoulder. "Oh, Marco," she crooned. "It's all right. It's all right." Kiera looked over Marco's shoulder. "Mosha, please."

Mosha left with a glare but closed the door softly. Kiera led Marco back to the chair and took his hand. "Marco, listen to me," she said gently. "These things are important."

He looked at her with quiet anger, but the love underneath stung her eyes.

"Oh, Marco," she said quietly, "I'm so glad you came." She smiled at him because it was true. She prayed he would understand. Understand and forgive her. "Marco, I left the manse because I had to, but this rebellion has no hope if I leave Fairbanks." He started to interrupt but she held up a hand. "Please let me finish."

She swallowed. "First, let me ask you a favor. No matter what happens, please teach the Alaks how to use magic like we do. Remember I told you they use earth magic already? Teach them to use the other elements so that this," she spread her hands, "will never happen again.

"Second, if something happens to me, please take care of Alex. I know you already promised, but I have to tell you what danger he faces. The truth is that Alex is my dead sister's son, Marco, and I owe it to her to see him safe. Alex's father is a shifter. His name is Hunter Daniels, and he is one of the Shunakah."

Marco looked stunned, but Kiera pressed on. "Hunter killed my sister, and he was imprisoned back home for it, but he must have escaped and now he wants Alex back." Kiera held Marco's eyes. "No matter what happens, Marco, Hunter must not be allowed anywhere near Alex. He's a monster. You have to keep Alex safe if something happens to me."

Marco leaned forward and grabbed her hand. "What in Nudd's Uffern are you planning, Kiera?"

Kiera shook her head. "What?"

Marco looked exasperated. "What are you going to do?"

Kiera leaned back and touched her tongue to her upper lip. "Well, Marco, this is the part you won't like. I need you to tell me when and where Vayu and Valen get together each turn. I know you're going to say that I can't take them both, but I know I can. I have a plan. I'm not going to tell you the details, so don't bother to ask. It would be easier if you just tell me what I need to know, but if you won't, I'll go hunting until I find out for myself."

Marco looked mutinous. She couldn't face him, so she closed her eyes. "I have to do this, Marco," she said, and her voice sounded surprisingly firm. "There is no other way. Now is the right time. The slaves will be killed when they rebel unless I do this, and if I run away, it will never stop."

After a moment he spoke. "They meet every turn at noontide for lunch in the great hall," he told her tonelessly. "And I'm going with you."

Kiera's eyes flew open. "No," she said, and grabbed his arms. "No, no, no!"

He pressed his mouth into a thin line. "Yes."

Kiera squeezed his arms. "No, Marco. You will not." She looked into his face and lowered her voice. "I am going to send them away. Someplace where they can't hurt anyone else, not like this. And God forbid, but if something goes wrong you have to be free of the taint of rebellion."

She stared into his face, willing him to understand. "Please, Marco," she pled, "please. I won't be able to do this if I'm afraid for you." She rested her hand on his cheek. "I love you so much, my friend," she whispered. "You're the best one I've ever had."

Marco shot up out of the chair. He stalked toward the door, running a hand through his hair. "You are going to get yourself killed."

"I sure hope not," she said, trying to sound light. "That's not part of the plan."

He turned to her. "Isn't it?"

"No, Marco," she said quietly. "It isn't."

He nodded once and picked up his coat. "I love you, too, Kiera," he said without meeting her eyes. "So you had better not mess this up. Don't go rushing in. Think it all the way through first."

Kiera snorted softly and Marco looked at her, a small smile all but smoothed away. He looked so handsome. Such a good man. Kiera stood and pulled him into a hug. When he started to pull back, she said, "Wait, Marco. I have something I want you to give to Laszlo. But not thisturn. Later."

CHAPTER 26

"GET YOUR THINGS TOGETHER," Kiera told Alex and Emmy when she closed the door to her room. "We're going to see someone, and you'll stay there for a couple of days."

A ghost of fear shaped Alex's mouth. "But not you?"

She summoned a smile from someplace. "No, I can't. I have to do something, Alex, but Emmy will stay with you while I'm gone, okay?" This would be their first time apart since—well, since Julia's death, and Kiera prayed he wouldn't balk. Or worse, feel sad about it. "It might even be fun," she added, and hoped it would be.

Alex looked up at Emmy, whose face looked a lot less serene than Kiera hoped her own did, but when Alex smiled at her she smiled back with such affection that the tension bled out of his shoulders. "I'll always stay with you, Alex," she told him with just the slightest catch in her voice, and Kiera turned to packing so they wouldn't see the tears that stung her eyes.

They shoved their clothes into bags, then dressed in the servants' wear Emmy had brought from the manse. Kiera hid her face with a scarf and led them outside and into the streets. With Alex's hand in hers, she took them south through the city toward the farms. They stopped to look at the houses, and the sky, and to remark about the people they passed.

When they entered the farming district, Kiera stopped at the first house she came to and knocked on the door. An older woman answered. "Good turn, mistress," Kiera said politely. "I beg your pardon, but I am looking for the home of the wife of the army captain. Do you know which one it is?" The woman pointed to a house at the end of the lane. "I thank you, mistress," Kiera told her, then left the porch.

That last house looked no different than all the others: small, a few hundred square feet, weatherstained, and cast of bleached wood. Kiera took a deep breath as she mounted the stairs, but her heart pounded anyway as she lifted a hand to knock. A woman answered the door far too quickly. A woman nothing like Kiera had expected.

This woman stood tall, perhaps two inches short of six feet, in a well-worn, russet dress that billowed but did not hide her rubenesque curves. Thick, nearly black hair streaked heavily with gray haloed around her head and trailed down her back. She must have been in her fifties, but looked ten years younger. Large dark eyes stared out from a pretty face. She looked kind, too, but somehow Kiera knew that this woman would make a frightening enemy.

The woman seemed amused by Kiera's perusal. "How can I help you?"

Kiera's voice shook a little. "Are you Laszlo's wife?"

The woman's eyes narrowed. "Who are you?"

Kiera smiled. "I'm sorry. My name is Kiera." She gestured back. "This is my son, Alex, and his nanny, Emmy. May we come in? I need to ask a favor."

Surprise flitted across the woman's face. "You may," she said, and stepped back. "But please take off your shoes," she told them, and walked into the house.

While the outside of the house might have been shabby, the inside was warm and inviting. A soft, blue couch pressed against the back wall and a sparkling stove against another, with a large pewter washtub sitting next to it. The woman had set a table and chairs in the middle of the floor, all well-crafted from some hard wood, and a curtain partitioned off a small bed in the back corner. A khaki-colored carpet lay the length of the room.

"Please have a seat," the woman said after they removed their shoes, and eased herself onto the couch. "May I offer you a drink?"

"Thank you, but we are fine," Kiera said, and sat down in a chair.

"I want a drink," Alex told her.

"Alex," Emmy hissed, but the woman smiled.

"Then a drink you shall have, young master." She got off the couch and poured a measure of water from a pitcher into a cup and handed it to Alex.

"Thank you," he told her gravely, and she nodded her head in return.

"What may I help you with?" she asked Kiera.

Kiera folded her hands in her lap to stop her from twining her fingers. "May I ask your name?" she asked.

"I am Amba." The woman's mouth twisted into a wry smile. "Why have you come here, Kiera, to ask help from a woman whose name you do not know?"

Kiera took a breath. "I am here to ask you to keep my son and his nanny for a couple of turns," Kiera told her.

After a moment of shocked silence, Amba roared with laughter. "Well,

Kiera," she said with a wide-mouthed smile, "that is a strange request for someone you don't know. I presume you have a sound reason for choosing me above, say, Salen next door?"

Kiera summoned her courage. "I do, Amba. Your husband, Laszlo, gave me his oath that he would protect my son, and the time has come. I am very, very sorry, to thrust this upon you, but I wouldn't have come to ask if my need was not very great."

Amba leaned back on the couch and laid her hand on the arm. "Who are you that Laszlo would make such a promise?"

Kiera looked at Alex. "Emmy, would you take Alex outside?"

Amba raised her brows as Emmy hurried Alex to the door and into his shoes.

When the door shut, Kiera turned to Amba. "I first want to tell you that I am sorry. I didn't know he had a wife or what happened would have never happened."

Amba's brows were still raised.

Kiera looked down at the floor, then made herself look back up. "I am Laszlo's mistress, Amba. Since late last cycle." She could feel her cheeks heat. "But when I found out he was married, I broke it off. I stopped seeing him," she corrected, unsure if the colloquialism would translate.

Except once, her traitorous heart reminded her.

Amba stared at her, face unreadable, for a long minute.

It's strange, Kiera thought, *how much they are alike. I wonder if that happens to people who are together for a long time.*

"Do you love him?" Amba finally asked, as Kiera knew she would. She had debated whether to lie about this, but it wouldn't be right to not tell the truth to the woman she'd harmed.

Kiera looked her in the eye. "Yes."

Amba pushed abruptly off the couch, and Kiera felt her heart go out to this woman.

"I'm sorry," Kiera said helplessly. "I really am. And I swear I wouldn't have chosen to do things this way thisturn if I had had any other options."

"Why are there no options?" Amba asked her, then turned around and folded her arms.

Kiera sighed. "Because there will soon be a war, and I must fight in it."

"You're nobility," Amba accused.

"Only because they made me," Kiera shot back. "And I left the manse, so I can't put Alex there because they'd use him as a hostage."

"You're the fire mage," Amba said, and sat down on the couch.

"Yes."

"And there's a death warrant for you."

"Yes."

"So why bring this to my house?" Amba asked her. Instead of sounding affronted, or angry, or any of a dozen other things Kiera thought she probably should, she sounded merely curious.

"Because as I told you, Laszlo promised me that he would keep Alex safe. Alex is innocent, and I can't think of anyone better able to protect him than Laszlo. And I trust him above all others to keep his word."

"You know that Laszlo is tasked to return you to Vayu."

"I know that."

"And yet you believe he will keep your son safe. Hmm. And how do you know, Kiera, mistress of Laszlo, that I will not take your son to Vayu? Let him ransom this child in exchange for you?"

Kiera lifted her eyes and held Amba's, but when she spoke, it was softly. "Laszlo would not choose a woman who would ever do something like that—let an innocent child be harmed."

Amba leaned back, smiling a little. "True. And I think you expect to die anyway."

Kiera shook her head. "No, I don't. But I could. Many things could happen." Kiera let her gaze fall back to the floor. "But no matter how things come out, I have to do this, and part of what I have to do is make sure that Alex is safe."

"Such brave words. Are they true ones?"

Kiera couldn't tell if Amba was mocking her or trying to test her. She sighed and looked at her hands. "Yes. They are. And again, I am sorry, Amba. Sorry for everything."

She looked up and held her voice firm. "If I don't come back in two turns, send for a man named Marco in the manse. He will take Alex."

Unexpectedly, Amba smiled at her. "So you have allied with Mosha."

Kiera hoisted a brow. "Who?"

Amba grinned, showing her teeth.

Kiera stood and turned toward the door. She jumped when Amba laid a hand on her arm.

Amba held her eyes for a long moment, something mysterious in her own. "Kiera, in part because he always honors his oaths, I love Laszlo very much."

Kiera looked away, pain and anger warring in her chest. She hated that any woman loved Laszlo, and hated herself even more for the knot of jealousy she didn't deserve to feel.

"I tell you this because I do not want you to worry for your son's safety."

Even knowing that Amba would see her pain and her fear, Kiera looked at her.

Amba nodded, acknowledging them both. "On my oath as well, Kiera, we will keep your son safe."

"Thank you," Kiera whispered, meaning it from the bottom of her heart, and let herself out.

KIERA'S HEAVY FEET remembered the way back. Hoping to avoid Mosha, she marched straight to her room. Completely exhausted in mind and body, she threw herself down on the bed and closed her eyes. She just needed to rest for a few minutes.

But then someone was shaking her, rolling her shoulder into the mattress. Still groggy, she sat up and tried to see in the dark. "Who are you?" she muttered as she pushed back toward the wall. "Mosha? What do you want?"

A light came on and she felt the blood drain from her face. "Laszlo," she whispered. "What are you doing here?"

His stared at her, all feeling locked behind a granite wall.

"Please, Laszlo," she began, but he lifted a hand.

"No, Kiera. No begging. Get up. You will come with me now." He looked around. "Where is Alex?"

"Alex is sick," she lied, heart pounding out of her chest. He couldn't take her now. Not now! "I had to take him to a healer. Please, Laszlo, please listen to me. I only want one day. One." Kiera lifted her hands in a silent plea. "I swear I won't try to leave the city or hide from you. I give you my word." She let her fear rise to the surface. "Please," she whispered, "Please, Laszlo, let me have one more day with Alex. To make sure he's all right. I beg you. Please."

Mosha slammed open the door. "Get yer ass outta here, Laszlo!" he yelled as he came into the room. "Leave her and go or I swear by the gods I will kill ye!"

Laszlo's face, in which Kiera prayed she'd seen a touch of sympathy rising, shut down. He turned to stare at Mosha for a measure. "Stay out of this, Mosha."

"Ye will give her till nexturn so she canna see ta the boy, ye bastard," Mosha spat. "Dunna make me throw yer big ass through another wall!"

Laszlo smiled coldly, then turned back at Kiera.

"Please Laszlo," she begged. "I will do anything you ask. Please. Just until nexturn. I have to make sure that Alex is okay. I'll go willingly with you after that. I swear."

He stared at her for a long, heartwrenching moment. "You have until two marks past noontide nexturn," he finally rasped. "I will come here for you then and you will be waiting."

She knew he had to do this. She knew. She knew Vayu would kill him if he didn't. She knew he hated it—and maybe even her, for not leaving the city. Hot tears spilled down her face, and she got up to touch his hand, to say thank you, to say she understood, but he stepped back out of her reach. His voice was cold. "Don't, Kiera."

Her breath caught as pain seared though her. She nodded and turned back to the bed. When the door shut, she sat on the bed and let her head drop into her hands.

CHAPTER 27

THE SUN WOKE KIERA THE NEXT MORNING. Well, the sun and the *plop* Mosha made when he sat on her bed. Her heart lurched as the fear of the day pressed down, but she opened her eyes and smiled up at him. He smiled back, a little sadly, and handed her some clothes.

"You'll wear these when ye go ta the manse." Mosha pulled his knife from the sheath at his belt. "And now we need ta disguise ye. Sit up and unhook yer hair."

He began to cut.

She flinched when the first broken strands slipped over her shoulder. Questions rose, ugly thoughts, but she set her jaw and let them them fall away, too. It was too late for doubting, for fear. No distractions today. No obsessing. And, she prayed, no mistakes.

When it was done, he gave her a scarf. She wrapped it around her head twice, leaving just her eyes and part of her forehead bared, then stood for inspection.

"With those clothes, and no hair, none will recognize ye. I am certain."

When the elements began to shift toward the second cardinal fire hour, noon, Kiera fell in with a group of slaves headed for the manse. Head down, she traveled behind them and focused on looking like one.

Scant minutes later she waltzed right in the door. No one stopped her. Not a soul even looked at her twice, though she felt as though alarms should have gone off. Just past the entry she held back and leaned against a wall to shake the snow from her boots and loosen the scarf. After the others disappeared, she took a breath and made her way to the great hall. Servants bustled, setting up for lunch. Kiera walked straight to a woman who held a leg of the stage for another who slid pegs into grooves to hold it in place.

"What can I do to help?" she asked.

The woman looked at her. "Who are ye?"

Kiera curtsied. "I'm Lola. Just up from the farm."

"Well, Lola, why don't you help in the kitchen. There's food to be prepared and brought out. It's down that way," she said with a flap of her hand.

"Yes'm," Kiera said, and hurried away.

She hid in the hallway for a while. When she caught sight of the approaching servers finally carrying out the food, she slid into an alcove. Right as the last one in line passed, she popped out and swiped the tray from the hands of the startled man, and smiled in a way she hoped look sweet. And not sick with fear. "Lola told me to fetch this. Thank you."

Completely disinterested, he shrugged and turned back. Kiera followed the others into the main hall, then up the stairs to the table on the stage.

As she took the last step, Vayu emerged from a doorway in the front of the hall. Valen followed. Vayu said something over his shoulder, and they both laughed.

Five more steps out and Kiera's breath caught, and wouldn't start. Agni. The last one in line for lunch on the dais.

Kiera forced a hard breath through her nose and set her dish down. Thinking hard, she hurried down the stairs and back into the hall. Another server bustled out from the far end, tray clanking as he trotted, his face knotted with worry. She stepped in front of him, hands up, and blocked his way. Abruptly he stopped and opened his mouth to say something. "I'll take it," she forced through a smile before he could speak. "It's my first turn here and they won't be nearly as mad at me."

He nodded gratefully and handed her the tray. It held gravy.

Perfect.

After a quick glance around, Kiera turned back and eased out into the great hall. She mounted the stairs, willing the men to look past her. To see only another servant. Face down, she scuttled to Agni's end of the table. The gravy's dark, smoky scent tickled Kiera's nose as she dipped out three cups. Chin to chest, eyes averted, she set a cup in front of Valen and one in front of Vayu, who, lost in conversation, never looked up. She padded back, used both hands to pick up the third cup, and walked around the far edge of the table to Agni.

And dumped the cup in her lap.

Agni yelped and pushed back from the table. As Kiera's fingers could attest, the gravy was smoking hot.

Kiera knelt down beside her until the table hid her face. "I'm sorry, my lady," she murmured. "So sorry. Let me help you."

"Clumsy slut," Valen remarked.

Kiera used the apron of her own dress to wipe spatters from Agni's skirt. Mouth pursed, Agni looked down at her, but her eyes widened when she caught sight of Kiera's face.

"Get out of here," Kiera mouthed. "Get out, Agni. Now."

Agni held her eyes for a moment, then pushed Kiera'a hand from her dress and stood. "My skirt is ruined. I am sorry, my lords, but I must return to my apartment to change."

Kiera remained kneeling and watched Agni dismount the stairs.

Someone slapped the back of Kiera's head and she fell forward onto her hands. "Stupid whore," Valen snarled. "Get out."

Head bowed, eyes on her fingers splayed on the floor, Kiera waited until his footsteps receded, then unsheathed her knife through the hole she had cut in her dress. She stood. Turned.

Fingers sealed the knife to her palm as she took two steps forward. Her hip bumped the table.

The men looked up at her simultaneously. Valen's jaw dropped, but neither face showed the fear they should feel, for even through the gold plating the manse's bones, she knew it would work. Even another world away, in a world without magic, it had worked. Even knowing, her breath still came too fast, because what she didn't know is what this magic would do to her.

So she held her breath as she crossed the knife over her body and pressed the blade to her shoulder, but it all gushed out in a sob as she sliced.

Fire erupted and Kiera flew through a snow-white world, but as in dreams, she never fell.

CHAPTER 28

PAIN. SO MUCH PAIN. SHE GASPED, but Kiera couldn't open her eyes. A voice from a nightmare. "You're awake."

She pried her eyes open.

Vayu.

His slap slammed the back of her head into the stone wall behind her.

Sparks danced in her eyes. She cried out, then whimpered. Why couldn't she feel her hands? Her feet?

She let her head loll back. Her arms veed above her, hands tied with rope to a bar that jutted out from the wall. She forced her head up, then let it slump down on her chest. A barrel. She stood inside a barrel of water.

She closed her eyes. Thoughts mixed, jostled, marched past, and none of them made any sense. She felt cold.

Fingers dug into the soft skin underneath her chin and pulled it up. "Wake up, Kiera."

The light seemed too bright, and she blinked slowly, trying to ease the sting.

His hand smashed into her face. Blood gushed from her nose, and she screamed as she yanked her head back and away from the pain.

Cheek pressed to an arm, she opened her eyes.

Cold, stone walls. Sparse lights. This was one of the magic training rooms. Vayu moved to block her field of vision. *Vayu. Oh God.*

"I see that you're starting to remember." He smiled thinly and moved back to sit in a chair he'd set a few feet in front of her. He crossed one leg over the other and folded his hands in his lap. "In case you're wondering, Kiera, I put you in water because you can't call fire from there. But please. Don't take my word for it. I implore you to try."

True panic now. Breathing too quickly, Kiera closed her eyes. She sent her sight up, up into the stream from the sun.

Instead of silky warm it felt cool, detached. She tried to pull from it, but the strands slipped and fell away, or fell apart, time after time after time.

Oh my God.

She opened her eyes to find Vayu watching her face. "You see, little Kiera. No fires thisturn. And without fire to buffer, you cannot call anything else."

Rage and despair warred inside her. Why hadn't it worked? Why hadn't he been sent back to her Alaska? Why hadn't she? What the hell had happened? "Fuck you, Vayu," she spat, hating that her voice shook.

He leapt from his chair and strode to her. "No, Kiera." His face looked serene even when he grabbed a handful of hair and yanked her head back. "You, traitor, will curse no man again. Instead you will die alone in this cell within the turn, straining and crying for the life fire you can no longer reach."

He allowed himself a small, malignant smile, then pressed all expression away. "But though you betrayed me, Kiera, I am not unmerciful. Tell me now where you have sent my son—" he gritted his teeth—"and how to retrieve him, and I will give you the mercy stroke now."

Another voice pierced the silence that followed. "I beg pardon, my lord, but she dunna know, and she canna help you bring him back. As I tole ye, we will have ta look elseplace for that answer."

Kiera looked wildly over Vayu's shoulder and at Mosha—*Mosha!*—standing back against the far stone wall. *What the hell is going on? Why is Mosha here? This is some trick! He has to be here to help me get free!*

Hope flared in her chest, and she turned a belligerent glare on Vayu.

He had been watching her face with a secret smile, and now, now that she had found hope, he dealt the crushing blow. "Do you know why I'm standing here, alive, Kiera, and you are bound inside this barrel of water facing your death?" he murmured as he leaned forward, eyes glittering with hate. His next words burned as deep as if they had been branded into the folds of her heart. "Because I knew to shield. And I knew to do that because my loyal servant Mosha," he gestured with his head over his shoulder, "revealed your plan to me."

Kiera's ears roared. What? *What?!* Her eyes sought Mosha, begging him to deny it, to give her some sign, some signal that this was all a ploy. A farce. *I'll play along!* she willed him to hear, to see on her face. *Oh God, Mosha, please! Please give me a sign!*

But Mosha crossed his arms and looked back at her. Not sadly. Not with fear. Impassively. Uncomfortably.

She stared at him for a long moment, eyes wild. After a moment he shifted a little, and the set of his shoulders became a little defiant, then settled back. Kiera's stomach knotted, knotted hard, and she couldn't breathe. She felt tears fill her eyes and spill down her face.

Vayu watched her almost hungrily. "I had hoped that would surprise you," he told her softly, then heaved a dramatic sigh as he returned to his chair.

"I fed you, Kiera, and clothed you and provided you and your mongrel son a home and a name. You betrayed me," he spat, "and for that you will die here, alone, and in agony as yet beyond imagining."

He leaned back and dropped an ankle casually over the other. His face mocked her. "And there is one final thing I'll have you know before I leave you to your fate. Mosha came to me, Kiera." He waved a hand. "He bled words, Kiera. He told me about your part in the farcical rebellion, and the curse that you wear, and he convinced me that he could convince you to sacrifice yourself." A smile curled one side of his mouth, but his eyes were filled with her death.

"My lord, please," Mosha ground out, then stepped past Vayu so that he could stand in front of Kiera. He looked at her kindly, and reached out a hand to touch her cheek.

She flinched back, screamed wordlessly, and spat in his face.

Vayu laughed from behind Mosha.

Mosha wiped the glob from his cheek with the back of his hand. "Kiera," he said, and his face was both sad and earnest, "I am sorry. I canna tell ye how sorry I am for ye, girl, but let this be your consolation: Yer sacrifice wunna be in vain. The slaves will be free, Kiera, upon my oath, and my Lord Vayu's. Free to marry and ta own land. That's our exchange, girl, and now thousands wunna die fighting."

"The price was me," Kiera whispered.

His gaze slid from hers as he nodded, then turned away.

How could he believe that Vayu would keep his oath to slaves? Beings he thought were little more than cattle? What the hell was wrong with him? Kiera's heart was screaming as it tried to pound out of her chest. "You're a fool if you think this demon will keep his word to you, Mosha." She was panting, and she paused because her thoughts were too jumbled, tumbling like stones carried by a current. One found an eddy. Settled inside it. *Oh God. I am so stupid.*

"You didn't do this for the slaves," she hissed angrily, and Mosha stopped but didn't turn around. "What did he promise you, Mosha? Gold? Women? What does a man like you want?"

Before her words could echo the chamber Vayu rose and hit her hard with his fist, smashing the side of her face, and she howled as pain shot through her head and the world swam in front of her eyes. "You have been nothing but trouble since you got here, Kiera," he told her briskly, shaking the sting from his hand. "You think far too highly of yourself, you stupid bitch, and I am that tired of your mouth."

Mosha walked out the door without looking back, and Kiera's heart died in her chest.

"He will be captain, of course," Vayu told her as he stared into her face. "Captain of my army."

Laszlo! her mind screamed. *Oh God. Oh God. Oh God. He's going to kill Laszlo! Oh God! Alex! What will happen to Alex?*

Kiera sobbed once, then flinched hard from the knife Vayu pulled from within his cloak—her knife!—and he chuckled as he cut the rope binding her hands. Before she could discern his intent he shoved her back, breaking her already precarious balance, and then down, down into the water inside the barrel.

Her knees buckled and her head slid under the waterline as he slammed a slotted lid over the top. She surged up, smashing her forehead, but the cap fit snugly and she had no strength to push it off.

She gasped, then realized that she could breathe if she stood still, half-kneeling in the water, and pushed her face up as far as she could.

Wondering what Vayu had planned next, she struggled until she slowed her breathing to listen, but he had already gone.

A scant handful of minutes later, earth changed to air as the hour passed into the next, but the first seizure hit Kiera before the green was gone from her sight.

What had Vayu said? That she would strain for fire?

Strain did not begin to describe what her body did. Her legs and arms spasmed, flexing so hard pain sang through her body, her limbs curling up and inward until she sank helplessly into the water. Her belly clenched so hard that she would not have been able to breathe even if her head had been above the waterline.

It was over in less than a minute. One long, agonizing minute, but Kiera knew the next one would be worse. Would she drown, she wondered, or would something inside her break the next time, or the time after that? Terror roiled inside her, and she wanted to scream her grief and her fear, but when she tensed she felt the pressure start, her muscles ticked, so she eased her breath and tried to still her thoughts.

Still shaking, she reached for air. Maybe she couldn't pull fire, but surely she should be able to pull something else. Anything. Something that would help her escape this prison.

Her sight left her and—fell back, lazily, slipped back to her like an exhausted child into sleep. Like the day on the field, north of the city, when she'd been hurt and worn out.

Kiera slammed her hand into the top of the barrel and sobbed once.

The next one came halfway through the hour. She did scream before her nose sank beneath the cold sheet, and she pulled an involuntary breath, sucking in as much water as air. When it was over she jumped up, coughing, and slammed her nose into the lid. Blood filled her gasping throat. She spat, and spat again, trying to ease the eddy twining through her guts.

Air turned to water, and brought another full-body contraction with it. This one lasted nearly twice as long, and when it lifted as abruptly as it came Kiera floated to the top of the barrel, body nearly drained of strength. Eyes closed or open, spots danced in her vision and did not fade. And the next one came soon after. When it was over she rose to the surface, choking, but couldn't open her eyes.

She felt so cold. She tried to take a deep breath, but expanding her chest sent spirals of pain through the muscles guarding her ribs. She gasped, gasped again and flailed weakly. Willing herself to relax, she took small breaths through her mouth.

As she quieted, she realized that someone was talking.

"—will not. The bitch dies."

Vayu? Was that Vayu? Had he come to watch her take her final breaths?

"My lord, he has said he will trade his life for hers."

Was that gentle voice Leith's? And who? Who would trade his life? Did she mean for her? Her legs trembled as she shoved them down and pushed her ear up to the slats, which left her nose halfway beneath the water. She canted her head and breathed slowly through her mouth. "He" had to be Marco, and she would not let him do this.

Vayu laughed, an ugly sound. "The cur's life is mine to take when I choose to take it. He has nothing to bargain with."

Leith's voice was gentle. "Vayu, if you agree, he will stand them down." She sighed over her next words. "My lord, he is your son. If they take the city, even the Skani nobles will accept his rule as the eldest saVayan."

Silence filled the chamber, and Kiera's heart lurched as she wondered if they had left.

A boom sounded, and the world quaked. Someone ripped the lid from above her and grabbed a handful of Kiera's hair and yanked her out of the barrel. The hand released her and she fell across the lip. Her head hung down and water streamed from her clothes and hair to puddle on the floor beneath the barrel. The thinnest stream of adrenalin sung through her. She choked and spat, then tried to push herself back up, but her arms shook and failed.

A rope snaked around her neck and jerked her upright. Her hands flew to her neck and she dug her fingers under the coil that cut off her air. The lifting stopped and she could breathe, though when her legs gave out again, which would be soon, she would hang.

Kiera forced her eyes open. The overbright light pierced her skull, and she fought to keep her watering orbs from slamming closed again.

A small, frightened sound escaped her throat. The space in front of her was filled with Vayu's face, frozen with hate.

Kiera began to wheeze as her breath came faster and faster.

His eyes said that he was going to kill her. Now.

He smiled a terrible smile. "I had wished to prolong this, little Kiera, but circumstances have forced my hand. But let this knowledge bring you what comfort it may: On my oath I will kill your paramour as painfully as I have killed you."

He raised a long knife.

She couldn't close her eyes.

A sharp movement intruded from the left. She flinched back when liquid splattered across her face.

And then Vayu fell back, gasping, a hand at his neck.

Leith stood behind where Vayu had, a knife in her hand. She looked down, then back up at Kiera.

"I am most disappointed, Kiera," Leith told her conversationally. "I expected you to finish this yourself." Her voice softened. "But then you were betrayed, and you have paid so dearly for it that I cannot find it in my heart to hold it against you."

She used the knife to hack the rope binding Kiera's neck. Twice and then it fell away. "Of course it is you," Leith told her, holding her eyes, "who will have done this. I will not be named kinslayer while my youngest son rules. And it cannot be Laszlo, Kiera. You understand that."

Kiera nodded once because she couldn't speak. And did not understand.

Leith put one hand on Kiera's shoulder, nodded in return, then plunged the knife into Kiera's sternum.

Kiera couldn't breathe. She tried to gasp, but air wouldn't come. Panicked, panicking, she reached out, writhing, flailing, desperate. There was no air. Kiera's hand thrashed, her body arched as she struggled, strove to pull a breath. Eyes still open, she reached for air. Blindly. Kiera rocked, lifted her legs, pushing and pulling, trying to force her lungs to open.

Air came, just a trickle, a straw's worth, but it wasn't enough.

She felt her mouth opening and closing, her face hotter and hotter. She pulled as hard as she could. Air. Fire. Anything. Her hand fell on Leith's, still holding the knife buried in her gut. And she pulled. She pulled air from Leith. And everything that would come.

Leith shrieked and tried to jerk back, but Kiera somehow held on, digging her fingers into Leith's wrist, finding strength from someplace, feeling skin break and blood flow, and still she pulled.

Her lungs burst open and she gasped as delicious oxygen filled her.

And then the seizure hit.

As she fell to one side her hand clenched around Leith's and the knife, and as her arm flexed it jerked the knife out. Hot blood poured from the hole, mixing with the water, and Leith slipped and fell backward, and pulled Kiera out of the barrel.

The back of Leith's head hit the stone floor with a wet *thunk* a moment before Kiera's forehead did, making stars slice her vision.

Leith lay still, but Kiera's body convulsed, straining, contracting, but backward. Instead of pushing something out her core pulled, her sight tearing out of her body in fragments, going everywhere and nowhere, desperately seeking fire.

The ground shook, and her body, a tight ball of clenched muscles, trembled with it. From far away she heard someone shouting. Or screaming. Pebbles bounced off her back, and the floor shifted and split open next to her with a loud crack from which she would have flinched if she could.

Her vision blackened as the loss of blood and the strain stole her strength, but nothing came, and Kiera felt muscles tearing inside her. Teeth meet teeth through her lower lip, and she slid backward into the welcoming darkness.

Chapter 29

Kiera floated above a still, white body lying in a small trundle bed. A man wearing a red robe knelt beside it, his hands flat on the body's chest.

She felt nothing. Thought nothing.

Like a breeze, she drifted out through the open door.

Sunlight sent square yellow spears through a window across the hall. She watched Marco pace, muttering under his breath. Laszlo stood, eyes shuttered, with his shoulders pressed against the wall just outside the door.

Kiera blinked.

Face contorted in rage, Laszlo had the man in red pinned against the wall. "You will not stop until she is healed," he shouted, thumping the man against the wall to emphasize his words, "or I will tear your head from your body!"

Marco laid a hand on Laszlo's arm and spoke so softly that she could not hear his words. Laszlo turned his head to listen, then abruptly let go of the man in red, who stumbled back, then away.

Kiera blinked.

The soft black of night bled through the window into an empty hall. Kiera turned back to the small white room.

Marco sat on his heels on the floor next to the bed. He held his shoulders hunched but made no sound. After a time he lifted his head. "Fire is coming," he whispered thickly.

"How long?" Laszlo asked from the somewhere in the darkness behind him.

"It's coming now," Marco said, standing up. "Less than a quarter mark. What do we do? I can call fire. Should I send some into her?" He lifted his hands helplessly. "But what if it hurts her? She can't spin it!"

Laszlo stepped forward. He looked at Marco, then at the bed, then back to Marco. "She may do it," Laszlo finally said. "Give her a half mark. If she

344

does not, you must call fire for her."

Marco nodded, then turned back and stared down at the bed.

"Leave us."

Marco turned back.

Laszlo spoke quietly and without inflection. "For that time. Please."

Marco's face pinched, but he laid a hand on Laszlo's arm before he slipped out of the room.

After Marco shut the door, Laszlo dropped to the floor and pulled the blankets back, revealing a naked woman. He leaned over and kissed her mouth, once, softly. With a shudder he pulled off his shirt and tossed it aside, then turned his head and rested his cheek on her chest, facing her chin. He laid his arms up and down the bed, one hand on her cheek, the other wrapping her bare skin against his arm, and closed his eyes.

His back rose as he pulled a deep breath. His jaw clenched, then relaxed. After a moment he began to chant softly. A soft green glow sputtered, then grew strong, a painted line where skin met skin.

Some minutes later Laszlo gasped and flinched once, the glow faded, but he pulled a ragged breath and kept chanting, and the glow surged and grew strong again.

Even later the hand on the woman's face spasmed, relaxed, then fell as Laszlo's breath stilled, and he slid to the floor, hardly making a sound.

Kiera blinked.

CHAPTER 30

THE SUN PIERCED THE ROOM, STABBING through her eyelids and shooting prickling rays straight into the back of her skull. "Ugh," she groaned, and draped her forearm across her face. She couldn't believe Emmy had opened the curtains before she'd even gotten up.

"Kiera?" a voice whispered. She opened slotted eyes and lifted her arm just enough to see under it.

"Marco." She smiled and tried to sit up, but her stomach knotted and shook when she tried to pull her chest off the bed. She tried to turn over, but her arms shook when she rested any weight on them. Kiera pressed her brows together in a frown and relaxed back. What the hell? Was she getting sick? She felt like someone had beaten seven kinds of hell out of her. The flu?

Marco watched her with an odd look on his face. He looked tired, too. Exhausted, in fact.

Alarm snaked through her. "Are you all right?" she said. "Why are you here so early? What's wrong?"

Instead of answering, he laid a hand on the back of her wrist. He squeezed once, then lifted his eyes to hers. "Do you remember what happened?" he asked softly.

Kiera furrowed her eyebrows and opened her mouth to ask what the hell he was talking about when they came. Memories, surging up like a wave from a stormy sea, swept over her, through her, washing away the soft fog and laying bare the ugly pictures skulking beneath. The stage. Her knife. Vayu's face, twisted with triumph and cruelty. Mosha's face. *Oh God. Mosha.* Kiera cried out and bucked in a rictus of pain. Marco caught her and pulled her up, then to him.

"It's all right," he told her quietly, rocking her back and forth. "Oh, Kiera. It's all right now."

"Is he dead?" she pushed through numb lips, desperate to know. She

346

raised a hand and tried to shove away so she could see his face. "Is Vayu really dead?"

Out of the corner of her eye Kiera saw a man rush in. He peeled Marco's arms from her and pressed her back into the bed. A lock of dark hair fell across his forehead as he looked down at her. "Tell me what is wrong," he said sternly, and laid a hand on the flat of her chest.

"Is Vayu dead?" she asked him, voice shaking as it rose. "Is he dead?"

With his shoulder Marco pushed the healer aside and took hold of her shoulders. "Kiera. Listen to me. Vayu and Valen are gone. They will never hurt you again. I promise you. No one will ever hurt you again."

Relief poured though her like water. Her breath washed out, and she closed her eyes as tension wafted away, piece by jagged piece. As the moments passed the shaking stopped, but her heart still pounded.

The healer's angry voice rolled above her. "Do not vex her or I will make you leave!" he commanded Marco. "She is still very weak!"

After the healer slammed the door, Marco sat down and took her hand. He spoke very gently. "I am so sorry, Kiera. But I swear to you that it's over."

She tried to smile at him.

He squeezed her hand. "Do you want to tell me what happened? Will that help?"

She closed her eyes. "No. Not yet," she whispered. *Maybe never.* "Is Alex all right?"

"Yes, yes! He's fine. With Amba. And Emmy. Don't worry!"

"Your mother—" she began, but he waved her off.

"No," he said to her, face earnest, and she realized he didn't know. "She is still very weak, but she will be fine."

Kiera started to speak, but stopped. That was not for today. "Tell me what happened, Marco," she asked instead. He lifted his brows in a question, so she added, "With the slaves. Tell me about the rebellion."

Marco smiled widely, pleasure written all over his face. "They did it, Kiera. Laszlo led the army into the city. They took the manse and declared themselves free. It's over."

Such joy washed through her that her skin prickled with pain. "Oh. Thank God. Thank God." She closed her eyes for a moment, but they flew open when his words sunk in. "Wait. Laszlo led them? Laszlo?"

Marco was still smiling, but something strange lurked behind it. "Yes, Kiera, but you need to know that it wasn't Mosha who was leading the rebellion. It was a woman named Amba. Laszlo's mother."

Still reeling, she moistened her lips with her tongue. "His mother? Amba is Laszlo's mother?"

He nodded.

She shook her head and tried to sort through her tumbling thoughts. Nothing made sense. What did this mean? "So Laszlo is the new governor?"

Marco stood abruptly and paced away. Stopped at the door. "No."

He looked so sad. Kiera stared at his face, trying to divine the cause. "Do you hate me, Marco? For what I did?"

With a bittersweet twist of his lips, he strode back and dropped down on the bed. "No. Of course not. How could I hate you, Kiera?" He snorted, but his eyes looked haunted. "You saved my life. From him. He was a monster, and so was Valen. No one grieves their loss, least of all me. Please stop worrying about me." He looked into her face and spoke softly. "It was just hard, Kiera. I almost lost you."

Kiera lifted a hand and rested it against his stubbly cheek. Emotion welled in him, and in her. Before she embarrassed them both, Kiera let her hand fall back and turned her face toward the window, welcoming the streamers of light that bathed her face. "I feel like shit, Marco. How long have I been asleep?"

She heard the grin in his voice. "Three turns."

The sun warmed Kiera's cheeks, kissed her lips. She wondered if she would ever stop needing that warmth. "That is a very long time," she murmured, and shook her head a little. "Do you know that I had the strangest dream? I dreamed that I was floating over—well, it must have been my body. You and Laszlo were standing outside the room and you were pacing, and then—" she bit her lip and tried to remember—"um, it was dark and you and Laszlo were in the room with me but I was sleeping. You said something about calling fire, but Laszlo made you leave, and then he, uh, did something. He made green light and—" Kiera looked up at Marco. "And then he fell, Marco."

Marco worked hard to hide his shock, his chagrin, but Kiera saw it, and her insides shattered. "He's dead, isn't he?" she asked him in a surprisingly strong voice. "It wasn't a dream. I must have seen it with my sight, or something, and he's dead and you're not telling me because you don't want to upset me." She hated that her voice rose, that it sounded shrill and as brittle as she felt. "You can just tell me, Marco. Tell me the truth. Is Laszlo dead?"

A sound whispered through the clap of silence that fell.

She turned her head, ready to scream and strike out.

But her breath caught.

Laszlo stood in the doorway. Inanely she noted his wet hair and fisted hands, though his face looked smooth and calm.

Marco squeezed her shoulder, then moved off the bed.

"Laszlo," she whispered raggedly.

He walked to her, slowly, his eyes never leaving hers.

He sat down beside her. Not touching her. Didn't try to touch her.

She tried to tamp down her feelings, but she started to tremble. She needed to touch him so much her stomach knotted. Would he let her? What would she do if he didn't? What the hell was wrong?

A thought came, though she tried to push it back into the lurking darkness. Had he let her believe that Amba was his wife because he didn't want her?

"Are you cold?" he asked her, concerned. He reached for the blanket.

"No."

His hand stilled, but he watched her. So softly that she almost couldn't hear the words, he whispered, "Can I touch you?"

Tears spilled from her eyes. "Please. Please hold me."

With a groan, he seized her, too hard. He yanked her out of the covers and crushed her to his chest.

She wrapped her arms around him and pulled as hard as she could.

In one fluid movement he lifted her up and into the lee between his legs, then, keeping one arm around her, he pushed across the bed until his back pressed against the wall. He yanked the blanket from under his legs, snapped it open and wrapped it around them.

"Leave us," he told Marco.

He held her tightly, murmuring sweet-sounding words into her hair as she wept.

WHEN SHE HAD SPENT her grief, Laszlo laid her down on the bed. He brought a wet cloth and washed the tears from her face.

"Please stay with me," she implored.

He touched her face with his fingers. "You must sleep. I'll be right here."

"Tell me what happened while I slept," she said, willing him to stay. Afraid that he wouldn't. Annoyed by the strength of her feelings and how much she needed things to be settled between them. "Tell me what happened."

He knelt down on the floor by her knees and rested a hand on her leg. "The slaves are free," he told her with a small smile. "Now sleep."

She tried to smile. "Laszlo, Marco said they took the manse—"

"A'kala," he interrupted gently, "you need to rest. We will talk about this nexturn. Tomorrow."

"I want to talk now," she answered, closing her eyes. "There are things I have to tell you." *And that I have to know.*

He sighed, just a small exhalation through his nose. "Kiera, I think there is nothing you will say that I do not know, and at this moment none of it matters." He rubbed her leg. "Rest easy, my heart."

Kiera opened her eyes. "What do you know? And when will it matter, Laszlo? Later, when I'm better?"

He looked at her for a long moment. In one fluid motion he lifted himself from the floor and sat down on the bed next to her hips. He took her hand, then looked down at her. "Why must you be so stubborn?" he asked her impatiently. "Please, *a'kala*. Rest. You are still healing and you have ten thousand turns to tell me all that you will."

"Because I have to," she told him. "I don't want secrets between us anymore, Laszlo. I have to know where we stand."

He sounded tired. "What secrets, Kiera? The lies we told each other? We each had good reasons, I think, and in the end they don't matter at all."

"You knew Alex wasn't my son, didn't you?"

He nodded once.

She felt the blood heat her cheeks. "And did you know that I am barren?" she whispered.

He nodded again, and she let her gaze slip past him and to the window. "Mosha told you. I knew he would." Kiera took a deep breath, willing the tears back. "Is that why you never told me the truth about Amba? Because you wanted to keep that distance between us? So that now that it's over, you can rule here with some other woman as your wife?"

Laszlo opened his mouth, then closed it. A muscle ticked in his jaw. "What else would you tell me, Kiera? That Alex's father is one of the Shunakah?"

Largely because he didn't deny any of it, Kiera flinched, then closed her eyes. "Yes. Alex's father is a Shunakah and he wants Alex back badly enough to kill me for him, which he's very nearly done twice, maybe three times, already. Please don't worry about me staying, drawing them here again, and making your wife-to-be uncomfortable. I will leave this city and find him when I am healed."

Disconcertingly, he smiled when she opened her eyes, although it looked a little grim. "And what else must you say before it is my time to spill the thoughts of my heart?"

"Goddamn you, Laszlo, don't make light of this!" she said hotly. "I deserve to know the truth." She stared into his face. "And so do you."

He stood abruptly, took a step, then turned around. "Kiera, do you love me?"

That was the last thing she expected him to say, and her thoughts skittered a moment before settling back.

"Yes," she said. *So much more than I want to.*

He grabbed her arms, startling her, and leaned down so that his face was next to hers. "Woman, I do not care whether you can birth babies. I do not care if Alex is your son. I do not care if all of the living and yet to be born Shunakah have sworn to track you unto death and beyond. Gods, Kiera. All that matters is the love that we share." He released her and sat back with a fierce set to his mouth. "I had sworn to keep Amba's secret safe until we had taken the city. I could not tell you, Kiera, because Mosha would learn it from you—"

"You knew about Mosha," Kiera whispered.

He shook his head. "We suspected him. But I was afraid that he would learn the truth from you, and perhaps others would as well, and all would be lost." He stood and paced to the window. "I was for too long a time without you, but that time was passing and I knew that I would reclaim you soon." He turned to her, face schooled, voice silky smooth, but his body almost vibrated with tension, and his eyes blazed. "Know this as truth, Kiera *a'Denaali*. I claimed you and you will remain my wife until you breathe your last."

Kiera rocked back, mouth open. "What?"

All emotion slid from Laszlo's face except for a slight stubborn set to his mouth that he did not press away.

Her heart beat too fast. "I think I would have remembered something like that, Laszlo, unless you did it while I was asleep. And even then, don't I have to, like, say yes or something?"

Even trying not to, he still looked fierce. He sounded it, too. "Three times I spoke my intent, Kiera, twice witnessed, and you heard my words and did not say me no. The night following the third you took me to your bed and it was done."

Kiera gaped. "It was those goddamned words you kept saying, wasn't it?"

He did not deny it.

"You can't just do that!" she wailed. "That's not fair! I don't know your customs!" Kiera gritted her teeth and shook her head. "Laszlo, the whole time I've been here I have been at the mercy of the whims of men." She lifted her hand and chopped the air. "First stinking Nick, then Vayu, then Valen, and Thesin and Gethor. Then Chanda—"

Laszlo grabbed her arm and pulled her forward, face hard. "Tell me he did not hurt you. The noise stopped him, and on my oath if it had not I would have."

Kiera's gaped and she tried to pull her arm from his hand. "No. He didn't—hurt me. And it doesn't matter now. Listen to me! I'm telling you that I don't want to be forced into anything. Laszlo, I hate it! Just like you would, or anybody!"

He let go of her arm and shifted back. "Kiera, I know that and I am sorry I did not first ask you in a way you would understand. I could not." He pushed further back on the bed so that she could see him clearly and smoothed all emotion out of his face. "Are you so opposed to being my wife that if I asked you would say no?"

Despite her best effort, her heart began floating up through her chest and into the heavens, pulling her lips up on its way. "Are you asking?"

He took her hand a little too roughly. "Yes."

Her smile was tremulous when she whispered to him, "Tell me the words again."

He held her eyes. "*Hyhi eeido, a'kala.* My brave, beautiful woman. Please be my wife."

She smiled from the bottom of her heart. "Of course I will."

He grabbed her and pulled her to him. "Gods, woman," he breathed into her hair. She could feel his heart pounding beneath her face.

After his heart slowed, and hers, she closed her eyes and spoke into his chest. "And now, as your wife, I have a demand."

His chest rumbled as he laughed. "So soon?"

"Laszlo, it's a serious one. Listen. You have made it very plain that you will not accept me taking lovers," she lifted a hand, "not that I would want to. But what about you? Will you take mistresses? Have sex, lie, with other women? That's what all the men here do." She pushed back. "You need to understand me. If you do, I will kill you. I mean it."

Laszlo shook his head. "Kiera, I am Alak." Kiera started to interrupt, but he lifted his fingers. "Please let me finish. I hold close the lessons my elders taught me. *Alak'shin katmodit dis'Alak.* 'Honor others first to earn honor in return.'" He brushed her breast with his fingertips, leaving a swath of sparks where they passed. "Does an honorable man dishonor his wife?" He shook his head a little and took her hand, watching as their fingers twined. "My people choose their *a'kala,*" he smiled without looking up, "with great care, because the choosing cannot be undone." He blinked, then turned his face to her and spoke very earnestly. "I waited forty cycles for you, my heart, and on my oath I will never touch another woman."

Kiera rested her head back on his chest, contentment winding through hers. "Where is Mosha?" she asked. "I never want to see him again, Laszlo. Please make sure he stays far away from me."

She heard the rumble of his laugh. "Waste no more worries on Mosha, *a'kala.*"

"Why? Did you kill him?" she teased.

"No. He has gone. But I will when I find him."

She tried to push back, but he wouldn't let go. "Please let me lie down. I can't see you."

He eased her out of his arms and laid her back on the bed. She studied his face. "Laszlo, you say these things, that you will kill these men, and I have always thought you were being—I don't know. Hyperbolic. But you're serious, aren't you?"

"Yes."

"Why?"

"He betrayed you."

Shock rolled through her. "You'll kill him because he betrayed me?"

His face was hard. "He betrayed all of us, Kiera." A cold smile lifted a corner of his mouth. "But yes, *a'kala.* I will kill him because he betrayed my wife."

Kiera closed her eyes and searched her heart. "Maybe I've become a terrible person, but it's not in me right now to try and dissuade you." She opened them as another thought followed. "That's why that last night you wouldn't let me touch you, isn't it? You were shielding. You were afraid I'd sense it, or what you were feeling, and things were just about to start."

If her words shocked him, he didn't show it. He spoke softly, but his expression was still fierce. "For certain. But Kiera, if Alex had been in that room I would have taken you both out of the city. I feared to take you without knowing where you had hid him because I knew Mosha knew and would hostage him. I searched until I found him, but you had already gone into the manse."

"I wouldn't have let you," she told him briskly. "I had to do what I did, Laszlo, just like you had things you had to do. Besides, that would have endangered everything you all have worked and planned for long for. I truly believed I could send them both away, and I would have if Mosha hadn't told Vayu what I was going to do."

He looked at her face. "Kiera, you are my woman. My first duty is to protect you."

That made her smile. "It's your duty to protect me? Is it my duty to protect you, too?"

His brows came down as he considered. "Yes," he finally said.

"That's the right answer." Kiera smiled again, but it was a weary one, and she closed her eyes and let her body relax. "Well, then. That means that you need to resign as captain immediately. No more traipsing around with the soldiers for you, mister."

He laughed, as she hoped he would.

"Okay. Now tell me what happened. The slaves are free. Is it a glorious story? Did you storm the manse? Who is governor? Is it Marco?"

She opened her eyes when Laszlo stood and walked to the door.

Kiera watched him, half hurt, wondering if he was leaving, and why.

He barred the door. "No," he said. "No more questions."

Holding her eyes, he kicked off his boots. He pulled off his shirt, then pushed down his pants and stepped out of them.

God. He was beautiful.

He walked back to her and sank down on his knees on the edge of the bed.

"There isn't really room for two," she said, a little weakly.

He grinned wickedly as he pulled her into his arms. "There's room for one."

CHAPTER 31

WHEN KIERA WOKE IT WAS MORNING, and she was still lying on Laszlo's chest. His arm lay draped across her back.

Someone knocked on the door. She started to get up, but he pressed her down with his hand.

"Someone's knocking," she whispered.

"Go away," he bellowed, and she laughed.

He pressed his foot inside her ankle and pushed her leg out. He pulled her up toward his face just a little, then reached down and lifted her hips just enough so that he could push his hardness inside her.

"Oh," she said.

THE NEXT TIME SHE WOKE with her head resting on Laszlo's stomach and her feet dangling off the end of the bed. He was snoring.

She smiled widely as she got up. She pulled on the big white shirt in which she had first awakened and reluctantly used the chamber pot. She prayed he didn't wake up while she did.

God. She hated these things.

Her legs still felt shaky, but she had to admit that she felt much better today.

She walked back to the bed and lifted the blanket to cover Laszlo, but he was gloriously bare and she had never been able to just look at him, all of him. So she looked.

He was as hairless as a man could be, and what hair he had, under his arms and framing his man-parts, was as dark as the hair on his head. She wondered why he didn't have more body hair, but then none of the shifters—the Alaks—she corrected herself, seemed hairy. His skin was a delicious umber, warmer and darker than hers by several shades. His chest was wide and big, as was everything about him. Not overmuscled, but hard and strong.

He was simply magnificent.

Laszlo's eyes slitted open. "Why are you standing there with that smile on your face?" he asked with a grin.

She blushed and looked away as she covered him with the blanket. She tucked it in around his waist and he grabbed her and pulled her down on top of him.

She laughed. And then she kissed him.

"Did you like the present I left you?" she asked with a smile.

The amusement fell from his face.

"I'm sorry," she said, abashed. "I didn't mean to make you sad. I worked really hard on it because no matter what happened I wanted you to know that I love you. I imagined that when you held it you would know how much I have loved you and what joy you have brought me." She touched his face. Smiled. "Maybe I was a little selfish, too. No matter how things turned out, I wanted you to remember me."

He closed his eyes. "I held it while he was hurting you, Kiera," he whispered gruffly, then lifted her off him so he could sit up.

He leaned back against the wall, grabbed the blanket in one fist and stared at something she couldn't see. Kiera stood on her knees and then straddled him, sat softly in his lap, and wrapped her arms around his neck. After a moment he put his arms around her. She kissed his cheek softly, then laid her head on his shoulder. "I love you, Laszlo," she told him, and they sat like that for a time.

"Tell me what happened while I was asleep," she finally whispered.

He lifted her head so he could look at her face. He leaned in, kissed her mouth softly, then hungrily, and she pushed back, laughing. "No! Stop being naughty! Tell me what happened!"

He nodded soberly, but she saw the twinkle in his eye. "We took the city."

Kiera grinned. "Wow, Laszlo. It was hard for me to follow all the twists and turns in that saga." She poked him the in arm. "Do you suppose you could provide me with a couple of details?"

He smiled widely, showing his teeth.

"I'm waiting," she said.

"Not thisturn, *a'kala,*" he said gently. "Thisturn you must rest."

"Laszlo, at least tell me who is governor. Is it Marco? You?"

"That is still being decided."

"You keep dancing around my questions," she complained a little hotly.

"It is tiring," he agreed.

"Why won't you tell me these things?"

He reached up and brushed her hair with his fingers. "I will tell you about everything, *a'kala*. Soon. But let us have peace for thisturn, all right?"

She looked down and then back at him. "Will Vrishka, or others, come to fight us after they learn what happened?"

His voice was mild. "No one will come thisturn."

She sighed and laid her head back on his chest. "When can I see Alex and Emmy?"

"I will bring them to see you nexturn."

"Why not thisturn?'

She heard the smile in his voice. "Because thisturn is mine."

"You could have chosen a place with a better bed," she griped.

He lifted her up, then stood, used the chamber pot (she closed her eyes and he laughed), and then pulled on his pants. "Get up."

"What?"

"Get up or I'll pick you up."

She crossed her arms. "You are the most bossy, high-handed man I have ever known."

He washed his hands, then his face. When he had dried with a towel, he pulled on his shirt and boots and walked back to the bed, leaned over and picked her up.

"Goddamnit, Laszlo," she complained, but her heart wasn't in it. She really did hate this room.

He grinned. "Are you going to punch me in the nose?"

She tried not to smile. "I'm too tired or I would. I'll have to owe you one."

He walked with her to the door, pushed the bar up with his foot, and then nudged it open with his shoulder. Leaving it open, he walked with her like a prize down the hallway.

They were apparently in the medical—the healers'—area. Like the room they'd just left, someone had painted the hallway walls stark white, and it smelled almost frighteningly clean. A series of rooms lined the hall, most with doors closed, but many lay open, and through the cracks in the doors she glimpsed slivers of people lying in beds as they passed.

And people stared. Some came out of their rooms to watch Laszlo carry her down the hall.

"Oh, God," she moaned, and buried her face in his shoulder.

"What's so wrong, *a'kala?*"

She whispered. "We had sex, what, four times? *In that room.* Everyone here must have heard."

There was a grin in his voice. "I would hope that they did."

"Goddamned barbarian," she hissed, and he laughed from the belly.

The hallway walls marked the exit of the healers' area. Instead of sterile white, rich, dark wood soothed the eye. She couldn't see the floor, but she was sure it was beautiful, too. Everything in the manse was beautiful. They had sure gone a long way, though.

"Aren't you tired?" she asked him.

"No. I slept well."

She sighed. "Aren't I too heavy? I can walk if you promise to walk slowly."

"No." He looked down at her. "And I cannot promise that."

He took her through the great hall, which was well-lit, though thankfully empty, but she shuddered as she caught sight of the platform on which she had—

"Shhhh. It's all right," Laszlo soothed. "We're almost there."

They exited the hall and went into the entry. He took her up the left stairs and turned left, then walked to the end and turned right.

"Are you taking me back to my old room?" she asked, delighted.

"Yes."

"Is that all right?"

He smiled without looking at her. "Yes."

She stiffened. "What about Nick, Laszlo?"

He was unconcerned. "What about him?"

"I was promised to him. I ran away. Does he have some way to—?"

"What would he ask? That you be forced to marry him? 'Tis too late. You're my wife."

With a heartfelt sigh she relaxed against him.

He stopped and opened her door. Once inside he laid her on the bed, then strode back across the carpet and barred the door. It felt so good to be back here that she wanted to sing.

"What will you have first, *a'kala?* Breakfast?"

She sat up, then pulled her shirt over her head. "You?" she asked with a smile.

He was on the bed in four beats of her heart. "Yes," he told her as he wrapped her against his chest.

THE NEXT MORNING Amba brought Alex and Emmy to see her. They stayed ten minutes. Marco came later and stayed five.

Agni came too, after lunch.

"You look wonderful, my dear," Agni told her as Kiera closed the door behind her.

Kiera hugged her. "I'm sorry," she said.

Agni pushed her back, but held Kiera's shoulders. "For what?"

Kiera was still too tired to stand for long. She pulled away and walked to the couch, then dropped down with a sigh. "I'm sorry. I'm still pretty weak. Will you sit?" she asked.

Agni nodded, then walked over and sat beside her.

Kiera's eyes flicked to Laszlo, who lay on the bed across the room with one knee up and his hands behind his head. He looked back, face blank.

Kiera looked back at Agni. "I guess I'm sorry that things didn't work out the way that—well, maybe the way the, uh, nobility would have wanted them to."

Agni folded her hands in her lap. "Lady Kiera, if you refer to what happened with Lord Vayu, then perhaps an apology is appropriate."

Laszlo sat up.

Agni flashed him a sharp look, but continued. "Lady Kiera, I say that because what you did frightened me." She leaned forward. "It frightened me very much. It was very brave, and very noble, but—" her voice trailed off, and Kiera realized that Agni was struggling to hold back tears.

Kiera put a hand on Agni's arm. "I had to do my part," she whispered. "There was no other way." Chagrined, she shook her head. "Lady Agni, these people have suffered so much."

Laszlo walked to the table at the edge of the couch and poured a glass of water. Kiera glared at him over Agni's head. "Stop hovering," she mouthed.

Agni patted her hand. "I do not dispute that, but it will take some time for the Skani to see things in the manner that you do, Lady Kiera."

Kiera sat back, trying to push aside her annoyance. "And I will never stop fighting until they do," she said passionately. "Vayu and his ilk enslaved people, Lady Agni, and stole everything from them that mattered. The Alaks are human beings with feelings and hopes and dreams, just like the nuwyr, like all of the Skani. But the Skani nobility have abused them so terribly, all of the slaves, and not just by stealing their freedom. I could tell you story after story of abuse and terror and pain." Kiera grimaced. "The slaves deserve so much, not the least of which is to be free, and I was honored to fight for that freedom."

From behind Agni, the white of a smile lit Laszlo's face and was gone.

"Lady Agni, all I ask for now is that the Skani respect the slaves' freedom."

Agni nodded. "And they will." She got up. "Though I must thank you, Lady Kiera, for not judging me cognate to Vayu."

There was an awkward pause.

Kiera used the arm of the couch to push herself up. "You don't have to thank me, Lady Agni," she said a little sadly.

Agni nodded and let herself out.

Laszlo barred the door behind her, and when he turned, Kiera raised a brow at his expression.

"No more visitors thisturn," he told her sternly. "Go back to bed."

"I'm fine," she said. "But I will lie in bed if you lie with me."

When they were settled, Kiera tilted her head back so she could see Laszlo's face. "She didn't even talk to you. You're my husband, and she didn't say even one word to you!"

He shrugged.

"Doesn't it bother you?"

He considered. "No."

"Liar."

He wrapped his arms around her.

"I love you, Laszlo."

"Sleep, *a'kala.*"

"Thank you."

There was a smile in his voice. "For being high-handed?"

"For being so good to me. I—"

"Shhhh."

She settled her head on his shoulder. "'Imperious' may be more accurate than 'high-handed.' Maybe even tyrannical."

His chest shook with laughter.

After a time, she asked, "Will there be war? Will they come to fight us because I'm—a fire mage is here?"

"Yes."

She tried to sit up, but he held her firm. "Shhhh, *a'kala.* Listen. Yes. They will come, but they would come to test the new ruler, or because the slaves are free, or because the sky is blue." He sighed. "The gods-cursed Skani do nothing but fight."

"What will we do?"

His voice was cold. "We will kill them."

"You and me?"

He laughed. "Yes. With our army."

CHAPTER 32

THE NEXT MORNING MARCO AND ALLIE came early, bearing breakfast trays. As soon as the four sat down to eat, Amba arrived with Alex and Emmy. Marco must have known they were coming, because there was more than enough food for all.

Alex chattered with Marco and Emmy. Kiera watched them contentedly, smiling, listening, while Laszlo sat behind her on the couch, his hand on her hip. Amba acted as server, refilling cups and delivering bread and cheese and other tasty morsels.

After they ate, Marco stood and pulled Allie to her feet. "We should go," he said apologetically. He looked at Laszlo. "You need to be ready by noontide, brother," he told him.

Kiera looked at Marco, then at Laszlo, trying to puzzle it out. "What does he have to do?" she asked Marco.

Laszlo suppressed a sigh. "Yes, Marco. Now go."

Without answering Kiera, Marco led Allie hurriedly out of the room.

Amba stood up, then glanced at Kiera and tried unsuccessfully to hide a grin. "We need to go as well." She took hold of Alex's hand and urged him up. "Don't you give in," she told Kiera conspiratorially, though everyone could hear her.

Kiera smiled back. "Oh, don't worry. I won't."

When they had gone, she got up and poured herself a glass of water, then seated herself on the opposite couch, facing him. "Tell me," she said, and took a drink. "Now. All of it."

"A'kala—"

"Laszlo, I am almost completely healed. I am not a delicate little flower who needs you to shield me from the rain. I want to know what happened. No more secrets." She took another drink. "Wait," she said. She sat her cup down and lifted a finger. "Let's start with this one. I know you're a mage, or whatever it is shifters who can use magic are called." She crossed her arms.

Laszlo smiled faintly.

"You knew I would figure it out. I know you did. Weren't you worried?"

He leaned back and extended his feet. "No."

"No? I thought you had used me."

"No."

"Yes, I did!" she said hotly.

He crossed his feet. "No. I meant that I never feared that you would reveal me."

"For God's sake, why not?"

He shrugged. "I knew you would not."

She was still angry. "That was foolish."

A smile tugged at his lips. "Did you?"

"What? Reveal it?"

"Yes."

"No!"

He laid his head back and closed his eyes.

Kiera made a frustrated noise. "Laszlo, you can't just trust people with secrets like that."

"You're angry because you're frightened for me."

"So what? That doesn't make it less true!"

His voice was gentle. "I only trusted you, *a'kala.*"

She stared at the ceiling, trying to rein in her temper. Her temper won. "Laszlo, Vayu tortured me! No one keeps secrets—" Her voice was too loud, so she made herself stop. She took a deep breath.

"Did you tell him?"

She knew she sounded sullen. "No."

Though his eyes stayed closed, a smile ghosted across his face. "I knew that you loved me, *a'kala.*" He opened his eyes and held hers, and his face looked resolute. "But I also knew that you would not tell him even if you did not." He opened his arms. "Come here."

She got up and sat beside him, and let him pull her to his chest. "Sorry to be such a grouch," she mumbled into his shirt.

"You should be very sorry," he told her.

She sat up. "Laszlo! You're supposed to tell me that I'm—I don't know. That it's not so bad or something."

He gave her an exasperated look and pulled her back to his chest. "I loved you the first moment I saw you, woman, standing alone against an army to save the lives of three children." He breathed out. "So brave. So beautiful. *She will be mine,* I told myself." He paused, and she could hear the smile in his voice. "Or do you think that when I saw you I thought, *oh there's a woman who will do my bidding?"*

Kiera laughed.

His voice was serious. "Do not doubt me, *a'kala,* nor your value to me."

"Tell me about your magic," she said, snuggling closer and then relaxing against him.

"There is little to tell. I can bring fire—"

She sat up. "You can?"

He smiled. "And I can bring air, though only a little of both. I can feel the—energy, yes?—from the earth, but I cannot make it come at my will, and I cannot feel water at all." He touched her face. "I learned a great deal from what you told me of your lessons, though I learned that I can send energy to another when I took your hand the time you called lightning. I could feel it crushing you and I thought I could help."

"How did you know that the fire I called wouldn't hurt you?"

He shrugged. "I knew it would not burn me."

She laid her head back on his chest. "I want to have sex with you."

He started to pull her up, but she pushed his hands away. "As soon as you tell me where you have to be at noon."

His voice was rough. "Lie with me now."

"Tell me first."

He grinned and snaked an arm under her bottom. She shrieked and tried to get away, but laughter made her weak. He pushed her down on the couch, then, with a groan, lay on top of her, pushed her knees apart with his and kissed her hard. Without further ado he reached down between them and opened her robe, and she let him feel her smile with his lips.

KIERA TOOK A BATH and slept for an hour. She woke when Laszlo closed the door, a tray in hand. She lay quietly and looked at him. He was pretty amazing. Beautiful. Smart. Gentle. Loyal.

My husband.

"Do you want to eat?" he asked her without turning around.

"How'd you know I was awake?" she asked.

"Your breathing," he answered, and started setting out food.

She sat up. "You smell better than—non-shifters? Would that be the right term? And you hear better, too?"

He shot her a grin. "Thank you."

It took her a handspan of seconds to understand his corny joke. She threw her pillow at him. He caught it with a smile and threw it on the couch. "Come and eat, *a'kala.* "

Okay. Corny but cute.

"So yes? To both?"

"Yes to both."

"Hey. Don't overload me with information here."

He smiled again.

"Any other enhanced senses?"

"No."

"You're stronger and faster than non-shifters."

"Yes."

"This is a lot like pulling teeth."

He looked up and raised his brows.

She sighed. "Never mind." She got out of bed and sauntered to the couch. She grabbed a piece of bread and a block of cheese and sat down. "Now I want you to tell me where you're going. Do I need to come?"

"After we eat."

She looked to heaven. "Laszlo, I have been really patient."

He faked a shocked look.

She laughed. "Okay. I have waited. So please tell me."

"A'kala, I have made you wait because you needed to heal." He looked away. "And because I have been selfish."

Kiera gaped. "I can't believe you just admitted that!"

He tried to keep his face still, but a grin pushed through, then faded. "Things will change. I wanted to treasure this time."

Kiera's heart softened. She put down her food and started to stand, but then a thought hit her. "Is there a bad secret you're keeping? Am I going to be mad at you?"

He looked at her a little sadly. "No. I do not believe that you will be angry with me."

"That scares me a little. Please tell me what happened!"

"Will you allow me to have until after lunch?"

There was just the slightest hint of vulnerability in his eyes. She got up and sat next to him, then took his hand. "Yeah."

He smiled at her so sweetly that it made her heart turn over.

"Laszlo, I love you. No matter what happens, I will always love you. And I will stay with you as long as you will have me."

"You will never get away," he told her ardently, but the smile he flashed softened his words.

After they ate he put the tray outside the door, then came back and stood next to her. He reached out a hand to help her stand. "It's time to get ready," he told her.

She took his hand and stood. He led her over to her closet.

"Where are we going?" she asked him.

"What color do you favor?" he countered.

"Red," she said without hesitation. "Laszlo! Please!"

Ignoring her, he plucked down a red dress, examined it, then tossed it aside. He chose another, held it out in front of him, and hung it over his arm. Kiera grinned and leaned against the dresser. He picked another, then another, then dropped the one on his arm. "This one," he told her, and handed it over.

She held it up. It was velvet, and more scarlet than red. It was square-necked and would cover her chest, she noted, amused, but it was undoubtedly very beautiful by anyone's standards. It was so long it would brush the floor in the front when she walked, and drag for a yard in the back. The sleeves would be tight to her elbows, and then bell out below and would fall to cover most of her hands. The top was fitted, but the skirt would fall thick and full. Its only embellishment was a thin gold cord that criss-crossed the bodice a half-dozen times, then wove into the fabric of the skirt below in two long, straight lines.

"I mourn your hair," he told her as she dressed. "You must let it grow long again."

She turned to smile at him. "I feel the same way," she admitted. "I will."

He helped her adjust the dress but stopped her when she would have walked to her dresser. "No paint," he said with a twist to his mouth, then leaned in and kissed hers.

"Where are we going?" she asked again, mouth against his lips.

"Soon," he told her without pulling away.

She leaned back. "All right. Let me brush my hair and we can go."

"Pull it up," he urged her.

"Tyrant," she called him, but did it anyway because it looked better than leaving the ragged ends hanging down.

When she was finished, he dressed in the clothes he had worn at the party. Fine black robes, black pants, and black boots someone had rubbed until they shone. He pulled on a long black coat and led her out and down the hall, then down the stairs.

He paused, started to go right, but changed his mind and led her to the front door instead.

"Wait here a moment," he told her, and went out the door.

She walked to one of the two teal couches set out for visitors, she supposed, and sat down on one. It was plush and soft, and she rubbed her hand back and forth over it, enjoying the sensation.

She still felt pretty tired, she admitted, though only to herself. It would be some time yet before she had her whole strength back.

Laszlo opened the door perhaps ten minutes later, then walked over and took her hand. She stood, and he walked her out the door.

The near-zenith sun burned brightly above, and she stopped for a moment to lift her face to it. She took a long breath, then another. Despite the bitter cold of the day the sun warmed her, and she felt herself strengthen under its gaze.

She opened her eyes to find Laszlo gazing at her, his eyes soft with love. Her heart swelled, and a smile lifted her lips. He led her to a horse, his big, black monster of a horse, and she laughed.

"I can't climb up in this," she told him, and motioned to her dress.

He grinned at her, then put his hands on her waist and lifted her effortlessly into the saddle, seating her sideways. "Hold on to the horn," he told her, then pointed to it to make sure she understood.

She took it in her right hand, which was closest, and hung on tightly. He walked to the front of the horse and took the reins, then led the animal, and Kiera, around the manse and toward the back.

"Will you tell me where we're going?" she called.

He ignored her.

"Tyrant," she whispered, knowing he would hear her, and he laughed.

They wound around the east side of the manse and toward the river. The crust of the old snow crunched with each step of the horse's feet. Crystals in the uneven berms on either side of their path shimmered in the sunlight.

Kiera lifted her eyes to the jagged mountains that lay both north and east of the city, where the white of old snow and the hard green of the pines warred for domination. She looked down at Laszlo, at his large back, his big hand wrapped round the rein, his hair that held the dark even in the sunlight, and at the sparks of ice that shimmered in the air around him as he marched on. She let out a soft breath as contentment wound round her heart.

As they walked she heard the buzz of many people talking and looked up. The coliseum loomed ahead, closer by the step.

She frowned, wondering why he would bring her here. *Maybe today Marco is going to be made governor?* she thought, growing excited, and leaned back in the saddle to try and see. Only a few people milled around outside, far too few to account for the noise, so most everyone had to be inside already.

To her surprise Laszlo led her around to the east side and through a door that led under the dome. She had to duck her head to pass under the first gate. He turned right and into the hallway, and kept walking.

He led her down the hall and past many rooms, all of which were empty. She was too high on the horse to see anything out the windows of the rooms between her and the field, but she could hear the unceasing susurration of the crowd above her.

After they had come halfway—she supposed—across the dome, she saw a door ahead and on the left. He turned at it and the horse followed. She had to duck her head again as they passed under the outer edge of the dome.

He led her out and stepped onto the field, which someone had cleared of snow. A crowd of perhaps a thousand people—most Skani in fine clothes, but some soldiers and some other slaves—stood in groups on the field. She glanced up at the stands. Another six or seven thousand there, and all of them standing.

"What is going on, Laszlo? Is this Marco's ceremony?" she murmured, but he kept walking as if she hadn't spoken.

Laszlo led the horse down the long red carpet that bisected the field.

Red carpet? She nearly laughed.

As they drew close to the middle of the field, the crowd ahead parted and she could see that a small wooden dais, perhaps ten feet to a side and that many tall, had been erected at the farthest edge of the field. It had been decorated with sprigs of pine and some other plants, and was pretty, but it looked a far cry from regal.

Just short of the stand Laszlo dropped the reins and the horse stopped on his own, dropping his head to whuffle the snow at his feet.

Laszlo walked around the horse's head and to her. He looked up at her somberly, put his hands on her waist and lifted her down. To her surprise he did not set her onto the ground, but instead shifted her so that he was cradling her in his arms.

She stared into his face, a small smile on hers, but he would not look back. He carried her up the stairs and onto the stage, then set her down gently on her feet and took two steps back.

And knelt.

"The Alak choose Kiera," he said, and whether he used magic or something else, his voice carried across her and out, where it echoed off the stone.

A cheer rose from somewhere as all of the Alak she could see, both below and in the stands around her, dropped to a knee.

Kiera stiffened and felt her eyes open wide.

Marco emerged from the crowd below her dressed in a king's finery. He walked to the foot of the stage and mounted the stairs, holding her eyes, and as he crested the top he fell to one knee, letting his chin fall to his chest.

When he spoke, his voice, like Laszlo's, carried. "The Skani choose Kiera."

Within seconds, the rest of the crowd below her knelt.

Then, as if choreographed, like a wave washing over a beach, all of the people crowded into the stands knelt.

The shouts, frenzied cheering, began someplace off to her left.

Kiera looked at Laszlo, who kept his face down.

"Stand up," she whispered. "Laszlo, I don't know what to do."

He didn't move.

"Stand up, Laszlo," she said with a little more volume, "right now, or I swear to God I will push you over the edge."

He lifted his head and looked at her, not quite suppressing a smile. "If I rise now," he told her quietly, "then you will have to share this rule with me."

"Don't you ever kneel again, goddamn you," she hissed, then took a breath. "Rise, Laszlo," she shouted over his head and let it carry across the field.

Faces raised, people shifted, trying to see.

Laszlo stood smoothly.

Cheers erupted from everywhere.

He took a step forward, but she lifted a hand.

He stopped, then stiffened.

Kiera bowed her head and smiled, just a little, hoping to quell any worries. "I have more witnesses than you did," she mocked softly, then looked up through her lashes and flashed a grin at his startled face.

She closed her eyes just long enough to pull a strand of air, then took a breath and straightened. She held Laszlo's eyes as she spoke, feeding air through her as she did, letting it carry her words across the stadium.

"*Hyhi eeido*, marry me, Laszlo of the Denaa. Please be my husband."

Silence thundered.

Laszlo started, blinked, then smiled, a glorious white swath that rose from somewhere deep inside, the raw emotion so rarely seen in him transforming his usually serious face into something heartbreakingly beautiful.

Blessing this moment, heart soaring, she swallowed back the tears in her throat. "Please share my life with me, my love, because it would be empty without you."

Kiera held out a hand, and he stepped in and took it, then pulled her to him, pressing her mouth roughly with his own.

When he released her she stepped back and turned to Marco.

"Rise, Marco," she told him, and he did, a wide smile painting joy on his face. "I name you brother, Marco, and you will also share the governance of this deconn with us."

He opened his mouth, probably to protest, but she lifted a hand to silence him and turned back to the crowd. Her people.

Her trip to find Hunter was going to have to wait for a little while. "Rise," she said, letting the love she held for all of them thread her voice. "All of you. You must never kneel again."

GLOSSARY

A'kala: "My lover/my woman" in Denaali.

Agni, Lady: Skani noblewoman who lives in Fairbanks. Magic teacher. Has red hair and green eyes. Sunwyr, but of which element is not known.

Air: One of the four elements. Travels in large streams and does not require a mage to expend extra energy to summon. It feels like a painless buzzing when touched with a mage's sight. The opposite of, and can cancel, earth energy. This element's symbol/sigil is a vata.

Alak (ah-LUCK): The indigenous shapeshifting peoples of Alaska, who are further denoted by tribe. Most have dark hair and eyes.

Alak'shin katmodit dis'Alak: "Honor others to earn honor in return" in Denaali.

Alaska: The country in which Kiera and Alex are transported. Geographically very similar to the 49th U.S. state, but the resemblances end there.

Alex: Kiera's nephew. Son of Julia, Kiera's deceased sister, and Hunter Daniels. Has dark brown hair and eyes. Age 6 in *Fallen Embers*.

Aliyah (Allie): Skani. Daughter of Lord Vriksha, Governor of Barrow. About 15. Blonde hair, blue eyes. Awyr.

Amba: Alak farming slave who lives in Fairbanks. Has dark brown hair and eyes.

Anchorage: A city/deconn in southern Alaska. Ruler is unknown.

Asana: Governor of Bethel.

Awyr (AY-weer): A Skani who was born under different, but complementary, sunsigns and moonsigns. These mages can manipulate, and sometimes summon, one or two elements weakly. Not ennobled, but not enslaved, this very large group functions as a middle class of Skani. Awyr make up approximately thirty percent of the Skani. *See also* **sunsign** and **moonsign.**

Barrow: A city/deconn in northern Alaska. Ruled by Lord Vrishka, a water sunwyr.

Bethel: A city/deconn in western Alaska. Ruled by Lord Asana.

Call: Part one of a spell in which a mage sends out her sight, locates and then summons an element into herself.

Captain: The leader of a deconn's army. Always a slave, but this person holds more authority than mayors and answers only to the governor.

Cardinal (hours) marks: The hours in which elements flow most heavily and with the most force. Plusses: Mages can do very strong workings. Minuses: Can overwhelm user. Cardinal marks are: 12–1 A.M./P.M. (fire); 1–2 A.M./P.M. (earth); 2–3 A.M./P.M. (air); and 3–4 A.M./P.M. (water).

Chanda, Lord: Skani. Nephew of Lord Vayu and Lady Leith. Has dark hair and blue eyes. Air sunwyr.

Cycle: One complete solar year.

Dagna: Skani slave woman who works as a farmer and who lives in Fairbanks. Has brown hair and blue eyes. Nuwyr.

Deconn (DEH-conn): The governed area surrounding one of four cities in Alaska, including Anchorage, Barrow, Bethel, and Fairbanks. A deconn's area extends approximately fifty miles in any direction from its city's center. Each deconn is ruled by a governor.

Denaa (de-NAH): "Big bear;" one of the Alak tribes in which the members can shapeshift into Kodiak bears. Laszlo is a member. Denaali tribal lands are located on an island in the southern Alaska nadeconn.

Earth: One of the four elements. Originates from all living things on the planet. Travels in very small streams and mages must expend extra energy to pull it, although Alaks apparently do not. It is heavy and thick and appears green. It is the opposite of, and can cancel, air energy. This element's symbol/sigil is a yar.

Element: One of the four types of energy that form the building blocks of everything in existence. They include air, water, earth and fire.

Emmy: Skani slave woman who works as Kiera's maid and Alex's nanny and lives in Fairbanks. Has dirty blonde hair and blue eyes. Nuwyr.

Fairbanks: A city/deconn in eastern Alaska. Ruled by Lord Vayu, an air sunwyr.

Fire: One of the four elements, fire originates from the sun and the stars. It travels in varying-sized streams and does not take energy to pull. It feels like a smooth jolt of electricity when touched with a mage's sight. Fire is the opposite of, and can cancel, water energy. This element's symbol/sigil is a xan.

Fixed (hours) marks: The hours in which the elements are the most balanced. They flow strongly, but not aggressively, and their flows are reliable. Plusses: Very stable magic. Not fancy, but reliable. During these marks, elements seem to seek stability and are more forgiving of mistakes. Minuses: Few. Fixed marks are: 4–5 A.M./P.M. (fire); 5–6 A.M./P.M. (earth); 6–7 A.M./P.M. (air); and 7–8 A.M./P.M. (water).

Gethor: Skani man who lives in Fairbanks. Friend of Valen. Has brown hair and blue eyes. Air awyr.

Governor: The ultimate ruler of a deconn, similar to a king or emperor. The governor owns all of the property, including slaves, in a deconn.

Helfarch (HELL-fark): Sunwyr Skani who have learned to use their magic to do very great workings. Very rare.

Hunter Daniels: Father of Alex, husband of (deceased) Julia, and brother-in-law to Kiera. Has brown hair and green eyes.

Hyhi eeido: "You are mine" in Denaali.

Julia: Deceased mother of Alex, sister of Kiera and wife of Hunter.

Kelktok: The fish camp/village in eastern Alaska where Kiera and Alex first landed.

Kiera: A woman who is transported to Alaska and learns that here she is a fire sunwyr. Has dark brown hair and eyes. Aunt of Alex, sister to Julia and sister-in-law to Hunter.

Laszlo of the Denaa: Alak slave captain of Lord Vayu's army. Has dark brown hair and eyes.

Laws, the two: (1) "All is power." Everything is made and operates by use of four types of power/energy, called elements, and elements are always flowing. Elements move and change because of the positions of the stars. (2) "Vessels of glass." Bodies are weak, so mages must not pull elements into themselves without having a reliable method by which they can deflect or send them back out.

Leith, Lady: Skani. Lord Vayu's—the governor of Fairbanks'— wife, and mother of Valen and Marco. Has blonde hair and blue eyes. Sunwyr, but of which element?

Lorgda: Skani slave man who works as a farmer in the summer and lives in Fairbanks. Has blond hair and blue eyes. Nuwyr.

Manifest: Part three of a spell in which a mage causes an element to appear in the normal world in a certain, predesigned manner.

Marco: Skani. Lord Vayu's youngest son. Age 16 in *Fallen Embers.* Has blond hair and blue eyes. Air sunwyr.

Mark: One full hour.

Mayor: A subruler of a deconn. A mayor is allowed to own both property and slaves, although he must answer to the governor.

Mek: The sigil/symbol for the element of water. When written it resembles a point-side-down triangle and is associated with the color blue.

Moon: One full month.

Moonsign: The word that denotes one of twenty-four periods of time during each day when the stars are in a particular alignment (but note that they are not otherwise named). Moonsigns are grouped into one of four categories by the element that dominates during the time they mark, including air, earth, fire and water. The first sign is fire, which commences at midnight. The second is earth. The third is air and the fourth is water. The fifth is fire, the sixth is earth, and so on. A mage's proclivity for magic is determined in part by the moonsign under which he or she is born. The other half of their magical ability is determined by their sunsign. If the two match, e.g., air sunsign and moonsign, the person will become a sunwyr. If the two complement (fire and air or earth and water), the person will become an awyr. But if a person is born under opposite signs (fire and water or earth and air), the person will become a nuwyr.

Mosha: Skani. Slave member of the Fairbanks army. Has dirty blond hair and blue eyes. Nuwyr.

Mutable (hours) marks: The hours in which the elements are the most changeable and their flows fluctuate. Weakest magic, but flows fastest. Plusses: Easiest to blend elements with others. Minuses: Can produce weak, unreliable spells. Mutable marks are: 8–9 A.M./P.M. (fire); 9–10 A.M./P.M. (earth); 10–11 A.M./P.M. (air); and 11–12 A.M./P.M. (water).

Nadeconn (NAH-deh-conn): The unincorporated area outside the deconns, which makes up most of the country. Peopled almost entirely by Alaks.

Naga: Skani. Lord Valen's paramour. Has strawberry blonde hair and blue eyes. Awyr.

Nakeetna: The abandoned city in eastern Alaska where Kiera first found Marco and Allie.

Nexturn: Tomorrow.

Nickinum (Nick), Mayor: Skani mayor of Talium, a Fairbanks possession, and Lord Vayu's spymaster. Has dark hair and icy blue eyes. Water awyr.

Nighttide: Midnight.

Noontide: Noon.

Nuwyr (NEW-weer): Skani born without magical ability, or possessing only very weak abilities. Nuwyr make up approximately two thirds of the Skani. Always enslaved, usually during childhood. *See also* **sunsign** and **moonsign.**

Pull: To seek out and summon, as in an element.

Saman, Lord: Skani healer who lives in Fairbanks. Mage, but rank and element are unknown.

Sen'ikcha a'kala achubruk: "Do not touch my woman" in Denaali.

Shatru: A group of invading people who persecuted and drove the Skani out of their home country approximately one hundred years ago.

Shima's tit: An exclamation.

Shunakah (shuh-NUH-kuh): "Snow dogs"; one of the Alak tribes in which the members can shapeshift into large dogs that resemble African wild dogs in both looks and temperament. Shunakah tribal lands are located around Bethel, which is in the southwest Alaska nadeconn.

Sigil: An element's symbol. Many types, broken down by cardinal, fixed, mutable and by working, and used to invoke an element's energy.

Sight: The manifestation of a person's magical ability. Mages seek out elemental energy using their sight.

Skani: A group of people who immigrated to Alaska approximately a hundred years ago to escape persecution in their former homeland by a people called the Shatru. Most are light haired and blue-eyed and many are mages of varying degrees, but none can shapeshift.

Slave: A person who is stripped of their legal personhood to become the property of another, generally including the governor of a deconn. In Alaska, slaves include (kidnapped) Alaks and nuwyr Skani, who may work on farms, as fishers, hunters, in the church, or in the armies. Slaves cannot marry, own property, choose their employment, or bring claims against any other person for any reason.

Spell: A three-part magical undertaking in which a mage uses her sight to call (or summon) an element, spin it inside her, and manifest it someplace else. Also called a working.

Spin: Part two of a spell. A mage first sends out his sight and summons an element to him, then pulls it into his physical body, where he shapes it inside his magical boundaries (called "spinning"), and finally sends it out to the "real" world (called "manifesting").

Strand: The smallest unit of elemental energy that a mage can use, it resembles a piece of thread or string when a mage examines it with her sight. Each element flows in this manner, sometimes singularly and sometimes with many other strands of the same element. Different elements flow differently, in different places, and exhibit different properties.

Sunsign: The word that denotes one of twelve month-long periods of time during each year when the stars are in a particular alignment (but note that they are not otherwise named). Sunsigns are grouped into one of four categories by the element that dominates during the time they mark, including air, earth, fire and water. The first sign is earth, which commences at winter solstice. The second is air. The third is water and the fourth is fire. The fifth is earth, sixth is air, and so on. A mage's proclivity for magic is determined in part by the sunsign under which he or she is born. The other half of their magical ability is determined by their moonsign. If the two match, e.g., air sunsign and moonsign, the person will become a sunwyr. If the two complement (fire and air or earth and water), the person will become an awyr. But if a person is born under opposite signs (fire and water or earth and air), the person will become a nuwyr.

Sunwyr (SUN-weer): A Skani mage who was born under the same sunsign and moonsign. These most powerful mages can summon and manipulate their element, and often one to two other elements as well. Cannot usually sense their element's opposite, much less summon it. These rare mages are ennobled and constitute the ruling class of Skani. *See also* **sunsign** and **moonsign.**

Symbol: A drawn sigil, generally used to display under what element a mage is born (and often used to decorate). In Fairbanks, the Skani child's symbol is tattooed or branded inside the left wrist three days after birth.

Talium: Protectorate of Fairbanks, located inside the Fairbanks deconn. Mayor is Nickinum.

Thesin: Skani man who lives in Fairbanks, and Valen's friend. Has blond hair and blue eyes. Air awyr.

Thisturn: Today.

Tikaani (teh-KAH-nee): One of the Alak tribes in which the members can shapeshift into grey wolves. Many Fairbanks slaves are members. Tikaani tribal lands are located in the eastern Alaska nadeconn.

Tribe: The Alaks, or indigenous shapeshifting peoples of Alaska, each belong to a group of shapeshifters called a tribe who all shift into the same animal. The known Alak tribes are Denaa (brown bear), Tikaani (wolf), and Shunakah (snow dog). There are others as well, including Nanuk (polar bear), Cha'ak (eagle), Aivik (sea lion), Yeil (raven), Tungak (black bear), Aabluk (orca whale), Kaviak (coyote), Gakut (lynx), and Kidjuk (goshawk).

Turn: One full day.

Valen, Lord: Skani. Oldest son of Lord Vayu and Lady Leith, and brother of Marco. Has white hair and blue eyes. Air sunwyr.

Vata: The sigil/symbol for the element of air. When written it resembles a point-side-up triangle bisected by a horizontal line and is associated with the color yellow.

Vayu, Lord: Skani governor of Fairbanks. Has white hair and blue eyes. Married to Lady Leith. Air sunwyr.

Vriksha, Lord: Skani governor of Barrow. Water sunwyr.

Water: One of the four elements. Originates from the great bodies of water both above and under the ground. Travels in large streams, largely underground, and takes extra energy to pull. Water is temperature sensitive and feels soft and metallic when touched by a mage's sight. The opposite of, and can cancel, fire energy. This element's symbol/sigil is a mek.

Working: Another word for spell.

Xan: The sigil/symbol for the element of fire. When written it resembles a point-side-up triangle and is associated with the color red.

Yar: The sigil/symbol for the element of earth. When written it resembles a square and is associated with the color green.

Yesturn: Yesterday.

ABOUT THE AUTHOR

L AURI OWEN IS A CIVIL RIGHTS LAWYER who grew up in Idaho's Treasure Valley. She started reading fantasy novels in the third grade, and
other than taking time out to sleep, never really stopped. The oldest
child of a homemaker and police officer, Lauri worked for more than a de-
cade in law enforcement. But Lauri's not-so-secret passion is social justice,
and so in 2002 she decided to become a lawyer.

After completing U.C. Berkeley's law school Lauri moved to the Alaska
Bush, where she fell in love with the magic and majesty that exemplifies her
new home state. She was selected in 2006 for inclusion in the *Who's Who of
American Women* directory in part for her commitment to civil rights, and
she now lives in metro Alaska with her elementary school-aged son and her
many rescued cat companions.

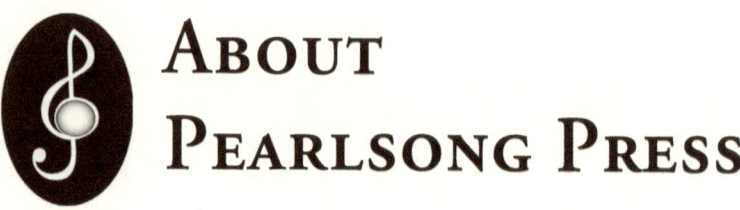

ABOUT PEARLSONG PRESS

PEARLSONG PRESS IS AN INDEPENDENT PUBLISHING COMPANY dedicated to providing books and resources that entertain while expanding perspectives on the self and the world. The company was founded by Peggy Elam, Ph.D., a psychologist and journalist, in 2003.

Pearls are formed when a piece of sand or grit or other abrasive, annoying, or even dangerous substance enters an oyster and triggers its protective response. The substance is coated with shimmering opalescent nacre ("mother of pearl"), the coats eventually building up to produce a beautiful gem. The self-healing response of the oyster thus transforms suffering into a thing of beauty.

The pearl-creating process reflects our company's desire to move outside a pathological or "disease" based model of life, health and well-being into a more integrative and transcendent perspective. A move out of suffering into joy. And that, we think, is something to sing about.

PEARLSONG PRESS ENDORSES HEALTH AT EVERY SIZE, an approach to health and well-being that celebrates natural diversity in body size and encourages people to stop focusing on weight (or any external measurement) in favor of listening to and respecting natural appetites for food, drink, sleep, rest, movement, and recreation. While not every book we publish specifically promotes Health At Every Size (by, for instance, featuring fat heroines or educating readers on size acceptance), none of our books or other resources will contradict this holistic and body-positive perspective.

WE ENCOURAGE YOU TO ENJOY, enlarge, enlighten and enliven yourself with other Pearlsong Press books, which you can purchase at www.pearlsong.com or your favorite bookstore. Keep up with us through our blog at www.pearlsongpress.com.

FICTION:

Bride of the Living Dead—romantic comedy by Lynne Murray
Measure By Measure—a romantic romp with the fabulously fat by Rebecca Fox & William Sherman
FatLand—a visionary novel by Frannie Zellman
The Program—a suspense novel by Charlie Lovett
The Singing of Swans—a novel about the Divine Feminine by Mary Saracino

Romance novels and short stories featuring Big Beautiful Heroines:
by Pat Ballard, the Queen of Rubenesque Romances:
  The Best Man
  Abigail's Revenge
  Dangerous Curves Ahead: Short Stories
  Wanted: One Groom
  Nobody's Perfect
  His Brother's Child
  A Worthy Heir
by Rebecca Brock—*The Giving Season*
& by Judy Bagshaw—*At Long Last, Love: A Collection*

NONFICTION:

Fat Poets Speak: Voices of the Fat Poets' Society—edited by Frannie Zellman
Ten Steps to Loving Your Body (No Matter What Size You Are) by Pat Ballard
Beyond Measure: A Memoir About Short Stature & Inner Growth by Ellen Frankel
Taking Up Space: How Eating Well & Exercising Regularly Changed My Life by Pattie Thomas, Ph.D. with Carl Wilkerson, M.B.A. (foreword by Paul Campos, author of The Obesity Myth)
Off Kilter: A Woman's Journey to Peace with Scoliosis, Her Mother & Her Polish Heritage—a memoir by Linda C. Wisniewski
Unconventional Means: The Dream Down Under—a spiritual travelogue by Anne Richardson Williams
Splendid Seniors: Great Lives, Great Deeds—inspirational biographies by Jack Adler